Th

Dear

Deceit

Christine Brooke-Rose

VP Festschrift Series:

Volume 1: Christine Brooke-Rose
Volume 2: Gilbert Adair
Volume 3: The Syllabus
(Edited by G.N. Forester and M.J. Nicholls)

Reprint Titles:

The Languages of Love — Christine Brooke-Rose
The Sycamore Tree — Christine Brooke-Rose
Go When You See the Green Man Walking — Christine Brooke-Rose
Next — Christine Brooke-Rose
Xorandor/Verbivore — Christine Brooke-Rose
Three Novels — Rosalyn Drexler
Knut — Tom Mallin

other Verbivoracious titles @

www.verbivoraciouspress.org

The

Dear

Deceit

Christine Brooke-Rose

Verbivoracious Press

Glentrees, 13 Mt Sinai Lane, Singapore

This edition published in Great Britain & Singapore

by Verbivoracious Press

www.verbivoraciouspress.org

ISBN: 978-981-07-9383-8

Printed and bound in Great Britain & Singapore

First published in Great Britain by Secker & Warburg 1960.

Introduction

JOSEPH ANDREW DARLINGTON

"The man who does not respect his ancestors is unlikely to do deeds for which posterity will respect him".[1]

Christine Brooke-Rose (1923–2012) is most commonly known as a writer of exploratory fiction. On first publication, her novels were often dismissed as difficult, overly intellectual, and specialist. As years passed her works have subsequently been reclaimed in the name of postmodernism, deconstructionism, third-wave feminism and digital hypertext writing, among other theoretical movements. After the publication of her fifth novel *Out* in 1964, Brooke-Rose's ideal readership has always seemed to be at least a decade behind her in its tastes and willingness to experiment. When considered in relation to this rather fearsome reputation, many critics have found it convenient to write off her first four novels as juvenilia, the work of a writer who had not yet found her voice. Richard Martin, for example, suggests that in *The Dear Deceit* it is "clear that Brooke-Rose was still uncertain about the direction she intended her fiction to take" (41). However, putting aside momentarily the academic concerns of narrative form and structure and instead considering the novel as a reading experience, Brooke-Rose's early works—most especially *The Dear Deceit*—exhibit all the wit, inventiveness, and sly humour of her later works, only in a more traditional (and more accessible) form. One suspects that the fetishism surrounding "highbrow" writers is to blame for this association of accessibility with banality.

---

1 The above epigraph is scribbled on the inside cover of a slim volume of family history; Roland P. Faulkner's *Descendants of Rev. Clement Moore Butler, D. D.* (1933). The hand is Christine Brooke-Rose's and the volume is now held in a folder marked "Research Notes for *The Dear Deceit*" in the Harry Ransom Centre's Brooke-Rose archive.

Set within the context of its initial publication, *The Dear Deceit* is undoubtedly part of a sub-genre one would describe as the "middlebrow". Concerned with English middle-class foibles, social expectations, and often parochial in setting, the late-1950s middlebrow novel—sometimes also described as the Hampstead Novel—provides ample diversion for the intelligent reader without ever becoming an intellectual ordeal. The novels of Margaret Drabble sit well in this category, as do many of Brigid Brophy's and some of Kingsley Amis' work. Against the "kitchen-sink" realism of the Angry Young Men, these novels can appear moribund; lacking in the life and vitality of angst-driven youth. The still waters of their surfaces, however, often hide profound hidden depths. *The Dear Deceit* is a clear case-in-point here, to which the reams of family history Christine Brooke-Rose amassed as research before writing testify.

In effect, two different interpretations of *The Dear Deceit* exist, depending upon the reader. For the majority of contemporary readers it follows the fictional narrative of a dissolute middle-class chancer from the awkwardness around the reading of his will all the way back to the hijinks of his youth. For those familiar with Brooke-Rose's family, however, it is unmistakably a retelling of the life of Alfred Northcliffe Rose, Christine's infamous father. A considerable number of letters held in the Brooke-Rose archive testify to the prevalence of the second interpretation among readers on first publication. Often, correspondents would address the text as if it were a straight biography. Peter F. Anson wrote to Brooke-Rose to tell her that "Your treatment of the Isle of Dogs—Lower Guiting incidents sticks very closely to the recorded facts, and I noted how you had even quoted verbatim here and there", commenting that the final work was, "SO true, but SO haughty!" Her research notes include a sheet of paper marked "Notes on Fiction vs. Fact" and acting as a key to the real-life references in the work:

> Vernon Manning = Rev. George Chambers, rector in Ventnor... Wld recognise himself, but wouldn't mind...
> Miss Harriet Ball: real, alive, Miss Florence Moss. She

comes out very well in novel, wouldn't mind at all, gave me lots of information...

Alfred Hayley is of course Alfred Rose...

Benedictines = Lambertines...

The Bertrand family is the Brooke family.

The list continues for a side and a half and carefully distinguishes the differences between truth and fiction as well as the likelihood of an outside reader recognising the references being made. Such an exercise is partly of interest concerning the processes of inclusion and exclusion that separate the "good story" told in the novel from the more scattered and indeterminate accounts of actual events. However, Brooke-Rose is clearly aware of the potential for libel cases to be brought against the novel upon publication. British libel law has always been notorious for its breadth of scope and it presents a very real threat to British writers seeking to incorporate the living within their fictions. Anthony Burgess, a friend of Brooke-Rose's at that time, had his novel *The Worm and the Ring* (first published the same year as *The Dear Deceit*) recalled and pulped after losing a libel case. Brooke-Rose's own semi-fictional "bifography" *Remake* (1996) had an entire final chapter removed by editors through fear of legal action (cf. Darlington, 2015). That none of the reviews of the novel make reference to its real-life inspiration—Alfred Rose and the Brooke-Rose family —shows the extent to which the "official" printed reception of the novel differed from the reading experience had by so many of those friends and acquaintances of Alfred Rose who wrote to Christine personally.

The research Brooke-Rose amassed in the year and a half preceding the novel's final version is notable for its scope and the persistence with which it was pursued. The work traces three family trees: Brooke, Rose, and Poulin. The Brookes in particular are notably prolific, featuring a line of ancestry going back to Charlemagne and an American side with three Maryland towns—Brookeville, Brooke Manor and Brookfield—named after them. Of Alfred's old associates, Brooke-Rose built up a variety of correspondents. One Henry Watts gives a notable description of his former work colleague:

> I will say this now: I do not think that he was a bad man. He did many bad things. But I do not think he did those things as does a hardened criminal. He had the makings of a brilliant mind; he also had the makings of a gangster and a crook. He was, actually, neither the one nor the other. But he fitted in between. Whether this was his final undoing, I do not know.

The closing image of Alfred in the novel as a young man, "A living statue, framed in the window", is taken directly from a letter of Francis G. Walton's; a neighbour of the Roses and a childhood friend of Alfred's, ninety years old at the time Brooke-Rose went to visit him. Much of the novel is a patchwork of Brooke-Rose's own writing and that provided to her by correspondents.

The most notable exclusion from the novel is that of Alfred's mother, Mary, and their childhood home. Mary Rose was a prominent scholar of William Shakespeare and, at the time of Alfred's youth, was custodian of the house which was Shakespeare's birthplace (cf. Liam Fox's letter). According to Brooke-Rose's notes, such a detail may have offended the current custodians of the birthplace, who may have believed the "living statue" referred to their own son and consequently sued for libel. The only surviving references to this in the novel are a couple of Mary Rose's real-life articles on Shakespeare that appear in Alfred's fictional bookshop. It is notable, however, that this character "in between" a crook and a genius conducts his first youthful acts of public indecency out of one of the very windows William Shakespeare would have peered through at his age. Truth is often stranger than fiction and deciding which of the accidents and coincidences of everyday life will prove "believable" on paper is a key concern of the writer as she goes about her strange craft.

In terms of narrative form, the unusual structure of *The Dear Deceit* should be of keen interest to readers practiced in the art of literary criticism. Other than the first couple of chapters providing the framing device for the novel (Brooke-Rose attributes her own research to a fictionalised version of her first husband), the rest of the chapters move chronologically backwards from the death of Alfred Hayley to his youth. This narrative structure is a reversal of a traditional *bildungsroman* structure wherein readers follow a character from youth to age, innocence to experience, and naivety to maturity. In reversing the standard presentation, Brooke-Rose subtly alters the experience of reading a "life story" and draws attention to some of the assumptions which the *bildungsroman* incites. When reading about Dickens's David Copperfield or Fielding's Tom Jones, readers the story tells every important formative experience and that each of these experiences come together to form the final character. However, placed backwards this cause-and-effect logic is less clear-cut. Is the reader *really* hearing of every important formative experience, or only occasional arbitrary episodes? How much impact should these episodes be assumed to have upon the formation of the character to which the reader is introduced at the start? Is something being related? Is that something now untellable, lost in the sands of time? In navigating the novel's unorthodox structure the perspective becomes not that of a reader of biography, but of the biographer her or himself; the reader is not being given answers, but rather going on a journey back through time to seek these out.

The powerful interplay of presence and absence on the shaping of history is a key concern of this novel, and it is something of which the Brooke-Rose lineage would no doubt be aware. In her earlier years, Christine Brooke-Rose had undertaken top secret war work at Bletchley Park, the centre of Britain's codebreaking efforts and other intelligence operations. Her work here remains secret although a testimonial from her former commander describes how she acted as "one of two pioneers in doing certain work which had never before been done" and that "the section which she helped to found [brought] to bear a direct influence upon, and in some respects guided, the work of many thousands of people". After the war, Brooke-Rose's considerable achievements remained unspoken by necessity. Her work would not even be communicable to her family; her mother, Evelyn Brooke-Rose, spent the war working for the Postal Censorship in Belfast and was thoroughly convinced of the propensity of loose lips to sink ships. Without any documentary material publically available or even held in family archives, it is near impossible to determine just how important and formative Brooke-Rose's wartime experiences were. Perhaps the attempt to capture her father's life in a fictional form was an attempt at recovering lost memories by Brooke-Rose? Or maybe it is just a good story.

A useful metaphor for the state of the novel, somewhere between history and fiction, can be found Shakespeare's Birthplace; the real-life location too dangerous to include in the final narrative. The reason for the Birthplace's protected status is not entirely due to its own historical merits, but that New Place—the house wherein Shakespeare lived with his own family and wrote a number of his most famous plays— was torn down "in an extraordinary fit of spite" (Winterman) by its owner Francis Gastrell in 1759 after he grew tired of tourists seeking it out. Shocked by this gross act of historical desecration, the Shakespeare Birthplace Trust was founded in order that some material remnant might be preserved. Over time, the Birthplace has come to take on the broader signification of "Shakespeare's house" in spite of its earlier second-place billing. The present stakes its claim over the past. The living trace is more powerful than a thousand lost and forgotten moments. In the words of Sarah Birch, "the process of constructing a story inevitably leads to falsification . . . this is both the 'dear deceit' which goes back centuries and the curse peculiar to modern-day society" (36). Perhaps this is the message of both *The Dear Deceit* and Shakespeare's Birthplace: the persistence of a good story over the specifics of facts. A well-written and entertaining novel will continue to return long after all those involved in its creation have passed on.

Works Cited

Anson, Peter F. Letter to Christine Brooke-Rose, 22nd October 1960.

Birch, Sarah. *Christine Brooke-Rose and Contemporary Fiction*. Oxford: Clarendon Press, 1994.

Brooke-Rose, Christine. Handwritten note included in book. *Descendants of Rev. Clement Moore Butler, D. D.* Roland P. Faulkner, author. 1933.

---. "Notes on Fiction vs. Fact". Held at the Harry Ransom Centre, Austin TX, USA.

Darlington, Joseph. "The Composition of Christine Brooke-Rose's *Thru*: An Afterlife of May '68". *Journal of European Studies*. Forthcoming, 2015.

Eastburn, C. J. Letter to Evelyn Brooke-Rose, 9th June 1942.

Fox, Liam (dir. of "Trustees and Guardians of Shakespeare's Birthplace"). Letter to Christine Brooke Rose, 14th November 1957.

Jones, E. M. Testimonial of War Work. To Christine Bax, 4th January 1946.

Martin, Richard. "'Just Words on a Page': The Novels of Christine Brooke-Rose". *Utterly Other Discourse: The Texts of Christine Brooke-Rose*. Ellen G. Friedman and Richard Martin, eds. London: Dalkey Archive Press, 1995.

Walton, Francis G. Letter to Christine Brooke-Rose, 28th August 1957.

Watts, Henry. Letter to Christine Brooke-Rose, 8th September 1957.

Winterman, Denise. "The Man Who Demolished Shakespeare's House". BBC News Magazine. 7th March 2013. Web. http://www.bbc.co.uk/news/magazine-21587468

1

M Y ADVENTURE began with a legacy, a very small legacy—just under a hundred pounds, in fact. But then it was only an intellectual ad‐ venture.

Of course, one could say that it began with my birth, or, for that matter, with my father's birth. An adventure, especially an adventure of the mind, can begin anywhere, as long as the mind exists to experience it, imagine it, invent it, or whatever the mind does with an adventure. And my mind did very little with the first inkling which came to it by chance some sixteen years ago. But then I was a very young man, and careless with inklings.

I was a captain in the Intelligence Corps at the time, and very proud of both my rank—for I was only twenty-one—and the letters I.C. which I would meticulously place after my signature on all but the most informal letters. This camouflaged the shame, mingled with relief, which I felt at not being employed in a more heroic capacity. The nature of the secret outfit—for so these sinecures were curiously called—with which I spent most of the Second World War, hardly matters here. I was drafted into it because I happened to speak fluent Flemish and French, having been brought up in Brussels, and Belgium was our special responsibility. We had requisitioned—for so these appropriations of property were curiously called —a palatial country mansion in Warwickshire, belonging to the sev‐ enth Lord Weirwood, who was away adding glory to the family annals.

Weirwood Abbey, which indeed included a wood weir in its grounds, had started as an elegant eighteenth-century house with a classical pedi‐ ment, and continued into a gothic fantasy of unusual wit and delicacy. My own office was way up in a round turret, from which I could see almost into Worcestershire.

Not that I could recognise a Worcestershire horizon when I saw one, but Jonas told me, many times, that it was so. Jonas was Lord Weirwood's old coachman, who had insisted on staying, until he was entrusted by H.M. Government with the collecting and burning of all secret waste paper. He would come round each day with a big sack, tunelessly muttering a direful song of his own composition:

Guar-dians of the fie-ry fur-nace
Shad-rach, Meshach, Abednego

And if work was in a lull between operations—for so our sudden bursts of activity were curiously called—I would look up and smile, encouraging a chat.

And, if the sun was shining, he would inevitably say: "That's a lovely view you've got there, sir, why, you can see right over into Worcestershire."

"Can I really? You're very fond of this room, aren't you, Jonas?" I fell easily into a lord-of-the-manor tone, for I was young, and an officer, and the room was now mine for the duration. And Jonas—as conditioned by his time and surroundings as I was by mine—seemed to enjoy playing the faithful-old-servant of nineteenth-century novels, almost as if he were living in quotes.

"I used to play up here, sir, with the fifth Lord Weirwood as he became, when we was boys together, I wasn't supposed to mind you, but he was a lonely little chap, and he used to smuggle me in, and some of the boys from the village too, now and again. We had plenty of larks up and down them stairs. And to think he went on ahead of me. Why, he'd only be sixty-six this year, and here's me at seventy."

"How old was he when he died?"—though I knew.

"Twenty-one, sir." That always knocked at me with a pleasurable guilt. The fifth Lord Weirwood had been killed in the Boer War and Jonas expected everyone to be aware of that fact. *"Ah, sir, the good die young. But they whose hearts are hard And dry as summer's dust Burn to the socket."*

Jonas could remember a deal of verse, but he never seemed to know just how often this dialogue—with minor variations of detail—was re-peated. Nevertheless he always managed to leave me staring out of the turret window towards that Worcestershire horizon which hung hazy and separate over the wooded rills of Warwickshire. And the wordless rhythm of an unwritten poem—for I really was very young—would lilt uneasily through my brain, starting from the nerve centre in the back of the neck, frustrating emptily to the brow above the eyes, until my green telephone would shrill suddenly and I would jerk it up and snap, "Captain Hayley speaking," and the colonelesque voice from London would crackle, "Wil-loughby here, will you scramble please?" For so the untappable line was curiously called.

One day I received two letters. They didn't at the time seem very excit-ing, yet the moment stands clear in my memory. There was a heat-wave on and permission had at last come through that year for us to work in our shirts, provided we wore belts and our sleeves neatly rolled up. It was already hot when I walked into the great hall of Weirwood Abbey just be-fore nine o'clock, and I remember experiencing a slight sensual shock at seeing so many men and women in trim khaki shirts, with belted waists and trim khaki bottoms; the fact that I was dressed in just the same way myself enhanced the pleasure. I pressed and half-fondled my way to the plain-wood letter-rack which, with the notice-board and wooden benches, anachronised the vast Gothic hall with a look of dead, governmental emergency.

I was hoping to find a note from a girl called, I think, Suzy, with whom I was derangedly in love. Love is always impossible to re-imagine, and often difficult even to believe, in retrospect. She wasn't a particularly rich per-sonality, but then, nor was I at twenty-one. She worked in the East Wing and we had arranged a system of notes; she had been on night-shift lately and hadn't left me any message for three days. I was frantic, imagining only too clearly what I called the worst, which was in fact the obvious, and I took, therefore, very little interest in the contents of the only two letters I found that morning in my pigeon-hole. Both were addressed, like all our mail from the outside world, to a P.O. Box number in London, where, from the outside world's point of view, we were supposed to be.

One of them was from a firm of solicitors in Stratford-on-Avon, informing me that my aunt, Miss Muriel Hayley, of the Ann Wardle Home, 102, Radnor Road, Weston-super-Mare, Somerset, formerly of Stratford-upon-Avon, had died on the 16th September, 1943, and that Chancery had awarded the residue of her estate to me as nearest relative. A cheque for £97 0s. 8d. was enclosed.

The second letter was from my father's other sister, Mrs. Cordelia Winthrop Blair, written in optimistically climbing lines and headed c/o Bank of South Africa.

> *Dear Philip* (it soared along),
>
> *Will you please let me know if you have heard from Mr. William Thornton who is my sister's solicitor? It is very important that I should see you soon, so would you give me some idea as to when this would be possible—in London?*

Instead, however, of luring me by leaving it at that, Mrs. Winthrop Blair could not resist telling me, in her own winsome old-world way, what it was she wished to see me about.

> *It appears that the residue of my sister's estate was intestate, and you are to benefit. As I had for many years to contribute towards my sister's living, it seems somewhat ironical that someone who never saw her or took the slightest interest in her should now benefit by her death, especially as the money did not come from my brother but from legacies left her by friends. I am the only one of her family left.*
>
> *Surely your Mother receives something from my brother's estate? I saw his Will, and she and you were provided for. I cannot think she is entirely dependent—as I am—on what she can earn.*
>
> *My love to you and please let me know when there is a chance of meeting.*
> *Cordelia Winthrop Blair.*

The big hall was empty. It was five past nine. In three minutes I had covered the silent corridor with my long legs and swiftly spiralled up the back stairs to my turret room, where an A.T.S. sergeant was trying to answer both my telephones at once. Operation "Puddle" was on.

The necessities of war taught me quite early in life always to postpone the answering of querulous letters, in legal matters if not, alas, in love. During the next few days I was so much whirlwinded by the unfairness of both love and war that the two letters remained forgotten in the private in-tray of my back trouser-pocket, where my batman found them a week later when sending my uniform to be cleaned.

Operation "Puddle" was over, the heat-wave was over, my love affair was over, and in the leaden lull that followed I sat at my desk catching up on private correspondence in the war-firm's time.

I acknowledged the cheque, and then, learning after all nothing from the lapse of days, wrote a curt note to my aunt, thanking her for her rather unpleasant letter, hypocritically regretting that I was not in fact stationed in London and so would be unable to meet her. There seemed little point, I added archly, in disputing a Chancery decision, especially over such an insignificant sum. I intended in any case to make the cheque over to my mother who, contrary to my aunt's belief, depended very much on what she earned, had received precisely nothing from my father's so-called estate, and had suffered quite enough through her marriage into the Hayley family to deserve every penny she could get out of it.

I felt rather pleased with the tone I had achieved, firm, distant, yet polite, or so I thought, a gentleman's letter.

Dear God, what a prig I was.

A vague unease must have mingled with my sense of righteousness, for I remember gazing long at that Worcestershire horizon, feeling oddly displaced in time. Why was I sitting in a stately home, looking out on the remains of the Forest of Arden, writing a Dickensian letter about the will of a nineteenth-century lady I had never known, to a nineteenth-century lady I had met precisely twice? Because of course, to me everyone over fifty was "nineteenth century", except my mother, who had been born in 1893 and had therefore only just reached her fiftieth birthday. Miss Muriel Hayley, formerly of Stratford-upon-Avon was, I had gathered, "peculi-ar", whether insane or simple-minded I had never inquired. It occurred to me that I knew remarkably little about my father's family, or, for that matter, about my father. The Hayleys of Kilbrae, I remembered him teach-ing me, and he had dressed me up in a bright red and yellow kilt which caused my schoolfellows in Brussels—who all wore plus-fours—to hoot with vulgar delight.

That Warwickshire view always set me daydreaming.

By return of double posts—since we both used camouflaged addresses—came an answer from my aunt Cordelia. I was to find out later that answer-ing by return of post in emotional matters was not one of the mistakes life had taught her to avoid. This time the letter was carefully typed in bright blue on bright blue paper, and folded in such a way that the last paragraph caught my eye, so that I read it first as I went upstairs.

... That anything my sister left should go to the son of such a man seems to me most ironical. It is the last thing she would have wished, but if you feel quite happy about it, then I can say nothing more. Had it been from any other source I should have been glad, but I doubt if you will believe or appreciate that.

With all good wishes,

Cordelia Winthrop Blair.

I don't know how or why, but that last paragraph remained engraved in the inmost recesses of my memory, to re-emerge word for word years later. It had hardly any effect on me at the time. I unfolded the letter, which was immensely long, and laid it out in front of me, on top of the re-ports which were neatly piled on my desk for me to read. Almost at once the telephone rang.

"Captain Hayley speaking."

"Phil, Derek here. What's the latest gen on Forger?"

"He's in Charleroi at the moment. Hold on, will you. I'll get you the de-tails."

I buzzed and a buxom private came in.

"Yes, sir?"

I put my hand over the mouthpiece.

"Oh, Miss Factor." I was supposed to call her just "Factor" or "Private Factor", but never stooped to it. "Bring me the last few cards on Forger, will you?"

"Yes, sir."

While she was out, I glanced at the letter, strangely unwilling to read it. My eyes kept leaping ahead to pick out words and phrases from different paragraphs: *you are so utterly ignorant of many facts . . . even at the risk of boring you . . . your father . . . do you think it was easy for my Father, who was the most honourable of men . . . when my Father was dying he said to me "I shall never be able to understand how we came to have such a son as Northbrook" . . . when Northbrook was sentenced to three years penal servitude I was a child in the schoolroom . . .*

"Here you are, sir."

"Eh? Oh, thank you. Hello, Derek? Here we are, erm, let me see. Forger. Reached Charleroi on 13th, from Namur, where *Theft* successfully accomplished. Contacted Barteau same day."

"Ah, he did contact Barteau?"

"Yes, on the 13th."

"That fits. Thanks."

"Any time."

I picked up the blue paper again, but hesitated. Although a lull was on my in-tray overflopped with routine, bumph, as we called the in-coming information which had to be mapped, indexed, analysed, co-ordinated, written up, distributed and (presumably) acted upon elsewhere. I was proud of my responsible job and at that age too conscientious to be capable of initialling a report without reading it, or writing one without having weighed the facts. My aunt's melodramatic style struck me then as "pre-first-war"—I remember that very phrase coming into my youthful mind: "pre-war" to me seemed long enough ago, when I had been a mere boy, but it existed in my memory, and so felt close and sensible as well as distant and unbelievable; but the First World War, before even the possibility of my existence had occurred, that was a suitable image of the old-fashioned, the blimpish, the irrelevant.

I stared at the letter with self-protective blankness, now taking in only the odd detail that my aunt used a capital F for her father but not for mine.

The war, as it so often did, made my decision for me. I put the letter by, not on account of my in-tray but because on that day at dawn our invading armies had landed in Normandy. It seems odd, looking back, that Derek and I and all the rest should have come in to the office at nine knowing nothing. But we were never told big things like that, certainly not dates, and we had long given up reading newspapers: since it was impossible to remember what one knew from the inside and what from the outside, it was best to read nothing and assume that all one's knowledge was secret. And yet, although the view we had of the war was thus curiously specialised, the "large sweep of events" as journalists saw it, still gave us much to do. Soon after nine-fifteen I was summoned to an emergency meeting and for many weeks I was working so incessantly and with such excitement that I forgot about the letter. When I did remember it, it was nowhere to be found.

I could have sworn I had folded it neatly and put it into my wallet. I acquired the filing habit young and had unconsciously turned my private person into a cabinet of folders, with a rough system of priorities for different pockets according to urgency, degree of secrecy, and degree of importance —love letters, notes about office intrigues, friends asking for help, just friends, and so on. A military uniform has many pockets. The wallet in the inside breast pocket meant *Top Secret—Do Nothing,* or at most *Top Secret—To be considered at leisure.*

The young are so easily prepared to swear by their memory. Who knows what happened to that letter—perhaps my friend Jonas, the guardian of the fiery furnace, picked it up near the waste-paper basket and assumed it had missed its intended target; perhaps it had fallen straight into the target; perhaps I gave it away with a pound note. I leave that question to the psychologists. Certainly I was not able to consider the letter at leisure, and although I didn't exactly do nothing, I let it remain un-answered, thereby losing touch with my Aunt Cordelia for many years—if touch there had ever been. I did, however, call on my mother.

I was quite unusually fond of my mother—unusually, that is, not for a boy brought up as an only child with no fatherly hand to help, but in comparison with the reactions indulged in against their parents by the adolescents of today. But then adolescents are always supposed to be having reactions, and difficult times, and problems of adjustment. We were not allowed any, under the Emergency Powers Act. Now that I am approaching forty, I sometimes wish one could read less about the problems of adolescence, and more about adjustment to middle age. Or, for that matter, adjustment to peace. Cer-tainly it was the breakdown I had, if one can call it that, which led me into all this a year or so ago, and it was my love for my mother which indirectly led to the breakdown as a delayed reaction, sometime after she had cut the umbilical cord I was myself unable to snap, when she left my world and me in it, alone. All that is obvious to me now, and as such uninteresting.

In those days, my mother was so close as to be actually working in the same outfit, at the other end of Weirwood Abbey, the eighteenth-century end. She had started the war by volunteering for the Censorship, which sent her, thoughtfully, up to Caithness to read the letters of fishermen, though she knew three foreign languages. I got her to Weirwood by the unlikely method of sending her some forms to fill in. For although war was a great network of pullable wires, so many people were so busy pulling them all of the time that the usual channels were sometimes quicker. She worked in the Foreign Office Section, and wore, thank good-ness, civilian dress. I used to give her most of my clothes coupons, and she always looked aptly elegant in well-cut country tweeds. My mother was, of course, beautiful.

I walked past the long range of french windows giving out on the tennis courts, where several arduous matches were being slammed back and forth, watched by posies of people sitting on the grass, civilian girls in summer frocks, men and girls in white, blue or khaki shirts, and Americans in dark olive green. Nature is so colourful, I thought, yet when man tries to find its essence, in order to protect himself and merge with it, chameleon-like, the colours he achieves are khaki, grey, and almost black.

It was six o'clock and I waited in the shady colonnade of the main entrance for my mother to come out, like a bee from a hive. Khaki buses and shooting-brakes were lined up along the drive almost as far as the gates, to take the day-workers back to their billets, which were scattered in many villages for miles around. I myself lived in the military camp built for the purpose just beyond Weirwood Abbey, and so did not depend on government transport. Those who did could not work late for just an hour or two, but had to stay till eleven, when the next lot of buses went out to fetch in the midnight shift. I could make my own overtime and had in fact done so every night for the last few weeks. It was a change to get off so early, in double-summer-time, and double-summer weather, but I felt very tired.

My mother came out wearing a cool-looking dress, redolent of the 'thirties yet somehow not old-fashioned—some kind of light silk, shantung I suppose, with a lot of stitching or small pleating, and long loose sleeves like a man's shirt only small at the cuffs. It was a very old dress, the colour of gold leaves, and she had had it as far back as I could remember, perhaps even in Brussels. Certainly she would never have been able to afford it later, in London, and one couldn't get silk in wartime. But she was clever with clothes and must have done things to it to make it look up-to-date—unless perhaps women's fashions had stopped with the war.

I saluted facetiously, then kissed her.

"Hello, darling. I managed to get a few rashers of bacon out of the mess officer for being out tonight. My contribution to supper." I tapped my gas-mask haversack knowingly.

"Oh, thank you, darling, that was thoughtful of you. I have a feeling Mrs. Walton's giving us baked liver, it's her party piece, and she was making terrible jokes about offal and the awful butcher this morning. The bacon should make it go further, she will be pleased."

We climbed into the bus, and at ten past six the motorised khaki file moved out, some turning left outside the gates, some right. Ours turned left to the village of Weirwood, which was almost entirely Elizabethan and Jacobean, and what was not had politely toned in. There was even a disused smithy under a spreading chestnut tree on a triangular hillock where the climbing road forked suddenly down and away, and whenever I passed it, which was not often, my throat tightened with sudden emotion about the Defence of the Realm and What We Were Fighting For, though admittedly it did so less and less as I changed from nineteen towards twenty-two and the war looked more and more won.

My mother was tired, and spoke little. I watched her as she rested her eyes in the rinsing green of the moving trees and fields. Her profile was still sharp and, though the skin round the chin and jaw had slackened, the effect was of tautness, not flabbiness, and her turned-up nose refused old age to the rest of the face. The thick grey hair waved gently back into a loose sort of chignon which seemed black compared to the rest, though I remembered her hair had been brown when I was small. She had just turned fifty.

"How's Suzy?"

"Oh, that's over . . . Weeks ago."

"Oh, darling, I'm sorry."

"Don't lie. You're very much relieved, really." I grinned at her and she grinned back.

"Well, perhaps she wasn't my dream daughter-in-law, but you know, very few girls are."

Her French accent was so very slight that only a phonetic recorder would have registered it. I used to strain my ear for it sometimes, out of love, but I felt it as an emotion rather than heard it as a fact.

"Very few girls are dream-girls anyway," I said. "That doesn't stop us dreaming."

"Come now, no cynicism. She wasn't really intelligent enough for you, and that never works." There was a sad certainty in her tone as she said this, but it vanished as she spoke again softly. "I really am sorry, though, did it hurt much?"

"At the time, like hell."

How like my mother to know, without asking, that it was I who had been jilted. How like her to leap several stages of retrospective sympathy and say simply:

"I see so little of you these days, and we're so near." Yet without a lilt of reproach.

"I know."

There was no need of explanation, of excuses, between us. We both disliked meeting for lunch in the crowded, clattering canteen, and if I worked late, or played late, she did not intrude. My love for her had never at any time been a creation of possessiveness. She was the most self-sufficient woman I have ever known.

Later, after supper, we went for a walk in the woods. She loved the woods, and had found herself a room overlooking them, on the outskirts of a village called Sutton Leigh, in the house of an old Methodist preacher and his large family, which my mother had chosen, she said, as a test of her faith. The local church, she told me, was so High it burnt a red light outside when the Sacrament was exposed, and the Methodists—according to the preacher—had been collecting indignant sheep into their flock ever since 1868, when a book called *The Priest in Absolution* had apparently started yet another bout of Roman fever and anti-Roman inoculation in the Church of England. There was also a small wooden but near the wood, built by a few Irish families with the help of some soldiers stationed nearby. This was the Catholic Church, where my mother went.

She did in fact step in for a moment on our way to the woods, and I sat on a stone wall watching the sun set behind the square tower of Sutton Leigh church. When she came out, the last glows of the sun caught her face, tinting her skin and hair and burnishing her brown eyes to onyx, so that she looked half her age.

I felt suddenly a little boy. Even the brown cardigan she wore over that golden dress reminded me of one she had possessed in Brussels, and perhaps it was.

"Tell me about Daddy," I said as we trod the pine-needles which re-called holidays in the Ardennes, "Who was he?" I had given her an ac-count of the lost letter, and what I remembered of its contents.

"I never knew much about your father." She always called him "your father", as if she had had nothing to do with him except through me, which made me think irreverently of the Virgin Mary. But then, she would dissociate herself in just the same way with the phrase "your Aunt Cordelia". Only her own brothers and sisters were Frédérique, Madeleine, Bérangère, Giselle, Maurice.

"Your Aunt Cordelia turned up in Brussels after he died, hoping, I suppose, that he had left her something. She stayed until even Grandad, who thought she was charming and enjoyed flirting back at her, got a bit fed up. Your father never spoke of her and the first I knew of her ex-istence was when she wrote me a letter to say how glad she had been to read the announcement of his death in *The Times*." My mother giggled a little, like a schoolgirl in class. "A charming way of introducing oneself to one's brother's widow, I thought. But that was fairly typical Hayley behaviour."

"And what's all this 'Northbrook' thing?"

"She always called him Northbrook, which was apparently his second name, though he never used it, even as an initial. Well, anyway, when she learnt there was nothing for her she really exploded."

I remembered wondering why she spoke so insistently about her sister-in-law, when I had asked her about her husband.

"Why did you leave him? What was he really like?"

"Oh, darling, it's such an old story." We had reached the stile at the other side of the wood and I helped her over it. She decided to sit on it, crooking her long legs into the second rung down. Mine were even longer and reached the third. It always seemed strange to me that I should be taller than she was, who had given me birth. "He was selfish and impossible," she went on, staring at a field of clover we were facing. She took the cigarette I offered and we lit up. "He was also much too in-tellectual for me. I was always left way behind."

The memory of her frequent helplessness saddened her eyes for a moment. She had such soft brown eyes. Brown eyes, I thought sentimentally, keep a face so much younger than blue ones, which glaze and go pale with age.

When she spoke again, it still wasn't about my father, but about us.

"You remember how poor we were, after his death?"

I remembered. 1936. My mother bringing me to London. I was English, she said, I must have a good, English education. But in fact I was only a pale prim little foreign boy, a Frog to my weirdly insular school-fellows who had barely heard of Belgium. I remembered those three years before the war in all their adolescent intensity of detail, if the years between thirteen and sixteen can be called by so pretentious a name as adolescent, instead of just plain silly. I remembered the fear I had felt as a boy when I first became aware of poverty's stark arithmetic: unemployment was high, my mother was over forty, and couldn't find a job except as a typist at £2 10s. a week; twenty-two shillings and sixpence paid the rent of our two-roomed, bathroomless flat in a grimy Pimlico block for which all the inhabitants borrowed Sloane Square as part of the address, because addresses still mattered in those days—especially to those who didn't quite have them; the coal, gas, electricity and telephone bills, the hire-purchase on the kitchen-stove as well as all her meals, or ours during my holidays, had to come out of the remaining twenty-seven-and-sixpence, which somehow never was twenty-seven-and-sixpence by the time she got it; one Thursday night she had only one penny left for her supper, went into Victoria Station to get a bar of chocolate from one of the machines, and drew a platform ticket. She had told me that as a funny story, but now I remembered it with an aching clang, as if that same penny had just dropped through a slit in the folds of my brain into a resonant nerve-machine. I remembered above all the innocence of her loneliness, not for herself, but for me: her doctor or a man on the floor above, who had lent her a shilling for the gas-meter and was something to do with the B.B.C., or her boss, a formidable lady engineer, even a chiropodist I had to visit for a verruca I had caught at school, all these and others set her dreaming of possible careers for me, or at least—since I wanted to be a musician—jobs to keep me going while I practised at the piano or composed the greatest symphony that ever was; and yet she never actually bothered any of these people, she was far too shy; charmingly, she rather expected me to do so, once she had given me the idea.

I had never quite forgiven the image of my father for all this. The war had indeed come as a blessing. I was not even ashamed of welcoming the war, thousands of others had done so too. But at that moment I didn't want to think of that bit of past. I wanted to learn about the man who had caused it. I tried to guide her back.

"Who were those trustees you always spoke about so ominously?" The word had acquired a whole weight of villainy for me as a boy. "I heard from the trustees today," my mother would say with despair in her eyes.

"Oh, Kingsley-Smith and others. I had been a nominal director of your father's company, which gave me a certain control, but a few years before he died your father replaced me by Kingsley-Smith, who turned up in London just about then. Anyway, they were rather unpleasant. You see, I had a document your father and I had both signed when we separated, to the effect that I was to get so much a year from the company if he died. But they said it was a very small company which would collapse if they paid me that much. They said they had the power to wind it up so that there'd be no money at all. My lawyer told me I could do nothing. In any case your father left so many debts the company couldn't even pay the dividends on the shares he left you. Yes, he did at least leave you something, however useless. I haven't heard since the war. I suppose the firm folded up when the salvage campaign put an end to mail-advertising. They did condescend to pay one small lump sum in 1938, which helped a bit, but there was no income. If it hadn't been for Elinor Jarvis, who found me a cheap flat and got you into Bramerton on reduced fees, I don't know what we would have done. Even so Grandad had to sell his last bit of capital to pay those fees. It was tough going."

We sat very still, puffing at the silence. Memory gives pride of place to sentimentality and nostalgic resentment, but sooner or later conscience follows too. I now also remembered, uneasily, how much more difficult I had made things for her at the time: demanding more pocket-money or the most expensive kind of tennis racket; refusing to wear my school uniform during the holidays—and what an expensive uniform, too—in case I met one of the boys and he told the others I couldn't afford mufti; grumbling because she left me alone all day, because we didn't go to any shows, or do anything interesting I could boast about at the beginning of term; always making a fuss, abusing her, accusing her family of being "bourgeois", Victorian, ordinary, hypocritical; flying into a rage and giving her no peace when I discovered she had become a Roman Catholic, which was a religion "for the Irish and Flemish working-classes". And yet I must have suffered from all these things, unaware that I was acquiring, at a smart English school, all the middle-class vices while my middle-class family was practising the virtues. I suddenly remembered my shock when I first noticed that my mother's hair was completely grey, on the platform at Charing Cross where she stood, slim in a long dark green coat and small grey felt hat, waiting with all the richer parents as the school train came in; I resolved to be so good those holidays, and I went on being selfish, demanding and cruel. Oh yes, I had my adolescence, like everyone else, but the war came, as I have said, as a blessing. Quickly I shifted the blame.

"Did you know anything about who he was?" I asked. "I mean, his going to prison?"

"No, nothing. I sometimes suspected something shady, but I had no idea what. I don't suppose I even formulated it. There were so many odd things about your father."

"But wasn't it more odd of you to marry him, at least in those days, knowing so little?"

Her anger, though always subdued as an ember, flashed quickly, but subsided even as she spoke.

"Those days, as you call them, weren't so fuddy-duddy as you seem to think. People were just as adventurous and careless as they are today, especially after the Great War. I was foreign, and very gullible. And I must say, he was always most convincing."

She was already smiling on the last sentence. Still, I changed my ground slightly.

"I wish I hadn't lost that letter now. There was a reference to some book, a biography of Sir Something or Other, which apparently mentions 'one of the many episodes in which he figured', or some such phrase. That would give me a clue. And I just didn't take it in."

"I should leave it be, darling. He caused much suffering, and not only to me, I'm sure, but whatever he did is no doubt recorded elsewhere, at any rate, our only business is to pray for him."

The swiftly fallen chill of the evening swept over her like a ghost and she shuddered. I put my arm round her.

"You're cold. We'd better go back."

We stubbed out our cigarettes carefully on the stile before throwing them away in the bracken, then I helped her down. Her hand was icy. I took off my tunic and put it round her shoulders.

"No, darling, you'll catch cold."

"Nonsense: zest of youth."

She smiled and looked into the darkness beyond the tender green of the young larches bordering the black wood.

"The edge of a forest always looks so mysterious, doesn't it, much more so than the middle is from inside. Marriage is a bit like that, or used to be, when we were more innocent."

A squadron of Halifax heavy bombers growled overhead, very high.

2

IT is now about seven years since my wife left me. Poor Jennifer. She couldn't cope, she said, with my mammoth mother-fixation. "They sure come in every size," she said, "but I never seen one that big, even back home where everything's bigger'n here, and boy do I mean everything."

She really was rather crude.

I am trying to be flippant about it, but actually I was very cut up.

It's true I was mentally comparing her, and sometimes verbally, but I could no more help it than avoid breathing. My comparisons were really contrasts, not identifications, indeed, how could they be the latter? My mother would never, for instance, have carried a pocket-wireless in her shopping bag for fear of enduring five unfilled minutes in the street. But then all this potted psychology everyone possesses these days leads to such over-simplifications.

The incident which, as she put it, finalised it, was of course trivial. Finalising incidents always are. I had expressed disapproval of her coral nail varnish, but she had kept it on, and that night to my amazement I watched fascinated and excited beyond my own belief her painted fingers moving over my thigh in the low lamp light. Dreamily I murmured:

"Pretty nails, playing at goldfish. I had a bath as a small boy once, and my mother wore nail varnish that colour. Funny she never did later."

Well yes, it was idiotic of me. This famous censor that suppresses so much, why doesn't it ever suppress those innocent actions and remarks that turn out to be destructive? Jennifer's hand stopped.

"And that's what makes the lacquer pretty now?"

I shall never forget the harshness of that question, hurled into the soft half-tones of our sensuality. Philip Hayley Es-quire, she always called me when angry. It was the manner of her leaving me, there and then in the middle of the night, which made me grasp, suddenly and irrelevantly, the possibility that American films might after all be based on American behaviour and not, as here, human behaviour on American films.

I had met her in one of those slow-moving lifts without doors, that you have to jump in and out of, in the I.G. Farben building at Frankfurt-am-Main, where General Eisenhower had his occupation headquarters in 1945, and where I was based as a liaison officer.

Most of the American girls in uniform were glamour-pussies with long, unpractical hair-styles; and sent there, frankly, for the boys, as an anti-fraternisation measure. She had arrived only the day before and was not yet used to "those kinda sleazy elevators". She jumped straight into my arms and, morals being what they were and the situation so Freudian, I kissed her at once. To my delight, she kissed me back and, morals being what they were and the situation so Freudian, it was some kiss.

Like all other conquerors, I had a fine old time. We lived well, many of us in requisitioned flats with central heating, and were waited on in the vast restaurants for officers of all services and sexes, by Germans evidently selected for their obsequiousness. We helped ourselves to their belongings, their books, their wine, their willing women. We could buy all our bribes, from stockings to cosmetics, at the American PX. We could get extra cigarette cartons and sell them on the black market. Life had never been so free and easy.

As for me, I had a car, a driver, the use of a jeep, and a job that took me from Frankfurt to Munich, Berlin, Hanover, wherever I chose to find documents to look at or prisoners to interrogate. As often as possible I wangled Jennifer with me and we spent much of our time catching colds in open jeeps and getting rid of them in Dakotas. Germany was in ruins, some towns, like Kassel, just a heap of rubble with only the tramlines running in between, and perhaps one upright building occupied by the American Red Cross, where one could get hot coffee and doughnuts on one's way through. My driver would rudely hoot the German civilians out of the road. But any sense of guilt we may have felt, perhaps singly, was quickly swallowed up in the general harshness released by long justified loathing and fear. There were no cinemas, no theatres except a few army shows, there was nothing to do except drive around and go to parties: the R.A.F. fifteen miles away one night, the Artillery another, the Americans, the French, the Intelligence Boys, the Control Commission, the Military Police, the Engineers, the W.A.A.C.S., the Red Cross, a dance-club in an old Schloss ten miles off, a night-club on a lake . . . And funny little accordion and violin bands playing *Sentimental Journey*. Nothing to do but loot, drink and fornicate.

Such was the atmosphere that produced our marriage, hard, easily romantic, artificial. She was enchanted by Europe, even in ruins, especially, perhaps, in ruins, and I was the perfect guide, with my vagrant job and my fluent German. We even managed Paris, Vienna and Venice on various stolen weekends. On my side, I was intoxicated by my own success with her.

We actually remained married for five long years of postwar realism, and I was passionately in love with her the whole of that time. At least, with her body. Her body seemed to contain all bodies, bodies of all the girls who had walked out on me before I could possess them.

So when she too walked out, I took it very badly. My lovely war was over.

The psychiatrist, who was a Jungian, said, "Yes, well, why not, if you want to?"

She said this after eighteen months of getting nowhere—at least, so I kept telling her. I said it was all so boring, my childhood, my dreams, me me me, it was all right at first, a relief, really, like a purge, but eighteen months, three times a week, what a cure for self-love, why one might as well be married to oneself. I was thirty-seven, and able therefore to make banal jokes about marriage. But psychiatrists always tell you it takes years, citing as examples their richest, unhappiest patients. I hadn't, she kept saying, come to terms with my dark side. But, as I told her, I had been holding Peace Conferences with my dark side ever since I could remember, with the usual dim results to be expected from Peace Conferences. Now, however, she said it was very interesting that I should have this resistance and let us analyse it, and in fact we were only just beginning (to get somewhere, she meant).

The next time I brought her my box-files.

She said very little as I enthusiastically explained, in great detail, the progress of my painstaking research on my father's life, but she watched me with that sharp foxy eye doctors always wear like a sudden lens when a patient is seriously ill. I felt it on me through the tremendous show I was putting on, but I didn't care. I knew I wasn't dangerous, and I loved doing my research. Then she said quietly, "Yes, well, why not, if you want to? But isn't it all rather a waste of time?"

I said, nothing is a waste of time providing one really wants to do it. Not even wasting time.

When I won a scholarship to the Royal College of Music just as the war began, I dreamt of becoming a great composer. I even had in mind one great theme, in descending fourths, which I used to play over and over on the piano, lest I forgot it before it could be brought in at a still moment of a future symphony. But the moment remained still for ever, and I became a solicitor, under the Further Education and Training Scheme of a grateful government.

It was thus that I came to read, over and above the surrealistic intricacies of Property Law and such, Marlborough's life of Sir Arnold Pettigrew, K.C., the last of the histrionic advocates. And it was thus that I discovered, on pages 110-113, the curious case of Alfred Hayley, defended by Sir Arnold just before he was made a Queen's Counsel. This indeed was the only clue as to the time, for Marlborough, like so many biographers, proved shy of dates. The reign of Queen Victoria seemed so very long ago that I at once dismissed the jolt I experienced as irrelevant. A common name, Alfred Hayley. The case, too, was so very petty, and only reported for an interesting ecclesiastical dispute behind the legal tangle. I couldn't help feeling that if any father of mine had gone to prison it must have been for something on a grand scale, something melodramatic, like murder, something novelistic, like ruining in bankruptcy thousands of trusting small investors, as the Town & County Bank had done in *Cranford,* or Mr. Frothingham in *The Whirlpool* or Ponderovo in *Tono-Bungay.* Strange how the reality of the past comes to our mind most immediately as fiction. Some even say that all our knowledge of the past is fiction. And so, like a novel merely glanced at, I laid the information aside.

Much later, when moving to a bachelor flat after the breakup of my marriage, I found at the bottom of a trunk full of my mother's things, a large yellow envelope marked, rather helplessly I thought, *To Be Burnt—A Briller*, in her hand. It contained great wads of writing, one again in my mother's hand —but much looser and less formed—one in pale mauve typing on thin yellowing paper,and a third, very thick, in an unfamiliar but bold feminine script headed *On Board SS La Lorraine, May 14th 1918.*

Laura, my dearest, it is sweeping over me that we are separated, that I am going away from you, that I don't know when you are sailing, and there is a catch at my throat and a strange feeling of numbness at my heart . . .

I read on fascinated. The style seemed quaint and Edwardian, or was it late Victorian, with forty words where ten would do and phrases like "my darling girl" and "angel child". I could hardly believe that the author was not after all a woman, but quite evidently my own father, writing a journal to my mother in the middle of the Atlantic. There were quite a few bits of verse, some of them quotations from Browning or Meredith, but one or two unknown to me and bad enough, I thought, to be by himself. It went on for forty-four pages.

The mauve typed document was much longer, in very close spacing on foolscap size paper, also written to my mother, or, lower down in the text, "You. My wife." It was all about religion and verbose enough to make a book. And it was dated, at the long-last end, *16th April, 1922.*

The pages in my mother's hand were written on the back of some office paper headed *Alfred Hayley & Co., Importers and Exporters—American, English and Swiss Merchandise, 16, rue de Lausanne, Geneve. Telegrams & Cables, Hayley Geneve.* They began in November 1920 and ended, curiously enough, also on 16th April, but 1921. They were also about religion, addressed to her husband and recounting her Odyssey of search, doubt, indifference and need, telling him over and over how much she owed to his guidance and to her love for him, and containing the surprising sentences: *I watched you play with words and arguments yesterday. I do not say that you were not sincere, I know you are sincere but was not the fun of argument leading you into absurd positions for the sake of keeping up the fencing and rejoicing at the agility of your own mind? I am glad I am not as clever as you are, glad I am able to trust others much more than I trust myself and to give myself up to the influence of God.*

My astonishment was both a puritan shock and a weird elation. I felt like a peeping Tom, as if these dullish documents were the very act that had given me birth. Here were two people living together who yet felt obliged to write each other great epistles on Affairs of the Soul. Couldn't they *talk*, I thought intolerantly, then remembered Jennifer, whose notion of man's immortal longings seemed to be comprehended in the word "goddam", and whose conversation, bright though it appeared, consisted of lively and intransigent views on politics, politicians and Cultural Life taken knock, sock and wise-crack out of *Time Magazine*. It was something, after all, that these two people who had been my parents could write about God at all, at any rate, to each other. And I pondered on that mysterious urge people have to write things down, regardless of ability. Diarists, grapho-maniacs, tree-carvers, note-jotters, who are they *really* writing to? Those anonymous hands that mark passages in library books and scrawl "Rub-bish!!!" or "But see St Augustine!"—are they telling God, the next reader, themselves, posterity? And posterity, was that not me, in this case? Why had all this been kept, though marked *To Be Burnt?* And this exact dating, as if an emotion acquired more reality for having occurred at a specific point in time, who was it for? There seemed to be something about Spring which prompted scribal and other longings. For each document ended: 16th April, 1921, 1922. My baby brother had been born dead on 16th Janu-ary 1922, exactly a year before my own birth on 17th January 1923.

What else was there? What clues did I possess? Precious few, at least in that envelope.

There were the three journals, two of them by him.

There was some later affidavit of my mother's, which gave her date of birth, Geneva 1893, the date of her marriage in 1919, the date of his death in 1934. At once I waved away the unjustly famous quotation which sprang with great obviousness to my mind. When lines of poetry spring spontaneously to the mind of a lawyer, I thought, they have surely ceased to be true. Life holds more than birth, copulation and death.

There was a copy of the Deed of Arrangement, 1938, resulting from a settlement in chambers between my mother and the trustees after the dispute over the Will. Four whole years of litigation, how typical of my profession. And then she had to withdraw her claims. Oddly enough, so had Miss Marjorie Maxwell, or "that woman", as my mother had always called her. So had Kingsley-Smith and other beneficiaries. Reading the document now, as a lawyer, and comparing it with the Will which I at once obtained in photostat from Somerset House, I could see that the settlement was in fact remarkably fair in the absurd circumstances. The Will was a madman's Will, for there simply was no money to leave, unless it had been embezzled. I was later to discover that such money as was left in the company went to settle out of court a somewhat un-savoury libel suit which was due to be heard just before my father died. Perhaps he had died to get out of the scrape, a child to the very end. But even from this document alone it was quite clear that those villainous trustees of my childhood had even put up money of their own and, together with "that woman", had done the best they could to save from the mess at least one lump sum, if not a regular income, for the provision of the widow and "the said Hayley Infant". That was me, a lawyer approaching forty, and accustomed to use that phrase in de-scribing the unwittingly litigating offspring of my only too wittingly litigating clients.

I was beginning to realise how dull and dirty my profession was.

Nor did this tedious bother over a few hundred pounds give me much information on my father's life. I took down the names and addresses of everyone mentioned in the documents and wrote, with maniacal meth-od, to all of them. Most letters were returned marked *Unknown at this Address* or even *Recipient Dead*. One or two replies came from business colleagues and casual club acquaintances. He had a caustic wit. He was extremely well-read. Most entertaining. But then, business men are easy to impress in non-business matters. Not a scholar, said a scholar. His book is useful for reference, though he had no discrimination, no idea of what to leave out. A little too plausible, said a Keeper at the British Museum. But then, scholars are hard to impress in any matters at all.

I looked up the Company Registration file at Bush House. It contained later addresses of shareholders and co-directors. Miss Marjorie Maxwell had become Mrs. Langtree during the war, just before the company was bought up. I wrote to her. "That woman" materialised into a gentle widow of fifty-eight or so, rather weak on spelling and strong on common sense, who wore two pips on the shoulder of her navy blue Red Cross uniform. A decent show of reticence turned slowly to gladness at my existence, an existence patently as innocent of grudges as it was of penury, so that, with the minute deposit of old guilt washed away, she gave me my father's Bible, a present from his parents on his eleventh birthday, heavily marked and annotated in pencil and red ink, with poems by John Keble and A. N. Hayley copied out on blank pages meant for notes. Inside the Bible at the back was an almost illegible pencilled note dated 1897, about a "Brother Theobald" returning. At the beginning of Isaiah, was a loose slip of paper which read, in yellowing black ink, *A. N. Hayley, P.O. Box 459, New Orleans, La., Nov. 9th 1905.*

Mrs. Langtree also gave me an oddly familiar but no doubt merely Freudian silver pencil belonging to my father, with red, blue and black leads that could be pushed out alternately. I was annoyed with myself for labelling it at once so self-consciously, but one is, I suppose, a child of one's ghastly time, and the pencil did curiously disturb me.

"A peculiar young man . . . of uncertain mental balance," the biographer of Sir Arnold Pettigrew had said of the Alfred Hayley there described. I turned up the account once more, and found that, although no date was given, the young man in question was said to be twenty-two. Sir Arnold had taken silk in the Spring of 1898, and the case had been fought just before that. If it was my father who was twenty-two in

1898, he must have been born in 1876.

I could hardly believe it. I quickly calculated that he must have been forty-three when he married my mother. Forty-three. Not very old, really, but it gave me a shock. It was as if I, who now felt that my life in its main features was more or less over, or at least set in a fixed bachelor course, were to marry again in a few years and give birth not only to a new being but to a whole new series of emotions. If we knew what the future held for us, I thought, we would be so frightened and incredulous we would never do anything, and perhaps never reach that future at all. And, paradoxically, that would be the end of free will as we know it.

1876. The best part of a lifetime before I was ever made possible. I began to resent that span of years, feeling obscurely that it was all right for parents to have existed as children and young people in love before one's own birth, but no more. And yet there was no doubting it: *The Times* Index for that year soon led me to the law report, and hence to other newspapers with fuller, more colourful accounts, all giving the whole name, Alfred Northbrook Hayley.

Soon I was even able to trace a few of the people concerned. One of them, called Felix Perkins, began sending me slow, repetitive and detailed instalments from a Jesuit College in Canada, where he is ending his days soberly as a lay brother, after a somewhat less sober life. He sends them to me still, and has not yet reached the incident itself. But then, I did ask for it. Earnestness deserves earnestness.

Another "witness", of whom I became very fond, was an elderly Anglican clergyman called the Reverend Vernon Manning, once a close friend of the man who prosecuted my father. He had, at eighty-two, a passion for folk-dancing and disliked Harvest Homes because the smell of vegetables interfered with the incense. When I asked him if he could identify one of the quotations in my father's journal as perhaps belonging to the period of his youth, he read out the lines with awe:

> *The hours I spent with thee dear heart,*
> *Are as a string of pearls to me.*

> *I count them over every one of them apart.*
> *My Rosary, my Rosary.*

And he said, "I say, that's *rather* good ! Your father was *quite* a poet, *quite* a poet."

A mistress, a few friends, some of whom mentioned other friends, including a certain Baroness Cuilth, now ageing, who couldn't remember anything about him; two journals, a posthumous dispute over a crazy Will, a trial. It wasn't much to fill up fifty-nine years.

Suddenly I remembered Miss Harriet Bell. At the end of the war I had received another small legacy, of 150, this time, the second of the only two legacies in my life, from the estate of a certain Miss Molly Wilson who had left this money to Miss Bell for her absolute use or to help Muriel Hayley if still alive. My aunt, Muriel Hayley, was by then dead and Miss Bell, not wishing to benefit, had given the money over to "the son of Alfred Hayley, in whom she had always taken an interest". I was considerably surprised by this interest, since I had never even been told of Miss Bell's existence. "She was your father's old nurse," my mother had said at the time, "she must be very ancient." I had written formally to thank her, and used the money for, my studies. After much searching I found her solicitors' letter and wrote to them.

She was not my father's nurse. She had come as governess to the two daughters of the Hayley household, at the age of seventeen, the Hayley son being three years younger. She was still very much alive, a sprightly eighty-six, minute and with intelligent blue eyes looking enormous under a straight white fringe, her hair being cut quite short like a little girl's. She ran single-handed a house that seemed all stairs, in Newcastle-under-Lyme, Staffordshire, where she had a great many friends, and seemed the incarnated answer to those who assume the aged are always lonely and should be allowed to die of their illnesses instead of being saved with modern drugs.

Finally, there was my aunt Cordelia. She had started it all, so many years ago. She was the very seed of my obsession, which had now grown into a dark family tree, filling my limbs with its poisonous sap. Should I try to find her? Would I regret it? Was she the branch that bore the fruit of knowledge? What would be the price of my curiosity? An ancient question this, which few have left unanswered, curiosity being, rather unfairly in the circumstances, one of God's strongest gifts to man. She had seemed difficult then, but now, what sort of old age was she having? In my legal experience, people who fussed about Wills, their own or those of others, were usually unloved. Would she be my responsibility? On the continent, certainly, but I was half English, and entitled to meanness. Perhaps she was dead. So many of my vital witnesses were.

She came up from Kent and I picked her out at once in the crowd that spilled out of the train. The first moment was like seeing oneself in a distorting mirror. She was so tiny I felt twice as tall, but I knew her from those pale glazed eyes in that pink and white English face. His eyes. And mine. All Hayley eyes were apparently rectangular, instead of rounded, like other people's. She *was* smartly dressed in a grey suit with a matching felt hat set straight over her blonde-white hair, and yellow gloves, and long, pointed, hand-made walking shoes that wrapped her feet like snakeskins. She was seventy-seven.

"You must think I'm decrepit," she exclaimed indignantly as I took her arm to help her into the taxi.

She was shy at first. How could I be so tall, she asked, when my father was rather a short man? Tell me about him, I said. But she wouldn't be so precipitous. She had answered my first letter with an old-world caution amounting almost to curtness, and it had taken several months of lively correspondence—chiefly about a charming old lady in Sittingbourne who was her very dear friend, and the roses in this lady's garden—to reach a stage of mutual trust and affection; and the affection was truly felt, for in spite of a certain asperity in her letters, I was enchanted with her in advance. The asperity, I discovered later, remained entirely confined to her letters, as if the pen moving across a page had the power to draw from a secret fountain of spite that mingled with the ink. But now I was in a state of suppressed excitement. Here was living my father before my eyes, caricatured by age but softened by femininity. It was like having a live model, she was so like him to look at, as I remembered him. She was so like him, in character, as I thought I remembered him, through my mother's feelings. But she was tender as he was, with the same engaging ways.

"How old were you when we last met?" she insisted, "fourteen, was it? You were only a little taller than me, then. I remember it so well. You collected stamps, didn't you?"

"Yes. And you gave me a stamp album for my birthday." She was pleased that I remembered.

"Let me take you to luncheon."

"No, my dear, I am taking you. I'm not an aunt for nothing. Besides, I don't eat." She said this with the same casual finality with which one says "I don't smoke" or "I don't drink". "I don't eat meat or vegetables, or fruit. I know a dear little place off Baker Street where they give me the only food I like." Which turned out to be rice and mushrooms.

"Miss Bell must be well over eighty," she said with glee, when I tried to draw her out by describing my researches. "Is she all right?" But we couldn't really talk in the restaurant because she was slightly deaf, and I didn't like shouting out my patrimony in public.

At last I got her back to my flat. It turned out, as I had suspected from her original letter, that she loathed her brother.

"You may be shocked, my dear Philip, I do hope you won't be, but do you know, it was a relief to me when I read of his death in *The Times.* I thought, well, now he can do no more mischief and bring unhappiness into no more lives."

"No, no, I'm not shocked," I murmured. "I'm very interested."

"You must understand," she said after answering most of my questions to the best of her fallibility, "I have no wish to dig up all the wrongs and evil that Northbrook did. His mind was diseased. He told Mother the most fantastic lies about me." She suddenly looked like a little girl about to cry. "He wrote terrible lies about me to Andrew, my husband, when we were in South Africa. Still, he died, only it was too late to bring back my happiness."

"What sort of lies?" I asked tentatively, but not loudly enough, or perhaps she didn't want to hear.

"And when Mother died, he stole a lot of things that should have come to me, including some silver hairbrushes. Your mother told me later that he stored them all at Harrods and sold them whenever he needed money."

Then her petulance veered to triumph:

"Did you know that we were related to Queen Amelie of Portugal? She was a Bourbon princess, you know, who lived near Stratford after the king's assassination. My mother never said a word about it, of course, she was like that. But later on, I met Queen Amelie again in London—she was a dear, dear friend of my parents—and she told me that she was my god-mother, and not only that, but apparently her mother—or was it her grandmother? I can't remember—and my mother's mother—or grand-mother—were sisters. Isn't that strange?"

"Very . . . But what about the Hayleys? Are they really anything to do with the Hayleys of Kilbrae?"

"Oh yes," she said airily, "we are certainly descended from the Hayleys of Kilbrae. My father was a keen genealogist and he had the family tree worked out." Aware perhaps that this didn't prove much she added: "He was a personal friend of the Royal Herald. Besides, Northbrook was named after the village of Norbrook, or Northbrook, in Warwickshire, where the family came from. It was there at the time of the Gunpowder Plot and is mentioned in Burgess' History of Warwickshire. Some of the conspirators hid there for some time."

"Did they really?"

"Yes." She was now very excited about the whole thing. "But don't waste time on all that. My mother's side is much more interesting. One of her ancestors is buried in Issois, Puys de Dome, did you know that?"

"No. No, I didn't." I wondered whether having ancestors buried in for-eign parts was considered rather chic in late Victorian times. But we were getting further and further from the point. She then confided to me that as a girl she always suspected that Northbrook was a changeling. "He's not one of us," she used to say to the others. And that seemed to dispose of him even now. She hinted at a dark secret, told her by her father on his death-bed."I can never reveal it, of course."

"Do please have some more tea," I said, "and a biscuit. You must eat, you know."

"Oh, my dear, darling Philip. It's so very good to have found you again," she said with sudden warmth, and she took my hand. "Be nice to your poor old aunt, who does love you so very, very much."

"Of course. I too. I'm so very glad also."

She had caught my enthusiasm for my research and wrote me many letters after that, though less about her brother than about family history. And I discovered that old age, far from making one wise and good and ready for one's Maker, merely emphasises, tenfold with each decade, whatever was wise and good before and whatever was foolish and bad.

And when I looked, with her written permission, into the papers of Miss Muriel Hayley deceased, I was not surprised to discover that my aunt, bless her heart, had done rather well out of my father's death. For in a Will dated 1921, Muriel Hayley had left all she had to her brother Northbrook, and £50 to her sister. Since my father died first, "all she had", which amounted to some £400, went to her sister, minus £97 0s. 8d. (not, therefore, a legacy in the strict sense) to me. I still remember her letter: *That anything my sister left should have gone to the son of such a man seems to me most ironical. It is the last thing she would have wished.* But as a lawyer I had come across far worse examples of family pettiness.

My aunt, I felt, was relatively angelic. Her fantasies delighted me, and had a quaint charm, especially in these days, when the only background one is permitted to boast about is lower middle-class, provincial and unmonied, provided, of course, that one has successfully climbed out of it. Be that as it may, I came to love my aunt Cordelia tenderly and true, as if to atone for not having been given a chance to love my father-for-all-his-faults, and be loved by him for-all-mine.

My picture of him was blurring and clarifying like stages in a painted portrait. He even, at one point, disappeared altogether, for my aunt's long withheld secret told her by her father on his deathbed turned out, a year later, to be that Northbrook was really the son of her mother's cousin,

Sophie Irwin, who looked very much like her, had made a runaway marriage with a runaway husband called Underhill, and died in childbirth. "Nobody knew about it except Canon Willoughby, our Vicar. That would explain a great deal, wouldn't it? You see my parents never really wanted children. I believe my father never quite forgave my mother for taking him on."

"But I thought you said, in your very first letter, years and years ago, that your father told you on his death-bed he would never understand how they came to have such a son as Northbrook."

"Yes," she agreed at once without the slightest trace of annoyance. "He said that, too. Isn't it strange?"

Of course no death under the names of Irwin or Underhill was recorded in or anywhere near the year of my father's birth.

Thus do many lies, white, grey and black, make up some sort of coloured truth. Journals, law reports, newspaper libraries, letters, solicitors' files, company registrations, certificates of death, marriage, birth, parish registers and tombstones, all making a trail of people, leading to more people, places, incidents, gestures and attitudes.

The analysts of dreams know as yet little of that sane insanity, that wilful entering into some reality other than one's own, by way of learning, searching, inventing, dreaming and becoming. Some call it truth, some creation, some fiction, history, memory or mere jingling of bells. Perhaps all these are one, beyond analysis.

3

ZING! ZING! Zing-zing-zing.

Back from school already. Laura glanced at the kitchen clock and realised with a shock that it was twenty-five to one. An hour and a half had gone by since the arrival of the telegram and all that huge time had got lost in the food-preparing mechanics that had orchestrated her anxiety. She had both heard and not heard the lift doors shut.

She lowered the gas under the saucepans and went to the door of the flat. There was no one there. Then the boy leapt at her from round the corner, with a "boom", coat, muffler and all, swinging his satchel round her back. His face was cold as an apple from the brisk November air. Today was the Thursday half-holiday, and soon the others would arrive for lunch. The lift was already humming its way down again.

"Mon chéri."

He felt the strain in her voice and disentangled himself, watching her.

"Come, I've something to tell you."

She closed the door. He followed her, not into his own room or the kitchen, or the dining room, or even the drawing room, which would have been natural at that time of day, but into her bedroom. She picked the telegram from her dressing table and gave it to him, saying simply:

mort "Daddy est mon, mon chéri."

She knew instinctively she must treat him as an adult, also that the shock might be mitigated if given first by ear and familiarly in French, next, by sight and formally in English.

> *Regret Alfred died pneumonia early this morning,*
> *Norah Frinton*

Philip had taken his grandmother's death very badly, the spring before last. It had been so similar, being greeted at the door with the news when back from school for lunch. Only then he was nine, and Granny had been living with them, here in Brussels, her body was laid out in her room in the very same flat. This was different, distantly in London. Laura watched his face and wondered how much he remembered. Tears filled his eyes but the expression was solemn, not sad.

He was still gazing at the telegram when the bell rang again.

"That'll be Marcel and tante Louise," Laura said. "You go, darling." She now lived alone with her father, but every Thursday her brother Maurice and his wife and son came to lunch, and the two boys played together all afternoon. She watched him as he tiptoed across the parquet hall to open the door. But he let them in without greeting them and walked back towards his mother's room, feeling both importantly tragic and genuinely heavyhearted.

"Alfred est mort," Laura said to her sister-in-law, who shook her head dolefully and kissed them both on the forehead in an awful silence. Then Philip, who had been slightly enjoying the dramatic situation created by the arrival of new people, suddenly burst into tears, remembering that he was half an orphan.

Maurice arrived from the office with Monsieur Georges Bertrand, It was "midi", that long continental lunch-break from twelve till two, when all the men came home. But lunch today was a quiet and hurried affair. The atmosphere was of formal respect for bereavement rather than truly sorrowful, for the sudden, and, by usual standards, untimely death of Alfred Hayley was an event no Bertrand could sincerely mourn except in so far as it might leave dear Laura in a worse plight than before. These mixed feelings were best expressed through the purely practical.

"I've got the ticket, Laura," said Maurice. He was director of a small but growing travel agency and Laura had rung him up as soon as she got the telegram. "You can pay me back later. The plane leaves at three forty-five, There's fog in London but they, seem to be able to land."

"Thank you, Maurice." She thought, 550 francs, it'll take ages to repay it. She had taken a single passage and was returning by boat.

"Louise will drive you to Evere," Maurice added. "Papa and I can go down to the office by tram."

Laura was sitting at the head of the white-clothed table, with her father on her left, and Louise on her right. The two boys sat beyond them on either side of Maurice, who was at the end. She found herself looking round at the solid mahogany sideboard and the oak china cupboard with its tall piles of matching blue and white plates, in all sizes, with matching graduated dishes, and wondering what her widowhood would bring. She gazed thoughtfully at her favourite brother. Why couldn't she have married a man like that?

Maurice was short but quiet and distinguished, with a touch of grey at the temples and rimless glasses like those of an American senator. Though dark-haired he did not look like Laura, for his skin was pale and his eyes blue. He was in fact a transposition, in a minor key, of his father, who flourished as the full senator, white-haired, ruddy-faced and jowled like a Boston terrier.

"Would you like to go and see your mother off at the aerodrome?" tante Louise asked Philip, who was dropping tears into his soup, and he nodded silently. Laura wished Louise wouldn't adopt such a patronising tone with Philip, as if he were a poor relation, even if he was in a way.

The small, square black Opel bumped along the lane that led to Evere aerodrome, which Philip was shocked to see was only a large field entered through a building like a country railway station, except that a long yellow sock floated from a pole on its roof.

"That's not the aérodrome, maman," he whined. "It was a much bigger one last year at the air tournament. Maman, that's not the aérodrome."

"Now, be quiet and don't worry your mother. She's got enough on her mind." Louise drove the car as if she were invigilating a schoolroom examination, sitting bolt upright like a teacher, which she had been.

"But it's just a field," Philip wailed. He evidently felt that only something out of Jules Verne could suit the solemnity of the occasion. Laura turned and smiled at him from the front seat.

"It's the same aerodrome, mon chéri. You were smaller then, so it seemed bigger. And besides, we saw the tournament from near Woluwe-Saint-Lambert, we were nowhere near Evere."

But Philip was crying with mortification.

"It's only a field, with a silly old building like a boathouse."

"It is a boathouse," Laura said almost gaily. "For boats of the air."

"Look, Philip, a Handley-Page W.8!" Marcel cried as they got out of the car into the cold autumn afternoon. He was a much more technically-minded boy, and thought Philip a crybaby, but had a child's instinctive tact. Philip looked up, sniffed, gulped, then watched with pride in his heart as the biplane, all wires and cloth-covered wood, circled over them, bigger and bigger, with its double-paired wheels down and its nose in an airscrew whirl, flying within touch, it seemed, and surely it was going to hit the roof of the building, but no, it cleared it and vanished the other side with a roar.

"Maman, is that your one, is that your one?" He was almost beating her with his woolly gloved hands.

"No, silly, she'll be going in a Fokker F. VII, three-engined monoplane, 163 kilometres an hour." Marcel scoffed knowingly.

The inside of the building looked a little more important, with ticket-offices and counters, but still it was remarkably informal. They strolled through exactly as if it were a small railway station and out onto the big field, where their faces caught the tingle of the cold air and the tint of the November sun. Hardly anyone was about. Laura seemed to be the only passenger, and she looked nervously around. Surely the plane wouldn't be empty, just for her?

"How many places are there on the plane, maman?" Philip tuned in to her thoughts.

"I don't know, mon chéri."

"Ten, if it's a Fokker," said Marcel. "But it could just be a Westland Wessex, which has only six. The Fokker's more posh. It does the Cologne-Brussels run first, leaves Cologne at two forty-five, should be here any minute." He wasn't his father's son for nothing.

Then a few more groups turned up, each with its one traveller or two. A blue official appeared, and moved from group to group, pointing at the monoplane which had come in to land out of the horizon and suddenly was throbbing in the green grass, some fifty metres away.

Marcel gasped.

"Comme il est beau! So streamlined and long, just look at that single undercarriage, and those side-engines tucked under the wings, 230 CV each . . ." he went into a technical rhapsody that Philip heard in a trance. And OO said the Sabena letters on the fuselage, and OO, Philip knew, this was the silver bird worthy to carry his mother to London.

The blue official came up to them and bowed politely. Laura turned to her sister-in-law, whose corn-yellow hair zigzagged flatly from under her hat, which hid the brown of her parting and tilted sharply over one eye. "Only a camomile rinse", Laura heard her mind cattily echoing Louise's favourite phrase, and then was angry with herself. In fact Louise looked very elegant in a long straight grey coat with the new square shoulders and a tall grey collar of Persian lamb.

"Merci, Louise, c'est bien gentil." She kissed her, then bent down and hugged her son.

There were already five people inside the plane and Laura got on with three others. She counted twelve seats, not ten, and three remained empty. She put her small suitcase in the luggage-net and sat down, strapping herself as she was told by the steward. It seemed ages before they took off, though in fact it was only ten minutes. Through the small square window she could see the little group by the angular modern building. Marcel was gesticulating towards the hangers, the field, the aeroplane, and Philip stood thoughtfully, listening and peering at the machine, obviously unable to see her. Then they started hitting and chasing each other, bored with waiting. Their knees looked very pink. At last the engines started up. Laura had never flown before and she felt sick with a lumpy mixture of death-wish and fear. The plane roared but seemed unable to move. It had stuck. No, it was moving slowly away from the building to the other end of the long field. But they were still on the ground. They were turning. She couldn't see Philip and Marcel and Louise at all, only the building. Then the building got bigger, yes, there they were, small and waving, Philip's blue muffler, goodness, there was the roof below her and suddenly she was alone in the sky, with the Belgian fields and the red houses receding into a patchwork of narrow strips, ploughed brown and yellowing green, which later flared for a moment into the bright tulip fields of Flanders.

Height rinses the soul, and flying brought paradoxically to her mind the childish notion that this was how God-in-the-sky must feel, looking with love but immense detachment, down at the troubles of men. It was not until she glimpsed the ashen sea between the newly gathered clouds that she forced herself to think of the dead man she was flying to.

For one thing, how was she to behave with that woman, who would presumably be there? Laura gave Miss Maxwell credit at least for subtlety in getting Alfred's secretary to send and sign the telegram. Not that the family didn't know, but she had been able to show the telegram to Philip. Children needed the concrete and the visible. "Maxwell" or "Marjorie" might have produced awkward questions. But how stupid of her, Philip would remember "Miss Maxwell", since Alfred had actually brought her on one of his visits to Brussels, four or five years ago, was it. Yes, 1929, or was it 1930? Not long after their separation, certainly, for Philip had been still very familiar with his father, she remembered. They had stayed, of course, at the same hotel. His nurse, he said, and his nurse it was throughout. She really was a nurse, too. Alfred suffered from gout and apparently needed a nurse. Nevertheless, this was the woman for whom she had been left. Laura thought her rather mousy—though undeniably younger—and merely wondered what effect the sight of such a decrepit father, who needed a nurse, had had on Philip. Fifty-five then, and nearing sixty now, a fat and flabby grey-haired man. Then she herself was forty, no, forty-one, now, good gracious. But children seemed insensitive to age. They always wanted to know—how old is Daddy, and how old is Granny—and age only meant big numbers, not wrinkles and loose flesh. Alfred had taken his son on his knee and showed him his silver pencil with the red, blue and black leads that came out to order, and blown open his gold pocket watch. It was only on that tram ride into town that Philip had been embarrassed, when his father had played the Englishman abroad who behaves as if a castle were his home, and made a fearful fuss, in atrocious French, about opening the windows when everyone clearly wanted them shut, so that even after the row, amused smiles were exchanged all round as he went on making angry comments in English. But Miss Maxwell had got on well with Philip, in her quiet way. Mistresses easily win the child for a while, they have the desire without the responsibility. And Philip had talked of her for several days. How odd she should have forgotten.

It was no use. Her mind refused to grapple with the future, or even with the next few hours.

"Good evening, Miss Maxwell," she made herself rehearse. Very dignified now, the woman with the Rights. "I'd like to go in and see him, if I may." Irony, that was it. "Thank you for letting me know." Silence up the stairs, or "Yes, thank you. I came by air, you know." Natural, gracious. Then the *recueillement* before the body, followed by quiet spiritual superiority. "I assume you saw to it that he received the last Sacrament?" No, no, forgive me. Oh, God, forgive me.

The plane was losing height in sudden plunges, and Laura held her breath to ease her nausea. She looked out and could see nothing but greyness like solid matter, a blanket which yet was empty space, through which they seemed to be falling, though the plane was horizontal as far as she knew, tossed in a blanket that wasn't.

The steward walked up the aisle and announced loudly, above the noise of the engine, that the fog over Croydon was too thick and they were making a forced landing in Kent. Everything was under control. Passengers would be taken to London by coach.

They crawled into London yard by yard, and it was nearly nine o'clock instead of five to six when the Imperial Airline bus deposited her at Airway Terminus, Victoria Station, Continental Departures. How often had she arrived at Victoria by boat-train, with or without Philip, how familiar it all was, how little changed, except for a few decorations, limp in the fog, and "Welcome Marina" banners left over from the princess's arrival the night before.

Laura loved stations, with their effusive smoky greetings, alike in every capital, and the curious feeling they gave one, of surprised recognition that so many others were arriving and departing on just that same day, and presumably on other days too, when one was cooking dinner or discussing school fees or reading St. François de Sale. But Victoria always seemed different, greyly impersonal, with so many busy people hurrying through only as a short cut under cover, just like herself, for her hotel was on the other side. Tonight all were muffled up against the fog which penetrated inside to mingle with the engine-smoke. Laura buried her nose in the big brown lamb's wool collar she had recently had fixed to her winter coat. The fog was almost as brown as the collar. Pneumonia. He must have choked to death. London at night, usually wet and luminous, with its high open-decked scarlet buses and its tall square taxis bearing their number-plates on the roof, still looking for all the world like those at the Battle of the Marne. Tonight the taxis were nothing more than their own headlamps emerging from a yellow wall. She was so tired and hungry that all idea of "Good evening, Miss Maxwell" was forgotten.

In any case, she suddenly realised as she tore at the tough, hotel-style roast beef and Yorkshire pudding, that no one would be there.

Of course. It would be an English funeral, with no laying out of the body in flowers on the bed, no one watching or praying. He would have been removed to a "chapel of rest". One couldn't have dead bodies lying around. And the woman, she would be staying with friends, with her sister, or with that dreadful man Kingsley-Smith perhaps—and death would not be mentioned, for death was an unmentionable thing, like sex in Victorian times.

Besides, even if that woman were there—she was a nurse, after all, and not squeamish—even if Alfred were lying on his bed at 28 John Street in all his elderly human glory, she didn't want to see him, if it meant talking to her. What could they possibly have to say to each other? Miss Maxwell was a very ordinary woman, she may even have tortured herself about it, Laura thought gloomily, and she would certainly be upset now, but what had that to do with her?

No, she would go later, with Kingsley-Smith probably, after the funeral. She didn't particularly want to sightsee their flat. She wished the woman well, and hoped life would treat her kindly. She would only ask her one thing, whether he knew he was going to die.

Although the night she spent in a little hotel near Victoria was restless, Laura was surprised to wake up much refreshed. Travelling was in her blood, and strange hotel rooms always stimulated her. The English breakfast, too, had the tang and special flavour of a forgotten ritual, exotic but traditional, strange yet familiar in the memory of some more ancient life, her own life, her young married years in London, tea, bacon and eggs, buttered toast and marmalade.

The fog had lifted during the night, like a block of stone by Samson's pillared hands, and she strode out into the pale sunshine with an incongruous joy in her heart, a tall and merry widow, in a café-au-lait winter coat, wearing a light felt toque.

Far from looking funereal, London was gay with red, white and blue bunting and golden decorations for the wedding of Princess Marina of Greece to the Duke of Kent the following week. The dress shops round Victoria unanimously proclaimed one colour theme, Marina Blue, all intertwined with Christmas beguilements that seemed to begin earlier every year, and Shirley Temple smirked cutely up at Gary Cooper on the posters of the cinema opposite, in "Now and Forever", which Laura thought she might see that evening.

A small boy approached her, in a tight little jacket, no shirt, and with bare feet on the cold pavement. He was selling matches and she gave him a whole sixpence, silently, watching his eyes grow big then look up at her distrustfully when she refused the matchboxes. She smiled and walked on. She knew that even if he really had no shoes, nevertheless shoes would have been found for him somehow, had he been sent on any other kind of mission. She also knew that she couldn't give to every beggar she saw, there were too many, and not all were really poor, though poverty was widespread enough. But today, today was special. Today there were gods to be placated.

And besides, England had become a foreign country again. The part of her which knew the value of every halfpenny had stayed behind at the hotel. She felt like a visitor, who didn't understand the crazy money, a rich American perhaps, or no, a little black girl from Africa, amazed by the solidity of the buildings, the glitter of opulence in the shops, and other evidences of wealth and comfort, a little lost girl from Sidney, thrilled by the heart of the Empire. London had always made her feel foreign, and insignificant, and poor, and, at the same time immensely proud to be after all part of it. Perhaps it was the numerous posters for Ceylon Tea. But today she felt foreign, and significant, and rich by a couple of sterling pounds, and not part of it at all.

The buses surprised her, for most of them now had their upper deck roofed over in white, like a mobile tennis pavilion, which made them look very tall but elegant and offset the long side-advertisements for Pear's Coal Tar Soap and such. But the steps up were still uncovered and still shaped like half a question-mark, echoing one's doubts as to whether to climb.

She chose an old open-decker and enjoyed the ride to Fleet Street. There was nothing quite like a late November sun hazing over Westminster and Whitehall, which now looked so pre-festive. From Victoria to St. Paul's by number eleven, it was the best ride in London, her father had said, when Alfred had taken him sight-seeing. Laura smiled tolerantly. It was only two years ago that *cher papa* had gone to London to persuade Alfred to provide for his wife and child in a decent will, and had come back talking of little else but his visit to the Houses of Parliament and how he had had tea-on-the-terrace with his son-in-law and his son-in-law's very close friend Lord Binnersley. Yes, Alfred could impress anyone.

When she arrived at 55, Chancery Lane, Laura stopped suddenly and hit her forehead with the palm of her hand, much to the astonishment of several bowler-hatted gentlemen who passed her and actually looked back.

"Complètement Tolle!" she muttered and walked rapidly on. Alfred's office hadn't been in Chancery Lane for years, not since she had left London. As if she didn't know the Bedford Row address by now. What an abstract affair an address could be, compared to the memory of physical stones and mortar.

Laura walked into the elegant new offices of the Medical Addressograph Company in one of the Georgian houses of Bedford Row, and suddenly became depressed again.

The young clerk at the reception desk seemed tactlessly startled by her existence and while he went out she caught a glimpse of the machine room through a half-open door. The sight of those girls stamping envelope after envelope with the address of every doctor in England filled her with apprehension.

Then there were the politenesses of the staff to endure, and Miss Frinton, the company secretary, greeting her with mournful condolences in Alfred's office. "So very untimely," she sniffed. "Why, he was still so young." Miss Frinton was a thickset woman of about fifty and fond of the gin bottle, whence the condolences evidently came. Laura gazed past her at the huge flat desk, the heavy silver inkstand (my Standish, he called it), the expensive leather blotter, the crystal paper weight, the small Nefertiti on the panelled chimneypiece, and her heart sank with the renewed load of his forgotten personality.

"*What* did you say?"

A word had leapt out of Miss Frinton's tearful monologue. "I said he's being cremated on Friday. At Golder's Green."

"Cremated?"

"By his own wish. His ashes to be scattered over London. It's—it's in the Will. I was one of the executors. So was Mr. Kingsley-Smith." She spoke quickly, visibly embarrassed at knowing so much more than the widow, and determined to keep off the money side of the Will. "It said, he particularly desired no religious ceremony."

Scattered over London. As if London weren't dirty enough. Laura couldn't help looking at the fire that smouldered in the grate. Tomorrow, it would be a little heap of ashes. The sequence of thought that followed the shock was almost illogical. He hadn't gone back. It was therefore as clear as a heart-thump that he had not changed his will. Without asking, she knew the date of that will—January 1932. He had written her a long beastly letter about it. He loved writing long beastly letters. So all her efforts since had been in vain. And yet he had been much more pleasant during the last year. She had even begun to think he might come back to her, and make a home for their son, a happy home, too. But then it was easy enough to be pleasant by occasional letter, all passion spent.

Miss Frinton was carrying a black deed-box, which she placed on the carpet in front of the fire.

"These are all personal letters, Mrs. Hayley, mostly from you, I believe. He kept them all in here. You may like to go through them." She hesitated, swaying a little, then added lugubriously "One never knows what might come in useful in a court of law."

"Oh, no, I really couldn't, Miss Frinton. You'd better destroy the lot."

"You just sit down here, Mrs. Hayley." She pushed Laura gently into the big brown leather armchair, so that her thin lisle stocking caught on the metal corner of the deed-box and laddered.

"Damn."

"Mr. Kingsley-Smith won't be coming in today, he's looking after the funeral arrangements"—with Miss Maxwell, Laura thought bitterly—"and seeing Mr. Hayley's solicitor. You've got all morning and all afternoon, Mrs. Hayley, I'll bring you a cup of tea and then leave you to it. Here's the key. One never knows what might come in useful," she repeated as she waded out of the office.

The first bundle Laura saw was tied up in blue ribbon, looking absurd in that black legal box. She untied it and read through the letters, half-hypnotised. They were all from Philip. Some were on children's paper with rabbits and bears on it and in tiny envelopes. Some were scrawled on big grown-up writing paper.

Dear Daddy,

I am not forgetting the Parter-Narsta and the Alfer-Beater, I wish you were here, so that you could tickle me every night when you say goodnight. I think it would tickle me at Upsillon and Epesillon and Omega . . .

They were dated by the day and month only, but neatly packed chronologically, the writing and spelling getting worse and worse as the years went backwards.

. . . I hope you still remember my name but if you don't it is Philip Daddy may I com to London at Crissmest do you know I am very glad to see a crissmest I have a new pen . . .

Laura skimmed through them sadly and tied them up again. She would keep those to read at leisure. No time for sentiment now. But then the bottom letter dropped out and fluttered nearly into the fire. Laura caught it and knew it at once. It was hugely scrawled in pencil on a large sheet of the blue writing paper her mother had always used, and it was written to herself. She remembered weeping over it and showing it to Alfred. They were preparing the new flat in Chiswick for what was to be their last attempt to live happily together, in 1927. Philip had been left with his grandparents in Brussels. He was four years old.

. . . very disegribbel Mumy that I never seen. leeving hir sun right to ckoohll the poor little thing. he could not breef a spec of crying. dyaar in that time I have been so much crying so much. but my pray my pray my pray my pray hummeny days bat hummany but hummeny days am I going to stay you'vo been touring me so much about going to London.
Mrs. Misstress disegribel Mother
Philip.

And Laura wept again. All the shocks of the last twenty-four hours jerked her body with sobs as she covered her face with her hands, the tears trickling through her knuckles.

"Now, Mrs. Hayley, you shouldn't get so upset," said Miss Frinton gently, coming in with a cup of tea, that rattled with the shaking of her hand as she put it down on the desk. "Don't read the letters, Mrs. Hayley, just search through them quickly. Would you like me to help you?"

Laura shook her, head, pressing her fingertips on her eyelids. The blue letter lay on her lap, between her elbows.

Miss Frinton looked at her for a moment, then emptied the spilt brown liquid from the saucer into the cup and crept softly out of the room.

Laura dabbed her eyes, blew her nose, lit a cigarette and drank the lukewarm office tea slowly. She inhaled, staring at the fire and flicking her ash into it. Ashes to ashes, she kept repeating. When her cigarette was finished, she slipped the blue letter back into the bundle and placed the packet beside her bag. Suddenly businesslike, she flipped rapidly through the piles of her own letters, glancing at each one and throwing it on the fire. The whole room flared up with the blaze, and every speck of dust shone as in a riot of sunbeams.

She was just going to light another cigarette and rest when she saw the document. She recognised it at once. His copy of the Separation Agreement. Dated 12th June, 1929 . . . the said Medical Addressograph Co., Ltd . . . in the event of my death . . . to make over to my wife the aforementioned . . . £300 (three hundred pounds) per annum out of the profits of the said company . . . Signed Alfred Hayley. The hugely aggressive A and the unreadable rest, the family name disappearing into an agonised wriggle and the whole pretentiously framed in dots and a grandiose curve.

"My darling Laura, my own dear wife, we're going to start all over again. We'll bring up our beloved child together."

His smooth soft voice like a tenor murmuring. Paris, December 1931. He had asked her to meet him there and bring her copy, of the document. "We will start all over again. There's no need for this document now." She had handed it over, with tears in her eyes and he had torn it up.

Then he had gone back to London, satisfied that he could now alter his will in favour of that woman. Only the document had stood in his way.

And now he had forgotten to destroy his own copy.

£300 a year. It was a lot of money. She was safe. She would be able to bring up her child.

Laura folded the Deed of Separation and placed it by the bundle of Philip's letters. The black box was empty, except for a large and thick yellow envelope. Mechanically, she put it with the other papers and picked up the whole lot, together with her bag. She was tired, and wanted to get out of this oppressive office. She looked round and wondered whether to take the small Nefertiti from the chimneypiece. He had bought it for her. But no, let them have it. What did she care?

The fire was flickering out, choked with black flakes, and gasping.

4

THE FIRE crackled deep inside his chest, the black flakes fluttered up and down his windpipe. The room seemed to be full of fog. He knew she had placed towels on the windowsills where the draught came in and drawn the thick velvet curtains, and the curtains themselves were the colour of fog, yellowy brown and as worn as muddy old roads. But he could see the fog nosing its way over the top like smoke from his pipe. He could even see himself hiding behind those curtains, smoking, smoking, puffing like a chimney.

He couldn't move. He was propped bolt upright and yet at times he couldn't see the room, it seemed to disappear. The thing to do was to keep his eyes open, though his eyelids were tied down too. But he must keep his eyes open so as to see the wallpaper. It was a dull buff colour, just like the fog, but there ought to be a bunch of roses that looked like a face. That's how it always was when he couldn't breathe, that's how it always had been, bunches of roses, lots of bunches, that all looked like smirky old men, except one which was God, facing the bed, on one side of the door so that when his mother came in it was on a level with her face.

But it was Dr. Vera Williams who had called and given him the injection. His eyelids weighed down over eyes backed with crushed ice, like the burning crushed ice lower down, in his back, that's where it came from, and they closed away the roses that weren't there. Because of course, how could they be, he was in the middle of now, it was all quite clear, he remembered leaping about the bed with that fire raging in his lungs, and becoming quite stiff. And the fear, he remembered the fear that he was going to be dead in the next second, and then the next, and then, but now perhaps he was dead. There was no pain any more. Probably that had been a dream, the whole of it a dream. It was all quite familiar, he had so often dreamt that his real self was rising out of his body, like a spiritual body out of thick, inert matter, then woken in the struggle to keep it back, with his will at least, his own body being inert matter to the last. So the dream had returned, that was all, and everything was all right now, except that he still couldn't move. His legs seemed to be in stocks, and his back was nailed to the wall with a cold burning pinion. But he mustn't fall asleep again or the roses would collapse into the fine orange waffle of the tall gas-fire that was drawing out of his mouth all the fog he had eaten. Otherwise he would have to eat the roses and become an ass.

The roses must have fallen for the noise was deafening. But that was because he was standing on a balcony with Pope Pius XI. The Pope had one hand on his left shoulder and held the other up to silence the pullulating crowds below, who had been shouting *Viva el duce* in rhythm for hours. He himself was holding a sheet of vellum covered with his own handwriting, holding it out for the Pope to read. It had come out of the calf-bound book that was still tucked under his arm, though in constant danger of slipping as he stretched out the sheet of vellum, at the bottom of which were sprinkled two rows of ants that said, "Read and publication allowed," with the signature of the pro-prefetto. There was no doubt at all that it was the same piece of paper, he had written it himself and got the pro-prefetto's signature in Rome last August. He contemplated his own handwriting with pleasure, and that of the pro-prefetto with scorn. And now he was telling the Pope all about it, and how he loved Marjorie. The Pope was all in white, with long white hair flowing from a golden mitre and he started reading what was written on the sheet of vellum, intoning it like the Good Friday gospel, all on the dominant and down a third at the end of each phrasing, with resolution to the tonic at the sentence stop. At least that's how Brother Sebastian explained it, who stood on his right.

"The compiler has been accorded the special privilege of making his own resear-ches. Among the shelves and in the cupboards of Bibliotheca Apostolica Vatica-na. Where every possible courtesy was shown and unlimited facilities were given to *him*. The famous Indices Librorum Prohibitorum Sanctae Romanae Ecclesi-ae. Relating almost entirely to heterodox works. Are known to all Scho-*lars*."

Then the Pope's voice changed to bass, like a response—perhaps it was in fact Brother Sebastian, or even himself—very low, and going up a third then a fourth to get home to the tonic. He said to Brother Sebastian, "it's rather like Porter King's piano-base at Madame Tonia's, that's all Porter King could do."

"Evil literature is to the Mater Omnium Ecclesia-rum What symptoms and diseases are to the Medical Profe-ssion And are treated according-*ly*. Rome August fifth nineteen thirty-*four*."

Then the Pope led him to a Hepplewhite shield-backed mahogany arm-chair and handed him a huge golden crown, which turned out to be a book bound in gold filigree with inlaid rubies. The Pope was holding it like a plate.

So he said : "I can't eat this, Your Holiness," and the Pope said "try", and Brother Sebastian led a chorus of robed acolytes who intoned "if at first you don't succeed, try, try and try again." The Pope picked out the rubies with an apostle spoon. "Now. One for Mummy, one for Daddy."

"No, no, no." He was choking, and the red square of gas fire looked enormous, like the door of a furnace. Marjorie was holding his wrist and looking down anxiously. He couldn't see her face, only her anxiety, which had a face of its own, all detached and swimming about. How silly of him to choke, he was all right now. She had done something very loving and soothing to his arm, which was stiff and cold, but spreading a warmth like water through him, so he said very loudly, but it came out as a whisper, "I love you, Marjorie, you know that, don't you?" And she said from the other side of the swimming face, which muffled her voice like a cloud, "Yes, I know, my darling. I love you too." But the cloud gobbled it up.

And now it was so difficult getting across that bridge. He had swum right across the lake of Geneva, with the mountains mocking him on either side, and then up the Rhone, upstream, every current against him. But the bridge across the chasm was only a slippery white strip, like a ribbon of rubber, as wide as his body, and he had to slither along it like a slug, though fortunately he could hold the edges. But he had to go so carefully, hardly moving, or the strip which was by no means taut, would turn and throw him down into the gorge below. There was, of course, the other bridge, a narrow but splendidly constructed modern affair in iron, also white and without any handrails, but at least it wasn't soft. Lots of people were crossing it, acrobats and stunt cyclists perched on top of each other, and it all looked so much easier than what he had to do. Slither. Slither. Slither. But he got there, and one of the acrobats, who was naked to the waist and wore white tights, helped him up. His skin was golden and his nipples well fleshed round.

It was no use walking, really, because the horizon went round the corner instead of straight on. Miles and miles of it always disappearing behind a mountain. And there was a big diamond inside each of his toes, that weighed so heavy he couldn't walk fast anyway. Then Reggie Kingsley-Smith appeared from under a waterfall and said "Don't forget to leave me your teddy-bear fur coat with the astrakhan collar." And he put his hand on Reggie's shoulder and said, "You are my only friend."

She must have moved Philip's photograph to the chimney ledge above the gas fire, so that he could see it when he opened his eyes. It was amazing, all he had to do was open his eyes, and there was the beige-brown room. He was sitting propped up, so he must be all right. He shut them again, because a voice hit his ears and he couldn't hear if he saw things as well. "It started with a rigor," the voice said but then got lost in a long murmur, which after a black while came through the blackness into his head more clearly. Who could it be? The voice must be his mother's. And the other one, Miss Bell perhaps. The words began to shape themselves from sound to sense.

"It doesn't seem like twelve years . . ."

Twelve years. I am twelve years old today.

". . . My youth really, but I don't mind that, except, somehow, it seems the whole of my life . . ."

The whole of my life.

". . . and also such a small block of time. Do you know what I mean?"

Of course, it was Marjorie. My beloved is mine and I am his. And her sister Iris, answering:

"Don't brood so much, my dear. He'll be all right."

I'll be all right.

The low murmur went on, but clear now, vibrant with meaning.

"I understand now what older people mean when they say 'it seemed only yesterday' about an event which happened, why, practically in history, or in my own childhood. Childhood always seems ages and ages, it's only afterwards that slips by. Now I find myself thinking that the Great War was 'only yesterday'. Do you feel that? No, of course you don't, you were only eleven when it ended. But I was eighteen. A few years of fun, fun that seemed like life itself for ever, then I met him. At twenty-two. And suddenly I'm thirty-four, like the century, yet it feels as if time stopped then. I might just as well still be twenty two, except that I'm not. Yet those years were full enough. He encouraged me to train as a nurse. I had my work, and him, and when I think of all the things we did together, well, places we went to . . . though he hated gaiety of any sort, we never went out, you know, to a show, or a dance, or the cinema. I sometimes wanted to, but it doesn't seem to matter at all now."

"Ssh, darling, you'll wake him. Why don't you get a little sleep? I'll watch for a few hours. Please, Margie."

"No, dear. I just couldn't sleep. Oh, bless you for coming, it does help to have you here. This time I just know, somehow. It's strange. Sometimes in the past when he made me so unhappy I even wished he would die, just to solve everything. Oh yes, I'm very wicked, really. And now, tomorrow doesn't even exist. I can't bear it, I can't bear it. Oh I do love him, Iris, I really do love him."

That was odd. He thought he was having 'flu, and now he seemed to be having death. It was impossible. The clock on his bedside table ticked highly into their murmuring, louder and louder, and he remembered how he had made her promise, once, not so long ago, that if ever he should be dying she would not send for Laura. Pity, that. Everyone around, nice. Everyone. Somebody was dying, evidently. But he didn't look good, no. Old. Flabby. His belly must be a mountain, or had it sunk? How did one rescind an order? If he moved his little finger perhaps. So heavy. How did one revoke a life? There shall be weeping and gnashing of teeth. But it was so heavy. His little finger, that was it. That was the thing to do. If only he could move it. Not that it mattered, really. Tomorrow he would wake up refreshed by sleep and his love would nurse and spoil him back to health. Someone else was dying, poor fellow, but not him. He couldn't die just like that, without having, well not now, not him, no, not just out, nothingness, him, his big familiar self that had kept him company all these years. He was young. There were still so many things. Weeping and gnashing of teeth. But of course. Only the teeth remained even when the whole body and bones burnt, and the teeth would rise again and gnash. Could it possibly be true, after all? Cast into outer darkness. Into the fires of hell, in a few seconds from now, going, going, gone. For two hundred and sixty five guineas to Mr. Hayley. An oriental metaphor with ornamental arabesques in gold filigree. In a few seconds from now, eternal sleep or everlasting flames. If thy diamond offend thee, pluck it out. But in fact it was only those frowning white eyebrows like two strips of cloud that offended him, and they got bigger and bigger, growing into a dark and angry bearded cloud that filled the whole sky. Gong, gong, gong! NO! But who is this that cometh up from the wilderness, leaning upon her beloved? Take up thy bed and walk. Rise up, my love, my fair one, and come away. And I would give my soul for this To burn in everlasting hell. To burn in everlas— His little finger, his little finger, where was it, he really must move his little finger.

No, that wasn't it. It made him choke. He coughed and spluttered and his brain was on fire with a white clarity of words which flowed all gravelled up into that gold frame of orange light, which was enormous like a big square gate, out of which stepped the Abbot, who said, "Repeat after me," and he repeated, shouting, it seemed, between gasps, but knowing completely that it was only a mutter, without sound perhaps, without any sound at all, In manus tuas, Domine, commendo spiritum meum. Redemisti me, Domine, Deus veritatis. In Manus tuas, Domine.

Because of course the white monks were lifting the square gold frame, which was on fire, and he had to leap through it on a white horse. And as he flew gracefully into the air, he realised that the vast gold frame was a mirror, towards which he could see himself advancing in a black and white cowl on his huge dapple grey horse, bearing a banner of closely scripted vellum. Nearer and nearer, he was about to crash into the mirror, without his black horse, and he saw only his own terrified eyes and the yell of horror on his face as he leapt through himself, through himself, through himself, for ever and ever, towards a cold white sea.

5

THE MIRROR in the reception office had flung a square of startling whiteness over the bare desk, multiplying the pale mingling of gaslight and September twilight that peered through the window from the dead Georgian silence of Bedford Row. A short paunched figure in a bowler hat moved across the room, limping slightly, then through another office and out again into the corridor, closing the doors quietly. All empty, that was good. No one was working late.

The machine room was like a morgue, but smelling of live dust rather than death. It was dark back here and he switched on the light. Six hand-printing presses stood side by side, unemployed by the night. The Medical Addressograph Company Limited. He always felt a twinge of pride when alone in his office. This was his achievement, built up from nothing, a nothing that began only eight years ago in one room of his earlier flat at 8 Stone Buildings, Lincoln's Inn. Of course, those had been easy times, in the wild prosperity of Baldwin's famous five years, before the slump. But he had somehow come through the slump, almost unaided. Now, however, there were rivals. Beresford & Co. for one. They had even taken from him the Doctors' Who's Who, which he had published when he called himself the Fairfax Publishing Co., so that they were able to supply a correction service to manufacturing chemists at a much lower fee, and were usually more up-to-date with their list of doctors.

Alfred Hayley walked on one tiptoe and a short drag, across to the first machine. He put down his black briefcase, removed his bowler, and sat down, chuckling.

He wore formal black and pinstripe with stiff wing-collar, for there had been a reception of medical publicity men at Worcester House, and he had dined afterwards with Lord Binnersley. He felt elated, not from drink—for he was an abstemious man—but from the company he had kept. His pale eyes bulged a little behind the round and thinly black-rimmed glasses as he sat grinning at the printing press. His mouth was a wide thick line pushing the flesh apart into a flabby neck, and short grey hair tufted disobediently upwards from a high, wrinkled and re-markably bumpy brow. A narrow red ribbon was sewn into his left but-tonhole, and as he stood there his belly protruded slightly beneath the silver fob-chain dangling from the short black waistcoat.

He bent down slowly as if in pain, took a large folder out of the briefcase and propped it on his knees against the addressograph machine, which looked something between a schoolroom desk and half an upright piano.

"I'll show them," he muttered like a theatrical villain, and even ad-ded a guttural "Ha!" which came out as a "Hmm", for although he often felt most histrionic when alone, here the large emptiness of the place quenched the very urges it gave birth to. He took out a few stencil frames from the drawer and removed from them the fitted lead plates on which the names and addresses were embossed, replacing the names with separate letters from the emergency box. It was slow work, for his fingers were unskilled and he had to check each result in a pocket mir-ror, comparing it with the prepared list in the folder. He had done this before at home, by hand on an ordinary stencil, but Marjorie had come into the study unexpectedly and he had had to push her out. The result had been a little amateurish but he had used it all the same. This, though more difficult, was safer and quieter.

The silence heightened the small fiddly noises and he began to hum a complicated passage from Schubert's Death and the Maiden quartet, inter-polating sombrely with pom-pom-pom for the base. When at last the press was set up, he took out from the folder a wad of wrappers, all marked Beresford & Co. in green on the top left corner. He looked at the marking with wicked glee, now enjoying his role and playing it full, for himself as sole audience. Then, patiently, and still singing pom-pom-pom, he fed the wrappers into the machine, pulling the lever and anxiously examining each one as it came out. There were about fifty of them. The addresses were unchanged, but each doctor's name was converted into a gynaecological detail, a medical student's joke, or an obscenity. He smirked with schoolboy pleasure. He'd soon show them, stealing all his doctors, Dr. Tucker, Dr. Lunt, Dr. Clitheroe, Dr. Buttery, Dr. Carter, Dr. Pendennis, Dr. Magel, Dr. Angus, Dr. Arne, Dr. Falkus, Dr. Ornast, Dr. Kee . . . The first twenty had been easy but by the fiftieth he had had to stretch his imagination considerably.

When they were all done, he picked the types out of the machine one by one and replaced the blocks, still humming. Quickly he stuffed the wrappers into the briefcase, gathered up his bowler, and, hardly aware of the pain in his toe, strode out of the room with a pom-pom-pom-pom-da-di-da-pom-pom as he switched off the light. Less confident suddenly in the contrasting dark of the corridor, he clicked the door to and met the silence with a brave but quieter hum, making his way to his own room.

The desk lamp flooded the crystal paperweight and the pink blotting paper in its buff and gold leather corners, so that the William Robertson inkstand with its silver wells, pounce box and pierced gallery sides looked like a miniature shining palace overlooking well-planned gardens and a sun-drenched fountain. He sat clown, opened his briefcase again and took out a packet of pamphlets about rubber goods and youth restorers. Then the wrappers. Then a sheet of green halfpenny stamps.

In the distance he heard the chimes of the Grey's Inn clock. Ten already. He must hurry.

He posted the wrappers, not in a bunch, but feeding them one by one into the grinning mouth of the pillarbox, bright red under a gas lamp in Theobalds Road.

At ten fifteen he was climbing painfully up the stone steps of No. 28 John Street. It was a tall dark house on a corner and the stairs were endless, smelling of iron and dank railings. Each floor had two flats facing the street, and every landing greeted him with the same polished brass numbers, knobs and letterboxes on their varnished black doors, which formed an inverted V together for no convincing architectural reason. At the top he paused to pant his breath to normal while he got his key out for the right-hand corner flat.

"Hugh?"

He hung up his hat and went into the sitting room.

"Hello, Boodles. I'm so sorry, my dear. I went back to the office and was working late."

They hated their own names, so they had chosen new ones. He picked on Hugh, and Marjorie, for some reason, fell for Pontie, but he called her Boodles when particularly affectionate. At least, that is what they both believed, though in reality Boodles meant that he felt defiant, and guilty underneath. Thus do Jack and Jill redecorate for themselves the ordinariness of their situation.

She was lying on the tea-rose coloured sofa, with her shoes off, black-stockinged feet up, and reading a nursing journal by the light of a standard lamp behind her. He bent down to kiss her and then sat down, holding her hand.

"It doesn't matter, darling, I was on duty till eight myself. Had a hard day?"

"Oh, yes, yes. Damn toe, you know, though it's nothing to what it was, when just breathing on it was agony. Had dinner with Binnersley."

"And what did his lordship say?" Marjorie asked, both facetiously and obsessively. She couldn't help being impressed by the people with whom he was on easy terms, and to have a lord and court physician for a doctor was quite something, even if the cause was business rather than blood. Binnersley had had a notion that Hugh's arthritic toe—due to chalk deposits of uric acid in the joint—was a legacy, not from his port-drinking great-grandfather as Hugh was fond of saying, but from a gonorrheal infection, and it had been quite a joke had them to imagine how his lordship would have put it had he known that she was not Hugh's niece, nor just his nurse.

"Oh, false alarm, as you thought. Clever Boodles."

She repeated "Oh clever, clever Boodles," and lifted his wrist to her lips, fish-kissing it quickly and playfully down to his fingertips. Gratified, he smiled and stroked her brown shingle behind the ear with the back of his forefinger, as if she were a furry cat. In the electric light she looked twenty-two, he thought, as young and pretty as when they had met. Twenty-two. He suddenly remembered that she was exactly as young as the century, that she was now thirty-four, while he was fifty-eight.

Why, when he was thirty-four he hadn't even met Laura yet, he was— dear God! And it all struck him as extraordinary, though of course it wasn't, and he thought, what is love anyway?

She was saying something about Kingsley-Smith and her sister Iris.

"I think he's quite smitten."

"What? Who?"

"Reggie, darling. I said, he's taking her out."

"Good heavens, at his age?"

"Well—" But she refrained from the obvious. It was true her sister was only twenty-six. "He is a widower, isn't he?" she added a little anxiously. "I mean, there are no . . . complications?"

He was rarely interested in anyone except in relation to himself, and just gave a dismissing "Hmm? Oh, er, no." Then he added as an after-thought: "The Smiths are just nobodies, of course. *Kingsley*-Smith! They were just plain Smith when we knew them. The father had a small business in Birmingham and left them almost penniless. We practically paid for their upbringing. As a matter of fact my sister Cordelia was once engaged to Reg's brother William, but of course we couldn't allow it."

He got up, lost in a preoccupied look, only formally smiling at her joke about the two Maxwell sisters marrying the two directors of the Medical Addressograph Company, who loved each other like brothers.

He was his own world, she thought, more irritated by her own irritation or, at most, by the familiarity, the absolute expectedness of his self-ab-sorption, than by the lack of interest itself. Other people's worlds had no real existence for him—unless he was at their centre, even for a moment—and his enquiries about them remained perfunctory, if he remembered them at all. But she knew very well that this self-sufficiency was only apparent. The knowledge even filled her with tenderness. He carried his own world with him, not as an inner strength but as a suit of clothes to be admired; he assumed that his views—even when they contradicted the views of his former selves—his reading, his experiences, were as right, as new, as fascinating to others as theirs were wrong and therefore uninteresting to him; and this assumption naturally needed those very others, if only to prove the point over and over again. Almost anyone would do, provided they played the game of ceasing to exist as individuals. She had seen the astonished or exasperated faces of his guests when he formally allowed them, with ill-concealed impatience, to have their way, then blithely went on as if they hadn't spoken. But then she never could follow difficult arguments. She herself went quite blank in his presence these days, he seemed to have drained her of character. All this she felt obscurely, unable to verbalise it to herself. Sometimes she even doubted his brilliance, wondering whether those who admired him were perhaps themselves not very clever, like Reggie. But sometimes his brilliance was the only thing she didn't doubt, it was the excuse for all the rest, even if it bereft her of intelligence. Then she simply loved him, helplessly, unthinkingly. The irritation, however, was only too conscious, even though she rebuked herself for bothering him, tired as he was, with such pettiness of conversation.

From the sofa she watched him walk over to what they called his den—a long low armchair of studded and well-worn leather to the right of the fireplace, with an adjustable lamp and a two-tiered revolving bookcase within easy reach; beyond, tall built-in bookshelves in the recess, lined with rare collections and first editions, and a pipe rack on the wall of the wide chimneybreast. A Sheraton drum table stood to the left of the armchair, at the moment carrying a sewing basket and some socks.

Alfred Hayley was a lover of antiques, and quite a connoisseur. His favourite period was the fashionable one, that is, 130 years at least before his own. Nothing Victorian, or Regency, and he preferred early to late Georgian. But alas, he couldn't afford to buy for himself, and his sitting room was mostly a rather messy library, for books he did collect. And silver, which was laid out in a glass show cabinet. Even these, he mostly bought to sell at a handsome profit, and he spent hours going through "Notes and Queries", item by item, as well as a great deal of time at Christie's, Sotheby's and Hodgson's. But he always said that had he been rich he would have turned his home into "a delicious marriage of Louis XV and Queen Anne, with perhaps a Charles II inlaid walnut casement clock as an elegant father-in-law."

He selected a pipe from the rack, took out his tobacco pouch and sat down with a weary stage sigh, filling the bowl as he stared absently at Marjorie swinging down her black-stockinged feet and fitting them into the flat black shoes that stood neatly waiting for them on the old brown rug. They were rather big, her feet, both broad and long, and the ankle-bone peered whitely through the thin black lisle, like a radish through the earth. It reminded him of one of the names on those envelopes and his eyes glittered. She bent down and buttoned the straps of her shoes, then rose, walked over to him and crouched at his feet to unlace his own shoes. She took the left one off with extreme caution, then the sock. The process was painful, which annoyed him.

"Darling, it looks better. That last bit of swelling seems to have gone down."

Which annoyed him even more.

"Oh, it's all right, leave it alone. Dear," he added quickly but not tenderly.

"I'll change the dressing. You'd better have a soak as well."

"Oh, really, Marjorie, don't fuss. What's the use? I got *no* result from doing the cure at Bath, why should this help?"

"Well, darling, it has helped."

"Oh, all right. But give me my slippers, for heaven's sake, my foot's freezing."

He lit his pipe with angry puffs and winced as she put his slipper on and plopped the large gas fire to a low flame, for it was a warm evening.

He found it hard to be gracious about her devotion, which he enjoyed as a man and resented as even that much of an invalid. He knew well enough he was rude, but because his rudeness never produced the martyred look his wife used to put on he got no satisfaction out of it, and stopped, still impelled, however, to begin again each time. Marjorie was trained with far worse patients, and though he took advantage of this, she simply went on with her business. It was both soothing and disturbing at the same time.

Soothing and disturbing, that was just about the sum of it all with her. He watched her as she walked down the corridor, from the kitchen to the bathroom, boyish in figure but trim in the ungainly blue calico of her uniform. He was off on a pipe-puffing dream, as on a journey. How much was their love affected by the convenience of their arrangement? How much was the convenience inconvenienced by their love? He couldn't help remembering the time when their urge to live together, as opposed to just meeting and making love, overwhelmed all else, and all else came to look not just unimportant, easy to sacrifice, but desirable to sacrifice, no sacrifice at all, positively disliked as a hindrance. And now, was it even as convenient as all that, the deception and furtiveness necessary still, society being what it was in this modern age, as tied as ever to rules and taboos the Edwardian era and the War were supposed to have overthrown? Or was society's censure really a reflection of one's own conscience, as Carstairs had maintained last Tuesday? The censure one attributed to society was really one's own, he said, the less conscience a man had the less afraid he was to defy society, and society's tenets survived only inasmuch as a sufficient number of people riddled by their conscience survived. At the present death rate of consciences there would be none at all in about fifty years, and everyone would live with whom they pleased, openly, and for as long as they wished. But that would be anarchy, and Alfred didn't want that at all. He preferred outward order, and secrecy. Secrecy was half the joy for all its torment. Carstairs, however, certainly had the courage of his convictions. Alfred's face crinkled into a smirking frown that framed the gleam of pleasurable disapproval in his eye. Pity, yes, pity she found the other way so repulsive, in spite of all his eloquent pleading. She had liked it well enough at first, or pretended to. But women were so conventional, they didn't understand these things. And they always had their own way in the end.

Fatigue swept over him like a sandstorm after the dry, electric excitement of the previous few hours, and suddenly he hated her, he hated everyone, he hated life, that is to say he hated himself. What a mess, he thought in a sick, yellowing despair, what a miserable mess.

Then she was kneeling by him again with the basin of hot water and the new dressing.

"Oh, my dear," he said, holding out his pipe like a symbol of oath, "oh, my darling, oh, Boodle-oodles, I do love you so."

She looked up and smiled, touching his free hand.

"I love you too, Hughie, so much."

Then she bathed his foot, and dressed the uric toe.

His lawyer was furious, and treated him like a child. "But Mr. Hayley, why, why? What did you do it for?"

"I didn't 'do it for' anything, as you put it." The trick was to throw every phrase back, as if only fit for quotes. "Because I didn't do it. And I have no idea who did."

"Do you realise that this constitutes Criminal Libel?" Mr. Croft ignored the dignified denial. The doctors had been very angry at receiving envelopes so addressed and handled by local postmen and servants. They had indignantly complained to Beresford's, who were appalled and examined the folders carefully. The type was not their type. It was Mr. Hayley's type, and although he had been careful to use only pamphlets from houses that advertised through Beresford's, the trick was too clumsy for real deception. Besides, it had happened before, in handwriting, and they had let it pass with apologetic disclaimers.

Alfred Hayley hadn't dared accuse anyone on his staff. He was known as an odd bird, a collector of erotica and an occasional but fairly typical practical joker, quick to find others lacking in humour, slow to appreciate humour against himself. Mr. Croft had been the company's solicitor ever since it had begun in '26, and that of the Fairfax Publishing Company before then. He knew his client well. "Publisher," Alfred Hayley used to scrawl grandly opposite "Description of Director" on the new company registration sheets eight years ago. But the Fairfax had been merely a cover to get catalogues and rare books at trade prices. It had one publication to its credit, The Doctors' Who's Who for 1923.

Now Alfred Hayley was delivering one of his tirades. He really was remarkably eloquent. Such a smooth flow of words, in that soft persuasive voice, with rotund phrases like "these relics of Victorian hypocrisy", "the quick suspicions of the Puritan mind that reflect only its own mud" and "a true gentleman need fear no slander." One forgot about his tired old face and the grey hair sticking up over his nobbly brow and the bleared eyes behind the round rimmed glasses, and the protruding belly as he paced up and down his own office, with gracefully forensic gestures of those well manicured hands that always returned to his lapels, holding them like the edges of a gown. "I am a Catholic aristocrat," he was saying.

He wore a high wing-collar, a gold tiepin, and the small red ribbon of the French Legion of Honour in his left buttonhole. A bloodstone signet ring flashed on his left little finger, a gold bracelet wristwatch, and a sapphire ring on his right fourth finger. His suit was in light grey worsted of excellent quality. Mr. Hayley never wore black and pinstripe when consulting his lawyer. And his lawyer wondered, as always, how Mr. Hayley managed to dress so expensively, on the directorship of a company that had only recently begun to yield him a maximum of £750 or at most £800 a year; for although that was a tidy sum, and he often called it a thousand, times were hard and uncertain since the slump, prices were high, he had two households to support, and one of them in John Street, Bedford Row, where few could choose to live; he belonged to three clubs he couldn't afford, he collected rare books and he moved in costly company. Perhaps he sold them his conversation? He was cultured, certainly, he could talk most plausibly on any subject. As now. And his lawyer, who had learnt from long experience that the caricatures of art and literature are not, after all, grotesque exaggerations, as one thinks, but that life is full of just such people, everywhere, watched him with envy and frank admiration.

"You ought to be a barrister, Mr. Hayley," he said sincerely when the speech for the defence was over.

"But I am, my dear fellow. I am. Classics at Christ Church, then Law. Never practised, though. I've forgotten a great deal."

"Evidently."

"Now look here, Croft, you know me—"

"Yes, Mr. Hayley, I know you. And I confess I'm surprised. Very surprised. I would never have thought it."

"Well, then, as I said—"

"You know it means prison?" the lawyer asked, cutting short the renewed burst of sweet unreasonableness.

"Prison?"

The word was like a switch turning on the light. The panelled room was alive with the sudden anger in that lined face.

"Well get me out of it," he said at last, sullenly. "You're my lawyer, for God's sake." He made a gesture of exasperation and sat down at his desk. "Bless my soul, some people just can't take a joke. Common little middle-class men with common little middle-class standards."

That too, the lawyer thought, that was the stock protest of the confidence-trickster out-tricked. And the man was, like himself, nearing sixty.

"Humour is the one quality no one will admit to being without," he said slowly. "Virtue, honesty, courage, patience, chastity, none of these are fashionable and we modestly forgo our claims to them. But not humour. And yet, you know, every one of us is without humour from practically everyone else's point of view."

"Oh, don't pontificate, my dear fellow, tell me what to do." Behind the arrogant tone, Alfred Hayley looked suddenly damp-eyed and crushed, like a schoolboy chided by a favourite master, and Mr. Croft looked at him compassionately.

"I'll have to think about it," he said gently, "now that I know that—well, Beresford are suing, and I won't deny that I'm very worried, very worried indeed."

When he was gone Alfred took off his glasses and put his head in his hands. Prison. The word made curious ricochets over the waters of his memory, yet no concrete image would come, although he knew it existed. All he could think of was that a letter from his son now lay in front of him, on top of a pile of papers. Laura rarely wrote now, except to enclose one of Philip's untidy scrawls, but even her letters were gentler. She always addressed them to the office. Owing to Croft's arrival he hadn't had time to read it, and he now replaced his glasses to gaze vacantly at the black King Albert mourning stamp still in use, together with the incongruously bright carmine one announcing the 1935 International Exhibition. But he already had the whole set. They had been issued in July, before the ones of the new king even, due in December. He had sold his collection ages ago, when he got married, in fact, but his fascination had remained. Such beautiful things, these bits of coloured paper, how tantalising the insufficiency of the one, as opposed to the six, or nine, or eleven, and how arbitrary the features that made them rare. He brought to his lips, then admired at a distance, the sapphire ring so honourably received from the dealers for handling old Darnley's collection and refusing a commission. It had fetched £3,500. And he thought of his noble gesture with a glow of pride, of his honesty with a tint of regret. Darnley was dead. King Albert I of the Belgians was dead. The king is dead, long live l'Exposition. No, that wasn't quite fair, the king had died in March. Philip had written him a long and solemn letter, rather obviously translated from a school essay, all about the funeral. Very moving, or rather, very emotional. But he might die tomorrow and Philip wouldn't care one way or the other. Or anyone else, for that matter. That was the summary of his life. But no, they would all care. One only says that, as one says one could die tomorrow. But one doesn't die tomorrow, one goes on. March was a long way away. He had been to Rome since then. Rome, eternal city. Prison. How long for? He was fifty-eight. Only fifty-eight. Old Binnersley was ten years his senior. The Prime Minister was sixty-seven, so was E. F. Benson. And Sir Oliver Lodge, he must be ancient. Jo Chamberlain was over seventy and Shaw was nearing eighty, active as a combustion engine. Prison. But it wouldn't be for long. His friend Lord Alfred Douglas had been to prison, after all, and for libel. They wouldn't allow him paper and pencil and he had himself smuggled some in to him so that he could write his poems, beautiful poems, they were. He too would write beautiful poems, another Ballad of Reading Gaol, only much much finer, in decasyllables, or alexandrines perhaps, the first successful alexandrines in English, to express the long long days.

But Alfred Hayley sat crumpled at his desk, staring at an unopened letter from Brussels, immobilised by the vast melancholy that pervaded not only his present being but all the beings he had ever undergone.

Some of these beings shook it off, however, and plunged into much intense activity during the following weeks. As far as possible he avoided the office, where Miss Frinton was going through one of her alcoholically arch phases since Beresford & Co. had started their proceedings, and he spent most of his time in the Reading Room of the British Museum, putting the finishing touches to his book and checking all the new material he had obtained in the Vatican Library that summer. He found the Reading Room comforting, lost and deep inside the vast building, for although the shiny black desk-rows that stretched out from the round centre sometimes reminded him of a giant octopus, the image he preferred was the usual one, the beehive, himself a bee manufacturing more honey to place somewhere in that enormous honeycomb. His precious book, on which he had worked so hard during the last ten years, would be published soon in a rare and limited edition, and find a place on the shelves, not just these shelves, accessible to the common herd, but in some secret chamber, the Private Case, where he himself had special permission to work as a privileged expert, together with the keeper of THOSE Printed Books, who would one day be the Keeper of HIS Book. I am the Keeper of a Book, he would say, that is unique and fabulous. For of course he, Alfred Hayley, would have donated his manuscript, the most beautiful thing of all.

The Reading Room itself was also a free extra club, where he could meet his more scholarly friends, and this led to more, invitations, more social calls, more wine-dining. He felt immensely popular. He went to Lady Cuilth's At Home—he was very proud of his acquaintance with Lady

Cuilth, who was a baroness in her own right and signed her letters "Cuilth", like a lord, which always gave him a thrill of pleasure. There he was introduced to Sir James Branley, who wanted to see his Wilkes collection. Lord Weston, who had always taken an interest in the Medical Addressograph Co., now wanted his son to enter the firm and had discussed it with him over an excellent dinner. His own little intellectual gatherings at John Street were very successful, mostly male, of course, but occasionally June Wimpole, the novelist, turned up, or Alison Frank, the first woman barrister, and some of the Bloomsbury types. He also helped young Trent to concoct a plausible denial of the homosexual charge he had been faced with at the music college where he taught. Had not Abraham himself pleaded for Sodom? Alfred Hayley disapproved, of course, but he was modern, broadminded, a gentleman who would not stoop to bargaining with God.

Yes, life was exceedingly pleasant. He sold for £200 a first edition of *Fanny Hill* he had come by, after lending it to Elinor Jarvis and warning her to keep it locked away and hidden from her husband. He didn't see much of Elinor these days, she had always been Laura's friend rather than his. But he had bumped into her in the city, outside the Stock Exchange, where her husband spent his days, and since he was holding the book, and since he had always loved shocking her, he pressed it upon her, using her, in a way, as a safe hiding place. He also bought a Wilkes manuscript he passionately desired, for £250. He fell in love with a Hepplewhite shield-backed mahogany chair with divided splats, costing 175, visited it every day for three weeks, then got over it. He gave £20 towards the education of a boy he met with Carstairs at a Queen's Hall concert, knowing he would inevitably be asked for more, looking forward to the refusal, enjoying the lordly gesture. Marjorie was always so annoyed when he did that. "You can't afford it," she said.

Today he was lunching at his club in St. James' Street, with Oliver Meridew, and he now emerged from his club in Pall Mall, where he had looked in to have a chat with Lord Binnersley. Yes, he really was immensely popular.

A chauffeur-driven dark blue Daimler slid past him bearing an ageing lady in fox furs; then a black Rolls with a tilted white beret over crisp yellow curls at the wheel—a vision which nearly took *his* breath away—both cars were long and rectangular, highly polished, elegant and modern, and he wondered why a girl alone in a large Rolls Royce should be such an exciting sight, while a woman over fifty in the same setting merely sad, even disturbing, reminiscent of death and hearses. A man now, that was different. A man could be attractive at sixty or more. He glanced sideways at himself in a window, and approved of much . . .

Pity he had to wear glasses these days. But he looked splendid in his large homburg and his old Canadian teddy-bear coat, nearly seventeen years he'd had it now, it was so good, and now men's coats were long again he had just freshened it up with an expensive astrakhan collar. There was quality for you! He walked up the Haymarket, with Grace Moore in *One Night of Love* on his left and Marie Ney in a play called *Touch Wood* on his right (last two performances), which the *Morning Post* had said would run for ever. He felt above it all, on top of ze world, as Maurice Chevalier would say, though actually he was walking uphill, half consciously keeping step with the tight white breeches of the Whisky Johnnie Walker, that walked and walked enormously, without ever advancing, across the tall black building at the top of the street. Huge and red-coated, white-gloved, cravated and monocled, Johnnie Walker smiled at him, nodding his head and removing his top hat, walking and walking. And Alfred Hayley strode goutlessly up to Piccadilly, zestfully along it, and then thankfully into his club.

"Ah, my dear fellow, good to see you," he said to Oliver Meridew who rose to greet him from a depth of brown leather. "See you've got yourself a whisky. Good. You'll forgive me if I don't? Bad for the old gout, you know. I'll just have a pipe. Thank you, Corley, nothing for me."

He put a book down on the table, wrapped in brown paper, and pushed it across.

"Ah," said Oliver Meridew. "Thanks." He unwrapped it and quickly replaced the flash of disappointment with a look of admiring absorption.

"I say, this really is quite something."

"Thought you'd like to see it," Alfred said, puffing at his pipe to light it. "It's all but finished. And it's only a beginning, you know, a sort of guide to the material. I plan to write a book on the whole subject."

The volume was calf-bound and the pages were vellum. They were covered from start to finish with lists of titles and numbers, all written out in a bold though not outstanding calligraphy.

"*Registrum Librorum Eroticorum,* by Farley H. Dayle," Oliver Meridew read out softly from the title page, "Privately Printed for subscribers, London —" The date was still a blank, to be filled in when printed. "Farley H. Dayle, why do you . . . Oh, I see, it's an anagram of Alfred Hayley. Oh jolly good. When do you hope to publish it?"

"Difficult to tell. My printer Yvan Evans thinks next year, or '36 at the latest. It'll be a very limited edition, and soon each copy will fetch fabulous prices. Have you noticed the letter in front, with the pro-prefetto's signature?" He was excited, anxious both to talk about his work and to sound casual. "It's going to be printed in front as a kind of Imprimatur-Imprimachure, as Yvan Evans calls it." He knew the letter by heart, from having composed it, and he longed to read it aloud himself, sonorously, as he had read it to Marjorie, or rather, to the roofs of Rome from the balcony of their small hotel at the top of the Spanish Steps. But he didn't dare, in the holy precincts of the club, so he waited as patiently as he could while Meridew read it politely and passed on.

"I say, old man, you've given all the British Museum Private Case numbers."

"I wondered if you'd spot that. They'll be livid, won't they?"

"Damn useful, though. It's maddening the way they won't admit what they've got. And when one does apply to see something, to the director, no less, they put you at a special desk and watch you, just in case you may actually be enjoying it." And Oliver Meridew raised his eyebrows rapidly twice, this being the only okay way he knew of underlining anything slightly *risqué* without actually smirking.

"I know." Alfred sighed. "The Victorian mentality. Damn lot of hard work I put into that, sheer cataloguing. No time for relish, no time at all. Of course, I'm only doing it for the money. It's bound to make heaps."

"I congratulate you, Hayley. Put me clown as a subscriber, will you? A most useful reference work."

"Well, thank you, of course I will. With pleasure."

"By the way, Hayley, talking of rare books, could you let me have that *Fanny Hill* I lent you?"

"What *Fanny Hill*?"

"*My Fanny Hill*. You borrowed it at Yarnley, remember?"

"But my dear chap, I didn't borrow it to take away. I took it upstairs to bed with me."

"There must be a misunderstanding. Surely you remember the conversation we had? It was in the library. John Carstairs was there. You and your niece and he were my guests that weekend."

"Yes, I remember perfectly. Splendid weekend."

"You picked the book from my shelves and admired it so much I said you could borrow it, but asked you to take great care of it and return it within a week."

"I don't remember your saying that. I must have been quite lost in admiring it. Good gracious, my dear fellow, it wouldn't have occurred to me that you could allow the book out of the house for one moment. I thought you meant borrow for the night. I took it to bed and then replaced it first thing the next morning. Before breakfast."

"I see." There was a silence which took exactly the time of the unspoken phrase. "Well it isn't there."

"Isn't it there?" Alfred asked with great puzzlement. "Oh dear, don't say I put it back in the wrong place."

"Where did you put it back?"

"Where it came from, I thought." His eyes went up into his memory and his fingers directed the traffic he apparently found there. "Left of the door opposite the french windows, about three shelves from the bottom, in the centre. But of course I can't be absolutely sure now. Oh, dear, I do hope you find it. Must be worth quite a tidy sum."

"Three hundred."

"Really? As much as that?" He looked genuinely surprised. "Well, I expect it'll turn up," said Oliver Meridew. "I'm sorry about the—misunderstanding."

"Not at all, not at all. If I had borrowed it of course it would have been disgraceful of me to keep it so long. But surely you weren't prepared to allow a book like that out of the house?" Meridew still looked worried, and Alfred raised his hands, saying genially:

"Come and search my flat, I do protest, my dear sir. Come this very evening. As a matter of fact there will be a few very interesting young men there tonight, please come."

They went up to the dining room. For the rest of the luncheon they talked of *The Sunday Times* Book Exhibition at Grosvenor House, of Winston Churchill's broadcast on the causes of war in the National programme the night before, of the smaller Disarmament Conference at Geneva, and of the curious resentment caused by the picture of Herr Hitler on the wrappers of oranges in a sale by auction at the London Fruit Exchange, so that the lots had to be withdrawn.

"Very odd, all the same," said Oliver Meridew to himself as he left the club at forty-five minutes past two. "Deuced awkward, in fact. Deuced awkward."

6

HER AWKWARDNESS made a silent pact with his in the cocoon of the hotel warmth, against the comfortless cold of the elements outside. The sea was the colour of mud and Calais was invisible on the dull horizon. There was not one wind-blown creature on the pebbled beach, and through the tall leaded windows between the oak panels they could see the spray blown right over the beach onto the seafront. Shakespeare's Cliff looked angry and alone, its chalk turned grey. Inside the dining room there was a roaring fire in the chimney, and much luxurious upholstery, "all plush and British Empire," Laura called it, which had annoyed him.

"Waitah!" He compensated with a British Empire manner. "This tea is pure dishwater. Take it away and bring us something drinkable."

"Yes, sir. I'm sorry, sir. I thought madam said China, sir."

"And don't be impertinent."

He made a magician's gesture over his plate of bacon and eggs. "You'd better remove this and keep it warm. We'll just have to wait. I refuse to eat cold bacon just because you don't know how to make tea. We'll have to wait! Really," he continued with the tight-strung larynx and heady resonance the upper classes use when they want to be audible to all without appearing to shout, "you'd think that with unemployment as high as it still is they'd make some effort to keep their jobs."

"Oh, Alfred, must you always make these scenes?"

Her eyes showed distress, her voice impatience.

"My dear Laura, what can it matter to you? I insist on getting tea that I can drink. Surely that's not too much to expect, even under a National Government. Besides, the place is empty, so there's no need to get so embarrassed, my little bourgeoise."

The dining room was not, in fact, empty, or he wouldn't have made the scene. An elderly couple were sitting at another table in the far corner, nearer to the door. She shrugged her shoulders.

"Oh, never mind."

"Damn fellow's got nothing to do," he grumbled on. "That's what comes of meeting in such a godforsaken place. Dover in late October, I ask you!"

"I don't see why I should come rushing to London every time you decide to ask me for a divorce so that you can marry that woman. I've said no a thousand times, it was you who insisted. This is more than halfway, for heaven's sake."

"Why wouldn't you discuss it when we met here in September?"

"Really Alfred, don't be exasperating. You know perfectly well why. I came to fetch Philip after his holiday in that ghastly place in Kent. You only came down for the day to give him a "family" outing. How on earth could we talk, scrambling up and down Dover Castle with the child?"

She paused as the waiter arrived with a teapot full of fresh tea and an obsequiousness full of controlled fury. Then he brought the bacon and eggs from the hotplate. She managed to give him a sympathetic smile before angering back to her own problems as she poured the tea.

"You were quite disagreeable enough anyway, grumbling, quibbling about everything the whole afternoon. We were both glad to see your train move out."

"We were both glad! Always hiding behind the boy."

"The boy, as you call him, was very upset."

"The boy, the boy! What about us? What about me?"

"Is your tea drinkable now?"

He snorted but missed the edge of her question, and they ate in silence for a while exchanging nothing more than the salt cellar and the mustard pot. He glared at her as he punctured his egg with the fork, so that the yoke ran all over the bacon like yellow blood. Of course, she enjoyed sitting behind that silver plate teapot, that silver plate jug and that silver plate sugar bowl, petite bourgeoise playing the gentle lady, smiling her empty comfort to the rebuked servant, wearing her martyred look in those velvet brown eyes, refusing to quarrel, refusing him everything.

They had argued till midnight, then gone to their separate rooms. He had achieved nothing, not by wheedling, whining, or caressing, not by boasting, threatening, or talking of God. Especially not the latter, which inevitably brought out "Whom God hath joined," and when he pointed out that in this particular case God hath not joined she said "As far as I'm concerned, He hath". And in any case, she said, that wasn't the point. He quite obviously intended to marry again, and perhaps have children—otherwise why bother about a divorce? When pressed, he had admitted at last that Miss Maxwell was not merely his nurse, and a ten-year pretence had collapsed which he alone had believed in. Well, she had said, there was the boy's future to think of, she had to cling to her legal rights—What legal rights? He's provided for! All you can think of is my will. Well I'm going to live, live, live, the way I want to live and with the woman I love, the only woman who's given some meaning to my life, etc., etc. And Laura had looked at him quietly and said: "I was hounded into marriage and I won't be hounded out."

She was staring past his head at the yellow sea on which she was to sail again in an hour or so. It would be a rough passage, probably, but she was a good sailor. He couldn't make up his mind whether the sadness in her expression was indifferent or, by gentlemen's standards, damnably reproachful. And whichever it was, he found to his annoyance that those dark eyes in that nut-brown face could still disconcert him.

He could see that she knew he was glancing at her each time his fork went into his mouth, yet her gaze was wearily but determinately travel-bound, as if he were making an unsuccessful pick-up in a dining car.

She hadn't aged at all, considering it was breakfast time. What would she be, thirty-eight, thirty-nine? A slightly fuller network under the eyes, but no sign of a double chin, and her clouding hair still brown in big waves and a short bob. Five years older than Marjorie, yet still prettier and more elegant. She was wearing a brown jersey cardigan over a cream jumper with the new low polo neck and straight tweed skirt. Well, not quite straight. A small triangle of stitching at the top of the back pleat had half hypnotised him when he had walked in behind her. It moved as she walked. She had kept her figure, though—a slight thickening all round perhaps, but all in correct proportion—middle-age seemed powerless against good legs and good carriage. Yes, there was an air of breeding about her. But it was only an air. Her mentality, her background were incurably middle-class. He sighed.

"Laura, my dear," he said at last in his most gentle voice, "let's not quarrel like this. It's as bad as the good old days. Surely we can talk it over calmly, without losing our tempers."

"Is that a royal plural?"

But the edge in her voice had gone and it was gentle.

"I want to show you something."

"What?"

"After breakfast. Something I . . . have upstairs, that I—er—want to give you."

The rest of the meal was civil. He told her about his projected visit to the Vatican library next summer, to catalogue what was there and include it in his Index. She did not ask if he would be going alone, but of course he now knew that she knew he would not. Pontie was officially his nurse, sometimes his niece, and as far as Monsignor the Pro-Prefetto was concerned she would be his assistant as well. To catalogue erotica with one's mistress in the library of Holy Mother Church was not anybody's achievement, and it was with some effort that he refrained, at this poise of their good humour, from underlining with statement, an idea which he could see in her eyes had flitted through and shocked her, though he himself found it so deliciously amusing that civility came easily.

How was her father faring after Madame Bertrand's death? Did she now run the house entirely on her own? Did she think the financial crises would be sending up the cost of living in (For he had been fortunate in that her parents had settled in Brussels instead of Geneva, the Belgian franc being as low as the French in relation to Sterling.) And was Monsieur Bertrand still dotty about Communism? Laura smiled.

"You know what Philip calls it when his grandfather listens to Radio

Moscow?"

"What?"

"Well," he says—but first I must explain that in French U.S.S.R., is U.R.S.S, and my father gets all those illustrated magazines called 'l'U.R.S.S.' So Philip says he's listening to the Great Bear, la Grande Ourse', you see."

It sounded rather lame in translation and at second hand, but he laughed outright, both gratefully and as a proud father. "Oh, very nice. Very nice indeed."

So they went upstairs in good humour.

"I'll fetch it and bring it to you," he said.

He came into her room where she was closing her suitcase. He was carrying a thick yellow envelope.

"Laura, my dear, I want you to read this. I've wanted you to read it for many years, but somehow, I could never bring myself to give it to you, even at the time."

He handed her the yellow envelope across the unmade hotel bed. She looked at it and said: "If that's one of your forty-five page letters I don't want to read it."

He flung it furiously into her suitcase.

"You shall read it. Really Laura, you're impossible. You don't even try to understand."

"What do you want me to understand?" She removed the yellow envelope and threw it back on the bed. "Why our marriage failed from the start? Why your giant egotism makes you impossible to live with? Why you sent me back to my parents and then took away the smallest assurances of future security I had, even to the nominal directorship of your company which you gave over to Kingsley-Smith? Why you tore up our Separation Agreement? I'm no longer interested why, the result is the same. I am thirty-eight, do you think I can get a job in all this unemployment if anything should happen to you?"

"It isn't that, Laura." He picked up the packet and fingered it awkwardly, like a boy handing in a school report. "I wrote this long before then. Don't you want to know anything about me?"

"Oddly enough, no."

She clicked her case to and sat down at the impersonal dressing table to do her face and put on her hat. She still powdered her nose violently, punishing it with the puff and sending a cloud all round so that she had to brush her dress afterwards. She still used the lip salve quickly, like a schoolmistress underlining a mistake. And her hat was brown felt, with a dented crown, and had to be put on at a special angle, with great care. He took all this in with a weird tenderness descanting his fury as he talked, walking up and down, and waving the yellow envelope. When she got up at last to fetch her light brown coat, with its huge lapels and cuffs, which was hanging in the solitary confinement of the heavy Victorian cupboard, he stopped walking but went on talking, opened her suitcase and popped the envelope inside.

She saw him in the cupboard mirror as she closed the door, but quietly put her coat on, without his help, for he was still talking. She buttoned and belted herself up, picked her travelling handbag from the dressing table and went over to the suitcase.

"I'll carry it for you," he said gallantly.

"Nonsense, it's minute, and I'll have to carry it later."

"Well, I'll take it as far as the customs barrier."

"All right," she said airily.

But downstairs he had to put it down at the reception desk while he paid the bill. She murmured sweetly, "I left something behind," and raced upstairs with the small suitcase before he could protest. She went to his room, opened the case and placed the yellow envelope fair and square in the middle of the half-stripped bed. But very sedate she was as she walked down the thick red and blue stair carpet of the hotel, and placed the suitcase innocently at his feet again.

He was livid. She hoped he would refuse to see her off, but hysterics have a miraculous instinct about other people's hopes and he doggedly accompanied her, barking all the way to the station-harbour.

The maids had removed the yellow envelope from the bed and placed it on the dressing table, propped up between his two silver hairbrushes, from which position it greeted him when he returned. And in his hands the yellow envelope looked larger than the yellow Channel boat that moved slowly into the opening between the harbour's crabclaw walls.

Forty-five page letter indeed! Admittedly the journal was rather thick, but how poignant! *On Board S/S La Lorraine, May 14th, 1918*, it began. He had read it late last night and wept over his sorry self. *February 24th, 1919*, it ended, *God help me and help you too Laura. The news I have been waiting and praying for has come, but what news. What have I done to merit this?* How well he wrote in those far-off days. What a terrible pity it was he had missed his real vocation. *I have had a terrific struggle to keep the shrine lamp burning. I have come to the end of my long rosary, which I have told all these months, and there is a cross with thorns there instead of a crown. God help me to kiss it. O hands I loved is this what you have wrought for me. Sight and sense seem to have gone, I am groping blindly, reeling from a blow which has stunned me. I am coming to you, just when and how I don't know. The world has suddenly gone dark for me, nothing seems left to me, only a spark of faith hope and belief remain. Yet! I blame you not for mine the fault is had I not been made of common clay I had climbed the higher heights unclimbed yet and seen the freer air the fuller day! And you have never known, never known.*

But the last line was even more heartbreaking:

I can never add another word to this. I can never come to it again.

The temptation to Free Will is always great, and at one in the morning, in the midst of tears in a lonely hotel bedroom near the wintry sea, it had not been resisted. He had come to it again, he had added to it, on the opposite blank page—but in pencil, which doesn't really count.

Fourteen and a half years and more since I wrote these last words.
Tonight I feel we have said the Mass for the Dead over our dead selves—

And I feel like the Ashes used at a
burial service
   Ashes to Ashes, Dust to Dust
   I cannot believe in the Resurrection
of the Dead.
   If any word I've said tonight has
hurt you, be consoled for it has
hurt me twice as much
   If your wounds opened mine bled—
   And so I fear it will ever be—
Our crosses are hewn from different trees
But we each of us have our calvaries
    But
The costliest Sorrow is all our own
For on the summit we bleed alone.
        A.   1 a.m.

It was beautiful. She would surely have been moved to tears if she had read it, then she would have relented.

He remembered for a moment just what she was to have relented about —a divorce—and the words jarred a little in their emotional overtone. He saw there was a space after the first sentence *Fourteen and a half years and more since I wrote these last words,* and after a moment's thought he took out his silver pencil and added in a slightly smaller hand, to get it all in: *I've read them again and again since you left me.*

Yes, that put the whole thing in the right key. It meant that she had "left" him last night after their talks, but also "left" him utterly alone and forever, groping blindly, reeling from a blow which had stunned him, with no spark of faith hope and belief, the world suddenly dark for him . . . and she had never known, never known.

7

B UT THEN, had anyone? Had he? And what was there to know? Truth is what we believe, even if what we believe is not always truth.

For whereas most people assume that they are more complex than most people, Alfred Hayley assumed that he was more complex than that. Which is not surprising since few can understand the algebraic progression of their own consecutive selves. And as for being understood by others, that was much to hope for, since life in its irony so arranges things that those who must try to be the centre of attention are invariably the most impossible really to know.

To Marjorie his mistress he had no religion, a not very unusual state though he thought himself in that respect rather advanced. Marjorie, a girl of conventional religious background, suffered at first much, then less, then hardly at all as he slowly replaced her code with an old-fashioned and mundane mixture of daring ideas like Free Love, Trust your Conscience, and Science has Made the Idea of God Untenable. For in spite of his many interests he was a businessman, and although he occasionally read a modern book, and of course *The Times,* he was hardly in the vanguard of intellectual opinion as to which emotions were fashionably significant and which ought to be suppressed as trite. He couldn't understand a word of modern poetry and therefore denied it the name—someone had shown him a thing called The Waste Land, written, as far as he could see, by an illiterate young hooligan, an American, of course—and he considered Futurism, when at all, as one more sign—if any were needed after jazz, half-naked Charlestons and screaming flappers—of the younger generation going to the dogs. For of course, Alfred Hayley was a Puritan, profoundly shocked by his own behaviour and therefore even more by that of others.

Nor was he a particularly successful businessman, except perhaps in his own eyes. In the eyes of other businessmen he was an original, an eccentric, an intellectual. In the eyes of his wife—well, she certainly knew one or two of his preceding selves. And yet not all. There was that journal he had once written her and never shown. Sometimes he even wondered just who he was, all things to all men and no one to himself, or no one to all men and all things to himself. Then there was his son. In the eyes of his son what was he? But he could only look forward to Philip's manhood for any answer that he really cared about, for he disliked small boys, unless they played like angels and talked like Christopher Robin.

And so it happened that Alfred Hayley found himself at half past six one evening parading up and down the nursery—or so he called it—of his shabby mansion-flat in Acton Lane, wearing a monocle, a mortarboard and an Oxford M.A. gown. Philip, at five years old, had never seen the like before, and his grey eyes stared in some alarm from between the pale fringe and the rim of the Tiger Tim cup as he sat up in bed in his blue dressing gown, all pink after his bath, eating his supper off a Winnie-the-Pooh tray and tucked up with a few more of those synthetic monsters of the modern nursery, as Alfred always called them, the teddy-bear, the gollywog, the cuddly kangaroo. When the lamb lies down with a fluffy lion, he would enounce with scorn, it will be the end of the British Empire. Yet it was he who had bought the toys and children's books, and he secretly relished the gramophone records of the Winnie-the-Pooh songs, often listening to them by himself in the drawing room out of his new mahogany box.

"You're a golliwog," the lamb said thoughtfully as his father showed off his academic dress. "Are you going to a party?" Then the lamb's alarm increased. "Mummy's not to go out, Mummy, you're not going out, are you Mummy?"

Laura smiled and shook her head as she refolded the pale blue bath-towel which had been drying on the fender round the gas fire, producing a familiar scorched smell that sent images from Alfred's nostrils, of big bath tubs in front of flaming grates in distant nurseries. Then jealous anger chased them away as he glimpsed her collarbone under the V-neck of her loose shirt-dress and he remembered the fuss Philip had made one of the rare times he was taking Laura out to the theatre and dinner with Elinor and Alan Jarvis. She had bought a new evening frock for the occasion—a stunner for her dark complexion, one of those low-backed, low-waisted affairs in cherry-red chiffon, or was it crepe de Chine, with a knee-length front and a long frilly tail. She had laid it out on their bed and Philip, who had apparently been flinging fits of temper all afternoon, had crept in while she was fixing his supper in the kitchen, removed the dress and stuffed it down the corner-space behind the chest of drawers in the nursery. Silly of him, since that was his favourite hiding place, to which he had escaped only the week before, after throwing his teddy-bear at his father in the drawing room and telling him to shut up making all that noise on the piano as all his animals were in hospital. And now he sat there saying "You're a golliwog." Really! Had he, Alfred Hayley, given birth to a monster?

But he caught back at his temper as it flapped out. Laura had said: "You're so seldom at home, come and say goodnight to Phil or he'll never grasp the concept of God the Father." As half a Bertrand, the child seemed incapable of grasping the concept of his own father, let alone the other.

"This is a Master's gown, from Oxford, Philip. It is a great honour to have the right to wear it."

"Are you a master, Daddy?"

"Well, not a schoolmaster, of course," he replied with a heavy stress of scorn on *school*. "A Master of Arts."

"Oh."

"That means I can put 'M.A. (Oxon)' after my name."

"Aimée Oxen," Philip repeated, thinking of the last cow but one in a stable on a farm in Pichonnat, Canton de Vaud, Suisse, Europe, the World, the Universe.

"It's short for Oxford," his father explained, thinking that his son looked remarkably stupid.

Laura had removed the boy's supper and he was brushing his teeth, spitting into a bowl on the tray. He announced suddenly: "I'm Cambridge."

Alfred sat down on the bed and took off his mortarboard.

"Oh? Why?" His monocle dropped and Philip stared fascinated at his father's left eye. "Why?" Alfred repeated.

"Because Tony says so."

A few weeks back he had been caught out not knowing, having in fact no idea what his friends at school were talking about. That made him feel terrible. "Well, which blue d'you like best?" they asked and he had chosen the light rosette like Tony's. As simple as that, and he was so relieved that although at first he had mentally resolved to ask his mother, he then forgot.

"Well, Tony's wrong," Alfred said firmly. "You're Oxford, because Daddy went to Oxford, you understand?"

"Is Oxford a place, then?" He looked disappointed.

"Yes, Philip, and a very wonderful place. I hope you will go there too, one day."

"Is it a castle?"

"No, it's a university. It's like school, only much, much more important, for grown-up young men. They go there to study Latin and Greek."

"Like party-nasty?"

"Pater Noster, Philip, yes, and alpha-beta."

"Let's do alter-beater, Daddy."

The tray had gone and he snuggled down, ready to scream at the tickling which descended on him like a bee at epsilon, ki, pi and ypsilon as they recited together: alpha, beta, gamma, delta, *ep*-silon.

"Daddy," he said happily, when he was lying quiet after the shrieks of delight had subsided, "were you born in Oxford Castle?"

"Why, no, Philip, it isn't a castle. I just studied there."

"But you *were* born in a castle weren't you, Daddy?"

"Of course I was." He had a quick sense of humour when flattered, or could quickly humour the flatterer; and seize the opportunity: "You belong to a very important and noble clan, Philip, you must never forget that. The Hayleys of Kilbrae. When I go up to Scotland next week I'll buy you a kilt, it's a beautiful costume for you to wear, so that you can say, when people ask you, this is the Hayley tartan, the Hayleys of Kilbrae."

"The Hayleys of Kilbrae," Philip murmured and fell asleep quite suddenly.

"It really is too bad of you," Laura said in the drawing room. "Filling the child's head with all this snobbish nonsense."

"My dear Laura,"—this opening usually introduced something unpleasant—"you know nothing whatever about it. No Englishman who's the son of a gentleman has ever been harmed by knowing something of his lineage." He seemed to have hit, by way of a pretension, on the odd truth that children are seldom harmed by what parents think will harm them, but by quite different things, and although he did not grasp either the pretension or the resulting truth, he nevertheless felt he had said something righteous and therefore profound.

He was filling his pipe, standing with his back to the gas fire, so that from Laura's armchair where she was putting away her sewing, she could see the small head of Nefertiti on the chimneypiece, staring every now and then from under his gesticulating grey worsted arm, and contrasting oddly in smooth serenity with his flaccid good looks and pale angry eyes.

"I'll have you know that I intend to bring up my son as a Hayley and not as a Bertrand, as an English gentleman and not as a little Swiss nobody. I didn't rescue you from the clutches of that 'bonne famille' of yours in order to have you plant their tedious little notions in the mind of my son."

"Their tedious little notions do at least include clean and tidy personal habits," she exclaimed furiously. "I suppose you want Philip to grow up with the idea that all a man need do is to laze about in his dressing gown all morning, smelling of bed, and never come home in the evening. What's happened to you, Alfred?" she went on, seizing the momentary advantage of his speechless anger. "You used to be so careful of your appearance, but now you've let yourself go completely, even when you do finally dress and leave the house you've got ashes all over your suit, or dandruff. Not that I mind, if only you'd leave early like other husbands and let me get on with the housework. And come home for supper. Who do you think you are, Sanger in *The Constant Nymph?*"

Though he seldom read modern novels, he had been pressing that one on her for months. She hadn't in fact read it, but had seen the recent film, alone one afternoon. She was anxious to show that her tastes were different.

"Ever since we saw that play, two years ago, when I last came over, what was it called, *Hay Fever,* you seem to think the only really *upper* class behaviour is to be rude, careless, lazy and utterly irresponsible. May I remind you that we are *not* living in a large country house to which we have invited a lot of crazy people."

It was all so true he was livid.

"Really Laura, you're so conventional it's practically impossible to live with you. Smelling of bed indeed." He whimpered suddenly. "You would never say a thing like that if you really loved me. That's what I've always said. You don't love me enough."

"By which you mean I ought therefore to leave you. You can twist anything, can't you? Well I'm not going to give you that pleasure. All I ask is that you should leave the house after breakfast and come home for dinner like—"

"—like every other husband," he joined in sarcastically. "I've told you before, Laura, you know nothing whatever about English life, and if you don't take to it kindly you only have to leave."

She raised her eyes heavenwards, then regretted it. He hated the gesture, which at once produced the expected sarcasm.

"And God isn't looking down on your martyrdom from inside that porcelain lamp in the ceiling."

"I'll go and serve dinner. Excuse me."

He wasn't going to let her off as easily as that. But nor would he actually follow her into the kitchen, which was a dark, messy place overshadowed by a fire-escape with a milk-lift perpetually clattering up and down and a large middle table always in the way and always covered with spillable, breakable things, and a dead old-fashioned range inside the chimney under a chipped mantelpiece next to the hideous modem gas stove which had rude iron legs. Yes, she was French enough to be good at cooking, if nothing else.

So that their meals were bitter in words. Throughout dinner, sitting on Empire chairs, they went on poisoning each other's hearts and eating her excellent *blanquette de veau.*

Or rather, she ate it. He toyed with it, criticising it. He complained of the way the table was laid. He said she had the mentality of a banker's daughter. He threw in phrases like "blood will tell", and she said "What, at fifty-two? Tell what, and to whom?"

It seemed to be one of life's dirty tricks, she thought in an angry torrent of silent verbiage, that those people who lacked the ability to notice, imagine or understand the effect they have on others, also needed, by way of further blinkers, to reject the only two possible reactions others could have to their goading: a loss of temper or an exasperated show of having exercised patience. Anger seldom encouraged coherent expression and left the goader with an illusion of victory—excellent, if only it kept him quiet for a while, but it didn't. And the claim to patience automatically produced, with some justification, accusations of smugness. In the past she had indulged both, frequently. Now little was left to her but passive silence, and although this often drove him to go on and on, it did in general enable their marriage to work more smoothly than before, by teaching her to agree with everything he said and keep her teaching thoughts to herself. The marriage worked, in fact, like the type of middle-class marriage he would most have scorned, because it had become unreal. And whenever reality bubbled forcefully from below, their conversation would degenerate to an insane shuttlecock of small prickly resentments, for she was aware that she too had come to interpret his every opinion as a critical slur, even though, as she also knew, it wasn't always.

He was giving her a little lecture on the impoverishment of the aristocracy—moving up one class by implication as by an elevator. "The war dealt us a final blow," he said with a tragic sigh, putting down his wineglass full of water, "from which some of us have not yet recovered. But we are the backbone of the country. I don't suppose you have much knowledge of English social history and the long struggle between the landed gentry" (going down, Laura said to herself as she gathered up the plates and dishes, but then I have a shopkeeper's mind) "and the crude fashioners of the Industrial Revolution . . ." At which point Laura got up and went back to the kitchen, bearing two plates and a bowl of stewed pears.

Always the woman's last resort when out-argued, Alfred thought; indeed her privilege, he added gallantly, and walked master-like to the drawing room. But misery and self-pity soon oozed out from the neurotic bogs below those puffs of angry mist.

And all because his mistress, smitten with scruples, had run away on his wife's return to London. Three blissful years, he had had, of fairly uninterrupted freedom, with Laura in Geneva, then in Brussels when her parents had settled there to be near the younger son who had started up some potty travel bureau, of all things—the whole happy family in one house, Laura and all, so typical of them. Even the father worked in the son's office. But now she had come back, determined to make, as she said, a go of it. And a go it had been, for Marjorie had gone. Marjorie had believed his story, for so long she had believed it, but then she had found out. Usually one lied to a wife about a mistress, not to a mistress about a wife. But Laura was so essentially remote, so uninterested, so continental. She never inquired, never seemed to suspect—whether from certainty of fidelity or from certainty of infidelity he couldn't tell. He lied to her, of course, but it seemed almost a waste of talent. Why did he always have to be wearing his life inside out, not daring then to change because it was unlucky? Or impossible. Once upon a time, there were arrangements. Men were made like that. Everyone understood, and wives were submissive. But the old double standards had collapsed. People expected all or nothing. It was the war, everyone wanted security and their ideals unspoilt. So they fussed about duty and bonds. Except the young and the rich, they didn't give a damn. But he was neither young nor rich—though he could hardly complain, he was benefiting from the general wave of prosperity and would soon be able to live the sort of life he felt he had always been accustomed to. But he was tied by the morals of two middle-class women who both naturally loved him too much to let go.

For of course, the one thing a person no longer in love dislikes to ad-mit is that his one-time love might be no longer in love as well. Rather does he believe he loves them both, as they both love him, and recites to himself snappy little verses like "how happy could I be with either were tother dear charmer away", assuming that neither charmer would in fact dream of being away. Or so it had been once. Now it was all much more confusing, though it seemed so easy. Look at the fuss everyone had made about that play they'd seen with the Jarvis's, *Young Woodley*, at the Savoy, all because a boy falls in love with his housemaster's wife. Yet in that very play she had mentioned, by that bright young man, what was his name—the husband only had to say he adored one of the lady-guests for his wife, a famous actress, to announce casually to both of them, "the time has come for the parting of the ways." It was as easy as that. And then when he found he didn't adore the lady-guest after all, everything *was* all right again. Shallow, of course, brittle, exaggerated. Men went around saying "Would you like me to make love to you?" It was prepos-terous. But perhaps the basic attitude was right, it was breaking down prejudices just as Oscar Wilde had broken down prejudices before, by amusing everyone out of them. Why then, did he find it so hard to tell the truth? Because his pursuit had been so ardent? Was that it? One could only end lightly if one had begun lightly? The stronger and the more eternal love he declared, the more unthinkable was a confession that it now no longer existed. At least, to a certain type of woman, with ideals, who would go to a drawer of her mind and bring out one's pas-sionate promises like marriage lines.

"This is London calling, 2L0 calling. Is Bartok Mad or Are We? Dr. Percy Scholes is here again in the Studio . . ." Am I mad or are they? Al-fred sat back in the rose damask armchair with his hand on his brow, looking dramatic for no one. His nerves were a flock of butterflies pinned down by every discord in the illustrated talk. He switched off irritably and looked at the black upright piano and the bound volume of the forty-eight that lay on top of it over a few thin sheets of music. So long, since he had really played, often and every day. So long since music had seemed his very life. Like God. Like Laura. The Eighth Prelude. Lento, Moderato. The quiet opening, still as daybreak, flowered in his mind so that his fingers stretched to shape the notes. But he didn't move. The new toy required no effort, and he switched it on again, waiting for the programme to return at the mere gesture. What a wonderful thing this wireless was, bringing the world into a room-sized awareness.

"And so you see, the apparent discord is resolved . . ." But his thought made more noise than all the discords. Hatred filled him as wine fills a hollow stemmed glass, rising from the legs up and poisoning his head with fumes. He hated his son, who was a nincompoop and picked his nose and still wetted his bed and even wetted the carpet in here last week when his mother lifted him to take him to bed and he had refused to go. He'd been holding himself in all that time. Disgusting. He hated his wife. He wanted the whole burden to be taken from him. Take away the burden or give me the strength to bear it. No, just take it away. Everybody fussing about duty and responsibility. Marjorie fussing, Laura fussing, her family fussing, society fussing. He hadn't seen Marjorie for ten months.

The sudden silence interrupted his desire like a knock on the door in *flagrante delicto.* What a horrible thing this wireless was, it could wake one up when it stopped. Like God. You seemed to hear Him most when you hadn't been listening, and found suddenly He wasn't talking any more. Then His silence leapt at you like a black panther. Bother God. Laura was always going on about God, even though she said she had "become an agnostic", like him; and not without a fuss, either—"a gnosis, lack of knowledge, I've looked it up!" But agnosticism was only the other side of the coin in her calvinistic soul. "All this pretence at gracious living!" she had said over his brave attempts to furnish their suburban flat decently, to belong to the right clubs and to bring up his son as a gentleman, with a private governess because he was picking up an accent at the local school, "what is gracious living anyway but a fine disguise for the absence of grace?" Rather neat, that, he had to admit, and he stored it up for use in a more suitable context. But then she had spoilt it by going on. "What is a club anyway but an English admission of social failure? Who on the continent would pay so much a year to escape women and to meet more men?" Well, really! Then the dance-orchestra burst in from Savoy Hill playing that jumpy little polka with horrible gusto, followed by the words from a smooth tenor with clipped vowels *I miss My Swiss, My Swiss Miss misses me. I miss the kiss That Swiss Miss gives to me. I lost her in the mountains. In the mountains she must be.* Ugh!

He switched off, got up and wound the gramophone with great energy. Then he put on his record of Beatrice Harrison making the nightingale sing to her cello in the Surrey Woods. And after a while he felt immensely purified, and that the *world* was beautiful. What a wonderful thing modern science was. All this joy in a wooden box. Laura had gone to bed.

The next day Alfred took his wife to Oxford, and she wore her new cloche hat, which had cost seven and eleven at Selfridges.

The visit had long been planned, ostensibly for William Kingsley-Smith's inaugural lecture as new Professor of Anthropology at Beverley College. William, he explained to Laura on the train, was Reggie's brother and had done very well. Both were childhood friends but he had rather lost touch with them until just recently, when Reggie had turned up from South Africa where he had been a mining engineer for twenty-five years. His brother, however, was a great scholar. No, they hadn't been up together. As a matter of fact, she mustn't mention his Oxford education to William, as he had been rather envious and bitter at the time, he had gone to Liverpool or somewhere like that. "They were rather beneath us in those days, don't you know, but of course society was much more rigid then. He's done very well."

The Kingsley-Smiths were certainly not beneath Alfred Hayley now. Reginald had been most useful by way of reintroduction to the Professor, and the Professor was most useful for casual-sounding introduction at the reception after the lecture, which had been on *Religion and Sexual Rites in the South Sea Islands;* a title which had filled Alfred with such adolescent delight that he had hummed *Where is my Rose of Waikiki?* all the way from London. But the lecture had been sober to an academic extreme.

Everyone was wearing gowns, except visitors from London and dons' wives, many of whom seemed to belong to a society for the preservation of the longer skirt, looking two and sometimes three years out of date. Such, however, is the power of numbers that it *was* Laura who felt shy in her knee-length pleats. But the Professor was visibly charmed.

"Well, well, I took you for a student, Mrs. Hayley. I'm delighted to make your acquaintance."

"I so enjoyed your lecture, Professor. Forgive my ignorance, but have you written elsewhere on the subject? Some of the allusions to comparative religion seemed familiar." She looked at Alfred, who scowled and tried to interrupt.

"I have written several books, yes, Mrs. Hayley, and one precisely on Problems of Comparative Religion. Perhaps you read it?"

"N-no, I—er—must have been given a great deal of its contents in my husband's er—conversation over the years."

"Well, I am flattered, North—er, Alfred, and how are you? Isn't it ages and ages? More than a quarter of a century. Reg was so pleased when he bumped into you, where was it, at his club, no? Where's he got to, by the way? Ah, there he is. Trying to get through without spilling his sherry. My dear Reggie."

"That was pretty impressive, Bill. Way above my head." He nudged Alfred. "And yours too, I expect, eh?"

Alfred turned primly back to the Professor.

"Nonsense. I enjoyed it immensely. I have hundreds of questions I want to put to you, my dear chap. One of them, for instance, I was most intrigued when you said—"

"I'm afraid I have to circulate. I'm very sorry, but I am, well, the guest of—" he made a small vague gesture to belittle it —"honour. Call round at my rooms later, do please, I'd be delighted. And come up again."

Laura was always puzzled, even now, at the ease with which Alfred felt himself affronted. He seemed to have no sense of humour and no sense of nuance, as he drew himself up, straightened his tie and glared at the Professor's hand which was being shaken by a white-haired man in a heavy gown. But then his angry eyes lightened as he caught sight of someone he knew and darted off.

She was trying to sound reasonably intelligent to Reginald Kingsley-Smith, a little man with thick lenses and hair combed carefully. sideways over a bald head, who was explaining to her in immense textual detail why he belonged to the Bacon Society—a subject before which many otherwise intelligent people go blank with boredom and embarrassment. And as she listened she watched Alfred's hand on some old man's shoulder and thought, he is fifty-two. Her father once said a person's character can't change much after thirty. The bad gets worse and worse, the good better and better, but if the bad is very bad it can drown the good altogether. And he was already forty-one when they'd met, what chance had she got, even if she had been the ministering-angel type? But Mother St. Jerome didn't agree with that at all. She used to say, there's always grace, which can illumine even the most sick. She always spoke of self-absorption and aggressiveness, of cruelty and vanity, as illnesses for which prayer was the only cure. Laura couldn't believe that, there must be some appeal to reason. But Alfred had no religion now anyway, he refused even to discuss it, and wouldn't allow Philip to be taught the barest outline of God's existence. "I'm bringing up my son as a lapsed Catholic," he had quipped to an atheist intellectual barely ten minutes ago, during a discussion about *The Golden Bough*, which everyone seemed to be mentioning. But even in her unbelief she felt that one needed a little more to lapse from than the learning of the Pater Noster as if it were a multiplication table. Which perhaps it was. She felt befuddled with sherry, and started reciting in French, just to add to the din of voices, *Notre Pere, Qui Nes au del, Que votre nom soit sanctifie, Que votre regne arrive, Que votre volonte soil faite sur la terre comme aux cieux . . .*

"I'm so glad you agree with me, Mrs. Hayley," said Reginald Kingsley-Smith, who could only see her nodding and moving her lips. "It's all so obvious. I really can't understand how anyone can still be so bigoted about it. All this national bard stuff, you know, they won't give it up."

"But if you're so sure Bacon wrote Shakespeare, Mr. Kingsley-Smith, doesn't that merely make Bacon into a national bard instead of Shakespeare?"

"No, no, Mrs. Hayley. There's something about the name you know. The emotional appeal of centuries and all that."

"Laura my dear." Alfred was back, suddenly jubilant. "I'm taking you to see my old college. And a very dear, dear friend of mine I just ran into. He's asked us round to his rooms for a drink before dinner. Old Dr. Darnley, he's gone on ahead."

Alfred was anxious to get Laura away from the Kingsley. Smith brothers, the only people in England, probably, who had known him as a boy. Max Darnley at St. Luke's, his old friend and fellow-philatelist, wouldn't spoil the act because he would never realise an act was on.

Indeed, most of it was built up, rather wisely, before they set foot inside Dr. Darnley's rooms. "My own beautiful college," Alfred waxed sentimental at its fifteenth-century frontage, and even the porter greeted him like a long lost friend. "Dear old Baxter," Alfred said, "he never forgets an undergraduate's face. Of course, I used to tip him handsomely."

And because the notion was unseizable that Alfred's youth must have occurred in the 'nineties, when she had only just been born, it never struck Laura that dear old Baxter, who had lost an arm in Flanders, looked roughly Alfred's age, and would in fact have been seventeen in Alfred Hayley's mythical student years.

When Alfred went up to Scotland on business a week later, he bought Philip a Hayley tartan kilt, which was bright red and yellow, with a bright red jumper and bright red socks, and a Hayley tartan tie.

On the way back he made a detour via Birmingham, where Marjorie had got herself transferred to another hospital. Women in love who pleaded scruples and succeeded, he had discovered, were not in love. And although many women had neither love nor scruples, mere scruples melted to the flattery of pursuit as surely as ice under the sun. So they stayed at the Arden Hotel and made love like long lost pigeons, first her way, to please her, then his way, to please him. It was a ritual, he said, for he had lately read or mis-read D. H. Lawrence, it was life-giving, and she smiled and answered, "I just love you."

In the morning he hired a Daimler and took her to the village of Weirwood, in West Warwickshire. He was so excited he could hardly sit still, and chattered all the way, staring out of the window and fingering her thumb as if it were a cud. But he stopped the car as it drove past the Abbey grounds, and stepped out to take a photograph of it, distantly through the trees. Then he got in again and sat very silently as they drove on.

It was a Jacobean village, mostly, with some Elizabethan cottages and a few later larger houses. He gripped her arm as he walked her round, so tight it hurt. They went past the old smithy in the village centre and up a lane which led to Manor Farm, a long, treble-breasted Elizabethan house with what estate agents called a wealth of oak-beams, but real. He had once shown Laura a very early photograph of Manor Farm, pretending it was his parents' house, and she had said, with continental innocence, what a pretty cottage. He had snatched it from her in disgust, tearing it as he did so, her grip on the edge having been firmer than he thought.

When he had photographed Manor Farm, they walked back, hand in hand, towards the disused smithy. There seemed to be nobody about. A wo-man came out of the village shop lower down the street, a man waited by a bus stop at the bottom, where the road turned left towards Warwick and right towards the Abbey and Birmingham and the North. Strange having buses. The village shop had an ice-cream placard outside. He stood in a trance at the top of the hill by the smithy, then turned right towards the Old Vicarage, where he was born.

It had a wide frontage with eight first-floor windows, three under one roof, three under the other, and two in the space in between. On the ground floor in the right half there was the door, then a space, then one window. There had once been another window, bricked up by the tax on light but more prettily than usual, almost invisible in fact, with only the keystone above it, like Nefertiti's hat. He had never noticed this, for the house had been covered with purple clematis and wistaria. The porch too, stood naked now, a small Queen Anne pediment on two elegant slim legs. The tall hedge had gone, but the house was still divided into two. He looked at it now with an expert eye and was astonished. A seventeenth-century brick house but with Queen Anne sash windows, all painted white, and a Queen Anne porch with glass at the top of the brightly-painted door to let the light in. He remembered it all as dark and gloomy and enormous. It was light and graceful and not very big.

But his room up there on the right, over the drawing room, who slept in it now? What was it like inside? Did it have roses on the wallpaper? He couldn't see. But it was still there. And the tall thin chimney flanking the house for the drawing room fire, like an index-finger warning from a clenched fist, that was still there.

He turned silently into the churchyard and walked past the tombstones to look through the hedge at the back garden. Marjorie followed at a tactful distance, trying to be both there and not there by looking hard at an inscription on the church wall. And after a while, that seemed to her not only interminable but a huge distance away, he went behind a yew tree and sat on a large flat tombstone marked "C. W. Braddon, R.I.P. 17th June 1889", and he wept.

8

THERE WAS, however, one person whom Alfred Hayley did not have to impress as an old boy when he took her once to visit Dr. Darnley in his rooms at St. Luke's. For Miss Harriet Bell had known him a very long time. His act in this case was rather vis-à-vis Darnley, and by way of previous introduction.

"She was my sister's governess," he had said—which was true —"and so utterly devoted to the Hayleys, you know"—which was fairly true—"We've always treated her as a friend of the family. Poor thing, she's come down in the world rather"—which was untrue—"and I'm giving her an outing. She'd be terribly thrilled to meet a real live Oxford don." Which was fairly true.

All this had to be considerably subdued in front of Harriet Bell herself, who was a pint-sized independent little woman of fifty-two with the sharpest blue eyes that ever darted about under a fringe of straight and greying hair. But that was all right too, since his easy-going charm and courtesy with her could only emphasise to Darnley what a perfect gentleman he was.

And when old Darnley had bowed gravely over Miss Bell's hand, and said, "Dear lady, the pleasure was mine," and when old Baxter had shaken his jovially and said, "Bye-bye, sir, come and see us again," Harriet Bell turned to Alfred in the High and said:

"Northbrook, that was delightful. And now let's get down to business."

"Ah, yes, I was afraid you'd say that. Dear Hetty. Playtime's over, back to your lessons, children." He put his arm affectionately round her and she was pleased, looking up at him with a shrewd and rakish smile.

"What I've always loved about you, Hetty, is that you never mind what appalling grimaces you make. Well now, funny-face, can't I tempt you to a drink at the Mitre?"

"No, my dear, we must catch our train." She looked at her watch, which hung from a breast-pocket. "If there's a dining car you can give me a drink there, and we can eat and talk."

"Yes, Miss Bell," he mocked in a girlish voice. "And Miss Bell," he returned to his own and murmured closely—"you are rather a dear."

They crossed Carfax towards the station, an odd-looking couple, like children dressed up; she minute, in a wide felt hat and a loose, low-waisted kimono Ulster that almost reached her gaitered ankles, though skirts had gone up to mid-calf that year; he not so very much taller, wearing a homburg and lost in a teddy-bear coat almost as long as hers, though men's coats were also shorter now. But he had bought it in Canada before the war, and it was much too good to have cut.

They didn't talk in the dining car, for there was none, and even the first-class carriages were full, so that Alfred grumbled most of the way about Macdonald and his damned Reds who wanted Everyone to have the Same Lack of Privileges as the People. Thank God the country had just shown them they weren't wanted, they'd done enough harm, even in one year, though fortunately they were dependent on the Liberals and couldn't do all they threatened. All of which was as good a way as any of forestalling the Talk on a Painful Subject. They arrived at Weston-super-Mare late that night, and Harriet Bell was much too wise to say any more until he had eaten and slept. It was something that he had come at all.

At breakfast, he was again full of optimism and flirtatious jokes about their naughty weekend and where the devil was the King's Proctor, spying on the Lord Privy Seal, perhaps, who was not a lord, nor a privy nor a seal, and so on and so forth.

"Northbrook," she said, "I haven't come all the way from Newcastle-under Lyne to banter with you. Do you realise that since Hannah Smith's death I seem to be the only one who's willing to look after Muriel's affairs? Mrs. Smith, I know, felt she had some sort of debt to repay, because your mother helped her with her children, but I have no obligation at all, you understand that, don't you?"

"Of course, Hetty, my dear, dear Hetty, you're very, very kind. I know that."

"No, it's not just kindness, it's a sort of moral duty, for I've always been very fond of you all, well, it's hard to explain, and I won't try, because it's not praise I'm after. I just don't want to be taken for granted, that's all. Old Miss Bell will do it"—she imitated him—"our dear old faithful governess, you know, absolutely devoted to the family. It's not like that at all. It's a sort of love I feel for Muriel because of what she is, which I don't feel for the rest of you, you're a selfish lot, and I love you in a very different way. But you're her brother, Northbrook, and you must be ultimately responsible, though I'll look after the little things. You can't evade that."

"No, of course not." He shrugged his shoulders. "Who said I was evading it? I've just been rather busy lately, that's all. I'm trying to keep two companies going, the Fairfax, which you know, but also the Registered Nurses Bureau. And I've got someone interested in an idea of mine for a third company, addressographs, it's the latest thing. I'll tell you about it later." He was so full of optimism he didn't notice her amused expression. "And then there's been the Dr. Stein case. As perhaps you may have noticed from the press I have been more than occupied, making myself obnoxious to the Home Office on his behalf. As a matter of fact I was there only two days ago," he went on after a quick gulp of tea, "and had a chat with Sir John Taunton, straightening out certain misconceptions he was labouring under. Personally we are friendly, officially we are at daggers drawn."

"Northbrook dear, could you return to the point?"

"Oh, er, yes, well. I did all I could at the time. I assure you that the three-and-a-half percent War Stock is the best possible investment for such a small sum. I had a great deal of work as executor of Mother's will, as you know. Challinor and Pring were most inefficient and the Regal Life held up the Probate by inquiring, like someone from Mars, by what right was I administering the estate, was I the son of the deceased?"

"The Regal Life? Wasn't that where you worked in Birmingham?"

"Now Hetty. Don't remind me of my misguided youth. Talking of which, Cordelia didn't make things much easier for me. Challinor and Pring kept getting the most extraordinary letters from Dr. Winthrop Blair's lawyers in Cape Town, called if you please, Van Dam, Smut and Temple, to the effect that I was to cease writing to them, that they had enough evidence, documentary and otherwise, about my reputation and past career, to justify them in refusing to have any dealings with me, that they would—"

"Northbrook. Have you been at it again?"

"At what?"

"You know what I mean."

"I've no idea what you're talking about. I thought it most unreasonable of Dilly, and very embarrassing vis-à-vis Challinor. I had to be very noncommittal, and just thank him for the extraordinary enclosure from Cape Town. I said, 'I am not impressed. I have answered it. I shall be in London on such a day.' For, of course, I was 3,000 feet up in Haute-Savoie at the time, with my in-laws."

"You answered it? Oh, Northbrook. So you *were* writing letters?"

"Writing letters? Of course I was writing letters."

"You know very well the kind of letter I'm talking about. Mrs. Hayley told me that Cordelia's husband had written to her to say you were for some reason trying to bring about an estrangement between him and his wife and that he would take action if it didn't stop. But that was five years ago at least, let me see, your mother died in '21, and you were already married, yes, it must have been 1920. So you started again after she died? Why, Northbrook, why?"

He sat grumpily like a schoolboy at fault.

"I only wrote about the Will. I had to. Besides, people don't think anyone's trying to estrange them unless they're estranged already."

Harriet Bell shook her head and looked at him with wonder in her sharp blue eyes. And a certain compassion. Writing, which might have been his saving grace, she thought, had always been his undoing. He had a pen and paper compulsion, he was the kind of person who had to write after a quarrel, in order to communicate that all communications would cease. He could never leave well alone. But then, nor could Cordelia.

"And she accused me of not going to the funeral," he went on, "and of stealing Mother's things. It's too bad. One goes wrong once and the only people who never let one forget it are one's own loving family. Of course I went to the funeral, you saw me there, didn't you, and Reggie Smith was there too, on leave from South Africa, you'd have thought he would have seen her and told her."

Harriet Bell refrained from mentioning that Cordelia had also accused Hannah Smith of stealing things, that what she had written, in fact, was actionable, so that Hannah's son would hardly be likely to seek her out. What a pair they were. She merely said: "But doesn't he live in Johannesburg? And I don't think they were on very good terms after William couldn't marry her."

"Wouldn't, you mean. She's impossible. Not at the funeral indeed. I adored my mother."

"I know you did, my dear. Perhaps Cordelia got it wrong. Hannah Smith wrote to her, and I know she was very shocked that you missed your mother's illness. She was seventy-eight, after all, and she had been asking for you. And you came so late. Muriel had been found wandering in the streets of Stratford, you know."

"Yes, yes, they told me about it, you may be sure. But I was in Haute-Savoie, I came as soon as I heard. My wife was expecting a baby—the one she lost—she wasn't well and—"

"How is your wife, Northbrook?"

"Oh, All right. Very well. She's in Geneva."

"Again?"

"Yes. She's working at the League of Nations. In the International Labour Office. Refugee Section, if you want to know. She's living with her parents."

"And the baby ?"

"He's with her. He's two years old you know."

"Good gracious, already?" She added cautiously, "So this hasn't worked either?"

"Yes, it has. It's just a modern marriage. We're on perfectly amicable terms. Only yesterday I got a most amusing letter from her, all about the lifts in the Palais des Nations. You have to jump in and out of them, you know, they don't stop and they have no doors. They go very slowly, of course." He met her steady gaze. "This is only a practical arrangement for the time being, Hetty, we're in the twentieth century, for heaven's sake. Well, no, it hasn't worked." He couldn't withstand her disbelieving blue eyes. "Oh, I don't know. Why does everybody hound me so? Why do you bully me, Hetty, you, of all people?"

The hotel dining room was quite empty, for they had talked long past their last cup of tea. He was smoking his pipe and waving it about. She said nothing, but pulled such a face at him he had to laugh.

"Oh, Hetty, my dear Hetty, I should have married you. But you wouldn't deign to look upon my hopeless passion."

"Hopeless passion! You might have told me." She was smiling, first facetiously, and at him, then dreamily, at some memory that hung visibly on some fixed point behind him. "You always got what you wanted. It was I who had a hopeless passion, rather."

"Oh, Hetty, for me?"

"No, Northbrook, not for you."

"Who then? Anyone I knew?"

"Yes, you knew him."

"Reggie? William? Oh, come on Hetty, who?"

"Jack Wilson, if you must know."

"Jack Wilson?"

"You don't even remember who he was, do you? Well, and why should you? He only came to the house once, and I met him one other time with his sister, Molly Wilson, you remember Molly Wilson? She contributes something to the Muriel fund, you know."

"Yes of course. Molly Wilson, the bluestocking. Good Lord. And do you mean to say you've been eating your heart out for her brother all these years?"

"Not *all* these years," she corrected him with a smile. "And I have plenty of heart left. He went to Australia, then came back to die in the trenches. So you see I was spared much."

He was silent, suddenly ashamed of his life. When he spoke again, it was gently.

"I kissed you on the tower of Coventry Cathedral, remember, on your twenty-first birthday?"

"I remember. Why don't you love your wife, Northbrook?"

"I don't know, Hetty, I don't know."

"Is there someone else?"

He hardly hesitated.

"No. No. In fact, I do love her. But she's so serious, Hetty, she has no sense of humour. And she's always tired, always got a pain somewhere. She was furious when I made her pregnant a third time—well, it *was* very soon after Philip's birth, I know, but still—she rushed back to Geneva to have an abortion, and stayed there, I ask you. And she always chooses my most job-like moments for her jeremiads."

"You, patient as Job?"

"Well, no, I meant metaphysical boils. Worries, troubles, pains and woes. You know the kind." And once again he looked remarkably genial.

Muriel was pleased to see them, in a metaphysical way, for she hardly seemed to recognise them, although she knew their identities. Their names, and most of what goes with a name, had been familiar in her mind since childhood, but to these she seemed to have attached new personalities of her own invention. Harriet Bell slipped easily into hers, but Alfred, who loved no one as himself, found his unnerving.

"I do not love thee, dear Miss Bell," Muriel greeted her. "The reason why I cannot tell, I do not love thee, DEAR Miss Bell." And she giggled. She knew, however, that she was joking, and hugged Harriet while Alfred tried to smile, and was mortally afraid of his mother's own flesh and blood. She seemed to have got worse. She was forty-seven, but had the smooth face and unformed features of a girl of twelve, roughened by time alone and not by life, so that although her wispy grey-brown hair was combed back into a high bun, one quite expected it to fall over her shoulders under a large Leghorn hat.

"Hello, Muriel dear. How are you? Look, Northbrook has come to see you."

"Ah, the Ruin of Us All. I'm so glad." Her mind was a houseful of family echoes, yet the words didn't seem to have the usual connotations for her. She stretched out her hand and smiled sweetly. "Good-morning, Narboo."

He winced at the pet-name.

"Good morning, Muriel, my dear, I hope you are feeling well?"

"Northbrook came with the Great Depression. Did you know that, Miss Bell?"

"For heaven's sake, Muriel—" but he stopped, catching Hetty's glance.

"And how is Harriet-your-dear-wife?"

Her dark eyes were velvety over him, like Laura's, but wider, and with the white more blue. He was about to correct her, then refrained, clenching his fists.

"Very well, thank you. She sends you her love."

"Oh, thank you very much, that will be nice." But she was sensitive to the edge in his voice. "What a pity you didn't bring it with you. Shall we sit down and have some bread-and-butter?"

"Yes, do let's," Harriet said quickly, though no elevenses were to be seen. "Tell me, Muriel, do you like it here?"

"It is the Fifth Heaven of Delight," she enunciated carefully. "There are seven altogether, did you know that? The seventh is for when we die. I bet Narboo hasn't reached the Fifth yet, he's much too cll-ever. That's what Mother says, it's better not to be too cll-ever."

"What do you mean? When did she say that?" Alfred asked brusquely, in spite of Harriet's signs.

And Muriel, who didn't mind what words meant, was frightened by his tone, lost track and became incoherent.

"The Second Heaven, but it was a secret and he didn't mean it, I promise you, Narboo, really he didn't, only don't tell Mother. I was going to do it, but the plate jumped out of my fingers." She started to cry.

"Oh, my God." Alfred groaned and put his face in his hands. "It shouldn't be allowed."

Harriet had her arm round Muriel and was giving her a handkerchief.

"Here, my darling, have this. There's a good girl. Blow harder, like the North wind. The North wind doth *blow* and we shall have *snow*. That's better, isn't it? Look at the dahlias in the garden, they're not sad." And the tears were gone without leaving a trace, like those of a child whose attention is deflected and who forgets to go on crying. "Tell me, darling, do you like Mrs. Wilcox here? Is she nice to you?"

"Oh, yes, she's very nice. She floats, you know. It's her special prer-rog'tive. We all have prer-rog'tives here, and that's Mrs. Wilcox's."

"And what's yours?" Alfred couldn't help asking, more gently this time, and leaning forward intensely.

"Mine?" She looked for it above the tasselled standard lamp, and after a while seemed to get lost. Her eyes returned to him, troubled.

"What's your prerogative, Muriel?" he repeated.

Then she smiled happily.

"Mine is blue. Something old, something new, something borrowed, something blue. Mine's blue like the sky and as big and as old and as new. Yours is borrowed, Narboo. But it's very nice," she added tactfully, "it suits you. Oh yes," she went on, tilting her head to admire him, "you look very nice in it, very, very nice."

9

"IT'S A terrible thing to happen to a man. Too terrible to talk about. Indeed, I never do talk about it. But you force me to. You make it very hard, my dear. But you're quite right, I do owe it to you."

The wheezy old gramophone was silent now, but the record of "Margie" had made them very sentimental as they shuffled around to it over the worn-out roses of the Brussels carpet. He hated modern dancing and could hardly do even a two-step, let alone a foxtrot, but he had bought her the record because of her name, and because dancing these days meant touching and even holding. All of which had led them to the fringed sofa.

He put one hand on hers and, resting his other elbow on his knee, sheltered his eyes which were now dramatically closed. But she was young, and the young love drama. Part of her wanted to giggle at his old-fashioned ways, but the rest was thrilled, flattered, attracted by his Experience. And he was certainly fair and handsome. So she unwittingly became many a heroine of the pulp-fiction she never read (for she was a serious girl), and she quickly placed her other hand on his, making a tall hand-sandwich, and said in a trembling voice: "I'm so very sorry. Please tell me about it. If it helps."

And so it came out, the sad story, which had to be very convincing. For she had written him a long renunciation-letter, of the type that young girls write who, having not quite stooped to folly, feel impelled to long analyses of why so many half yeses are to be after all followed by no. If a wife existed, she had written in her wide-eyed scrawl, then she would not consent. And if there were children, she would not see him at all. Her heart would break, she loved him so, and she would always love him, but

God would give her the strength, and He was giving it, then taking it away again for many pages.

So he had called at her lodgings, as indeed she had known that he would, for even innocent girls did not expect renunciation-letters to be taken literally, at least not without a touching last scene, full of elo-quent pleading and noble abnegations; followed, perhaps (though this thought was pushed away in horror) by such overwhelming passions that she might forget herself, unwillingly, and yield to a fate written in the stars and stronger than her long virtuous resistance could bear. Which of course would change everything, and nullify the letter.

"Oh, you're so sweet," he said, sitting down again beside her. "You're so good and true and right for me. And you're so very beautiful." He stared obsessively at her young skin, white and pink, smooth as a child's. "Marjorie, my own dear darling, you must believe me when I tell you that I want to marry you more than anything in the whole world. But you're quite right, I can't, or I would have asked you months ago, when I first met you. I would have proposed to you on that very night, at that very party, do you remember? Oh, I do, so very well. It was love at first sight. My darling, I've lived a good many years more than you have, but I can truthfully say I have never experienced any-thing quite like that. It was such a Bright Young party, full of Bright Young Things, wasn't it? Golden Youth. But you, you stood slightly apart, you looked, Different Somehow. No, it wasn't that you were more beautiful, I'm not a flatterer, I assure you. I expect there were more beautiful girls than you in that room. But I didn't see them. I just had no eyes for them. You looked so—how shall I put it—modern and yet modest. Not like the shy maidens of my youth, nor like the brash half naked fly-by-nights of today. Intelligent. Sensible. And lovely. As young as the century. Twenty-two." He seemed fascinated by the number and repeated hypnotically, "Twenty-two. Sweet and twenty-two. My Mod-ern Girl." He had been stroking her beck beneath her excitedly bobbed brown hair, then he moved his fingers to her underarm. This new sleeveless fashion was wonderful, the bare arms, the cross-over neck-line, the boyish Greek effect of the tunic with its low loose waist, and the white stockinged ankles just visible below the tubular underskirt. Youth, oh youth. Had not somebody said that the modern girl had ceased to be a woman but had not yet become a gentleman?

She shuddered, with the acute pain, low down in her tummy, that she had come to recognise as the thing they called desire, and wondered if he were going to try and seduce her now or produce his big secret first. She must resist, she said to herself firmly. But her lips parted and turned to him.

"You see, my darling girl," he held her chin now in a more paternal way —"I couldn't propose to you, desperately though I wanted to. I have a wife."

She started and looked away. Then to prevent her from getting up primly and beginning, "So all this time, etc." he himself rose and paced theatrically up and down between the sofa and the small round table that was draped in green velour.

"But it's not the way you think. You see my wife—" he gave a deep sigh and shook his head—"is in a mental home. She's been there for years. Incurable. It's quite tragic. She'll never come out. Oh, don't think I drove her mad. It's hereditary. Her grandmother was the same. Of course, I didn't discover all that until it was too late. Her family were only too glad to let someone else be responsible. Though sometimes I think they can't have been so wicked and I give them the benefit of the doubt. After all, she seemed quite normal even to me at first. It happened gradually. Oh, my dear, I simply can't tell you what I went through. I go and see her sometimes. No, I can't talk about it."

But he did, in much convincing and histrionic detail that could only have been based on experience. Even if he was touching it up, she thought —she knew he had an embroidering imagination, and loved him for it—he couldn't be simply inventing it. There were too many obviously authentic touches.

"And so, I'm stuck with this terrible fate. Insanity is not a cause for divorce, at least not as our law stands at present. One day, perhaps . . . But you understand, my darling, how I suffered all these months. I didn't want to tell you, neither did I mean to deceive you. I love you too much." He fell at her feet and put his head in her lap. "Oh, so much. But I have so little to offer you, so very little. Only myself, and my love."

Women are said to be mercenary, and yet for some reason a large majority of them find this appeal irresistible, as a large majority of men have found out. When he felt her lips and fingers in his hair and heard her tender murmurs, his hands travelled up her white-stockinged legs, unbuttoning the lower skirt and, after a little while, and only the usual protests, Alfred Hayley had acquired the mistress of his longings.

His supposedly insane wife was at the time sitting in the Reading Room of the British Museum, brushing up her theology and Church history. Or rather, trying to find a middle way to the Essential Truth. For theology was so bedevilled by philosophies she couldn't grasp, and Church history so bedevilled by laws and wars, councils and inquisitions, that there too one lost track of just which bit of the Essential Truth they were all disagreeing about. And as for the so-called history of thought, she always seemed to stumble on the sort of book that said things like "at the end of the nineteenth century, when mankind had taken a new leap towards material progress, advanced thinkers identified civilisation with hygiene. *Sanitas sanitatum, omnia sanitas,* they cried triumphantly." But she could never find out which advanced thinkers had thus cried, and where.

She had in front of her an enormously long letter from her husband, twenty-five pages of close purple typing on thin foolscap paper. Half of it she couldn't follow, but books were mentioned in it and she had put in for them. She was always so bored in London, with nothing to do all day, the best place was the Reading Room. Even now, with a baby on the way, she preferred to come here, though she had to be careful, having lost the previous one.

That had been last year. A terrible year, when she was sick with fatigue and horror at knowing, ineluctably and beyond self-persuasion, that her marriage was a dreadful mistake. With her upbringing she knew that there was no way out, that she just had to go on trying.

At least, that is what she had said to Elinor Jarvis at lunchtime. Elinor had told her some strange things.

"I had no idea you existed, you know, nor had Mother. He posed as a sad divorce until you came to London."

"But Elinor, why, why? We've been married three years! Or was he perhaps . . . ?" She tailed off, and looked into her soup with a sigh of exasperation to cover her embarrassment. Elinor was attractive, with a daring fringe of short dark hair and a long Persian looking nose. Exotic and cool. Today she looked marvellously slim and bosomless in a long, tubular tangerine coat-frock fastening up the side under a rim of brown embroidery —absolutely the latest thing—and a tall Tagel hat. Laura felt very much five months gone and ugly. It was only on Elinor's persuasion that she allowed herself to be seen in the West End at all. Bloomsbury was different of course, Bohemian and daring. But Elinor was so elegantly modern. Elinor, however, was smiling.

"No, my dear, he wasn't after me." Laura could feel her nearly adding, he's old enough to be my father, but the phrase remained merely in her eyes. Elinor was four years younger, twenty-five. "It's Mother, really," she went on, which made it worse. "It's an odd relationship. He met her in Liverpool, at the end of the war, I think, yes, 1918, when Jenny was born. They're both about the same age, I believe, and they struck up a tremendous friendship. Mind you, there was never anything between them, you know, not, well, not love or anything. I assure you, it's quite impossible. I remember Mother telling me, when I got married, that she had absolutely hated '*that* side' of marriage, it made her almost ill. Can't understand it, really, I do think parents are odd. Still, I *was* an only child." She mused for a while as the waitress came to remove their plates and bring the next course. They were lunching in a West End teashop specially designed to attract the new clientele of lady workers who once had nowhere to go, even when shopping, except quiet and well-hidden family hotels, the dining rooms being then wholly for men, while people of the artisan class went to the grubby coffee shops or the cook shops. Now even the Strand was sprouting a few restaurants with paper lace mats and wickerwork tables, and only the City remained impregnably male. "It's impossible to find anything up there," Elinor had said, though she was going to shop in Paternoster Row later, and meeting Alan for a drink somewhere.

"I still don't understand why he had to pose as a sad divorce," Laura persisted.

"My dear, it made him more interesting. Mother is a widow, and she was good for three dinners a week. That is, until he met some Baroness Cuilth, who no doubt gave him better dinners."

"Elinor!"

"Laura, my sweet, you must wake up. You've married a very nasty man. Until you came earlier this year and he couldn't very well hide you (though he moved with you to North London), he was a sad divorce, living in a very elegant bachelor flat in Stone Buildings, Lincoln's Inn—"

"Number 8, I know that. It's his office now."

"And he came to dinner several times a week. He was very poor, you know, had some story about having lost all his money in the Hudson Bay crash and being left with only the coat on his back—that gorgeous furry thing he wears, which was a gift from all his friends and admirers there, or something like that. Alan never liked him. Nor did I for that matter, except for that marvellous way he has of kissing one's hand after dropping his eyeglass. What a poseur, my dear. But he's much too self-centred to have real good manners. Why, if one dares to disagree with his opinion about anything, even a book or a play, he takes it as a personal affront to his taste and bristles like a hedgehog."

"Look, you don't have to tell *me*."

"I know, my dear, I'm sorry. He just got under my skin, that's all. We certainly had our fill of him and he never seemed to feel we didn't like him much. And yet I don't know, perhaps he did feel it. He was always trying to prove how many friends he had. D'you know, he once returned a book I had lent him and left several old envelopes in it, covered with names and telephone numbers. It was so childish it made me quite sad for him." She smiled, though, as she said it, and Laura couldn't help smiling back, recognising the strange sad-funny effect Alfred's absurdities always had on her own family. Elinor shook her head, as if at a hopeless case. "And then he was always talking about his erotica books, trying to shock me, I suppose, and would draw me aside and tell me the oddest stories, watching me closely."

"What sort of stories?"

"Well, just odd. How he'd met an Indian prince in the street at night, for instance, and taken him home for a week. That sort of, thing. I never quite saw the point, really."

"I've never understood him at all, I feel completely left out. He talks and talks, and I just don't know what he feels, what's behind it all. At Lissogne, with my family, he was so rude! Those long discussions on religion, railing against Protestantism and the Bourgeoisie, you know I honestly believe he wouldn't have chosen just those subjects if my family hadn't in fact been, well, liberal, but Protestant in background. Something seems to drive him to pick on the one thing he shouldn't pick on in any one instance. And of course, always in English." She laughed. "His French is terrible. My brothers and sisters all speak English, of course, and so does father, but naturally, not all that fluently, so that they were easily defeated in argument."

"Or gave in politely, wearily?"

Laura smiled.

"Yes. But they were worried. Very worried. I was completely worn out—and terribly depressed. I remember my sister Giselle spoke to Alfred about me, trying to drop some hint about his lack of consideration. Do you know what he answered? He said he knew I was tired, but it was quite natural since I worried so much about his health!"

"Good Lord!"

"And then he heard of his mother's death and rushed off to England, leaving me pregnant. I went back to Geneva, and . . . lost the baby." Tears filled her eyes and she couldn't quell the self-pity in her voice. "He wasn't even there."

"I'm very sorry. I can't think why you didn't leave him at once, I would have. These modern times, you know, people don't pretend any more, about marriage, and all that."

"Oh, I couldn't do that. And besides, in a way I do love him." Unused to discussing emotions, she said the word shyly, blushing. "It's a sort of pressure he puts on me which oh, it's difficult to explain. I always seem to come back. His very insensitivity is a kind of strength, you see. He assumes that I love him, that I want to be with him, and so I do, the assumption is the fact, it's irresistible. It was the same about meeting when we were engaged. He'd say 'Shall I see you tomorrow?' in such a tone, I'd say yes."

"That, my dear, is usually called emotional blackmail." Laura looked shocked.

"I'm sure the baby will make all the difference," Elinor said soothingly, "both to you and to him." She swept up the bill, waving aside Laura's protests, and Laura let her. She had, after all, been invited, and they were very poor. "In the meantime," Elinor said when they were out in the street, "you must just keep on trying. Courage, my sweet, I'm sure everything will be all right. You're much too nice not to come out of this with flying colours."

Laura at once wished none of this conversation had taken place. She hardly knew Elinor, and felt obscurely that even the kindest of women enjoy an emotional heart-to-heart for ever-so-slightly the wrong reasons. Elinor was younger, and yet so much more knowledgeable, more sure of herself in every way.

Perhaps, it was children that did it, perhaps she too would be like that next year. But why had Elinor seemed so voluble against Alfred? It wasn't terribly helpful of her. After which, she had just said, you must simply keep on trying. But how could she now believe a word he ever said? She had only recently discovered he was some seventeen years older than herself, not fourteen as she had always supposed, from his lies at the time they met and his skill in somehow never letting her see either his passport or any other documents, even when they got married.

She was annoyed to see that none of the books she had put in for before lunch had arrived. There was only her notebook on her desk, and this huge wad of typing folded inside an envelope. Last year she had written him a long hysterical letter from Geneva, after the still-born baby. All about their marriage and religion. And this was his reply. Pages of it. Mostly irrelevant.

Yet somehow it had brought them together again, the mere fact of his having written it perhaps. Twenty-five pages of attention. All about himself.

So now she was with him again, in a small garden flat in St. John's Wood, pregnant once more, trying to understand.

Ever since your letter of March 22nd reached me, the main subject of it, viz, the question of Religion has weighed more than heavily with me. I feel that I must give some account of that within me.

She started as half-a-dozen books fell on her desk with a clatter. The attendant, who was distributing from too high a pile, apologised in a profuse whisper and she smiled nervously, helping him to collect them. Several were for her. She felt sick. The five month embryo inside her seemed to be screaming. Perhaps it had just died, as the other one had died. Perhaps she would die in childbirth, like the young mothers of heroes in Victorian novels. She was nearing thirty after all. "The doctor's lady departed this life very soon after Sylvester's birth." She remembered the absurd phrase in an old paper-covered sixpenny novel called *Sylvester Sound*, which was among the books Alfred had brought back from his mother's house. Yes, she would surely die. Or perhaps she would have a miscarriage, there and then, and stream blood all over the Reading Room floor, with all the bearded scholars and the bald heads looking on. She gripped the shiny black edge of the desk and shut her eyes, holding her breath. Nothing happened. The pain passed. Philip/Philippa—a name she had chosen because it was one of the few she liked that occurred nowhere in the four-layered ramifications of the Bertrand-Guiset alliance—had evidently not heard a sound. But then, she smiled, he/she probably had no ears as yet. Hence no sound had occurred. The whole fright and pain had been in her own mind and body, not his/hers.

Which brought her back to her search for the Essential Truth.

You, at least, to whom this is not only addressed, but for whom it is an outpouring of heart and soul, should be able to understand it, and follow me with sympathy and compassion, for you did the same for me once with regard to your own wonderful experience, and you know how much I treasured and treasure that .

Yes, it was so unfair. Was it only for a Pygmalion's pleasure he had filled her ready mind with the fantastic beguilements of the Roman faith, only to destroy what he had fashioned like an outgrown toy? It was as if he had led her through a mysterious maze of new ideas, which had then at a wave of his wand turned to a petrified forest, a ruined Pompeii.

She turned to page 18, where she had marked his own account of this, and read it again.

When I first met you, you will remember your own attitude toward all religion. You had none yourself, and could hardly comprehend others having it. I seemed to visualise and acutely realise all you had missed, all you lacked.

She found his trick of saying everything twice intensely irritating.

I wanted to share something of that treasure with you, to lay something of it at your feet. In my blind and groping way I tried to do so. I can't explain it, you will I think understand it now.

Yes, she understood it now, he had been showing off, but what he was showing off did not belong to him.

I never wanted to convert you to anything, I had nothing to convert you to.

There was then a great deal about opening of eyes and seeing wealths of glory and discovering untrodden fields like a lovely child hastening to gather all the flowers therein.

My heart sang with the joy of your joy . . . You know you were always my "wonder child". You had now become my wonder woman, my wonder wife. And you my darling . . .

Then there was more about playing fields and travelling dubious roads together and taking different forks. She turned back to the beginning with a sigh.

. . . What is the real reason of this attempt to explain where I am and for what I stand? YOU. My Wife. Only You, a thought of you, anything connected with you can stir me now. And nothing, not the deepest experience which I have met in life, has ever stirred me as you do. When you wrote "It is a source of much pain to me that we should think and feel so differently", that very knowledge found an echoing Pain in the heart of me. And oh believe me, I suffer from it too. But I suffer far more when you say that the short time when we seemed to think alike was the "only really happy time in our married life". If that is true—and I refuse to accept it—the knell has rung for us, and all that remains to us both is a shell. That alone would prompt me to dare anything, to lay aside the covering of my heart and let you watch its throbs. But when you add "Don't try to take away the only thing that brings me a little peace", not even you can fully realise all such a cry means to me, for I have uttered it myself in bygone years, and know only too well the force and agony which can be behind it . . .

There was no force, no agony. Just a melancholy humble realisation that life was not its own reward. Why did he make such a huge drama, both out of hurting her, and out of comforting her, out of loving, and destroying? And what kind of scribal devil of self-love got into him when he took pen and paper, or worse still, a typewriter? He was bad enough when he talked, but at least he was witty then, at any rate his English friends always laughed—and she wondered suddenly whether wit and humour were perhaps different in kind, not just in degree, so that an outlook informed entirely by the one could never merge with an outlook informed entirely by the other. Wit seemed to her a verbal affair, mechanical, all, as it were, done with mirrors. It vanished like a light if a man stopped talking, or wanted to be serious or tried to write down something of his inner self. Witticisms then had to be imported, like ready-made parts of a machine. But humour—she couldn't even define it—humour was more like listening to God's jokes, and laughing even when they weren't very funny.

There followed a detailed account of Alfred's religious views from earliest childhood.

> *The faith I was reared in was the old Evangelical faith of the English Church differing intensely from the cold formalism of the Genevese Reformers. In that same faith were reared those two famous sons of the Church of England who in after years left her and lived to weal the Roman purple —Newman and Manning. As a child the latter was taught from the same books as I—"Peep of Day", "Line upon Line" and "The Story of the Bible".*

The account continued in this vein, through *that great English classic "The Pilgrim's Progress" and the glorious epic of Milton which were his constant joy in early boyhood*, to the High Anglicanism of his youth, when he was *very near to the chief actors in the great drama of the High Church Party, the (uncial) approach to Leo XIII with the request that he look into and recognise the validity of Anglican Orders as a basis of Reunion.* He could write volumes on the subject but the story had been told often enough by others, better qualified than he, and Laura even wondered sceptically whether these others were his source rather than his own experience. He described *the awful silence which immediately followed the publication of the Papal Bull "Apostolicae Curae" as electric in its intensity. We literally gasped in horror*, whoever "we" were, presumably the people mentioned a little lower down, whose friendship saved him from any precipitate step, *Robert Hugh. Benson, Father Maturin, Fathers Benson and Page of Cowley, the Duke of Newcastle, Lord Halifax, Fathers Stanton and Lowder* . . .

Nevertheless, the whole course of his life was changed and the memoir went on, to relate his final conversion to the Roman faith, on a train journey from Mobile, Alabama, to Kansas City, so sudden and intense that he got out at St. Louis and called upon the Archbishop, no less, whom he had met once at a luncheon party. *Our conversation lasted until late that night. I dined with him and the whole evening was given to discussion.* She could well imagine it. *He finally told me he would receive me himself early the next morning, and he did so in his private chapel.* He told me that never in his experience had any convert come to him who knew so thoroughly the Catholic faith and position, and that I needed no instruction. It was an extraordinary position for both of us. Strangely enough it was very similar to the circumstances of Newman's own reception.* He couldn't for the life of him remember the exact date of this conversion.

The Archbishop had then written to the Bishop of Mobile, with whom he, Alfred, *formed a quiet friendship, very necessary in a small town like Mobile, where an educated convert is certainly a rarity,* where indeed his reception caused something of a stir. He had, however, to pay a price for it, and the first year of his Catholic life was a *very sad and hard one in Mobile,* since all his friends *were distinctly anti-Catholic without knowing the reason why, and ignorant prejudice is always strong and bitter, unreasoning and the most difficult to deal with.* He made no attempt to deal with it. It caused a definite breach in his household and estranged his friends. Laura thought it very odd that Alfred should admit to having had ignorant friends, but then, it was the suffering that mattered here.

Ah, suddenly he had remembered the exact date, it was on *the Feast of St. Jeanne Frances de Chantal (Foundress of the Visitation Order) August 21st 1909 that he was received.* And he made his First Communion *with the Jesuits (by permission of the Bishop) on the third Sunday of the following month (Seven Dolours of the B.V.M.) and was therefore confirmed in 1910 on or about the 12th October.* And because these dates somehow tied up with his other lies about other dates, such as those giving away the duration of his first marriage, Laura found herself automatically subtracting four years.

Then, of course, came the falling away, though praying earnestly for light and guidance, past the Infallibility, the *Anathema Sit's,* the *Syllabus Errorum,* the Index. Laura couldn't help wondering how these could have become such stumbling blocks when he *knew so thoroughly the Catholic position he needed no instruction.* And the falling away was for some reason more true than the first acceptance, which yet had been so true, indeed, he always talked of his early piety as if its earliness were proof of its invalidity. But what was, to her, the crux of the matter was given only one paragraph, with, oddly enough, little rhetorical embroidery.

> *It must surely make the most devout Catholic gasp when Rome issues such a bull as the "Ne Temere" dealing with the whole question of marriage, in which she lays down the most drastic statements and propositions, which set at nought the civil laws of many countries, and makes these binding on the conscience of all catholics, BUT deliberately excepts certain countries from its operation. Truth cannot be Truth in certain places, and the opposite elsewhere. If a given thing is a mortal sin, it is so regardless of place. Why is this done? simply for political reasons, because the Papal representatives of Germany and Austria informed the Vatican that it was absolutely hopeless to promulgate such propositions in those countries, as they simply would not have them. As far as the British Empire was concerned, it did not care one way or the other. This finally finished me as regards Rome, and threw me back on the old position, with which I will now try and deal.*

Then came twelve long difficult pages in as close-typed foolscap as the rest, of the so-called Higher Criticism—though she wasn't clear what it was supposed to be Higher Than; of Biblical Scholarship that proved the Bible couldn't be revealed by God, since it was "axiomatic" that revelation must be of facts and not of mere speculation; of Comparative Religion, Krishna, Buddah, Osiris, Apollo and the rest; of scientific theories—determinism, cause and effect, evolution which is the utter negation of any theory of a "Fall" of Man, and therefore cuts at the root of the corollaries of that notion . . .

Laura looked at the books she had ordered and despaired. She knew she would never read them. He was too clever. And yet, and yet. All this when stripped of its verbiage seemed to her remarkably like the "common sense" view most people she knew had always held, indeed, which she had held herself. And "common sense", she had read somewhere, usually represented the popularised and petrified science of thirty or fifty years back. Perhaps there never would be an answer, perhaps human discoveries would merely continue to provide both sides with arguments for ever and ever amen. He just happened to be using this particular set. Could it be that having been to school more recently than he, she was unwittingly more advanced? If not what was the point of having generations succeed-ing each other?

But no, he read so much, he met so many eminent people, Even during those first few months in London, when they lived in such poor lodgings in Bloomsbury, before she had fled to Geneva, he seemed to know every-one, Lytton Strachey and Lord Alfred Douglas, who edited *English* and shook hands like a fish. And there was this bit here about Professor St. George Mivart, "a very dear friend of his," a lifelong Catholic who had ap-parently been excommunicated and cursed by Rome for an article on evolution he had written in *The Nineteenth Century*. What was it Monsieur Thibaudet had said about evolution? She wished now that she hadn't sur-reptitiously read *Peliens et Milisande,* or Le Conte de Lisle's *Fames Barbares,* during so many biology classes at the Lycee de Geneve. And she thought suddenly of Mike, who taught physics in California, and whose idea of the universe positively demanded another reality beyond that analysable by science, and more, a mathematical creator.

Then the bell rang and she realised with a shock she had read nothing but the great Hayley himself. She might just as well have stayed at home. Except, perhaps, for Elinor Jarvis.

What did she care, she thought as she gathered up her books and took them back to the centre desk, whether the Creator was a mathematician, an equation, an emotion, a blob of jelly, a whirl of atoms or a carpenter? She was so confused that until very recently she didn't know the differ-ence between atomistic and Thomistic philosophy. All this elaborate intel-lectual edifice of his was irrelevant, for she only wanted her marriage to be legitimised in the Church, so that she could be received. Surely that wasn't too much to ask?

For some weeks after writing this verbose Apologia, he had co-oper-ated, rather like a parent humouring a child. He had come with her to see Mother St. Jerome and even Father Hobart. His first marriage, he had ex-plained to them, had never been consummated, his wife had been extremely delicate, suffering from haemorrhages of the womb, and he had been advised ... there followed a sad tale of this brief but tragic union, that did much to credit his courage, his consideration and and his continence. Then, quite as suddenly as he had agreed to co-operate so he had ceased, with no explanation save a renewed and savage attack on that "fons et origo of all persecution, bigotry, superstition and cruelty, the Church."

The explanation, however, did not lie in books, but in the carefully flattened breasts and buttocks of a Young Modern Girl.

So that he thought, as he came out elated into Gower Street and the July sunshine—after a gallant kissing of the hand to show that no respect, at any rate, had been lost—things will arrange themselves. Perhaps she will die in childbirth, she's no chicken, when all's said and done. Or perhaps she will leave him, stay in Geneva after having the baby. She always ran to Geneva when anything difficult happened, as to a great Calvinistic bosom of predestined consolation. Or she might, he thought as an electric brougham nearly knocked him down, be run over. The ways of Providence were so mysterious. He walked on debonair, past the British Museum, towards Holborn and his office in Stone Buildings, Lincoln's Inn, missing his wife by four and a half minutes.

And Laura thought, as she came out from under the high grey colonnade and down the wide stone steps like a quaver on a bar of frozen music, what does it matter how one sees God? Even professed atheists sometimes call him Providence, when the thing they are hoping for seems too worldly or too wicked for prayer.

Chapter Ten

Contents of wallet—
One printed prayer to St. Thomas Aquinas
One photograph, family group
One photograph, dark girl in white blouse, signed
    "Come back to your loving Sally"
Seven letters signed Sally
One letter signed Mom
Two dollars
Pay record
Unit record
One newspaper cutting, *SURRY, VA. HERO*
                CITED.

Laura stopped typing and wiped the tears that blurred her eyes. She could stand everything, the smell of ether, the military ambulances pulling up outside the Abbey to bring in the wounded, and sometimes to take away the dead—in fact she wasn't so closely in touch with the hospital life as the nurses were. She could even bear typing the official reports back home, which never went straight to the family but always to a higher authority. But when a dead man's personal belongings were brought into the office for recording, she found it hard not to get more wrought-up than her job as stenographer, United States Army Medical Department, allowed. Especially if he was very young. She looked at the photograph. A blond, earnest boy. Student, Agricultural College of Virginia, the record said. And the beautiful scholar's prayer to St. Thomas Aquinas, that must have been to help him master the geology and mechanics and statistics and other difficult subjects deemed so oddly relevant to modern farming.

And having mastered them he would have married Sally. But now he was dead, of a bullet through the lung and just a little too near the heart.

She blew her nose and went on typing, quickly, impersonally. It was too hot to get worked up. Her heavy serge khaki skirt clung to her knees and ankles and she could feel her legs sweating in the black stockings and buttoned boots, though she had removed, her jacket and was typing in her blouse.

Space. Robert Camberley, Major M.G. U.S.A. Commanding. Space para. Base Hospital No. 41, St. Denis, France. Damn. She'd forgotten the recent order. The typewriter's so fast one can't think. How careless. She looked round the old abbey anteroom which had been turned into an office. The other two girls seemed to type away without even looking at the keys. Well, she wasn't going to do it all again. Exasperated she looked for the slips of paper she kept for the purpose. Oh, there they were, underneath the prayer. She placed them carefully between the carbons and rubbed out the place-name three times. Then she typed instead, "A.E.F., A.P.O. 702," murmuring to herself "Par Monsieur Saint-Denis certes ce sont des times, Qui passent dans les airs sur ces vapeurs de flammes."

When she went at four o'clock to receive her pay, which was thirty dollars a month "paid to include Aug. 31, 1918, by 2nd Lieut. M. S. Trevor, Q.M.R.C.", Second Lieutenant M. S. Trevor gave her an almost imperceptible nod with a very slight downward movement of his eyelids as he handed her the money, and she lowered hers, ostensibly to count, but actually to say she would be there.

And when they walked that night through the large Abbey grounds and along the country lanes between the hospital and Saint-Denis—lanes that seemed full of convalescent soldiers, arm in arm with girls—he talked to her of the stars, and how there were many systems, not just ours, about two million of them visible through the giant telescope on Mount Wilson back home; and how the universe was a thousand million time as big as what we could see through that telescope; and how each of these two million times a thousand million nebulae contained about a thousand million stars; and how the heat in the centre of the stars was so intense that protons and electrons were being annihilated, so that the universe was wasting away; and how ultimately, in millions of years, there would be no sun or stars but just a cool glow of radiation.

And when she said she didn't know what an atom was, meaning she didn't care because she was so happy to be with him, he said well nor, in a way, did the scientists, at least not so far, since the atom could only be inferred from all the events that occurred where it was not; and being earnest plunged into a detailed exposé of the Quantum Theory, until she said, as women do, "It sounds like you and me: you're the electron, whirling round the proton of love, first in one orbit then, quite suddenly, in another, which is me, without any predetermination. And no one saw you jump, it was like dying in one orbit, and being born again in another, wasn't it?" And he said, "Oh you darling, I sure do get lost in it." So she put her head on his shoulders and said, "Oh, Mike, what shall we do?" And he put his hand on her cool hair and answered quietly, "Let's just enjoy the stars, honey, their light takes so damn long to reach us, why, we may well be looking at something that's gone plumb out of existence."

Because he had described himself, modestly, as a schoolmaster, the United States Army had, in the general rush to get everybody to France, drafted him into the pay department, the meagre mathematics of which he worked in his head, under the wide lock of lank brown hair that fell into his eyes, and much to the astonishment of his sergeants. He was courteous almost by instinct, even when lost in thought. He was quiet, intense and very much in love. He was twenty-six and, of course, married.

When the Armistice came she was almost disappointed, and felt oddly American, coming into the war like that, at long last, then hardly seeing it. But that hadn't been her fault, and she was European enough to know her feelings were base and selfish.

"Yes, they are," Mike said to her in their favourite shabby little café, now shabbier still from the celebrations of the night before. "All those thousands that died, and all those thousands more that suffered. What's one small sorrow compared to theirs?" The scientist in him tended to sidetrack moral problems with truisms and she made an exasperated gesture.

"Oh, for heaven's sake, Mike, you know what I mean. Sometimes I wonder whether perhaps you love me less than you say, or less than I love you."

He stared hard into his cup of bean-coffee. "You shouldn't say a thing like that. Maybe I just don't express my feelings as you do. I guess I—well, I just never had this kind of problem, you know, I'm not a lady's man. A lady's man would know what to do. I married so young, at nineteen, I'd known Elaine all my life, everyone back home expected us to marry, I never thought this could—did I ever show you a picture of my son?" His hand went automatically to his breast pocket and Laura nodded quickly and moved to stop him, and he gripped her fingers hard. "There's so little time, honey, I just hate to spoil it with Big Problem Talk."

"I know. And I've tried not to. But it is a little different now. Sooner or later I shall be discharged from the A.R.C. and go back to Geneva, to my family."

"What about this Englishman you said was in love with you? Remember you said you were 'kind of' engaged, and I said I was 'kind of' married, and we both laughed. I guess we were both protecting ourselves because we knew it was too late." He kissed her wrist gently on the blue veins. "What happened to him?"

"Oh darling, he's nearly forty! Besides, I don't love him. I love you." She looked at him mock-suspiciously. "Are you trying to fob me off on him?"

He shook his head, but her own question had disturbed her. She felt clumsy and unfeminine in her khaki uniform. Believing that her only strong point was her thick brown hair which she wore rolled over on her cheeks and turned up at the back into a loose chignon, she took her hand away from his and removed her military cap, then patted the side hair nervously.

"Why did you seek me out when you knew you were married? Why did you say you loved me?"

A question so many women had asked, and so few men had known how to answer. Nor did he answer it, but looked at her like an animal in sudden pain.

"I was attracted to you, of course," she went on, with female relentlessness. "But I would never have fallen in love with you if you hadn't said anything. Women don't, they only—respond. Or if they do it's just too bad, they suffer in silence and at least nothing happens and no one's any the wiser. Except God. Whose wisdom," she added with a wistful smile, "is of course infinite."

"Oh, darling! When you say things like that, and laugh with your eyes like that, I love you so very dearly." He took her hands and kissed them all over. "My little nut-brown maid." And they both thought, but didn't repeat aloud, for it had often been said already: "And I must to the wild woods go, Alone, a banished man."

She had hardly written to Alfred since her arrival in France, or rather, since that embarrassing meeting in Paris. But she received numerous missives from him, "brief and unsatisfactory letters," as he called them, protesting that the Censorship inhibited him and that to expose the true depth of his love for her to another eye would be sacrilege. Indeed, the love bits were so metaphorically rendered that the Censor might well have been forgiven had he suspected a code. Otherwise the letters contrived to be mostly about himself, his job and the important people he was meeting. They made up, however, in length and numbers what they lacked in originality. She found it difficult to get through them, partly because she really did work very long hours, but also, she knew quite well, because she was no longer in love with him. And she wondered if she had ever been under his sway was perhaps a better description. But no. She remembered, even, how she had longed to receive a love-letter from him, when he had seemed all voice and body—something concrete that she could read at leisure, away from his touch and the great tentacles of his mental activity. And now she wondered whether her growing coolness had not after all begun the moment he put pen to paper. His beguiling voice, his good looks, his funny little gestures-in brief, his charm—all this vanished from those numerous pages he could cover so fast with that big bold hand. And as she lay in her hard iron bed, aware of eleven women breathing and dreaming around her, she stared at the tigerskin of moonlight thrown by the tall, shuttered Abbey window on the pitch-black wall, and realised that the love-letter must surely have been the creation of women. Poor women, supposed to be so artful and yet always outwitted, out-talked and outmanoeuvred: men might win on tactics, but women won on strategy, for a letter could be studied, analysed, compared, and few men came out well in love on paper.

Then she realised that Mike had never written to her a word of love, and spoke, for that matter, almost as little.

They were not discharged at once after the Armistice, in fact there seemed as much work as before, bureaucracy being relatively unaffected by the direction in which an army may be travelling. But they enjoyed much time together, for regulations were considerably eased up and the town was an amiable chaos of wild nightlife and remaining shortages.

Then suddenly in December, the whole unit at Saint-Denis was disbanded, and they both got new marching orders, which gave them a shock, for they had visualised it differently: he was to have gone first, returned to California and talked to his wife about a divorce—yes, he had to break it to her in person, he said, he owed her that. Laura was to have stayed behind, then waited in Geneva to join him later. But now she was "relieved from further duty at Base Hospital No. 41, A.E.F. A.P.O. 702, pursuant to Par. 4, SO 234, Hdqrs. S.O.S. A.E.F. dated Dec ember 3rd, 1918," and was directed to Commanding Officer Hospital Center, Bazoilles-sur-Meuse, for duty. He was to go to Orleans three days later. It was very frightening. She probably wouldn't see Mike when he left France, and the thought filled her with anguish. So Alfred had been convinced, when they both joined the American Red Cross, that she would be leaving first; and then it was him; and somehow this had changed everything.

Christmas 1918 in Bazoilles-sur-Meuse, Vosges, was very, very gay and very filled with people and their wild relief at being left alive, their wilder hopes of everlasting joy. It was the saddest Christmas ever spent in the twenty-five years of life called Laura Bertrand.

Five frantic letters, two cables, even—she gathered from one of the forwarded letters—a telephone call on official lines from London to Saint-Denis, all these "pursuant" reached her in Bazoilles-sur-Meuse, Vosges, during the bitter cold of January and February, when her fingers were so chilblained she could hardly type, and her heart so heavy she couldn't bring herself to write to that mad Englishman who was so passionately begging her for news.

Then at last her discharge came through, and she spent an exciting morning collecting unbelievably numerous bits of paper from unbelievably various offices, and receiving from a sadly anonymous pay officer vast sums of money due to her from the parent-like economy of the American Army, which had given her, like a child, only thirty dollars a month out of an appointment salary of seven hundred and twenty per annum, plus quarters and rations.

Few but the most spiritually rich can resist that all-solving excitement of suddenly possessing more money than one is used to handling. As for the materially rich they have forgotten, or have never known it. Laura felt happy for the first time in many weeks, not from the thought of all the worldly goods this money could buy, for she took less interest in worldly goods than most young women of her age. Indeed she had laughed for long at a story of Mike's about a priest who had had to stop a marriage ceremony because the bridegroom in his confusion had said "with all my goodly words I thee endow". "Goodly words are enough, for me," she had declared, adding quietly, "as long as the fellow's not a millionnaire in them, breeding them like money." Now she felt only a warm confidence spreading over her mind like wine, so that she went about her last minute tasks repeating to herself: "I'm going home. I'm going home. Everything will be all right."

Mike too had gone home, and written to her from Le Havre, a letter so tender, that although his handwriting made it look like a series of mathematical formulae she knew that it represented, as he would say, "another reality behind the symbols used to represent the appearance of phenomena."

And so she dispatched to Alfred Hayley, all unease washed away by the sudden urgency of her departure, a brief note saying that she was going home and no longer regarded herself as engaged to him. She couldn't even be bothered to express the usual gratitude for the acquaintance or the beautiful friendship. "I'm sorry," she stooped to, "but there it is. Please excuse rush, my train leaves in twenty minutes."

Alfred Hayley, "pursuant" to Geneva, was generously welcomed by Madame Georges Bertrand, who would not have her daughter in love with a married man.

"Oh Maman! Don't be so old-fashioned," Laura reproached her mother as many daughters have done, probably since Cain had a little sister. She was standing in front of the mirror, in black silk stockings with peach-coloured clocks, and a jupon of soft ivory satin, her hair much dishevelled from the constant trying on of a new tea-frock her mother was helping her to make. The feel of the dark green charmeuse had been exquisite, and she admired the new elegance of the skirt, narrowing round the ankles just like before the war. Only now she really was a grown woman, and would know how to walk in it. She looked at her body dubiously. Her skin was so brown! And her bosom altogether too aggressive. She must get one of those new flatteners. On the other hand, he liked her as she was. She added solemnly, but trying to sound casual, for the worldliness of the thought really frightened her: "He's going to get a divorce."

"That's only what he says, my dear." Madame Bertrand spoke through a lot of pins. "And that's neither here nor there, I will not have you marrying a divorcé."

"But Maman. Alfred is a divorcé!"

"Well—" She was a little put out by this sudden information, and took the pins out of her mouth one by one while her mind did a quick somersault, differentiating to her purpose. "He did not, I presume, divorce his wife on account of you?"

"No, no. It was ages ago. Oh, Maman, he's so old!"

"Nonsense. Forty is the prime of life." Alfred was in fact forty-four, but had lied about his age when he first met Laura, and so had had to keep it up. "Your father was over forty when Maurice was born. Is his wife still living?"

"I believe so, I don't know. I think he said the marriage wasn't consummated," Laura added through the green charmeuse as the loosely tacked panels passed over her head once more.

"Well, there you are," Madame Bertrand said with satisfaction, kneeling to make a deeper tuck where the lower skirt was caught in below the knee to give, the fashionable barrel shape. "My darling Laura, you do see that it is a most immoral thing to break up a marriage, don't you?"

"Yes. Yes, I do," she said dutifully, and thought that her mother's distinction between two divorced men a bit hypocritical. If someone else had clone the breaking-up, that was all right. "But it's not a happy marriage," she went on doggedly, remembering at the same time that Mike's letter had been getting more and more cryptic, "and, oh, Maman, I do love him."

"My dear, I thought I loved someone else when I married your father. How can a young woman know what love is until—" She stopped, aware suddenly that her daughter was twenty-five and there had been a war. "Laura, my child, you didn't—"

"Mais non, Maman, voyons!" And she thought, how irrelevant virginity had become in the modern world, wondering at the same time what it felt like actually to lose it, instead of just having it as a thing one must not lose.

"Ah!" Madame Bertrand sighed with relief, and stripped her daughter once again. "Love comes with marriage," she went on, gently expounding the maternal philosophy of her girlhood as if it were the wisdom of all ages, which perhaps it was. "Though many a man may take our fancy, fancy is not enough to get you through all those long and difficult, discouraging, wonderful years of growing responsibility. Only real love can do that, and real love is that which is slowly aroused in a woman by a strong and loving man." Her own experience had become a fixed and universal law that omitted, in its enunciation, the enormous variations in the human capacity for happiness which even her marriage had undergone.

Laura's hair had half fallen down over her shoulders and she looked at her more than *déshabillée* appearance, which Alfred had wittily called disabilitated, when she had once shamefully let him get that far in the Studio. Her hands moulded her body downwards and she tried to remember which hands she most responded to. But desire is hard to reconstruct and it was Alfred's presence she felt beneath her touch, being also the most recent. Mike gave her peace. She switched away from such abysmal thoughts and said violently:

"Maman, he eats me up. He eats me up spiritually."

"He has a strong personality certainly," said Madame Bertrand, handing her back her old blue alpaca dress. "So had your father. Just think, he started as a sculptor. You will learn to guide it, as I learnt to, guide it, with experience." Thus she dismissed Monsieur Bertrand's youthful aspirations. "And you must admit," she went on even more persuasively, "that he does love you deeply and sincerely."

Madame Bertrand had the same Guiset brown eyes she had given to Laura and all her children save Bérangère, who came after Laura, and Maurice, the youngest, both of whose eyes were Bertrand blue. Brown was in fact very much Madame Bertrand's colour, for though her wide face was waxen, her hair was a smooth, greying pile of silky brown, and her favourite song was a sentimental ditty by Jacques Dalcroze on the four seasons of woman, who wore white when married, blue or pink when children came, brown when a grandmother and black when left all alone; Madame Bertrand's eldest son Frédérique, a heavy, sombre, intelligent man who was following in his father's business, had also married a sensible, domesticated and sweet-natured girl just like herself, who had recently given birth to a daughter; and finding herself a grandmother at fifty, Madame Bertrand Père obediently took to brown, sometimes, however, anticipating wistfully in soft black *peau de sole*. And what with Alfred's slight subtraction of years from his age and her own proud awareness of being a grandmother, it naturally did not occur to Madame Bertrand that in fact she was not herself very much older than the suitor she wanted as husband for her daughter.

In effect, they all said much the same thing. "I can forgive him a lot," said Frédérique, who loathed him, "for at least his love is sincere." Madeleine was in America, so couldn't say anything. Bérangère said, "He plays the piano beautifully—" though in fact both Giselle and Maurice played it just as well, and didn't thump so—"and his love for you is quite overwhelming." Bérangère had been teaching dancing in Paris, and had come back with a very intellectual but grumpy young man, who seemed to take it out of everyone, and especially her, because England and America, he kept repeating as if he had coined the phrase himself, had won the war by fighting to the last Frenchman. Compared to this particular Frenchman, who had not been fighting, Alfred Hayley had considerably more charm. "Il est drôle, ton milord," Giselle said, "mais comme it t'aime." For though Alfred had modestly represented himself rather as a *milord manqué*, a younger son of a younger son of a second son of the twelfth Lord Hayley of Kilbrae, this twelfth lord occurred frequently enough in the conversation to create the necessary confusion. Maurice, who was only nineteen, said nothing.

As for Monsieur Bertrand, he took to Alfred at once, as Alfred *saw* to it that he would. Monsieur Bertrand, who had for many years edited two Geneva newspapers—one serious and one funny—was now director of the best bookshop and publishing firm in the city. His mother, a widowed lady from Maryland, had settled in Geneva when he was a boy, and he spoke fluent but accented English. He had the good looks of an American senator as envisaged by Europeans, and the good taste of a European intellectual as envisaged by Americans. He was liberal, atheistic, tolerant, revered the aristocracy but believed in a homogeneous body of righteous opinion called the People, and was therefore both shocked by and passionately interested in the Russian Revolution. A cultivated, respected man, and a very easy prey to the well-practised Hayley method of capturing with cul-ture. Old books and collections of prints were admired—some were sold at an unexpected profit on the Englishman's expert advice—a recent public-ation called *Eminent Victorians* was enthusiastically recommended, then presented as a gift, Creative Evolution and the Life Force were discussed, as well as the dramatic collapse of the Hapsburgs, over which all who had hated and fought the Germans for four terrible years were so irrelevantly rejoicing. The peace negotiations in Paris, Wilsonism, the Swiss and Amer-ican Federations, the educational theories of Pestalozzi, the fables of La Fontaine and the subtle delights of French Grammar, all these were aired in the comfortable, cluttered and dark drawing room of the big house in rue d'Amiel, though on some of the themes Alfred Hayley had to bluff or, better still; politely defer to his host.

And when Monsieur Bertrand remembered to inquire tactfully about the prospects of his future son-in-law, the future son-in-law replied, that at the moment his affairs had suffered a considerable setback from the war, but that he had always done well for himself, and that "blood would tell". Whereupon Monsieur Bertrand went to fetch a chart that unfolded all over the green plush cover of the dining room table, under a low drum-shaped centre-lamp of wrought-iron with long yellow fringes hanging from a yellow silk lining. And Alfred was shown to his slight chagrin, how the family tree had been traced back, as indeed all family trees can be, to Charlemagne. His keen eye very soon, however, fell upon the undeniable fact that the first Bertrand, in the sixteenth century, had no antecedents at all, had indeed merely married a younger bud on a branch of this large sprawling Anglo-Norman family that bore such a heavy burden of distant royalty. Of course this first Bertrand could also have been of noble Norman descent, but there was nothing but a blank on the chart. He could have been a Huguenot refugee, or a poor Picard weaver set up in England. He could have been a bastard. "He was a Lon-don merchant," said Monsieur Bertrand, with a blue twinkle in his eyes, "who did rather well for himself."

So when his daughter said to him one day, as she sat between two tall stone jars on the balustrade of the terrace, wearing a Greek looking tunic of pale orange while the others played croquet on the lawn, "Don't you think he's a bit too old for me?"—he replied, perhaps a little knowledgeably, "At least he'll be faithful, my dear. Besides, forty isn't all that old, it just looks old from twenty—what is your age now, twenty-four, twenty-five is it? Twenty-six this summer. Why you're no longer so young yourself, you know. And he really does love you." Yes, he really loved her, with poems entitled *"Mon Espéronce"* and "Resurrection", Petrarchan sonnets to his Laura, with letters, flowers and courteous calls, with *No John No* at the piano and very gentle manners, with outings in coffee-coloured fiacres or chauffeured landaulettes and trips on the Léman pleasure-boats. And women's eyes hovered attentively over him from beneath great mushroom hats of tagel straw with paradise feathers or big blue begonias, whenever he entered a tea-room with her or walked in Pont du Mont-Blanc or the Promenade of the Jardin Anglais in a twirl of Japanese paper parasols. For though he was not tall, and his mouth was too wide and his nose too big, the general effect was pink and white and clean and handsome, with sandy hair that stuck up boyishly in front, like a brush, but greying at the temples, and the lines around his eyes and mouth testified only to the added mystery of those few extra years. He was, besides, exquisitely tailored in light grey, with a wide silk cravat and a panama hat: and the small red ribbon of the Légion d'Honneur in his buttonhole, about which he was modestly English.

And so it was that one day in June he came to her miserably and said that he had lost all his money—for even the American Army was not a widow's cruse. She didn't understand the full story, something to do with securities he had in Canada, or shares in a Canadian firm which had gone bankrupt, and the cost of living which had shot to 160% from a pre-war hundred—a proposition which her mind refused to grasp.

"Now I have nothing to offer you," he wailed, "now you'll never marry me."

And she, like a child denying an allegation, said, to her own astonishment: "Well I will marry you, just because, so there."

The family haste was perhaps a little precipitous, but since they were providing everything, including the Bertrand chalet for the honeymoon, no one could accuse them of grabbing. The couple was married in July, before a drowsily twanging clergyman in the American Episcopalian Church, then again at the Hotel de Ville, where the clerk called her Mademoiselle first and Madame when he handed her the pen. The bride, modern and defiant, wore a red silk dress of such wartime brevity that even her shins were visible, in white silk stockings and white satin shoes. Everyone thought, but nobody said, that red was unlucky, or unseemly, or just un-Bertrand. Giselle said the effect was very Swiss and patriotic. Perhaps it expressed, rather, the bride's sympathetic affiliations with the Scarlet Whore of Rome.

Nearly four thousand feet up, facing the Mont Blanc for breakfast on the veranda, it was easy to be happy and in love. This indeed was her childhood, the mountain playing tricks, scintillating so white that one could only look at it broken up in the squares of the dining room windows; or disappearing altogether, or blushing deep at sunset, and puffing out irreverent pink clouds; then the last rays would switch off like a light and it would look like a dying swan, clutched at its base by a huge black bird of prey, with claws as large as forests.

Even so, there were difficulties. Alfred didn't like climbing, or picking bilberries on the wooded slopes, or hunting for mushrooms, or the expedition down to the valley for provisions. It annoyed him that she should be doing so much housework instead of sitting with him, and indeed, the place was geared for large family parties, who could share the chores. But he just wanted to be idyllic all the time. And to make love. Over and over, that is, after the usual honeymoon catastrophies had passed. So much so that when one night at eleven a party of German students clumped down the mountain path outside their bedroom door, singing *Wenn ich komm, wenn ich komm, zvenn ich wieder wieder komm,* she started laughing helplessly, and he was livid with affronted masculinity. So she got some sleep that night.

But it was the family who, as families do, came in the curious but common belief· that newlyweds need only two weeks to "get to know each other", after which mysterious knowledge they are then equipped to face "life" together, life being, in this case, the fact that this summer was ·the first gathering of the chicks to the Bertrand nest since before the war. So came Monsieur et Madame Bertrand Père, Monsieur et Madame Bertrand Fils with their baby daughter; Bérangère with her French fiancé and her Isadora Duncan eurythmics in a rude Greek tunic on the grass; to a tin-can piano from a teeth-grinding phonograph; plump and bosomy Giselle and Jean Duclot, the earnestly Calvinistic son of Monsieur Bertrand's publishing partner, to whom she was unofficially engaged; Maurice, who hummed and whistled Brahms incessantly, so that Alfred felt impelled to come in with a loud *di-DA* if he got so much as one note wrong; and a small newly acquired white dog called Rimski, over whose yelps Monsieur Bertrand composed a ditty which went (frequently):

Rimski, tu n'es pas Korsakov,
Rimski, tu n'es qu'un petit boeuf,

much to everyone's amusement.

And they climbed all day, in hobnailed boots, and bifurcated skirts which, Alfred thought disgusting. And they sang as they walked up, and they sang as they walked down, great hearty songs, yodelling songs, sad sentimental, songs, gay tripping songs, from an inexhaustible repertoire and each with innumerable verses, always, in a faultless, tediously simple harmony, always about the, beauty of their damn big mountains. They even sang around the fireside in the evening. It was ghastly.

And so the splendid impression of comfort, and culture which the Bertrands, had made on Alfred began to wane. Their family jokes, for one thing, were incomprehensible. Even Monsieur Bertrand became a bit of a bore, with his amateur etymologising from the local patois; his collection of the seven, hundred and nineteen ways the name Bertrand had been misspelt, so far, on envelopes; his cornering of any non-Bertrand in the woods with an illustrated lecture on poisonous mushrooms; his attempts at English humour which were still at the level of "When is a door not a door? When it's ajar"—a craze which had surely died with the, old, century—or his proudly repeated English story of the gentleman who asked another to call him a cab; and a mock-heroic circular poem which sent everyone into fits every time the beginning came round again: *C'était en mine huit cent treize, sombre treize.*

Happiness is usually ordinary and the happiness of another home can make some people feel very superior. Slowly he began to dislike them for the very things he had momentarily admired and envied in them—momentarily because Alfred Hayley never admired and envied for long without belittling. *Une de ses Alfrederies*, the Bertrand would call, behind his huffed and frequent back, the many examples of his bad manners, his endless talkativeness, his childish annoyance when contradicted or proved wrong in argument, his total lack of interest in anyone or anything unless relevant to himself. Indeed, one of the characteristics the Bertrands never quite forgave him was his duck's back indifference to their extraordinariness as a family, since everybody thought them extraordinary, original, intelligent, lively, talented—everybody, and especially themselves.

And though he adored, of course, his darling wonder-child as much as ever before, slowly he became insufferable, as all do whose overwhelming love for another person is only a diversion of self-love, causing a great big dam, since others can never love one as one loves oneself.

Poor lodgings in Bloomsbury, in that big black sprawling London where numerous connections were to set him up in business; strange little firms in London or Geneva, buying and selling, what, she had no idea, created it seemed as mere names and changing into one another at the touch of a bold signature, and all lodged in the same set of rooms, at Number Eight, Stone Buildings, Lincolns Inn; lateness at the office, meetings at his club, loneliness. And when she inquired, shyly, after her in-laws, she was made to understand that she didn't quite exist as yet in their awareness, and that were she to do so they would regard her, probably, as a mere adventuress. He himself might well be outcast on her account—hence their present poverty, he dared not go to them. Families were always a little difficult about that sort of thing. She must be patient, and let him handle it in his own way, when the time was ripe.

11

THE SUCCESSFUL businessman is an adventurer with a creative mind, but the adventurer in Alfred Hayley had been dead some years and he had never created anything except—like God, he used to say—a world of trouble for himself. And, in fact, for others, but himself was all he noticed. He was, therefore, a businessman, but only moderately successful, in a routine way.

And so he came to ask himself just where he was, as men do on reaching forty, forty-one, or forty-two, which they regard, according to the food they ate for dinner and the flattery they drank that day, as the beginning of the end, the end of the beginning, or just a comfortable halfway house.

America, that European's dream of untold wealth, had not, after all, provided him with a fortune. Yet he had been richer here than anywhere else and even now after many ups and downs he was comfortably off. He shared a rented apartment with a young publisher called Carey Wyatt—it was very small, but at 46 Fifth Avenue, and expensively furnished in the best Boston Directoire. He belonged to the Metropolitan—even he was not eligible to the University Club, which favoured Yale and Harvard men, and was rather snooty about Oxford England. And he had an office of a sort in John Street, on the wrong side of the Bowery perhaps, and a little too near the wharves, but with a breathtaking partial view of Brooklyn Bridge. Yet he was not, at present, a happy man.

How did one make that jump into big business, he asked himself? Some people just saved, then bought, like peasants with coins under the mattress. But he was no saver. He liked living just a little above his income, assuming, not altogether wrongly, that spending money in advance attracted more, because more jolly well had to be found. When he did have extra he invested, but his money never seemed to treble and quadruple like other people's: he had no taste for Wall Street games and, apart from the dull safe securities which provided him with a small private income over and above his salary, he had tended rather to indulge such gambling instincts as he possessed in putting up, say, half the money for some-body's small wild scheme, or the whole money for a small wild scheme of his own. There had been that unfortunate cotton-wood box mill experi-ment of Carter's—Hayley, Carter & Co., Inc.—in New Orleans. And his ex-cursion into the staves business. And the Twain Transportation, his very particular contribution to the craze for reviving the waning river com-merce on the Mississippi; but the higher insurance and the freight delays had offset the savings as against the railroad and killed the scheme stone dead; and although the Federal Government was now talking of operating a fleet of barges from St. Louis, nothing had come of it yet, and in any case it would hardly help private companies. Then he had dealt on the side in Real Estate, but that too had somehow become unreal. His only success had been as an exporter of lumber—the job he had mostly been doing all along, first in the South, then back in Canada—and the moral of that seemed to be that except in very big business a new firm needed more than just capital, it needed all one's time and all one's love, two things that nobody who had not put up the money was prepared to give. Mere investment might just as well be impersonal, like Government Stock, if one's time and love were already taken up. For time and love meant among other things powers of persuasion, and these he possessed to a fine art.

But the exporting of lumber was somehow not quite so gentlemanly an occupation in New York as it had been in the deep South, unless of course, one was so high up the ladder of Success that nobody cared what one had been a Success In.

And so, after a brief and triumphant return, as Sales Manager, to the New York Headquarters of that very same originally Canadian firm, the Summerson-Dupree Co., Ltd., which had given him his first clerical job, he had in one rash evening at the club, become a publisher, leaping, as it were, from one extreme of the wood-pulp trade to another. Always selling, as he said to his partner, Wyatt, what other people produced. For though he then came into close touch with men of much more cultured tastes, he could muster little interest in the trigonometry textbooks and nursing manuals which Wyatt insisted were much more lucrative than modern novels. What modern novels produced he dared not think, he only knew about old books which could, with care, fetch high prices. Evidently some modern novels made money—one, called *The Rosary*, had been selling in its thousands for nine years, and every publisher mentioned it with awe. Certainly he got considerably less out of trigonometry textbooks and nursing manuals than he ever had out of what he called "real" business, though hopeful authors kept sending them the oddest things—manuscripts on theosophy, thrillers and Ph.D. theses on the Great American Novel: "Moby Dick is like an onion," Wyatt had read a passage out of one of these, amid great guffaws, "from which layer after layer of meaning can be peeled. And at its tearful heart lies our face reflected in a mirror." Alfred Hayley couldn't help feeling that publishing was a bit like that, too.

They had a smart office in the city, though, so high up he always got a shock when he walked to the window and found that the street was not, after all, a few floors below those windows opposite—some gymnasium or ballet-school where young men in tights were constantly practising—but way below like a mountain crevasse.

Wyatt had in fact put up most of the money and though he owned some shares he was, in effect, Sales Manager again, at a much lower salary. He got more and more depressed, and couldn't understand it, since he had always loved books, all books, and always excelled at selling, whatever he was selling. And yet he felt he was getting nowhere. At forty-one, with once a home and a business of his own, where was he now?

Although he knew in his heart it was the approach of middle age, he blamed this destructive mood on the general restlessness, for the whole of New York had for long been abuzz with the thought of war. Ever since those absurd Lusitania notes it had been getting clearer and clearer that the United States would sooner or later have to enter the War. Nobody wanted it. And yet in that mysterious way public opinion has of feeling both one thing and its opposite, everyone also wanted it, at least by now. And some, certainly, including Alfred Hayley himself, hoped to profit by it. He felt he had made a mistake in a small moment of romanticism about the respectability of publishing. And so, quite recently, and without relinquishing his shares in Carey Wyatt Books, or indeed his claim on Carey Wyatt's easygoing friendship and useful apartment, he had rented this much drearier little office in John Street and set up once again in "real" business, the buying and selling of timber in the hope of navy and army orders, a little late perhaps, though he had contacts, and a certain weary optimism. But the adventurer in him had died, and he felt very tired as he walked to the elevator, still muttering "I don't care, I don't even care."

It was that time in a man's life when he discovers to his surprise, gratitude and regret, that the blood really can lie quiet. Has done so, in fact, for several years.

The cold hit him in the face and he turned up his fur collar. This new central heating mania was most dangerous—background heating, they called it, instead of getting roasted by a fire, and he would quip, who wants to live in a background? He walked briskly along Wall Street and into Broadway which was a clatter of streetcars with much honking from the modern rectangular black taxis. So rectangular, everything in New York, so tiring, hardly a curve except on the more mature women, and one didn't see many of them in the city, only rectangular young stenographers in boot-top length tailor-mades with rectangular loose jackets or rectangular military pockets and flat rectangular hats. He looked up at the sheer cliff of Wall and yearned for a few striped summer awnings that would bulge like eyelids over the sun-flooded stone.

He decided to be English and walk, without a purpose, or rather with the vague purpose of letting the crowded lunch-hour slip by and of finding, ultimately, a quiet restaurant, far from his usual haunts. He was not in the mood for businessmen's war hysterics.

He spotted her at once as he entered the long narrow restaurant. A great cloud of brown hair like puffed silk, held mysteriously by a small golden band over the clear brow. And a pouched, almost transparent white blouse with soft striped revers like an effeminate sailor, and a loose knot of dark foulard between the breasts, the pointed shape of which seemed to shout at him already through the ninon or whatever it was and the fumey distance. She was alone at a small table for two, and with a quick look round he made sure that no other table was completely free. She was reading a book on her knees, but looking up quite often to stare thoughtfully at nothing as she ate her soup and a piece of bread. Then she smiled at him and he approached the table.

"May I join you, or are you waiting for someone?"

She went quite red in the face.

"No. No. I mean yes. The seat is free." Her grave eyes travelled round the room quickly and she saw that other single seats were free, but no complete table. So, while he took his coat off, she surreptitiously brought the book up from her knees and placed it by her plate, fixing her eyes on it as she went on eating.

"Now come, that's not very polite. It's such a small table we might just as well talk."

She looked as troubled by the rebuke as by the evident pick-up.

"I'm sorry. I don't talk to strange men." This sounded so absurdly prim in the modern circumstances and the wicked city, and he, looked so amused that she added, even more apologetically. "I—er—have to read this in my lunch-hour. I'm a—I'm studying."

"Oh, I see." He was mock solemn, then suddenly looked mischievous. "Then why did you smile at me when I came in? I took it for an invitation."

"I didn't smile at you!" She looked both shocked and alarmed. "I must have been smiling at my own thoughts, and you just got in the way." But then she really was smiling, at her own statement.

"I do apologise. Next time I'll put a pebble in my mouth."

"Like the Invisible Prince."

He was delighted.

"The Yellow Fairy Book! Did you read those too? They were the joy of my childhood." He was pleased to be able to appear younger. The Blue Fairy Book and the Red had indeed been the joy of his teens, but the later ones he had started collecting, quite recently, in America, as a full-grown adult passionately interested in Frazer and in Andrew Lang's *Magic and Religion.*

She smiled.

"Some. I learnt English from them."

"You are not American, then?"

"Half. And you?" She discreetly tossed back the ball. "You sound English."

And so the game of acquaintance began, service, love-fifteen, fifteen all, thirty-fifteen, thirty all . . . your advantage. His advantage all the way, really, for her obvious reticence was a challenge and he excelled himself, thus learning much about her while retaining his charm as a mystery man.

And what was she studying? Well, she wasn't really studying, she had just said that, but she really did read as much as possible in her spare time. The book on her lap? Well, it was St. John of the Cross—*o dichosa ventura,* she murmured when pressed to show it to him. She worked at the Hispanic Institute, and before that she had been a cataloguer in Yale University library, and before that—he smiled at such youth, so anxious with its testimonials of experience, too few to be yet lost count of. Before that? Was she so old? Oh yes, she was twenty-three. He had thought her younger, perhaps twenty, but that was no doubt her shyness, and her seriousness. She shared a room in Little West 12th Street with a girl-friend called Mary, who wrote poetry and knew a lot of artists and writers in Greenwich Village and had met Edgar Lee Masters and Ford Madox Ford. They shopped at the big market or at Wanamaker's, and on 14th Street at the big store for ribbons and stuffs and household things. Yes, she liked New York. Her name was Laura Bertrand. "Do you mean to say you're not eating a main course?" he asked when his arrived, and she shook her head and said she never ate much, and anyway she must be going and it was a pleasure and goodbye.

"What absolute nonsense, my dear girl. Are you trying to starve yourself?" And as she got up he stretched out his arm to touch hers and guide her down again, and was shocked by the rush of forgotten desire at that mere contact. "Sit down," he said weakly. "I beg you to sit down." She looked startled by his tone. "Listen, I desperately need company. Your company. You're hard up, please, please, have lunch with me."

"I'll do nothing of the sort."

But he had recovered now and used all his charm. And finally she accepted, wine and all, saying:

"It's just like Antoinette."

"Who's Antoinette?"

"Oh, she's a character in *Jean-Christophe*, you know, she's very poor, and a governess in Germany and there are no tickets left for the concert." Her dark eyes were shining as she got carried away in the story. "Then Jean-Christophe, who is a composer, has an empty box and doesn't know what to do with it, and he sees her and insists on sharing it with her. She protests a lot, of course. Oh, non monsieur, and all that, but she goes, and she loses her job because the family is furious with Jean-Christophe for having been seen in a theatre box with their governess. And she goes back. to Paris, and loves him terribly of course, all the time, and works and works and works for her brother to finish his studies. Then she dies. It's all terribly sad. We always used to play at Antoinette when we went to concerts."

"We?"

"My sisters and I. We always played at books. We played *Little Women* for ages because there are four of us—well, and two boys, one above and one below, but we're sandwiched in between. And it's funny, I was always Jo, partly because I'm the second eldest girl, but mostly because I was such a tomboy and could never keep tidy. You wouldn't think so now, would you? Or would you?" She started fussing about her hair and arranging the knot on her bosom. She was flushed with the wine and the warmth of the room.

"I think you're enchanting. Tell me more about yourself. What brought you to America?" (and me), he added to himself.

"Well, it's easier for a girl to work here, I mean a girl of good family. Though that's changing now, with the War. When war broke out I worked in the Red Cross in Geneva for a year, in the Prisoners of War section. But in any case, we have a lot of cousins here. My father was American, you know. He came over to Geneva as a boy with his mother, who remarried there. Then he married there too and after a while he got naturalised. It's usually the other way round, isn't it? But of course originally the family came from England and settled here. In Maryland, you know. Still, we were all *born* American citizens. Anyway, we've always had an urge to come, and we all did, at least the girls. My older brother's in the firm now and Maurice is only seventeen. My elder sister Madeleine is still here, she's a nurse in Detroit."

"But you're not telling me about yourself."

"No."

Suddenly she was quiet, aware of having talked too much. She always did when she tried to overcome her shyness. He offered her a cigarette, which to his surprise she took, lighting up and smoking inexpertly though obviously not for the first time. She said slowly, between two puffs.

"I don't think one ever tells a complete stranger really about oneself. Only what's all around."

He wanted to say, It's a spiritual fan-dance, but he was afraid of shocking her, and while he thought, There isn't a girl in the world, however innocent, who doesn't know how to do it, it's an instinct—he said aloud, "How right you are." He was put off by the sudden quiet, aware of his heart thumping and a cold sweat from nowhere on his brow, like stage-fright. But he forced himself to go on. "I do want to know more of you. I would like not to be a stranger." He recited as if in a trance. The atmosphere seemed electrical, isolated from the restaurant which was probably empty by now, but he didn't want to know. Damn it, he tried to break it up inside himself, am I falling in love? Then he said intensely, "Please, may I see you again?"

"Well—"

When in doubt, say no. She who hesitates is lost. And so forth.

She was not exactly lost, for she was a good girl, but she did fall in love, rather fast, and was terrified of him. She became more and more reticent, and he more and more talkative. Thus their roles were gradually reversed, yet still they revealed little of their inner selves, unless inner selves consist of all the books one has read and the cities one has seen and the concerts one has heard—a problem which philosophers have not solved yet.

And he talked of all these things, how New York had touched the heavens since he first saw it, when there were few skyscrapers and these were only twenty or thirty storeys high, before the Singer Building went up with forty-seven, round 1908, and the madness began, rather splendid really, and the views were almost Alpine, though he would rather see the real Alps, especially with her; and how London was all sprawled out low in space, compared to this, an amorphous protoplasm of dirty villages, adding unto itself more and more cells, though he loved it dearly, and there was nothing in the world quite like the London parks, except perhaps—and he roved around the Americas from Alabama to Peru.

And he took her to plays she had never heard of, to barbaric performances of Wagner, who was all the rage, and coy performances of Maeterlinck and Barry, whom she liked, and Shakespeare in a weird Boston English.

He spoke of God and the catholicity of Latin and the Onlyness of the Roman Church. He spoke of John Henry Newman and Archbishop Whateley —who was his great-uncle on his mother's side, and of whom she had never heard. "The Victorians religious?" he echoed with mock surprise, "Come, with men like Darwin and Tyndall and Clifford? The ordinary people, perhaps, but they weren't really religious, just hypocrites. Of course, there was always a nucleus of the more sensitive, more artistically inclined, who turned, in their despair, to Rome. Oh, my dear, Rome has so much of the truth, that could enchant your innocent pagan soul, and yet, and yet, I shouldn't be surprised if God had created the Church as a thorn in the flesh of true believers. Christian apologists can apologise for God, but how in the name of God can they apologise for the Church?" And he spoke of W. H. Mallock's *New Republic* and Gibbon's *Decline and Fall of the Roman Empire,* especially chapters 14 and 15, on the Ancients and the Immortality of the Soul, which he said had been a turning point in his life. But there were so many turning points in his conversation she felt giddy.

"You are my higher education," she said, though formally speaking hers was higher than his, French lycées being what they are, and the English catching up at University, to which he had not been. But her ground of reference was very different, and she was uncertain of herself. He seemed to be part of a mysterious inner circle, in touch with unknown powers who sent him books and catalogues and theatre tickets and who were in the know about everything. Indeed he even hinted once that he was employed by the British Secret Service, to keep watch on neutral aliens like herself. New York to her was one tall hive of anonymous bees all alike and buzzing very loud, then flowing like honey after office hours into those funny subway kiosks that like miniature conservatories. Yet she met none of his friends, except Carey Wyatt, and he met all of hers, even the Caldwells, rich family connections of some Bertrand cousins, who lived in Madison Avenue. During this ardent courtship, the president of the United States made a stirring speech in Congress, calling for war to make the world safe for democracy. And she said, why does he drag party politics into something so important? A week later, America had entered, and the feverish excitement all around poured also into their turmoiled blood, making a heady mixture of patriotic fervour, sexual desire and the Roman Catholic faith. Their love seemed a thing apart from hatred of the Kaiser, or the call-up of American youth, and indeed it continued in spite of these things, almost insulated and yet continually suffused with them. And he gave her two photographs of himself at thirty-two, slim, romantic and Southern in a white linen suit, as older men do who fall in sudden youth, and she fell more in love with him through the photographs; and more in love with him when he tried, but failed, to learn the energetic struts and stomps and two-steps she could do, because doing them meant holding her. And a bit less in love the more he talked.

When he got tired of talking in drugstores, in tearooms full of sweetened cakewalks and diluted rags, on benches in Central Park or Battery End, in her room when Mary was out, in his flat when Wyatt was away, he so wanted to touch her, to strip her naked of more than the mental labels she had lived by, that when one day, a scribbling friend of Mary's said that he knew a painter who had a studio in Greenwich village and who was going to Mexico to escape the War, Alfred quickly got in touch with this brave man and arranged to rent the studio from him.

It was in Patchin Place, and outside it there grew an ailanthus tree and the Elevated Railway, which he said looked just like a Swiss Chalet, and she said, horrified, oh no, but which made, at any rate, a noise like a mountain crumbling. Inside the studio was another elevated stairway and balcony, much more like a Swiss chalet, leading to a primitive bathroom and cabinet bed; below, a kitchenette, a table and chairs, two chintz armchairs, an open fire, easels and canvasses stacked thick against the wall, a huge roof window, and of course, a couch.. Her tiny hand was seldom frozen here, for coal and sticks were brought all the way upstairs by exceedingly obliging tradesmen.

And they would sit for hours in each other's arms, first in the firelight, then with the summer moonlight streaming down through the vast glass panes. Saying nothing. For her reticence was so affecting him that when at last he was truly alone with her he felt nothing, nothing but terror at the empty space between them, which all his words had been so unable to bridge that words now became as empty as the space. And although he mentioned eloquent silences, and took refuge in murmuring frequently, "All day the same our postures were, And we said nothing all the day," which gave poetic authority to his sudden helplessness by implying that soul was speaking to soul, he felt that something was wrong, for his desire had gone. So he lay her out on the couch, and knelt by her, and said, "You are my shrine, my goddess, I worship and adore you." And she smiled and asked, "In all my flawful beauty?" For she always said she had a nose like a potato and a skin like a coffee bean. So then he protested, "You're beautiful, don't you know it? You're beautiful. Oh my wonder-child, my darling little girl." And he unbuttoned her blouse, stroking her neck, and unclasped, with recently acquired expertise, the new brassiere she wore because all American women were now wearing them, she said.

And so it always went, she allowed so much, and not much more. And he seemed not really to want it. Sometimes she even came to breakfast with him, and they would play at being married, she more shy than ever, sometimes even unhappy, he chattering of toast and maple syrup and of wanting to see her face over the coffeepot every day, unlike all other married men. Once he was ill and she nursed him. He loved that, it was just like marriage, but with an unbelievable angel, naturally.

For so a girl could preserve her virtue, that great prize, for need be, out of fear, innocence, distaste and an ancient years spirit of barter. A gentleman loved her the more for it, and both could learn how to make the pleading take up most of the time.

Then one day, not long after a highly emotional joint attendance at Midnight Mass in the Jesuit Church of St. Ignatius, she slipped down to Virginia where she had some cousins and there volunteered, just like that, for the American Red Cross. So he volunteered too, when she told him of it. It was a very dramatic gesture. He even called on his lawyer to make a new will, leaving "everything he had or might inherit or get" to her. "At present there isn't much," he said when revealing this generously high bid for her. "I have lost heavily through the War, and many of the Securities are at present practically worthless, but they would cost little or nothing to hold, and later on I believe they will come back again." And she didn't know what securities were, having always assumed that people lived, like her, on a weekly wage packet which just got bigger and bigger—as they got older.

In practice, neither of them was called till April, when first she had to report to the Nurses' Mobile Station, Holley Hotel, and later he, to the Red

Cross Headquarters in Madison Square. He called her his brave, plucky little soldier. He was quite certain she would be leaving first and carefully put aside for use on the occasion a most ingenious French pun he had worked out, proudly: *Je pense à toi, donc je te suis.* But in the end it was she who was to follow him.

The rush was enervating, to the New York docks, the day he sailed. She had spent the last few evenings quietly marking all his clothes and sewing strong red shoe-bags for him with A.H. embroidered in yellow. He seemed hardly to have talked to her, properly, that is. Then that fool Wyatt and a girl called Violet got in the same taxi with them. The dock entrance was closely guarded and no one was allowed even in the enclosure, so that he had to go sadly aboard, and the ship didn't leave for ages. Then he dis-covered that a thermos flask full of excellent whisky had been smashed in the general push, though wrapped in leather gaiters and packed at the top of his grip. Everything was soaked and the cabin stank and his tobacco pouch was ruined, "The tobacco will sure smoke good," said his cabin companion, a Red Cross man from San Francisco, who looked rather a bore, and later exclaimed innocently, "Ho, ho, you rascal," when he saw that Alfred was reading *The Way of All Flesh.*

He went up to the lounge, which was full of people—army and A.R.C. of-ficers, jolly Harvard boys going to Italy as ambulance drivers, some civil-ians, and the personnel of the French Commission to the United States, returning to France with their families. Through a small window he could glimpse the troops still filing up the gangway with their kitbags on their shoulder. All around him rumours were bandied about, and people who had never sailed before were exclaiming at everything they saw. But he was too experienced a sailor to feel excited, and his heart was heavy.

He sat down in a corner of the lounge and started writing to Laura.

The letter grew and grew, and turned into a journal as the days went by, days when the sea got rougher and the passengers sicker, and every-one more anxious as no news was put out and no convoy appeared. "Most odd with so many important people on board," he said to the man from San Francisco. But soon he made friends with those higher up, especially the French High Commissioner who invited him to his table, much to the annoyance of other Red Cross men. There he met equally delightful because important people, including the director of the Credit Industriel de Paris, who was now Controller of Supplies for France, and wore the Legion of Honour in his buttonhole.

But his journal became a private chapel, where he worshipped his madonna. And he arranged to carry this private chapel upon his person in an oil-skin water-tight bag, so that if they were torpedoed it would reach her, somehow, in Geneva. For it was beautiful and very spiritual.

There is a great deal about me, dear heart, which you do not know and I have not been able to tell you, but which I will tell you one day, and if anything is not clear to you or seems hidden or a little uncertain it will be clear then. Trust me always dear as you have so wonderfully trusted me in the past. For as you have given yourself so also have I given myself to you. I feel I have not made you realise this and the thought pains. I feel I have assumed things and taken things for granted, yet that can't be so. It is your modesty which makes me feel this way at times. You do not go out to meet happiness and you seem to fear and doubt it when it does come. And yet I close my eyes and see you now as compared to what you were when I met you. Then you were a promise of a bud., now you have opened into a wondrous and beautiful flower. And your beauty my adored one is so perfect without spot or blemish issuing and proceeding from a pure and perfect soul illuminating me and all about me. That is what I see and worship in you.

So, as the week passed and they approached the danger-zone, still, inexplicably, without a convoy, and rumours growing more colourful as the ocean became more grey, he whipped up his emotions to an orgy of self-indulgence, what with his anxiety about her sailing, about his own proximate heroic death, about her reticence and his, which made him uneasy that he had never quite impressed on her his remarkable personality or the unusual depth of his feelings.

A few romances sprang up on board.

Everyone was ordered to keep on their lifebelts.

If I should die think only this of me, he wrote on. *Thank you from my heart and soul for all you have been to and brought to me, for all you have done for me without knowing it, for all you have wrought in me. Then there are things of which I may not speak, there are dreams which cannot die, the very sacred, holy moments of communion we have known, when soul spoke to soul. Their memory is with me as I write this and I bow my head in reverend adoration of my wonderful little girl. You have become a creed and a religion to me. "I love thee to the level of every day's most quiet need by sun or candlelight, and if God choose I shall but love thee better after death." They say we may land late tomorrow, the Bay is now like a sheet of glass, but no land is as yet in sight. It is the most dangerous of all times now I hear. I may not be able to write more so if this should be my last, dear wonderchild, goodbye, God have you ever in his keeping. Keep my memory green, I know you won't forget me. I love you, I adore you, my every breath is yours. Alfred.*

And then at last, nine days after leaving New York, a destroyer came alongside in the silent dawn and everyone woke with lighter hearts to a new sense of safety. Alfred stood on the bridge with some of the more eminent passengers and watched as the ship sailed up the river to Bordeaux. The disembarkation was chaotic, with no system for handling baggage, followed by an equally chaotic train journey across the city to the station, a few hours to wait, dinner and then all aboard for Paris. There were, of course, no sleepers.

From the unlit corridor of the night-train to Paris he saw the Castles of the Loire loom past in the black and green daybreak, and murmured "Full rose the silver moon on the tranquille fields of France"—which sounded like a quotation so he went on, as if it were—"those fields unreached as yet by the ravages of war." But the moon was not shining. Only Laura, who by now was twice as large as life and many times as intensely bright.

In the end he was sent to London after all, and left Paris with mixed feelings, for the chestnuts were in bloom but the long-range bombardment shells burst about every fifteen minutes.

Home. Everything seemed the same on the familiar skyline as his train approached Waterloo. Parliament, Whitehall, Northumberland House, the horrible Charing Cross bridge everyone had fussed about for years, Adelphi Terrace thank God still there, Hotel Cecil, the Savoy somehow taller and denuded of its terraced balconies with their granite columns and coloured pillars; Somerset House, Cleopatra's Needle. But he could hardly recognise the London beneath the skyline. So many cars, black taxis, no carriages, the Strand much wider and Kingsway, which had been mostly a string of vacant sites on his last visit, now actually in use, lined with stately buildings all taken for granted; the hideous London Opera House Mr. Hammerstein had opened a few years back had just been turned into a picture theatre called The Stoll—thank goodness the American musical seemed to have had its day, though moving pictures were hardly an improvement. The new Australia House was only half finished—in fact most of London seemed to be full of gaping buildings left like skeletons, for the war effort. But the rest of Aldwych was still the same heap of rubble it had been in 1901 when the plan was begun, a real disgrace to London, now covered with horrible huts for the American Y.M.C.A. And Villiers Street filled on both sides with ambulances and private motorcars specially commandeered, with Red Crosses on their glass fronts as they waited for wounded heroes coming in to Charing Cross. And practically the whole of Northumberland Avenue, including the three great hotels, requisitioned by the Ministry of Munitions or something equally ghastly.

No guardsmen in scarlet, the troopers of the Royal Horse-guards in blue. No blazing lights. Impossible to get cigarettes after eight, or a whiskey after nine-thirty, except, it seemed, in secret clubs.

And now, in Stratford-on-Avon, he could hardly recognise his mother. He had always thought of her as stately, statuesque even, and so, surely, she had been. Now she was a portly little woman of seventy-five, with off-white hair, who seemed to have shrunk, not so much in breadth, but in height. She had always seemed a little taller than her husband, taller than himself, or was it just his memory of her that had grown? Perhaps his father's death, seven years since, had removed those psychological inches.

Yet they seemed to have little to say to each other, though he talked a great deal, and she called him "my dear, dear boy" and "my very own darling". Muriel got on his nerves by asking several times, "How is Harriet-your-dear-wife?" And he was shocked to see how simply they lived, in a dark and narrow house over their antique shop, called, rather lengthily, *The Books, the Arts, the Academes,* a quotation out of context, where the subject so described was actually women's eyes. But the shop was full of Shakespeareana. She had written all about it when they first started it, and yet he had visualised it more romantically, especially the house itself, which made their old furniture look out of place and dingy. He glanced round with an expert eye: it had never been very good anyway. He noticed his mother's two local lectures, Women in Shakespeare and The Baconian Myth, beautifully bound in red leather on the most visible shelf, together with the Complete Works of Marie Corelli and, on top, a dreamy photograph of her in sepia mist, signed, To my very dear friends. His mother was much respected in Stratford society.

They talked, mostly, of family news. Uncle Septimus had died, and so had Aunt Charlotte. Dilly was married, as he knew, the year before, his mother's tone of relief being unmistakable, for Cordelia was now thirty-six. "To a charming doctor," she quavered, "a very good family, the Winthrop Blairs. They met in France. She is a trained dispenser, you know, she was doing very valuable work."

He couldn't understand why she was treating him, behind the darling boy-ing, as a complete stranger. He knew all this from her letters, and letters were a family's lifeblood. There had even been a time when she confided a great deal to him of her worries, about Dilly's character; Miss Grey had been a very bad influence, did he remember Miss Grey, she would write, the governess who came after Miss Bell? Miss Grey would tell Dilly about, her previous jobs, and how her pupil's father had fondled her on his lap. Then Dilly had wasted her dispenser's training and gone off to Bradford as a governess, and later to Ireland with two men. But after a while the confidences stopped as Dilly grew older and got so angry at his letters to her, such nice, elder-brother letters, too, full of serious advice. Then Dilly had written him some of her prize catclawings, at their father's death, for instance, in 1911, when she implied a deathbed disowning vow and enclosed an obituary from the *Stratford Herald* which said that Mr. Hayley had left two daughters. Correspondence had more or less ceased after that. Petty, petty, petty, it all was.

"Have you seen her?" his mother asked anxiously. "She is in hospital in London, you know, she had an operation."

"Yes, Mother. I saw her."

"I know you two have never quite hit it off, my dear. But you're no longer children, and there is quite enough fighting and hatred in the world. She is going to Cape Town after the war, you know. The Winthrop Blahs live there."

"Good."

"You shouldn't say things like, that, Northbrook dear."

"But really, Mother, she's impossible. Do you know, I had hardly been in London a week, when she wrote a letter to the secretary at my club telling him I ought not to be a member, and why." This was not true, Cordelia had merely called at his club and he had found her chatting flirtatiously with a gentleman in the hall. But the sight of her as a grown woman had dissociated his time sequence for a second and the idea of what she might have been saying had given him such a shock, that grew into such a fear of what else she might so easily have done, being her, that by now he truly believed it had happened so. His mother watched him sadly and murmured, "You're so alike, you two," which he most indignantly denied, and quite forgot to mention that he had then visited his sister in hospital and made a most unpleasant scene.

"When Dilly got married I said to her, I hope you will never have any children."

"Oh, Mother."

"She denied her parents once," Mrs. Hayley said, in a trembling voice. "I heard about it by chance, later. She was asked, in Birmingham, if her parents were the Hayleys who lived at Over Marstaple, and she said no."

Alfred was silent, for he had done the same, not once but several times.

"There is so much hatred in the world today," she repeated. "Charity begins at home."

And so, he thought, does the lack of it.

Something that starts with the snatching of a doll can be nurtured so skilfully as only families know how, so that as life's conventions hide it more, the canker grows larger with age.

Why should he have to see someone he didn't get on with, who didn't get on with him, merely because she was his sister? Surely by now they could accept the fact that they just didn't like each other much?

Muriel said suddenly:

"But Mother, at least he always thinks twice before saying the wrong thing. Dilly thinks only once. I don't think at all, but that's only because I'm not clever."

Only the very wise can re-enter an abandoned world and feel at home there, without help from sentimentality and lies, at least of omission. Few can blend past and present, or their many different selves. He did not, therefore, mention his great secret love, but wrote instead in his journal:

I spoke of you and yet even with her I feel a strange reticence. What is it? On my way back to London I spent a few hours at Oxford, and as I walked its famil-iar streets I saw once more its grey and hoary shrines and the spots I love so well, I had a wild desire to have you there with me, to show you Oxford as I know and love it. Through Christ Church fields and Merton's Meadows to Mag-dalen Bridge, along Addisons Walk I went, recalling the years that have flown, and realising how empty they all were, but how full the time is now because I have you. I sat in the gardens of Worcester, my own college, and wrote a few lines to you. The way you and I have travelled together dearest is a very sacred and holy way to me, and I feel I cannot speak of it to others. All my ideals all my half formed abandoned hopes all my inspirations my desires to do and ac-complish have all gone into it. Here in these pages I feel I am showing you what you have not seen before, I feel as though I were taking you into in soul and showing you everything there.

Still there was no news of Laura. He had no idea when she was sailing or whether she had sailed. His job as Director of A.R.C. Motor Transport for Great Britain and Ireland kept him very busy in a small office at the top of 39, Grosvenor Gardens, or travelling round the country on tours of inspection for the Purchasing Department, or taking over a lot of old stables in Eaton Mews and getting them converted into garages, or going up to Liverpool, or down to Southampton, to supervise unloadings. Touring cars, ambulances, trucks, vans and lorries, mostly Fords from America, all had to be imported, and about two hundred cars a month from British Government stock also had to be shipped to France. He worked long hours and would collapse on the bed at his club in St. James' Street, over which were fixed two small flags, one with a red cross on a white background, the other with a white cross on a red background.

I want to go to Switzerland with you, he wrote, *to meet and know and love all your people, for your people are now my people, and I especially want to go to the chalet you have told me so much of, there and in Geneva where you spent your childhood, I feel I can let you see and know so much of me which I feel you don't know now, my dear little wonder-child, my own precious Laura.*

But still there was no news of her, and he wired Madison Square in despair. By now his great and secret love had become a holy of holies, an inner tabernacle, a veritable Song of Songs.

She came, she went, in a leaden August. It was all so casual, their greeting at Southampton where he rushed to meet her. They talked of this and that, of her sailing from Hoboken, of torpedo scare, of a nurse called Jean who had shared her cabin.

He pulled some strings and changed his job, so as to be in Paris, where they met again, two and a half months later. But alas, she had not read his journal and seen his inner soul. There was distance in her eyes.

Würöüü

Would that I could hush all the loud confusion in my heart. I have seen you, but what is it, what is it, Laura? I have not been able to say one word, or to give you or even tell you of this, though I brought it to give to you. Am I to lose myself in the grey tumult of these after years? Why can I not speak, when every fibre in me is crying out for utterance, when all my pent-up devotion is travailing for birth? Oh, Laura, Laura, surely you must feel, must know, must understand.

He caught a severe cold in France, and after his return collapsed into bed and self-pitying hysteria as all London celebrated the end of the war. And in no time at all the cold became pneumonia. And there in the Hospital for Officers, Lancaster Gate, he slowly convalesced his body and his love, reinventing and recreating it in his own image: it was the absence of marriage that weighed so heavily upon his sense of responsibility towards her, it was the passion of his devotion, here at last he had found the phrase, the words, and he was so happy. Devotion, adoration, love, service, unselfishness, every thought and feeling one can have for another expressed in or through or because of passion, this was passion transfigured, transmuted, the very personification of the spiritual.

For Alfred Hayley had faith, against all evidence, and his shrine was alight once more.

12

"HUMOUR, THEY say, dates fast, and no doubt they are right. But seriousness dates too. Only the very truest artists can still move us or amuse us when generations have passed, for the artist, though a man of his time, is, at his best, in touch with more universal ways of laughing and crying than those of his own day. And even so we sometimes smile where we are meant to weep. It takes an artist great indeed, my friends, to cut right through the notions of his time—notions of behaviour, of righteousness, of love and spiritual truth taken most seriously by serious, intelligent and devoted people—and to come out the other side and speak, meaningfully, though still in the idiom of his age, to generation upon generation for thousands of years. Such an artist, dear brethren, is Jesus Christ. And why? Because He is not just an artist, He is the son of God, whose compassion is eternal, whose sense of humour is for all time. In the name of the Father the Son and the Holy Spirit Amen."

The abrupt end of the Abbot's peroration was a very good trick, for while everyone in the congregation confusedly crossed themselves, he vanished and the pulpit was empty when they looked up. Already the Abbot was being revested with his pontifical robes, by half-a-dozen acolytes in red and white.

It is certainly effective, at least in New York, thought Alfred Hayley, who knew just where the Abbot had borrowed the idea, and had watched him as he started his descent backwards already on the words "for all time", then turned and raced down the remaining steps in his slippers. The Abbot always wore slippers indoors for he liked to move swiftly and silently as a Recording Angel, and was fond of the line, "the moving waters at their priest-like task." There was indeed a very slight hint of undulation about his gestures. The congregation, however, had been electrified by those staring black eyes, that looked more piercing, if possible, under the tonsured skeletal head.

In the evening there was a reception in the big ballroom of the Plaza Hotel, to which Alfred Hayley, as a Catholic businessman with connections, had contrived to get himself invited, and he listened intently as the young Abbot, looking like a handsome ghost in his white habit and black scapular, made a picturesque plea for funds towards the costs of having already built, out of pure faith and a few donations, the entrance arch, guesthouse, Glastonbury kitchens, refectories, chapter-house, abbatial lodge and a spacious chapel in Edwardian Gothic on the very spot where Saint Lambert of Alfringham had appeared to their beloved founder exactly eight hundred years ago, in 1110, standing on a shrub—in brief for his mad dream of a medieval abbey, now £15,000 in debt, on Mynyddglan-mynachloggwyn, Wales, now renamed Monsalvat. "Or what man in there of you, whom if his son ask bread, will he give him a stone?" Stones, however, would have been quite welcome too.

"Well, I hope you like our begging friar?" Alfred asked Mr. Quentin P. de Vere, in a tone equivalent to a Latin *num*, expecting the answer no.

"He's crazy," said Mr. Quentin P. de Vere, "crazy," he repeated, sipping Bourbon with a bemused stare, for he was clearly impressed by the size of Father Cynewulf Huxley's impudence.

"It's kind of a cute idea, though," said Jerome Winterton Junior, who looked as inapt as he sounded, a large-bellied man in tails. He had been much taken with one of the lantern slide lectures, and kept calling the Abbot—amid great guffaws—Father Kinema, the Prior of the Peep-Show and Bishop Bioscope.

"The Modern Neo-Medieval," Alfred said, as archly as a chancel roof, "probably seems less absurd to you Americans, because you haven't got the real thing and when you want it you have to imitate, sometimes transporting stone by stone. But I assure you it's nonsensical in Europe."

Jerome Winterton Junior looked very offended, and drank umbrage with his whisky in polite silence, reviving only when somebody quoted Oscar Wilde on the youth of America being its oldest tradition, having been going on for three hundred years. He was a railroad king, or arch-duke rather, in a system as great and widespread as the Hohenzollerns, who had managed, as the rich do, to stay rich despite all government measures against railroad kings, and he liked, beneath the jokes, to salve his conscience with big donations, the bigger the better, for a needle's eye was very small indeed, and he was bulkier than a camel.

But Alfred Hayley would go on, with obsessive tactlessness. If America's youthfulness had been, going on for three hundred years then it was time America grew up. Surely they weren't going to be romanced into paying vast sums of money for this crackpot notion, Neo-this and Neo-that, good-ness, they had enough Neo-European over here without contributing to it in Europe as well.

"Well, this is called the New World," said Quentin P. de Vere amiably, "and the new always owes more than it likes to the old, but it's new for all that."

"Yes, of course, my dear sir, and all the more reason why you should concentrate on your own culture here." This was much better. He felt the atmosphere relax. Poor babes, so anxious to have their own culture, their own literature, as if the whole thing weren't a pale, provincial echo of England, why, only four or five generations back these people were Eng-lishmen; no individual culture can be produced in that time, it takes cen-turies. "Let the stones of Venice remain in Venice," he went on, "and the stones of Cynewulf's dream Abbey remain Abbot Cynewulf's worry. Per-haps," he added wickedly, spoiling his whole effect for the sake of the pun, "he ought to address the Masons on the subject." He was suddenly delighted with his joke. "That would shake old Barnaby to his masonic foundations." Barnaby was a powerful oil magnate, and nobody laughed. Alfred raced on, expertly. "But to get back to the point, do you really think that all this vast expenditure is necessary for a couple of dozen young men to lead a life of prayer on a mountain in Wales?"

"I guess it can't do no harm, if those guys pray for us guys who spend so much on lobbying and advert-izement," said Jerome Winterton Junior, and immediately looked embarrassed. "I mean—" he shrugged to re-express his idea of a profitable contract, but was fortunately interrupted.

"Would any of you gentlemen like to meet the Abbot?" It was a husky voice, almost a whisper, and it belonged to Paul Summerson-Dupree, a tall, big man in his fifties, head of a large lumber firm which had started in Chatham, Ontario; moved to New York and now had branches scattered all over the United States. He was of French-Canadian origin, and a prominent Catholic. "You, Hayley?" His tone cooled audibly as he said the name.

"Anybody for the Abbot?" Alfred mocked, "not me, thanks. I know him too well already."

"You do?" They looked incredulous. This fellow certainly got around.

"I came across him in England you know," he said, pleased with his effect. "But I was involved in, how shall I put it, a little—*lèse-majesty*—with the venerable Lambertine."

'Why do I do it ?' he thought furiously when they moved away to meet the Abbot. 'What got into me ?' 'Quite apart from anything else, it was a terrible impression to make.' He, the enigmatic Englishman, with the impeccable manner. For so he imagined he was called. But then he reflected that *lèse-majesty* with a Lambertine could add spice to the enigma. He started playing at alliteration: a *contretemps* with a Carmelite, a brush-up with a Benedictine, a dispute with a Dominican. *Lèse-majesty* with a Lambertine. Yes, that was a good exit line, though the others had performed the exit, bowing politely and moving away through the crowds. Even so, tears of rage pricked his eyes as they always did after a loss of temper, or when he felt he had made a fool of himself, or like now, a bit of both. Why had he tried so hard to undermine Cynewulf's efforts? Father Cynewulf, he should say, no, Abbot Cynewulf. 'My Lord Abbot,' he found himself muttering as if in rehearsal of an imagined meeting. He would kneel and kiss the ring, looking up at those coal-black eyes, murmuring 'traitor', then he would rise as the Abbot recognised him with a start, and he would smile contemptuously and turn away.

It was too silly. Had he been talking to himself? Two ladies were staring at him oddly—both daringly elegant in dresses that seemed to get narrower and narrower all the way down—and he was suddenly very much aware of his own eyes, glaring, indeed staring fixedly at the band of tulle over the rounded décolletage of the more mature of the two yet he had not seen her until this very second. He screwed his eyes shut, drank down his whisky, opened them again and looked loftily in another direction. Then he took out his gold pocket-watch, raised his eyebrows at it and started pushing across towards the big glass doors. What did he care? He had forgotten all about Cynewulf Huxley. He didn't even know Huxley had gone over to Rome until he read about his picturesque arrival in the *New York Times*. Everyone seemed to end up in Rome, but he, Alfred Hayley, was clearing out of it.

That night before his train he wrote nine letters of abuse to the Abbot, each begun as a fair copy of the previous, which had become illegible with changes and improvements, anger breeding its own details like mice. Each was torn up, and for once, he tore up the last copy too, suddenly bored, and very much exhausted.

"Hello there," he called in a friendly mock-American voice as he walked up the veranda steps, straw hat in hand, and hailed his wife. "You look as pretty as a picture." She was lying in a wicker chaise-longue, fanning herself slowly with the *Alabama Recorder*, and reading a fashion-paper. He bent down to kiss her, perfunctorily goggling at all those mincing ladies. "Oh, dearest, you're not going to wear *that*?" He read the caption aloud, " 'The transparent corsage should prove one of the most distinctive features of this season's seductions'. And who are we going to seduce this season? 'In one or other of beauty's features,' " he read from the opposite page, " 'you may count yourself less well favoured. But you have (or you would not be reading this), a *sense* of beauty: all other things therefore can be added unto you.' They're certainly making sure of a very wide public!" She turned the page pretending to read as he stroked the back of her neck playfully with one finger, so he straightened up again and declaimed, "O, picturesque persuasions, o elegant confections, o requisite suggestiveness!" He liked to finger through her magazines when she was out of the room, to look at the satin knickers, silky pantalettes, the camisoles of calico, the taffeta jupons with narrow plissé flounces in shallow vandykes, the persuasive tea-gowns and lace bodices. "I'd like to see my darling girl step upon an omnibus in *that* skirt."

"Alfred Hayley, you're a depraved, unnatural man and pray get off my dress pleating."

He had sat down on the edge of the chair extension which creaked, and she had immediately moved her legs away, but a fold of the lemon-yellow muslin draped closely around them was under his thigh.

He shifted it.

"Now Hetty, that's no welcome for a tired, hot and dusty man. My God, this city suit! I should have taken a lighter one to change on the train, but it does make so much more luggage. Oh, bless you, Linda Jane." He had been staring wistfully at her empty glass on the low wicker-table near her, half-longing to scoop up the minted, whiskyish syrup at the bottom, like a child, with his finger, half disgusted in advance by the sweet thirst it would give him. He didn't want Madeira from the carafe either. But here was Linda Jane, trim in her long black gown and stiffly starched cap and apron, carrying an iced tumbler full of freshly sprigged mint julep on a tray. He looked up at her gratefully and immediately felt uneasy. He was always oddly disturbed by the brown blackness of Linda Jane's skin, combined with the black blackness of her dress and the sharp movements of her svelte body. Negroes never affected him one way or the other outside, but here at home, or standing before him now with her waist at eye-level, bob-curtseying and smiling in that parlour-maid outfit, with the white frills and those straight sparkling teeth, she made him each time start too familiarly and end up too brusquely. She knew it, moreover, and was gone in a flash, straight as a young birch. Harriet knew it too—how often had she told him not to say "bless you" to a Negro servant. But she said nothing now and he shrugged.

"What a journey!" he said, mopping his brow. "I travelled down with Benson, you know, Homer Q. Benson." After all this time American names still tickled him, and he repeated it twice with different emphases, which irritated her.

"How was New York?" she asked, not wanting to know, and staring at a photograph of a woman wearing the "Wright" hat, a large straw affair with pointed wings stretching across the front, apparently inspired by the shape of the biplane.

"Hot. Much, much hotter than here, a nasty damp heat. O, for the bal-samic pines, and the gulf breezes, where the great rivers meet at the golden gates to the world of waters," he mimicked the Mobile Hotel ad-vertisements. "And my beloved sits like a fragrant bloom under the richly scented magnolia grandiflora." There was no magnolia immedi-ately around, only a huge oak and a Japan plum, but he got quite worked up by his own parody, so that the thought passed through his mind as he spoke, that her bosom looked most Biblical in its square-necked plissé, she who had sworn—agreeing, for once, with the Vatican—that the new fashions were hideous and indecent and she would never wear them. He thought, too, that the straight cut of the gown made her belly bulge in this sitting position, and that he even wanted her, in a tired, mild way, beyond the grit and clamminess of the journey. She's pretty, he thought. I used to love her, what have I done?

She rose and straightened her dress. "You'd better change, dear. Jack and Ada and the Carolets are coming to dinner."

"Oh, no!" But he was pleased. Pretending before others was easier than pretending to her alone. Either way, she insisted on not being taken in, but at least before others she played the game, and much too well. There was nothing in Europe quite like the American hostess, for conviviality in food and conversation: the more she fed them with the one, the more she devoured them for the other.

As it happened, the Reciprocity Bill was the chief subject of conversa-tion, but Harriet aired her views like a man, a truly modern woman, still, however, in the "Alfred says" stage, though she had ceased to acknowledge the source. And in theory he let her have her way these days because it made a better impression. In practice, he too frequently claimed his due, even correcting her, like a footnote popping up into the text. Tonight, however, he felt tired after his journey and let her hold the floor while he warmed up, butting in only with a grumbling, "This damned government interference," which he would repeat if no one had heard in the general hubbub. "This damned government interference. Typical of the Civil Service mentality." And Jack Morley said something polite about "your author Kipling having loved the British Civil Service so well." For Harriet's father, Mr. William C. Cottrell, was one of the Chief civilian employees of the U.S. Army Corps of Engineers, Mobile District.

But Harriet hadn't been listening. "I just don't get it," she said. "If Taft unites with the Democrats, to reduce duties on imported Canadian lumber and wood pulp and all the rest, in exchange for lower Canadian duties on —well, whatever it is, what's he gonna do when the Democrats go on trying to lower the tariff against protected industries? Which they will, if they get control of Congress this fall."

"Oh, they won't get control, Harriet," said Morley, who was a chubby lawyer, "maybe the Republican majority will come down a few pegs, that's all."

"And who do you think you are, William Jennings Bryan?"

Everyone laughed. The Hayleys had shared a house with Jack Morley and his young wife Ada in their early days of marriage, and the foursome were on very easy terms. Surprisingly the arrangement had worked well: Jack Morley admired Alfred, Ada loved and admired Jack Morley, Harriet adored Ada, admired Morley, loved and respected Alfred. Alfred loved himself, adored Harriet, admired Morley and so on. Mervyn Carolet, however, owned the large sawmill that Alfred bought from, and had taught him much about the different qualities of yellow pine. Their relationship was more distant, more intelligent, more complicated.

"You mark my words, Jack Morley, the Democrats'll make it weigh awkward for the President, and what'll he do then? With half his own party against him! *And* all the lumber states." The second opposition group was clearly the one that would topple the President down.

They were marking her words a little too much, Alfred thought, and decided to recapture the conversation.

"Canada will throw it out," he said oracularly, and added with weight, "I saw Summerson-Dupree in New York. Had dinner with him as a matter of fact." Carolet looked half impressed, half incredulous. Alfred went on: "And he said, 'Hay-ley my friend, don't worry. Sir Wilfrid Laurier may champion it till he sees stars and stripes in his morning tea, but the Maritime Provinces will block it. Canada will throw it out, my boy,' he said." Under the guise of a dinner table imitation he casually revealed the friendly relations still existing between himself and the great Summerson-Dupree. "And I may say," he added, "I agree with him."

"So those damned Loyalist refugees will have their uses yet," said Jack Morley jocularly, and Alfred pretended to look affronted.

"Sir, you are insulting the feathered brood of the Mother Country, sir, you are speaking of the woman I love. I demand an apology in the name of the British Empire, that unique, unprecedented and sunsetless scattering of lands and peoples, that—"

"That great and glorified co-operative store," Jack and Harriet came in together, and though he laughed with the others, for the phrase was his, he also felt annoyed. It was all right for him to use it, he felt, but not for them. The Little Englander vogue had passed and hardly touched him here, and, not being a progressive intellectual, he had never really fallen for it, smart though it had once been. But there was always a wavering double standard in Alfred Hayley which enabled him to be moved by and believe in the subjects of his own parodies. Harriet rang for the next course.

"How was New York?" Carolet asked as Linda Jane came in with the dessert. Alfred looked steadily at Mervyn Carolet, and gave a careful summary of his business achievements, followed, after Linda Jane's exit, by a humorous version of the Abbot's visit. He was glad of this opportunity to account for his time in front of Harriet, without appearing to be doing so.

"And he's only thirty-nine, you know. It's a strange story altogether."

"He should have come to Mobile, he'd have been lionised," said Mrs. Carolet, who was a Catholic. "I hope he was successful?"

"As a matter of fact, I don't think he was," Alfred replied with satisfaction. "New York seemed to be far more interested in the arrival of Teddy Roosevelt, after all that time in the African jungle and all those splendidly platitudinous speeches to every crowned head in Europe. Everyone was asking, would he run again for president? No he would not, but he would talk, and talk he certainly did. A lot of people are finding the Abbot's visit very awkward, and what with the Ballinger investigation, well, a Lambertine abbey in Wales seems rather remote."

"But what about the Catholics?" Mrs. Carolet persisted, shocked by his levity.

He smiled.

"Some of them, I believe, even hinted that his lordship should stop begging. I read that one anonymous benevolence is paying his fare on a luxury liner to Trinidad, where he will sing a pontifical Mass on the Feast of the Assumption. I can just see it, five dozen pretty negro choristers and acolytes in scarlet cassocks and snow-white cottas, the clerks of the crozier and mitre in white, those of the book and bugia in black. Typical of Urbs Eterna, and Father Cynewulf Huxley will love such 'picturesque persuasions'."

His tone had become so wicked that the ladies looked embarrassed, without quite knowing what by. Mrs. Carolet assumed that her religion had been affronted and was silent. Ada was puzzled and looked at Harriet and Harriet, who had been trying to stop her husband with glares as matriarchal as she could muster, decided it was time to withdraw.

'She hasn't the figure for the scabbard line,' Alfred thought as he watched the women hobble out past Carolet who was holding the door. He remembered the two ladies at the Plaza reception and now quite unaccountably recalled overhearing the older one saying to the other, "My dear, his beard tickled my décolletage." Yet he could have sworn he hadn't heard it at the time, so lost was he in his own thoughts.

He had a feeling there would be a scene that night and there was. He hated scenes, for he always came out of them in a more hysterical state than she did. It was as if she created them solely in order to unload her own hysteria on to him, for after the scorn, the sarcasm and the implied accusations, she emerged calmly as she had begun, leaving him to plead or cry with rage or fling out of the house in a fury that took hours to abate. But then she always said he started them, with his goading, and his boasting, and his cutting remarks. And above all, his lies. "Why can't you ever tell the truth, Alfred Hayley," she would ask, more like an impatient mother than a frantic wife, "at least to me?" Yet it was to her of all people that he had to tell lies, meaningless lies, pointless lies, lies sometimes just for the sake of lies, he never even knew why. If she asked what time he had left work he told her half an hour later, if she asked, had he stopped by at Mrs. Mudie's, he said yes if he hadn't and no if he had, and if she asked had he remembered to pick up that book he'd promised, he would hide it and say he'd forgotten, and then bring it the following day. It was an obsession, of which he knew the cause, but not the cure. The cause was past—he had got into the way of it when he was seeing Cleo, Cleo, whom he called Leo (and himself Sylvester Pope), Cleo who let him love her any way he liked.

It was no use, he had to go upstairs, he couldn't drag it out here much longer, merely in the hope that she would be asleep. She wouldn't. But still he lingered.

He picked up the novel she was reading from the table by the settee: *The Rosary*, by Florence L. Barclay. Oh, yes, everyone was reading it. He flicked through it idly and was suddenly absorbed. The hero, called Garth Dalmain, who wore a purple shirt, was obviously going to fall in love with the Hon. Jane Champion, who had just exquisitely rendered, seated at the Bechstein among aristocratic guests in a country house, a beautiful song :

> *The hours I spent with thee, dear heart, Are as a string of*
> *pearls to me,*
> *I count them over, every one of them apart, My rosary! My*
> *rosary!*

That was rather fine, he thought. And a brown slender body with small pointed breasts and buttocks came before his eyes, between his hands, between his thighs, with a bare-teethed laugh.

How fast we think and dream—only a few minutes—though fantasy can last a lifetime. She had been brushing her hair and was twisting it round and up for the night when he went in, so tired that for one flash he saw his mother there—no, it was a trick of the brown hair on the plump neck-line and the old-fashioned dark bedroom gown with a peplum skirt effect. The face in the mirror was Harriet's, watchful but not tender. "What have you been doing? Dear?"

"Oh, just finishing off a pipe, jotting down notes for a report."

She placed the last hairpin in silence. Then at last:

"Touching, the Morley's belief in you as a man of contacts, isn't it? Sir Wilfrid Laurier indeed!"

"Oh, God, Harriet, don't start on that."

He gazed ceilingwards in exasperation and with an exaggerated sigh sat down on the clothes-chest and started unlacing his shoes.

"And don't you pretend God is on top of that closet looking down on your martyrdom. 'Cos He ain't." She overdid the lowcaste Americanism just to annoy him.

"Oh, really, Harriet, this is too much. I'm very tired. Do I have to ac-count for every thing I say to my guests?"

"How can I believe a word you say when you just never tell the truth?"

"SHUT UP, will you?"

"And don't you shout at me, Alfred Hayley, how dare you! And you might consult me before you write back home to that aristocrat family of yours that your marriage is breaking up. Look what your kid sister had the nerve to write me." She threw a letter at him, all crumpled into a ball, and it hit his nose. He muttered, "Kid sister, indeed!" but Harriet had sud-denly smashed through her own isolationism, and nothing could stop her. "Oh, I can just imagine what you wrote, one of your weighty packets, pages and pages to *Dearest Mother*"—she imitated Victorian English—"all about your poor dear wife whom you are forced by tragic circumstances to leave, for though she is a dear dear girl and means well, she really isn't quite-quite, or up to your social and intellectual standards, indeed she is just a little bit imbecile—or perhaps the lady is no lady sir, and ran off with a bounder, sir, to your eternal shame and sorrow—or maybe you discovered a past for her, as a fallen woman, in the sporting houses of New Orleans, things too terrible to speak of, too sullied for your mother's ears. Your heart was broken, of course, but you managed to slip in a page or so on divorce being not quite so unacceptable socially on this side the Atlantic, indeed not at all in some states, that she must understand, we're in the twentieth century now and things have changed since the death of the old Queen . . ."

In spite of much experience with him Harriet had not yet learnt that one must never hit the nail on the head.

He stood as if his feet had taken root in the rushwork matting, and stared at her with bulging half-demented eyes. His face went pale, then would flush suddenly and go pale again as her words poured hot over his mind and his mind refused to melt or flare to anger but kept iced and isolated in the one idea, how to behave as becomes a gentleman, that she might feel outdone, worsted, humiliated, small. Slowly he came to life and moved nobly to the door, opened it, stepped out, shut it without a sound, and even downstairs allowed himself only the gentlest slam, just loud enough to let her hear, and know that Linda Jane would have heard, that he had gone out. He started walking towards the town, gripped with suffused pleasure under a deadly calm.

The fury came through gradually, like a blood-transfusion.

"How does she expect me to read a letter if she insults me the whole time?" he justified himself as he walked, and his anger rose and lasted all the way into town before he realised he had nowhere to go. The car-lines of Dauphin Street stretched away in a glitter between the narrowing parallels of smaller and smaller gaslights. He walked for two hours, down to the harbour and out into a suburb and back again along the broad oak avenues and on beneath the banana trees until at last the warm breeze made him languorous, so that his rage evaporated in the fragrance and he only felt foot-sore. He didn't quite know where he was, but a saloon was open and he went in, just to sit down.

It was pretty dismal. Three girls in low bright bodices sat together drinking, looking bored. Two men were asleep with their heads down among the glasses of another table. A morose game of poker was being played next to them and beyond that a gentleman was drunkenly pawing at the transparent corsage of a bosomy woman with yellow hair piled like a bird's nest from her eyebrows upwards. Behind a segregating slatted screen a presumably Negro or Creole pianist was strumming a slow drag with a monotonous base on an upright that sounded as tinny as a nickelodeon. The carved walnut of the vast Victorian bar matched the face of the man behind it.

The darker of the three girls got up and swayed towards him but he waved her away and she skulked back with a toss of her Spanish-looking head. He ordered a large bourbon-and-water, drank it down and ordered another, then settled down to read Cordelia's letter to Harriet, smoothing it out on the table. It was just as he expected, ingratiating and mock innocent and all about the joy they had all felt that their brother was so happy at last, and married to such a sweet and sensible girl, and surely she was not going to throw all that away. Her brother, she knew, had a difficult character. Then followed a detailed analysis, with poisonous hints on how to manage him. Her mother, she said, never read his huge letters, but gave them to her to prune. Thus she had come to understand him, perhaps better than anyone, even his wife, for sometimes it happened that a man could pour out his soul to his mother yet be a stranger to the woman he loved. And so on. It made him ill with rage, and suddenly he felt that hot tears were streaming down his face underneath the hand that shaded his eyes from the gaslight.

He was face to face with himself, and wanted to escape. He glared through his fingers at the blonde woman's low corsage and the plump gentleman's white hand roving over it as he kissed her, and he felt nothing but disgust.

How could he have entered such a place, dragged here his innocent little sister's letter to his dear sweet wife, now of all times? He called for madeira and thought tearfully of Cleo, suddenly, obsessively, oh my beloved sits beneath the cedars of Lebanon, she is black but comely, listen, oh ye daughters of Jerusalem, as the tents of Kedar, as the curtains of Solomon, and her breasts are as two young roes that are twins, her lips drop as the honeycomb, honey and milk are under her tongue and the smell of her garments is like the smell of Lebanon spikenard and saffron, calamus and cinnamon, myrrh and aloes. Awake O north wind and come thou south. O felix culpa. Well, God made us mortal and imperfect, didn't He? What does He expect? The wages of death is sin. Mortal sin. A sin is only mortal, surely, if it dies, and one no longer suffers agonies at the mere thought of it. Other men, he knew, took this sort of thing in their stride, but he was not as other men. He had a soul, a great spirit. He Suffered.

He was in a blabbering state by now, not from drink, but from emotion: "My God, my God," he reiterated, and thought he was praying, but saw only two slim white hands on the hips of a crimson satin skirt. Then a finger touched his ear. He jerked up and gestured her off, looking down fixedly at his pocket as he fumbled for money.

The stars were so bright and he didn't know where he was. On the glass door was a small and dog-eared notice in clumsy print, *Porter King, player of ragtime, from* 12.30. The houses were low, mostly one-storey, a few sticking out from the row with a second. Where could he go?

Not the Motleys, who thought them the happiest couple aside themselves. It occurred to him as he walked away that if he and Harriet were to divorce after all they would have to leave Mobile first, pretend to go far north to one of the lumber states there, and in fact go and get divorced somewhere. Then New York, and freedom. A big anonymous city. Cleo had gone to New York. But he would never find her.

Where could he go? Carolet? He'd be shocked. He'd read him a lecture on the Church and divorce, what could it matter as long as he didn't remarry? As if he would, good Lord, no never again.

As a matter of fact Carolet wasn't a bad idea. He could talk to him in such a way that he would certainly keep his mouth shut should they want it kept secret, yet have the right version should the secret leak out. But no, after all, her parents lived in Mobile and they'd have her version. He was back near the centre of the town. A late hackney carriage cloppeted slowly down the avenue, back from its last hire. He hailed it and the driver shook his head.

"I'll make it worth your while," he shouted. But he didn't want to go home.

"Take me along the Bay Shell road," he ordered, "until I tell you to come back."

"The horse is tired, sir."

"So am I. And I have to think. You can go slowly. I'll pay you double, man, three dollars."

"Night rate's two dollars, sir."

"Four then, five, you scoundrel, move on." He sank back on the soft plush, and cried silently, as the oak trees moved slowly on either side, and the city was left behind, with its tropical plants and its hothouse smell. "Oh God, I love her," he muttered without having a clear image of anyone, as the large Spanish-style residences passed by, their gardens full of Japan plum and feathery china vie. "Oh God save my marriage," he prayed at the magnolia groves and the moss-laden cypresses, "it's such a beautiful thing, the most beautiful thing I know, I've ever known," he murmured soundlessly at the dark bay that glimpsed at every turn of thought between square minarets and baytrees, beyond the orange groves and vineyards of scuppernong.

It was four o'clock when Alfred Hayley crept back into his own small house, up the stairs, and into his dressing room, where he slept exhausted on the couch, like many a married man before and since.

His great daredevil tempt-God plans had quite dissolved into the night, the devil being bored and God, at this particular moment, understandably deaf.

13

THE GIRL looked like a prince from pantomime as she stepped proudly out of her changing cubicle on the pier at Daphne. Her bathing dress was of white washing-satin braided with black and scarlet embroidery. Her black hair was tucked into a white cap of almost Gainsborough size and style, with only the sweeping feather lacking, but a few curls peered from the top with a carelessness that must have taken twenty minutes to achieve. Her legs were crisscrossed with black braid and she was carrying her bathing robe like an unwanted cloak.

Every single person sitting along the pier, in front of their fretwork cabins or under the colourful belvederes, turned to stare at her as she walked boldly past them towards the end of the pier that stretched on pilings far over the tidal flats to where the water was deep enough for swimming. It was as if she had chosen one of the first cubicles on purpose for this parade, and her eyes, but not her face, smiled straight ahead at the western shore just visible on the other side of the bay, or at the Belle of Daphne, which puffed slowly over from Mobile, bringing more visitors to the popular resort. But she was really smiling at herself, for stirring as much interest as a famous beauty entering a carnival ballroom, possibly more.

"Disgusting," said Harriet Cottrell, who was sitting on the wooden steps of the Cottrell cabin. She wore a considerably more wholesome array of red and navy serge, with a pouched front and a big sailor collar, and though the skirt was short, at least the knickerbockers reached below her knees and besides, black stockings made all the difference.

The eyes of Mr. Cottrell and Mr. Alfred Hayley followed the white prince, their lips murmuring something appropriate like well, well, what will they think of next, though Alfred Hayley was in fact more shocked than he showed. Satin, he had noticed, became like skin when wet, and this girl seemed to have—he wondered, had she *anything* on underneath?

Mrs. Cottrell, who sat, like them, in a wicker chair, under a huge pink and yellow umbrella, had plenty on underneath, and looked voluminous in black and white stripes, with enormous sleeves and a veil over her straw hat, as if she were going driving. And indeed her straight-front corset gave her a curious air of bowing to the populace from a royal carriage. She had placed the unpacked picnic basket on the table when Harriet had emerged in her bathing dress, so that from where Alfred sat he could hardly see more than the top of Harriet's head. To prevent him seeing even that, Mrs. Cottrell kept leaning forward and shifting her white lace parasol, which she carried even in the shade of the big umbrella.

"Harriet, dear, you must either go down into the water or put your clothes back on. You can't sit around in that."

"Oh, Marm, plenty of people do. See there?"

Mrs. Cottrell turned her head regally first to one side, then to the other. What went on below and beyond, in the sea, since this mixed bathing had come into fashion, she preferred not to find out, she could hear it all from a distance, for all she knew they even touched each other. But the family groups were all sitting fully dressed around the bathhouses or outside their cabins, protected from the sun by coloured awnings or wooden roofs with arabesque ornamentations like frills. Further along the pier, right out in the open, four adventurous young men in white flannels were playing shuttlecock and battledore, looking very red in the face, trying perhaps to develop a British colonial tan. And down on the flats a party of young people were ostensibly looking for shells or crabs in the driftwood and the sandy pools; there were five or six girls among them, all in wet and bathing dresses, red, blue, black, and one very gay in black and yellow, surrounded by at least ten men, also straight from the sea. It was no doubt very smart and daring of them, there was much laughter, chattering, giggling and screaming just audible as sand was thrown over the wet galatea and the black stockinged legs, and bold male hands patted it away.

Mrs. Cottrell's eyes paused in their round for one moment of horror that was immediately censored into ladylike distaste. "Harriet, child, you do as I say."

"I'm *not* a child, Marm."

"Just so," said her father, who added quickly, under Mrs. Cottrell's glare, "and don't you argue with your mother."

Alfred had kept carefully out of it, his head tilted slightly back as if he were admiring the rich men's houses on top of the tall red buffs or red and ochre clay, with pines and willow-oak clambering up and the rickety wooden steps with driftwood railings clambering down. He was torn between two poses—that of the worldly-wise and courteous gentleman for the parents, and for Harriet, that of a slightly *roué* young charmer, with an expert eye for women, but enslaved now and ready to be reformed by a dear sweet girl. She was looking at him, so he risked a sidelong glance of appraisal over the strange goings-on down on the tidal flats, as well as a quick turn of the head towards the prince-girl, who was wading out in the water. Then he said amiably:

"Well, dearest, since you've changed, you might as well have a dip. Why not come along with me? May I, Mrs. Cottrell? I promise to look after her, and will give my life, if necessary, to rescue her from drowning." He got up and bowed with exaggerated courtesy, as if he were begging for the honour of a dance, which was rather absurd since he had been waiting for her to change. His sandy hair tufted up on his bumpy brow, and he looked pink and white and very skinny in his long blue striped bathing costume. But Mrs. Cottrell couldn't help smiling and gave a motherly nod.

"You run along, you two young people, why, that's what we came here for. Such a charming young man," she said to her husband as she watched him escort Harriet up the pier and help her down the wooden steps that led into the shallow water. "I'm so very glad Harriet's gotten herself affianced to him, and not to that unpromising Judd boy, why, I wouldn't trust him with my daughter any more than I would trust a bandsman in the park. He's a nobody, a second son of a small town buggy-maker that's gotten wealthy scraping a few hundred dollars to place a new brand of horse-less carriage on the market. My word, anyone can do that, and Johnny

Judd don't even want to do that, he's kind of aimless. But Alfred, he's alto-gether different. A little older, for one, more serious."

"Yeah, he's doing fine, for twenty-eight. But that about trusting, you know, it's funny, but that's just one word I wouldn't use about my future son-in-law."

"Why, Mr. Cottrell, what *do* you mean?"

"I dunno, it's hard to explain. Oh, I like him, I think he's fine, just fine. Very entertaining, and cultured, oh yes, very cultured, and a most proper young man. I guess he'll go far. Very far. I'd even say I have faith in him. But trust, is that quite the same thing, I wonder?"

"There you go again, Bill Cottrell, splitting hairs and playing with words. Why can't you talk so's other people can understand, and say just what you mean in black and white?" She heaved a very understandable striped bosom.

"I don't mean anything much, Sarah dear. It's just that he seems to ex-cite some suspicion in business circles. And yet, when I press it, nobody can lay their finger on just what it is. He's never been in trouble or any-thing like that. It's just a kind of vague unease people feel about him. 'The reason why I cannot tell. I only know and know it well, I do not love thee, Dr. Fell.' That's what one guy said."

"Well, I declare, if you go listening to guys! He's a most civilised young man, and by the bye, I don't approve of your remarks about Hetty's, well, womanly attributes, it was *most* embarrassing for her, *and* in front of her future husband too."

"I guess he must have noticed them by now."

"Why, you depraved unnatural man, Bill Cottrell." But she threw him a pleased flirtatious look, for she had a tendency to take all his references to unmentionable female attributes as a sign of awareness and therefore a compliment to herself, since she had them too. "He's only a boy, for all his grown-up airs, you know, a most proper young man. And a real gentle-man. You wouldn't want him to think we're barbarians, would you, Mr. Cottrell?"

Meanwhile the civilised and proper young man, the boy, the gentleman, was jumping the gentle waves so as not to wet himself, and sending in between them great splashes of sea water over his future wife, who screamed with delighted shock each time and splashed him back, and jumped the gentle waves as well.

The group of young people from the beach had rushed down for another bathe, and the water seemed to be full of white arms like windmills and sailor collars and large colourful caps bobbing up and down, though some of the men actually swam, and quite far out. Showing off, Alfred thought sourly, for he couldn't swim. But the prince-girl was also swimming, at least, she wasn't among the bobbers and paddlers, and a white cap floated in the distance.

"There's going to be a jubilee," one of the young men was shouting, skipping with great splashes from one person to another. "Tonight, probably, the old fisherman said so, from the way the dolphins are fidgeting. You must come, are you coming? We must all come. You coming, Ted? You, Herb?"

"What's a jubilee?" Alfred asked. Harriet as they sat chest deep in the water, wet at last, and hand in hand.

"Oh, it's wonderful. Whole walls of shrimp about two miles long come marching up on the beach. Then crab, about an hour later. They hide under the logs and driftwood. Then the flounders, like a silver barricade. Last time I was fifteen, and we were here on holiday, we'd taken one of those houses up on the cliff, with my cousins, and we all sat up round a huge fire with all the shore people, who were ready with baskets and big boxes with ice. We cooked flounder over the fire and ate crab gumbo for weeks. It sure was wonderful." She had got very excited as she described this fairytale scene, and he watched her glistening arms gesticulating the whole crustacean cavalcade, and the small waves lapping at her navy blue bosom.

"Oh dearest, can't we stay up tonight for it? Just you and I? A sort of silver jubilee, in advance, and in secret? To celebrate our future happiness?"

She looked at him tenderly, touched by the pretty compliment. But at once she said,

"Oh no! Ma would never let me do that."

"I know she wouldn't, dear. I meant, couldn't you escape, after they'd gone to bed, for a few hours?"

"Alfred! What can you be thinking of?"

"Oh, my sweet, nothing, nothing wrong, I do assure you. It's only that, well, I never seem to be alone with you."

"You're alone with me now!"

"Alone! Sitting in the water surrounded with two dozen people?"

"Well what *do* you want?"

"I want to kiss you. I want to hold you." His tone was so intense and he had moved up so close she was frightened. But he held her down tight as she moved to stand up out of the water, and she fell back in, losing her red cap and her head went under for a moment. She came up red and spluttering, her piled brown hair soaked, some of it crawling round her neck like small Medusa snakes. His shock at seeing her like this, no maiden-blossom now, was almost as great as hers for the violence, and he could only stare at her in fascinated horror. His mind below his mind kept repeating a four-letter word like a bass drum to what his upper mind was thinking, which was that she looked dreadful, below the words his voice was saying, which were, "Here is your cap."

"Hetty, my dear, forgive me, I didn't mean it." He splashed after her as she waded towards the steps. Thank God, he thought, they were almost under the pier when it happened. "It was horrid of me," he panted, "oh dearest, it was the beast in me, it's been so long, oh my dear, dear one, forgive me, you must understand, all men are beasts, it's the ape in us, but women are angels, oh please, it was only because I love you so, you're an angel . . ."

In spite of his fondness for the *grande passion* line, with its dark hints of uncontrollable desires and rich interior life, he didn't like to shout too loud, and his voice seemed to be lost in the rumble of the waves and the yells of other bathers further out. But she turned on the word angel, having decided to smile bravely through the tears, some of which at least were of sea water.

"I forgive you," she said with the water pouring down her serge suit and black stockings. "I forgive you."

He was a little disappointed, but he said with a tremor, "You do, don't you? Oh, what a dear sweet girl you are," and became swiftly and truly overjoyed.

But as they splashed their way out he saw emerging from the waves, up the next steps further down the pier, Venus in white so clinging that her breasts almost showed through, and, as she turned, her shoulder-blades and the hollow of her back. He couldn't resist taunting Harriet, and stopped to stare openly. Some of the young men had swum after her and were hailing her from the bottom of the steps, inviting her to join their party, but she was already on the pier. She picked up her bathing robe, wrapped herself up and walked on with her wide-capped head held high.

"Alfred, how dare you!"

He was pleased.

"Well, my dear, you must admit she attracts the eye, if nothing else. But as a matter of fact I was only trying to hear what these people were saying about her, the little hoyden. Listen."

An animated discussion about the origin of the white prince was going on among the young men swimming about between these steps and the next. A lady from New York, a Senator's daughter, a Florida beauty, a Mexican, a Southern belle from New Orleans, no local lady.

"No lady at all," Harriet said to Alfred, firmly.

"One last dip?" he suggested casually.

And the noise of their quick motion as they emerged together from the water was like the sound of a rushing mighty wind, so that he felt immensely purified.

"I'm getting married to my beloved soon," he said, "to my darling, sweet, forgiving, understanding girl, oh, you can't know, my angel, in your dear, dear innocence, how much I love and adore you, worship and want you—at my side, in my daily life," he added quickly, for she had looked slightly askance at the word "want".

She did, however, escape that night, very quietly, for two hours. And they crept down the ghost-brown cliff, along the driftwood steps where every clump and stump was overhung with sad Spanish moss, and from behind a willow-oak they watched the crowd down on the beach, sitting on old raincoats and carriage rugs and logs around the roaring fire, waiting for the crabs and silver flounders, singing and talking. And there he held her at last, and raised her moonlit face to his and kissed her so that now at last she knew what he meant by "want", and guessed, with a thrill of shame, what all those hints of the beast in man were about.

The crowd was quietening into drowsy silence, dropping off one by one, then suddenly someone shouted. For a mile or more down the beach, a wall of tiny shrimp came up out of the sea, surging up and falling back with the waves. The people woke up and shouted, scrambling for their baskets. The silver jubilee had begun.

"You shall not crucify mankind on a cross of gold."

A William Jennings Bryan slogan for Free Silver shouted at him from the station platform, scratched and tattered from the depression years, as he stepped out of the train at St. Louis, and he said to himself dramatically, This is It, This is the Sign.

Of course, he could have interpreted the Sign in precisely the opposite way, the cross of gold signifying Roman extravagance. But it was the moment that mattered, the blurred spiritual connotation of the words so clearly thrown at him, and him alone, in such a prosaic and materialistic context as a business trip, which made him see at once that this was the end of the journey, peace and virtue and holy matrimony, love is God and God is love, and all roads lead to Rome.

He called at once on the Archbishop, whom he had met at a luncheon in Mobile, and the Archbishop received him of course most graciously. They discussed for many hours, in the archiepiscopal library, Transubstantiation and the full meaning of *Tu es petrus*, which George Tyrrell had suggested might be translated as "You're a brick", and how it was such a pity that the Church had never really recovered from not listening to St. Hilary; and the objectivity of absolution and the curious fact that the word "mass" originally meant dismissal, which was a divine paradox indeed; and how Catholics in England now tended to say "the Sacrament" or "going to Church" because "mass" had become so terribly Anglican. And the Archbishop was profoundly interested in his opinion on all these things. They continued talking well into the night, covering the Pauline idea of grace and the inscrutable wisdom of the Church in both having and not having Saint Augustine; and the Augsburg and Würtemberg Confessions, and how the ending of the 17th Article in the Anglican Prayer Book, on Predestination, contradicted the beginning, which was typical of perfidious Albion, who wanted to be both Catholic and Protestant at the same time; and how now some people were even trying to establish communion with the Schismatic Eastern Church; all of which led, rather neatly, to the Athanasian and Nicene Creeds, the *filioque* clause and *theoticos* versus *Christicos*, so that he could slip in his excellently witty *mot* about St. Cyril, "who was a cad, if ever there was one." Then the Archbishop said he had never met a convert who needed less instruction, and he offered him a bed in the Palace for the night, and received him into the Church early the following morning, in his private chapel.

All this occurred in Alfred Hayley's richly furnished mind as he walked past the cascades of the wide avenue, flanked with pleasure-domes like sugared wedding-cakes, in the Louisiana Purchase Exhibition scheduled for 1903, which had opened only the previous week, a whole year late. He was trying to find the Lumber Pavilion, but the crowds were steering him like a ball in a mechanical game, from one brass bandstand to another, from *The Washington Post* and *The Union Forever*, to the *Hunky Dory Cakewalk*, *Smoky Mokes* or *At a Georgia Camp Meeting*, with flugelhorns and silver comets, euphoniums and sousaphones, but at last to the Lumber Pavilion. For he had come to St. Louis, as he had quipped to his young wife, whom he adored, to see a man about a log, and now it looked mightily as if he were also and subsequently to see another man about a dogma, or two.

The actual facts which Alfred Hayley lived and then somehow forgot, were that the Monsignor assisting the Archbishop was in conference, but a Jesuit priest called Father Le Gardeur, S.J., gave him the name of another priest in Mobile, Father Larkin, who would be very pleased to advise him and instruct him in the faith, of which he must first make quite sure, in view of his recent marriage into an episcopal family, which came, moreover, as he said, from Pennsylvania and of Quaker stock. "By all means mention my name," said Father Le Gardeur, a little, as if that name were to send great herds of swine crashing into Mobile Bay, "and God be with you, my boy."

Which He was, for a year or two.

But what is that devil that gets into a man when he is visiting a town on business, away for a day or so from a happy married home of two or perhaps three years' standing? Spots he would never even have entered when he was living in New Orleans, now called to him from a distance, turning him into a frightened but imaginative sightseer, with one hand holding, in the safety of his hotel bed, a Blue Book of the Red Light district, and the other absentmindedly caressing his own body under the sheet.

There were bagnios, cribs and honky-tonk saloons, and clubs called parlours and vaudeville theatres and pool halls and restaurants and confectionery stalls, and minstrel shows and buck and wing dancers and the negro bands up in Lincoln Park and Milneburg the dance resort up on Lake Pontchartrain. There was a photograph of some dancehall or amusement arcade, next to a shop which had RUBBER GOODS in very large letters right across the top, and Toilet Articles in very small letters above that, and Electrical Batteries in even smaller ones on the glass below. The caption said "Everything in the line of hilarity."

There was the Rosebud Café and Frank Early's, and Lulu White, Mulatto proprietress of Mahogany Hall in Basin Street, and Madam Mame de Ware who had two houses, one with white girls and one with coloured. But that was all beyond the pale, uptown, North of Canal Street, West of Basin, in the district so thoughtfully set up by Alderman Sidney Story for the segregation of vice. Where, as Charlie Watts had described to him once, the negro boys swept out the honkytonks at dawn, after the cattlemen, the business travellers, and the rich idle, local sports had gone, the dapper macks and sweet-back men in their stetsons, box-back coats and St. Louis flat shoes, the earliest pool-playing sports not due as yet, the shuttered bordellos quiet, the madams and the girls all fast asleep. Perdido Street, without even a sidewalk, where the negroes lived in squalor in low little broken houses, by the gasworks.

He turned to the French Quarter. That was more like it, everything civilised. He saw himself for a moment as a rich plantation owner, lordly freeing in his Will his negro mistress and all their sons, thus creating a noble line of the Creole Aristocracy, as described in the novels of G. W. Cable; and they would live in one of those magnificent Old Creole residences that piled up arches as on a square coliseum.

It was, however, a little late for the freeing of slaves. But not too late to —he looked at his watch. Just once.

And once upon that time was Cleo, and Cleo was truly amazing. And the Louisville and Nashville great Trunk Line was called the old reliable, only five hours from Mobile to New Orleans, leaving at 4.30. And of many business trips to Birmingham, or Montgomery, and especially Tuscaloosa, to see to the lumber rafts sent down the Alabama, or to St. Louis, to hand in for some reason in person his reports to the Forestry Conservation Commission, somehow did not end up in Birmingham, Tuscaloosa, Montgomery, or St. Louis.

"And what has my intelligent darling been reading in my regretted absence?" he asked on the evening of his return from what looked, alas, like the last of these trips, shortly after they had moved into a new house, leaving the multiplying Morleys to theirs.

He was sitting at the upright piano, playing softly but watching her out of the corner of his eye as she sat sewing in the big basket-chair, in the light of the muslin-shaded standard lamp. The question sounded natural enough, for Harriet belonged to the Ladies' Browning Club and to the local Women's Suffrage Society, which, however, was a very genteel affair, since women already had the ballot in Wyoming, Utah, Colorado and Idaho, and the rest were bound to follow. So useful, a Federation, Alfred would say, one can achieve progress without anyone noticing. But in fact he was trying to get her onto the subject of a particular book, which he hoped she would have found in the silk pocket of his wicker suitcase. Surely she couldn't have missed it?

"As a matter of fact I've been reading your Bible, your English Bible, your Revised Version, that is."

"Oh, really?"

That wasn't what he meant at all, and he didn't feel in the mood for another religious discussion. His fingers moved rapidly over the keys in a sudden bit of extempore that would either drown further conversation or provoke into words the unspoken tension between them. But then he caught the mockery in her glance, and stopped.

"I trust you found the Bible as—er—illuminating as ever?"

"Certainly. That was your intention, wasn't it?"

"My intention?"

He got up, took his pipe from the ashtray on top of the piano and walked over to the centre table, which was covered with faded damasc reaching down to the ground. Some of her sewing things were lying on her side of it, though she had a small worktable of her own in front of her. He picked up her scissors and started cleaning out his pipe with them.

"Alfred, do you mind?"

"Oh. Sorry darling."

There was a silence.

"What did you mean by 'my intention' just now?"

She smiled to herself. Then she put down her sewing, got up and walked over to her desk, with such a swish of her accordion-pleated skirt along the floor he half expected it to wheeze out a tune. Suddenly she was facing him on the other side of the table, holding his Bible.

"*This* was lodged, like a pressed flower, between the pages of Solomon's Song, which describes, as you know, the graces of the Church. I guess it has some kind of spiritual, or perhaps a sentimental value?"

She was grinning as she waved before his nose a slip of paper on which he had written, years ago it seemed, the address used for messages both by Cleo and Dan Carter, whose flat he sometimes borrowed: *A. N. Hayley, P.O. Box 459, New Orleans, La., Nov. 9th 1905.* He laughed. Was that all?

"Well, what about it? That's my business address in New Orleans."

"Nothing *about* it. I just wondered why it was among certain much underlined passages in The Song of Solomon, and why the Bible was left on *my* bedside table. You were certainly making sure I'd find it. Like the other book."

His heart missed a beat.

"The *other* . . . book?"

So she had found it. He felt slightly sick with excitement. What luck about that address in the Bible. He hadn't intended that, but now it would give added spice to her suspicions.

"Oh yes, I found it all right, just as you hoped I would." She dived down into the deep silk pouch of her worktable and fished out the little Blue Book. With a great gurgle in her voice she read out the passage he had marked down the side ("you sure do like marking things, Alfred Hayley," she said by way of introduction):

" 'Antonia P. Gonzalez, Corner Villere and Iberville Streets. The above party has always been a headliner among those who keep first-class Octoroons. She also has the distinction of being the only singer of Opera and Female Cornetist in the Tenderloin. She has had offers after offers to leave her present vocation and take to the stage but her vast business has kept her among friends. Any person out for fun among a lot of pretty Creole damsels, here is the place to have it.' And what exactly did Madam Antonia P. Gonzalez sing for you, *Ritorna Vincitor* from *Aida*? Did she perhaps play *Creole Belles* for you on her silver cornet? Or *When the Saints Go Marching In*? No doubt she is one of those pious Latin Senoras who have a holy picture of the madonna overlooking the proceedings? Or a crucifix, perhaps? Alfred Hayley Es-quire, what *do* you take me for?"

Somehow he didn't notice that gurgle in her voice, and put his face in his hands.

"Oh, my darling, I'm so dreadfully ashamed. Such depths of iniquity, oh, if you could only understand how a man's soul needs to sink into the abyss, it's a sort of purification, a—"

"Don't you give me that mud-nostalgia stuff. This isn't the eighties in Paris France, it's the twentieth century in Mobile Alabama for heaven's sake. You bore me, Alfred Hayley, what are you trying to do, make yourself interesting? You'd interest me more if you could behave like a normal, home-loving, domesticated American husband."

He was furious, but after a smouldering of silent rage, followed by a pathetic attempt to convince her that his sins were scarlet, he took his cue and confessed that it had all been a childish subterfuge to make her jealous, because of course he loved his dear sweet girl more than anything in the world, he had been so afraid of losing her love, she was so true and straight and good for him, his need of her was greater than ever, and he would take her to England, to meet his people, and they would have a little Queen Anne house in a quiet London square and lots of little Queen Anne children. At which she smiled dutifully and said, "What nonsense you do talk, my love."

But a cold misery of humiliation penetrated him for days and even weeks, though he managed to cover it up, and the outer covering eventually melted it away. For his Shulamite Octoroon was real. But he had found her gone, to try her luck in Harlem, backed, it was quite clear from Madam Tonia's shifty eyes, by a visiting New York pimp. And without a word to him. "What about Rita," said Madame Tonia, "or Marie-Claire?" But he had turned away in anger and disgust. As if that was all he wanted.

He kept, however, the slip of paper with his Box Office address, which Harriet had so ironically replaced inside his Bible. But he moved it two pages on, at the book of Isaiah, just about where the great prophet proclaimed, Come now, let us reason together, saith the Lord.

14

"COME, SIR, be reasonable, and hear me out at least."
"I have heard all I wish to hear, young man, and just about seen enough of you too." Sir Cedric drew himself up on his undoubted dignity. "And you have heard all that I have to say, which is, since you insist on prolonging this discussion as if I had not said it, you are to leave my house immediately. Not tomorrow, not after dinner, not after luncheon but Now. Good morning."

The planners of scenes-in-the-library always assume that the defeated party will retreat first, leaving them in possession, especially since they usually do own the place in fact. So they lord it by the fireplace while the underdog stands sheepishly near the door—a position quite untactical in modern warfare. And Alfred was a most modern young man.

He stood in front of the door, just by the brand new Globe Wernicke bookcases, and spread his arms dramatically.

"It's all a terrible mistake." He spoke breathlessly but fast, as if well rehearsed. "My mouth is sealed by a sense of honour that is stronger than the mere desire to clear my good name. But one day you will find out the truth, Sir Cedric, and then I hope you will suffer, just a little, in the hardness of your heart over the man whom you so unjustly allowed to be wrongly accused."

"Will you let me pass, sir!"

"I will, sir." He stepped smartly aside and opened the door, intoning at his lifted finger, "Surgentes testes iniqui, quae ignorabam interrogabant me. Retribuebant mihi mala pro bonis, sterilitatern animae meae."

"The man is mad," said Sir Cedric to himself as he walked down the carpeted corridor to the breakfast room, where he had left his wife in a state of distress.

"Oh, there you are." She fussed over the teapot to give him the sustenance she was sure he needed. "I've been so worried, Cedric dear, what did you say to him?"

"I told him I wouldn't prosecute, out of consideration for his mother. But I ordered him out of the house. Within the next hour."

He took the cup she had filled and strode to the head of the table, accompanied by a titter of the delicate china.

"Oh, dear," she wailed. "What will the poor boy do?"

"My dear Winifred, he's no mere boy, he's twenty-five. I already exercised great restraint in not speaking to him yesterday evening, so as not to turn him out late at night." It was true that Sir Cedric had carefully decided on a morning scene, since he would look rather foolish saying, "NOW sir," and then, "Well, no, you'd better stay the night" even if he did excuse it with "you're so unreliable you'd probably fall into bad company."

"I know, dear, you were most thoughtful. But I can't help worrying. What shall I write to Mary Ann?"

Sir Cedric buried himself in the *Toronto Times* and pronounced, like a disembodied oracle,

"We are not responsible to your cousin for the misdemeanours of her son, Winifred. We welcomed him with open arms and gave him the full freedom of our house. But he has more than abused our hospitality. I could have borne the constant disparaging remarks about our way of life, our beliefs and outlook, our friends and my methods of governing the province. I could have borne his arrogance and even his bullying of Beatrice. But theft I will not stand."

"Yes dear, of course, you're quite right." She added fearfully, betraying her daughter's confidence in order to win that of her husband, and perhaps a little mercy, "He's very fond of Beatrice, though."

"What do you mean, fond? He has no right to be fond of my daughter."

"No, dear, you're quite right. Indeed, she *was* complaining to me about his behaviour towards her."

"Winifred. WHAT do you mean?" The *Toronto Times* came crackling down like a dropped veil.

"Oh—oh, nothing, dear. I mean, she allowed her feelings to, shall we say, respond to his ardour. Well, no, perhaps it was only a playful pursuit. There was no harm in it, dear. But she regretted it—he does, as you say, bully her. And being still rather young, she didn't know how to get out of it, or hit back. They were only playing," Lady Handsworth added anxiously. "But even children's games can be painful. She has been avoiding him of late."

"Children's games indeed! Beatrice is nineteen, Winifred. That just about does it. The scoundrel! To play with my daughter's affections, then steal her stamp collection—my collection really, I devoted half my life to it—and sell it in Williamville, then blame her by implication! What enrages me most in the whole affair is his stupidity. Do you realise he went to the most notorious dealer in town! He left traces everywhere! He must have known I would start private inquiries at least. Did he *want* to be caught? And he got such a bad price for it, such a bad price."

"That's what I feel, dear, he's only a boy really, he didn't mean it, he didn't know what he was doing. And what will become of him?"

"Really, Winifred, are you out of your mind? Has this 'boy', as you call him, charmed all the good sense out of you? He can find his way around Canada by now. He has certainly managed to, impress enough influential people here in my house to get a footing on some fifty ladders of success if he continues to pester them as skilfully as I have watched him doing. I'll hear not one syllable more on this young man. The subject is now closed."

The word of Sir Cedric Handsworth, Governor of New Dorset, was law.

Alfred, however, had enough tact or pride, or paranoid suspicion, not to go at once to any of Sir Cedric's influential friends, and besides, he had already learnt, in his brief career, that a first footing is precisely what no influential man is ever willing to give; a third, or a seventh or a tenth perhaps, but the first one must reach by oneself. So he went to see Shand instead.

It was pouring with rain when he slunk out of the Governor's House, without so much as a phaeton to take him to the station. Lady Handsworth had agreed to have his trunk sent on as soon as he let her know of a forwarding address, and he promised himself that the forwarding address would be as grand as possible. So he was carrying only a portmanteau, and hired a cab as soon as he got into Williamville, in order to arrive at the station like a gentleman. But he was very wet, nevertheless.

He went to the station restaurant and drank a double brandy. He felt a little ill from nervous shock, and was frightened for his chest. That would teach them if he got pneumonia and died. Beatrice, in black, sobbing at his grave as the coffin was lowered, and Sir Cedric standing pale beside her, with all the staff of the Governor's House and Lady Handsworth looking tragic and reproachful; and then his mother arriving weeks later, and cutting them dead, and placing a wreath with one carefully dried and pressed Warwickshire rose, and ordering a stone with an inscription, "Let them be ashamed and brought to confusion together that rejoiceth at mine hurt." Or perhaps it would be better if they all gathered round his deathbed, Sir Cedric very stirred, with a pompous apology that was a great effort to utter; and Beatrice dabbing her eyes and Lady Handsworth mopping his brow with a lace-edged handkerchief dipped in lavender-water. Then he would recover, and wanly forgive Sir Cedric, and be invited to convalesce at the Governor's House.

The Ottowa Express steamed in like a hissing dragon, breathing fire. His porter took him to a first-class carriage and received a tip which produced an obsequious salute and a firm conviction that he had just handled the bag of a lord who was "something to do" with the visit of Prince George and Princess Mary, Duke and Duchess of Cornwall.

Alfred made straight for the diner, a fine long room with red plush fauteuils and a gilded ceiling. He chose a seat by the window, opposite a big and prosperous-looking man wearing a Norfolk jacket, and ordered a very expensive luncheon. He had enough money to show off, at least for a day or two. It had not even occurred to Sir Cedric to search him, and he had been clever enough to scatter about his person the money he had made from the sale of a book or two—these Canadians knew nothing about second-hand books—picked up for a song here and there, the song being sometimes a purely spiritual one called *Steal Away*. As for the affair of the stamps, it had been most unfortunate, but only some of the money had been found in his drawer—quite obviously planted there, he said—and Mr. Babbington, the dealer, having taken his cut, had been helpful about not mentioning the full price he had paid. And as the train trundled through the pinewoods, saying, rather unexpectedly, *malignitate, malignitate, malignitate, revereantur, revereantur, revereantur,* he watched the trees from the window, racing back to Williamville with the news of his innocence and of his great future successes, at least, the trees in front were running, those just beyond were walking fast, those beyond them moving majestically and those in the very background standing quite, quite still. And the telegraph wires were playing arpeggios over each other, up and down, throwing their messages from wire to wire to confuse all recipients with a ringing harmony, *revereantur, revereantur.* His elation rose with them and the excellent chicken broth warmed him through and through. By the end of the meal he had won the cautious admiration and interested curiosity of his table-companion, a Mr. Paul Summerson-Dupree, tall and broad with a small husky voice like a tiny kernel in a very large nut. He was on his way back from Labrador to Chatham, Ontario, where Summerson-Dupree & Co. had its headquarters. "Shortleaf and Loblolly," he said, when Alfred politely opened the conversation by admiring the view.

Then, tactfully drawn out, he flowered shyly into a whispered paeon of praise for the great forests of North America, the evergreens, which were soft wood, and of four main species, and the deciduous trees, which were hardwood—red gum, tupelo gum, sour black gum or pepperidge, willow oak, water oak, willow magnolia. These here were just toy woods, he should see the great pine forests of the North and West, the Douglas firs, the redwood, the hemlock and spruce, some of which were six foot or more in diameter.

The train began to say, for no reason at all, Cedars of Lebanon, Cedars of Lebanon, Cedars of Lebanon.

Businessmen are seldom poets, but Paul Summerson-Dupree's view of wood was more lyrical than that of most wholesalers, who tend to talk of grades, and structural lumbers, of strips, boards, dimensions and timbers, of felling, and bucking and skidding and hauling, of storage ponds and jackladders, scalers and turners, dry kilns, moving tables and green chains. And though these too make poetry, Summerson-Dupree had a way of whispering the names of trees as though he were the high-priest of all the forests, or he himself had clothed the earth with all these wonders at a gesture and a word. Perhaps the good meal helped, and the whisky and the slim young man's ardent eyes. At any rate, he suddenly remembered that he had a first-class convertible sleeper, with two bunks, all to himself, and that he would have to sit alone in it that afternoon, staring at all that loblolly, and sleep alone in it at night.

He did not sit alone, and they talked late into the night, and in the morning he gave Alfred Hayley his card.

Shand was worse than useless.

For one thing, he was drunk.

"Hang it all, you brought me to this damned continent, you've got to help me." Alfred's tone, was rather impatient, for he had very nearly gone on to Chatham with Summerson-Dupree, at a moment when Shand had somehow crumbled in his mind from a big rock he had to reach to a mere stone not to be left unturned.

The turning of the stone, moreover, was not only physically difficult, Shand being prostrate and rather large, but socially awkward too, Alfred being cleaned right out of cash. He had of course insisted on paying for his sleeper himself, in spite of Mr. Dupree's invitation and offer, for one had to be, above all, a gentleman, and a poor gentleman can be ruined by the pretence he feels obliged to keep when in the company of a rich gentleman, who hardly notices which of them has done the paying.

Shand turned on the couch and stretched for the bottle of Bourbon.

"Don't you think you've had enough?"

"Whooodjer THINK you are, telling me when I've—had-nough?"

"All right, old boy, keep calm."

Which was a silly thing to say, as Shand was about to fall asleep.

Shand was in real estate, and doing, in fact, quite well. His apartment was in the centre of Ottowa, near his office, and solidly furnished in the best Grosvenor Hotel style, where he always stayed when he went to London. It was spacious, too, for a bachelor, indeed it had a curious air of not being a bachelor apartment at all, with its corridor full of closed doors that always remained closed. However that might be, Shand was not a happy man, or at any rate, he was one of those innumerable people, no unhappier than anyone else, who yet believed they can be less unhappy with a bottle and who unload their tediousness over others instead of living with it.

Alfred launched into a long and dramatic account of how his uncle, the Governor, of New Dorset, had advised him to leave his house and province because his daughter Beatrice had fallen desperately in love with him, a first cousin, whom they couldn't possibly allow her to marry, they were very strict; Sir Cedric had been very friendly about it, of course, but there it was, and the fact that at the moment his nephew happened to be a penniless young man hadn't helped. The story was much embellished with romantic encounters and plots for elopement, but really, he went on, he couldn't have gone through with it, his career came first and his affections had not been as deeply involved as the girl had imagined. It had all been very difficult, a little polite flirtation she had taken seriously. "Oh, all right, nothing to sing about," he answered Shand's querying gesture about shape. "You know how these things are, old boy." Shand knew, and nodded many times.

When, however, Alfred tried to find out about any possible openings in real estate, or any other businesses Shand might be in touch with, Shand became oddly morose.

"But you told me, don't you remember, how easy everything would be, and how you'd be able to help me."

Shand said, "Whatsyer name?"

Alfred was annoyed.

"You know what my name is."

"Yea. Lovell. Gee, that's funny, Lovell Brook. Pretty name, Lov'llll. Prettier'n Alfred."

Alfred was even more annoyed.

"All right, I gave you a wrong name. Does it matter? I always wanted to change my name, I hated it. I thought America would be a good chance, but it didn't work. Letters came. And then I decided, on your own advice, to go and see my uncle, so I couldn't keep it up. How can you possibly mind a little thing like that? You of all people, so broad-minded and free-and-easy. Oh come on, Shand, pull yourself together."

"Hmm." Shand raised a papal hand. "Canada, and England. 'Sall changed. The Boers'll finish you. That is, they'll begin to finish you. An' all the others'll FINish finishing you. Liss'n ole boy, you, ole boy, that's funny, that is, liss'n ole boy, it's the ping—" his index finger moved sideways—"of the swendulum."

"Oh, don't talk rot, Shand, wake up. I thought my uncle would do wonders for me, would set me up. You've no idea all the promises he made. And to turn me out of the house like that. As if it were my fault!"

Shand shook his head sadly.

"It's the ping! of the SWEN-dulum, ole boy."

His index finger moved metronomically in front of his nose.

Paul Dupree was an American citizen, of French Canadian stock, who had inherited the almost defunct British firm of Summerson-Dupree & Co., Ltd., from an uncle in Liverpool, who had come over in 1880 to open a Canadian branch which had not gone very well. Paul Dupree reassumed the old name Summerson and quickly detached the Chatham branch from its Liverpool parent; then, a little less quickly but nevertheless very efficiently he set it on its feet again. Recently he had opened an office in New York, and another, two years earlier, in New Orleans, Louisiana, where the company was engaged in the export of hardwood lumber. He was therefore delighted when that most interesting young Englishman he had travelled with came, after all, to see him, and was shown into his office, wearing an elegant grey ulster and yellow kid gloves. Shand, after all, never looked at the smartly bound books on his shelves and one of them happened to be fairly valuable. Alfred knew for it had been his own gift, in England, to impress Shand, and now he felt it had done its job, or failed, according to which end of the relationship one looked at.

Paul Summerson-Dupree was visibly impressed, as businessmen so often are by accidentals of personality. He got up from the big roll-top desk that stood against the wall near the window, and shook Alfred's hand.

"Well, it's good to see you, young man." His husky voice sounded comfortingly confidential. But he turned at a tangent. "What a dreadful business, this shooting."

"Oh, shocking, sir." Alfred caught on quickly. "The whole of Ottawa was aghast. At Buffalo too, everyone felt it was practically in Canada." But Alfred was almost glad of it now as a neutral stepping stone to easy conversation.

"Well, we must pray the president will survive. But he's critically ill. Terrible business. So completely pointless, too. There one goes, getting on with a difficult job and then—poof, a madman. The ways of providence, dear me. However, tell me now how were your affairs in Ottawa?"

"I'm afraid they couldn't be worse. In fact, that's why I'm here, and so promptly. My partner made of with the funds in my absence. Oh, I knew he was a drunk, of course, but this I did not expect. My dear sir, I will not bore you with the details, but, I must admit, I began to wonder whether our so delightful meeting in the train was not perhaps providential."

"I'm most sorry to hear this, Mr. Hayley. But can't you do anything, find him, and prosecute?"

"Not worth it, sir. For one thing, everyone was too concerned about McKinley to worry about my small mishap. For another, well, when I say the funds, you must understand, it was a very little firm, nothing like your own great enterprise here, indeed, not a firm at all officially. I do believe we hadn't registered it yet. We were just beginning. Real estate, you know. Oh yes, I told you about it, I beg your pardon. I put up most of the money, a great deal of it in cash, then went to see my uncle, the Governor of New Dorset, you know, to see if he could help at all with a temporary loan. However, I don't wish to take up your valuable time with my tales of woe. It was entirely my fault. I'm a trusting soul, and perhaps a little inexperienced in such matters."

"Well, we all have to learn from experience and I guess you have learnt a little now."

"Indeed, sir. From now on I intend to be a hardheaded and hardhearted businessman, paying for my success in broken friendships, ruthlessness and unscrupulousness all the way along the line."

He had a great talent for getting on with men, especially men who were his superiors. By an instinct unusual in one so young he could estimate just how bold he could be in his jocularity. Some businessmen might have been irritated by the familiarity, or offended by the personal slant of the banter, but Summerson-Dupree was an honestly religious man who knew that business was like that, basically, and had to be. The only real wrong lay in letting that eat up one's life and spirit. He laughed with good humour.

"I wish I'd had the opportunity to be as unscrupulous as they say one has to," he whispered. "I'd be ten times forreder."

"I don't see how, sir. Ever since I met you I seem to hear and see nothing but the name Summerson-Dupree. It's funny how that happens."

"Really? Well now, Mr. Hayley, and have you at all considered the idea of entering the firm? It is quite large, and you'd have to learn the ropes of course, but there are openings and opportunities for an intelligent young man."

"It's very kind of you to suggest it, sir. As a matter of fact I had considered it, and that's why I came. Of course, I would be quite willing to start in a very modest capacity. I must be honest and say I know nothing of lumber. But you got me so interested, sir, I even did a lot of reading about it."

"Aw, you won't learn anything out of books. You've got to be there, in the yard, and if possible at the sawmill, right the way through from the log storage pond to the sorting table. The sawyer's the man who can teach you all you have to know—most important man in the mill. So's the filer. Anyway, it's best to learn all that later, and start on the clerical side. That moment," he continued like a wind in the trees, "when all those grading numbers and classifications you've been entering and transferring for months suddenly begin to come to life as real long heavy logs, all shorn of their bark and lying white and naked in the sun, I'll never forget that, my boy, not as long as there's breath in my body." Breath was about all there seemed to be, instead of voice. His lyrical mood had come on again, due perhaps to the young man's pale but intense blue eyes.

"And what about the forest end of it, sir?"

"Yes. You can go in the forest, but it won't help you much at this stage. Anyway, I plan to put you in hardwood—swamp black gum and cotton-wood, and Southern cypresses. Practically disappearing, those, very sad, isn't it, cypresses mourning the death of their own kind. How is your health, by the way? You look pale."

"Er, all right." He was taken aback and hovered between diplomacy and hypochondria. "Only my lungs, that is, they used to give me trouble as a child." He gave a Camillean cough. "But not for a long—"

"Capital. The piney woods of the South and the gentle gulf breezes. Just what the doctor ordered and you, young man, are just the person I need for the foreign department of my new branch. How would you like to go to New Orleans?"

Alfred thought, what a fool I was to spend so much on a thick winter Ulster.

Charles Watts, who had been sent to New Orleans in 1899, to open the branch office of Summerson-Dupree & Co., did not like the new arrival at all. The Englishman put on airs, for one thing, and for another, he seemed to be a great favourite with Mr. Summerson, who had, it seemed, come across half a continent to introduce him, though officially it was to "see how everything was getting on".

Everything was not getting on. The company had bought a mill near New Orleans for the manufacture of cottonwood boxes, and since he,

Charles Watts, had been sent only in connection with the exporting of hardwood lumber, he was very much against the cottonwood box experiment which therefore or, rather, as he had always predicted, soon ran into difficulties, and he said so in no uncertain terms. When he heard that the newcomer was to work in the foreign export department, and not in the cottonwood box business, he was quite annoyed. But Mr. Summerson was full of big plans, for future expansion into export of pitch-pine lumber as well as hardwood, and didn't seem to mind about the cottonwood box flop at all.

Soon his enthusiasm spread amicability all round, and Charles Watts introduced Alfred to Dan Carter, who took him down to the levee, where "millions of feet" of lumber, as he called them, were piled high into little square huts of crisscross waiting to be shipped abroad. Ten or twelve Negro roustabouts were heaving a log onto a long cart drawn by four oxen, then another log, and then another from the edge of the water where a big raft floated empty. They were trying to do it in rhythm but it wasn't the kind of job you could sing to and they just grunted, besides, though he wasn't allowed to use it, a man stood by with a whip. The freightyards seemed to be endless. A crate the size of a room stood below a crane, labelled "Do Not Drop". Further on two schooners were being unloaded of cordwood and further on still, the steamboats were lined up one behind the other, each pointing two tall and slim black funnels to the sky like the long horns of snails. There the longshoremen were trucking bales of cotton and some kind of weird wailing could be heard through the shouting and the clanging. Beyond those were the banana boats with one funnel only and beyond them a pleasure steamer like a wedding cake, again with the tall H-line funnels. The air was inter-wafted with smells, of burnt coffee, and grain and saw dust, of sweat, of lavatory and railroad grit.

Carter was eyeing him oddly, and said,

"Charlie Watts made a mess of that cottonwood box business. The boss is angry. What's more, there was no need for a flop. My guess is there's more than enough demand and all that's required is a little ingenuity.

Wow, if I had the capital, I'd run that mill very differently."

Alfred was in a complete daze. The unfamiliar smells, and noises, the heat and the peculiar exhalation of human politics in a new set-up, petty but impressive because mysterious, baffled and stimulated him as. Carter intended they should.

Soon he was sharing Carter's apartment in Camp Street, and Carter showed him round the city, took him to the French Opera House, talked a great deal about the Secret Societies which organised the Mardi Gras, the hierarchy of French or American business aristocracy in the town; and of course the forestry of intrigue in the lumber industry, largely invented by himself as an explanation for his lack of startling success in an industry which had recently shifted its centre from Michigan and Wisconsin to the South, where it was enjoying a big boom. He was really an overgrown schoolboy cultivating the newcomer, partly to dazzle him with knowledge of established procedures, partly to train him as a future ally for his own mediocrity. And possibly for something else.

Alfred, who had never been to a boarding school for long enough to learn the ritual of the passing years, was taken in and flattered at first, but gradually his own natural flair won him back his independence. And as his confidence grew, that of Carter diminished, so that when on Carnival Night, with a vast quantity of Sunday Punch inside him, Carter tried to make his new friend realise the nature and extent of what he called their interest in one another, he somehow failed to get beyond intensely uttered but vague generalities accompanied by rhetorical gestures. Alfred disliked drunks, and after a few weeks of unspoken awkwardness and cooling companionship he moved to an apartment of his own in South Rampart Street, which he could ill afford.

He worked extremely hard, not only to master the different grade numbers and classifications he had to deal with at his own desk, but many other things as well, such as what sort of firms were the largest customers, both inland and abroad, the methods of sale and transport, the tariff systems of all the countries that bought lumber from them, and indeed the entire processing from the first decision to fell an area of forest to the final wagonloads or shipments of the slender white boards and timbers, rough lumber, surfaced lumber, worked, shiplapped and patterned lumber.

He made friends with a man called Carolet, who was sawyer in one of the mills not owned by Summerson-Dupree. "The sawyer's the man who can teach you all you have to know—most important man in the mill," Mr. Summerson-Dupree had said. Carolet, moreover, was dealing with pitchpine, which Alfred had gathered was Dupree's next step down here in Louisiana; the long-leaf and slash particularly, which produced resin and turpentine as well as excellent quality lumber. And Carolet knew everyone, and arranged for him to be shown over the largest and most modern mill in the world, at Bogalusa, North of Lake Pontchartrain. Bogalusa was always establishing world records for daily production, Carolet said, its aim was to to the mark of one million board feet.

When the Spring came round Alfred started disappearing at weekends, taking an early riverboat up the Mississippi and visiting a station in the middle of the forest, to make friends with the lumberjacks. The first time he was most unwelcome, for he turned up in the middle of a birthday party when everyone was singing "For he's a jolly good fell-ER" . But slowly he won them over with his boyish charm and his zeal to learn.

He made such quick progress that after a year he was being sent abroad as representative, especially to South America, which knocked him for six.

"There's no doubt about it, the Roman faith really is universal," he said to Carolet. "It's a wonderful experience to hear the same Mass and know what's going on. I was thrilled to hear the *Mea Culpa* in Peru."

"Grievous faults are much the same in any language," said Carolet, who, though a Catholic, had always thought that this argument tipped the scales into fallibility. "Fears, not faults, that's what some of the more advanced thinkers are beginning to call them nowadays."

"Good heavens," said Alfred, rather shocked.

But he loved the Delta City—Crescent City was the name he preferred, it had an optimistic ring. He liked the weird wrought-iron balconies in the old quarters, and the Cabildo opposite Jackson Square, and walking amid the mad Medusa oaks in Audubon Park, and sitting quietly under the palms in Lafayette Square. But above all he liked walking up St. Charles Avenue and looking at the big houses, just as he had done in Park Lane, thinking, some day, I shall live in one of those.

His health improved considerably, as Mr. Dupree had said for the blighting and moist east winds of the Atlantic coast had to pass through such vast expanses of yellow pine that they arrived quite dry, and North winds were soon succeeded by warm Southern ones from the tropics. The sea air and the Pines, he said, were saving his life, for he rather liked to hint at a mysteriously Keatsian background. At any rate, he now felt truly a new man.

Just before the next Mardi Gras holiday, he told Carter he was going away. Carter was hurt, and Alfred enjoyed that. "But you can't miss a Mardi Gras!"

"Why not? I saw it last year."

"Good heavens, man, you talk like the guy who was offered a book for Christmas and said no thanks I've got one. Every Mardi Gras is different, unique."

"There are, however, my dear Carter, some variations of the same books which I do not wish to re-read every year."

He and Mervyn Carolet went to Mobile on the Louisville and Nashville railway, to study the possibilities. Carolet was saving to buy his own saw-mill, and Alfred felt that sooner or later he would have to branch out, either as a wholesaler and if possible an exporter, or with his own retail lumberyard. On the whole he preferred the former. He had confided his ambitions to Carolet, but felt he was not yet ready, or strong enough, and might well be put right out of business by an angry Dupree, who behaved as if he owned him, without at the same time giving him as much advancement as he wanted within the firm. Carolet also, was not ready, but had his eye on Hayley as a promising future buyer, and they tacitly agreed that together, and away from New Orleans, they would stand a good chance, at least in perhaps a year or two, or three. Both were cautious, for much could happen in the meantime, as indeed much did—Alfred's disastrous sideline experiment with cottonwood boxes, for one, as Carter, Hayley & Co. Carolet, in fact, did not altogether trust this Plausible Englishman, but was somehow fascinated by his optimism, and by his unparalleled enthusiasm for his own person, Hayley & Hayley & Hayley limited.

"What made you come to the States?" he asked, with the usual mixture of flattered pride and suspicious curiosity Americans have about new additions of undesirable aliens to their spicy melting pot—especially if they themselves are of old and very respectable French or English stock.

"Oh, I was advised by my doctor to go on a sea-trip—my lungs, you know. New Orleans or Mobile seemed just the thing. My uncle, the Governor of New Dorset—"

"What were you doing in England?"

"Well, I wasn't working, or in business, if that's what you mean." His tone implied that only tact and politeness prevented him from adding, that, only in the New World would a gentleman stoop so low. "Oxford took four years, then there was the war. I was wounded, you know."

"Oh, dear. Where?"

"Have you a passion for seeing scars too? Like my young sister."

"I meant, where in South Africa?"

"Oh, I see, forgive me, my dear chap. I was with the Kimberley relieving troops. I could have been sent home then but I opted to stay, and convalesced in the house of an uncle who had made a fortune in the goldmines of the Rand. Then I went back to help the mopping up. Such a stupid war, dragging on like that a whole year after Mafeking. But I came home earlier, in the Spring of 1901, just about two years ago, then straight to Canada. My other uncle, the Gov—"

"You mean you saw the new century in out there? Oh dear, even we felt sorry for the British boys who had to do that."

"I did, my dear fellow. And it was pretty grim, I can tell you, the new century."

15

THE ASTRONOMERS had decided, much to everyone's disappointment, that the new century was to start, not at the beginning of the year 1900 but at the end, in 1901 in fact, which seemed unreasonable of them since the Christian era had presumably opened in the year of God's Incarnation, zero A.D., and not on His first birthday. But God's childhood is so relatively undocumented, anything might have happened, and He may well have decreed a new century on His first birthday, as a sort of present to mankind, and told only the astronomers about it. The astronomers, at any rate, are usually in the know about time and the universe, and as they can always throw millions and millions of light years at us if we protest, it is best to take their word for whatever they choose to say.

It was true that seeing in the new century was not quite as hilarious an affair in South Africa or in England as it might otherwise have been, for everybody felt rather wearily patriotic, whipping up their British Empire optimism for the occasion but secretly wondering when the old Queen would die and whether she might perhaps take it all with her, unlike other people, or at least the spirit of it.

Alfred Hayley, however, was neither in South Africa, nor in England to welcome the new century, but on his way to a new life in the New World, on board ship in the middle of the Atlantic, being thoroughly seasick, much to the scornful amusement of Shand.

But the New Year which ushered in the false new century—when everyone went around muttering nineteen hundred in order to get used to it, and to console themselves for not being allowed to say twentieth century yet—that New Year was celebrated by Alfred Hayley in his college rooms at the oldest University in England, the city of dreaming spires which those who see things a little differently call Parkhurst Prison, Isle of wight.

It was not a bad place. He would often head his letters home with "My diggings in the Isle of Wight" or "Hotel Sea-view", or "Island Haven", much to his father's annoyance. The sewing of rough khaki jackets and trousers for the soldiers going to Africa was what he hated most, for it hurt his pride—after all he would have been an officer if he had volunteered, and of course, he would have volunteered. Before the war began they were at least sewing mailbags, which was less personal. But otherwise he got on surprisingly well with the other prisoners, the milder ones, anyway, and the really rough lot were somehow kept apart most of the time, in different workrooms and in another wing of cells. Three prisoners besides himself were gentlemen, who had picked each other out by an irresistible instinct, like Englishmen abroad, and formed a little club segregated, as it were, from the natives, a club which Alfred by the same token was very soon invited to join. A few of the others were allowed as occasional guests by courtesy of the social shortage—a sad little hatter, for instance, who was doing five years for bigamy—but the temporary nature of the privilege was never in doubt on either side. A gentleman was a gentleman, and there were only four of them. Two were in for theft of different magnitudes, and one for fraud. He was the only cynic and therefore a bit of a bore, while the other two, like Alfred, were of course innocent, they had been framed by their enemies, and were therefore more interesting. The Governor, Colonel Plummer, also believed in Alfred's innocence, and took much interest in this well-spoken and immaculate young man, who was so deeply religious and so gentle in his manner. And although such favouritism as he showed him came officially as a reward for good behaviour, the young man's charm and undoubted good lineage may have had some influence on him too, charm and good lineage not being met with every day in his profession. So all in all it wasn't too bad a place, and it reminded him in some, well, selected ways of an all-male college or boarding school, which had somehow never really come his way, as it had for other men. Old boys left and new boys came, who could be lorded over and shown the ropes—for even prisons have ropes; parcels from home arrived and letters were censored and the padre listened to one's inner illuminations and the Governor had one up for a little talk. Indeed he found to his surprise that, with certain reservations —and are there not reservations to everything?—he actually enjoyed prison, at least for an unexpectedly long time. But now the time was beginning to become a little too long.

He had served nearly two years of a three-year sentence, and although he didn't know it, much was being done on his behalf. The solicitor for the defence, for instance, Mr. Copplestone, who was a widower of fifty-nine, had fallen in love with Cordelia.

He did this on a brilliant sunny afternoon in April 1898, when he stopped the dogcart he had hired at the small yellow brick station of Over Marstaple, and asked a little girl on the road if she knew where the house of Mr. and Mrs. Hayley was.

At least, she had seemed a little girl from the back, with her Leghorn hat and her black-stockinged legs, and Mr. Copplestone, being rather short-sighted, had not noticed the exact amount of leg showing. When she turned he saw from her well-cut bodice that she must be quite seventeen, and that her frock came well below her knees. She had the calmest blue eyes he had ever seen, pale but reflecting the sky and with the top lids almost straight under straight fair brows; her skin was of milk and roses and her flowing curls seemed of spun gold in the sunlight. At least, he said all this to himself later.

Actually, she was sixteen, as he discovered, to his astonishment and confusion, when she walked into the Hayley parlour to say how-do-you-do with a slightly mocking look—or was it just delightfully mischievous?—in her oh-so-blue eyes.

Mr. Copplestone had come all the way up to Birmingham from London early that morning, then out on the branch line to Over Marstaple after lunch, and he felt a little dazed. He had come to explain in detail to Mr. and Mrs. Hayley exactly how their son had been caught up in a web of intrigue and made a scapegoat, all of which he had already explained to

Mrs. Hayley in London at the time, but Mrs. Hayley had invited him to come and explain it to Mr. Hayley as well, who wouldn't believe it from a mere mother. And self-repetition being the professional weakness of solicitors, here he was in the parlour of Monwode Farm, Over Marstaple: talking about the prejudice of the judge who had given a much heavier sentence than their son deserved, even supposing, he added quickly, he had been guilty; emphasising the great likelihood of getting the sentence shortened, for he knew Colonel Plummer, the Governor of Parkhurst, well, who was most impressed with their son, and had said it was only a matter of legalities, providing the young man also continued in his exemplary behaviour; listening to Mr. Hayley who declared he didn't care how long the boy was in prison, the longer the better, and either way he was a disgrace to his family; watching the daughter, Cordelia, who sat on the other side of the big oak table, holding her teacup like a little lady, taking in every word he said with a frightening alertness in her eyes, then being suddenly remembered and told to leave the room; and being called Dilly darling by her mother, Cordelia dear by her father. ("So young and so untender? So young, my lord, and true.") Dilly darling, Dilly darling, Dilly my darling.

Mr. Copplestone threw himself into the business of young Hayley's earlier release with a speed and enthusiasm unusual in his profession. By the autumn his end of it had been achieved and the rest was in the hands of the powers that be as slow as they wish. But it all looked very hopeful and a good enough excuse to visit the Hayleys once more. By then they had moved to Gravelley Hill, Birmingham, where they ran a small boarding-house. "An impossible time for farming," Mr. Hayley explained sadly, "it's never been the same since '76. I've tried and tried, but I'm too old, I give up." Muriel said, "Northbrook came with the Great Depression, you know, Mr. Copplestone," and Mrs. Hayley said "Hush, dear." Cordelia met him coming out of his room and walked down the dark narrow stairs in front of him, saying breathlessly, "We had to leave Over Marstaple you know, and come to this horrid place, on account of the terrible disgrace my brother brought upon us. He ruined my father, you know." Mr.

Copplestone did not know, or rather, he knew she was lying, for the cost of the defence had not been paid by Mr. Hayley. But his fingers were hovering fearfully six inches away from her hair, then withdrawing, and he loved her all the more for having taken her brother's defection so dramatically to heart.

That night he asked for Cordelia's hand in marriage and Mr. Hayley, to his surprise, gave it, though Mrs. Hayley's pale eyes, so like her son's and like Cordelia's, looked a little unhappy in that round fair face under the sandy hair.

In spite of the cloudy, pale effect of Mrs. Hayley's colouring there was no doubt she was the stronger character, a rotund little woman in black, who always looked "appropriately" dressed, and who seemed taller, because larger, than her husband. Yet her almost visible sense of superiority was perhaps more apparent than real, at any rate, she always deferred most gently to her husband, who was very much the gentleman farmer, even here in town, lean and now grey-haired, with brown eyes like those of his other daughter, in a high complexion. He seemed a little lost in the small dark house, wearing Sunday black all day instead of tweed or gaiters.

Mr. Hayley was also fifty-nine, but unlike Mr. Copplestone, he seemed a disappointed man, which was not altogether surprising in the circumstances. Even his youngest and favourite child, so hopefully named Cordelia, was not quite so beautiful or loving or true as he would have wished and he could not, in any case, give her the handsome dowry without which no Englishman of any standing ever married even the loveliest and most accomplished of women—at least not in his own day, nor would he himself have done so, but times were changing and Mary Ann even talked of letting Cordelia take up a training for some position or other. She was not really clever enough to be a governess, besides, neither he nor Mary Ann relished the idea, but there were new openings for young ladies these days, in nursing, and dispensing, as travelling companions, in libraries, some even went into offices as typewriters. Marriage, nevertheless, was always the best solution, and there was much to be said for solid respectability and security at once, instead of a young man who might yet have to make his way or wait for his not very large inheritance. There was much to be said for a man his own age, who was gentle and tender and wise like himself, with all the nonsense knocked out of him. And who might die in the next ten years—though Mr. Hayley skidded over that thought, for he himself felt young and tough and did not think Mr. Copplestone's heart's desire at all unseemly, in a widower, that is. There was in fact, a curious blend of practical convenience, relief, love, sincere concern and spite, in Mr. Hayley's ready acceptance of Mr. Copplestone as a suitor for his daughter's hand.

The old-young couple had of course to wait, at least until Cordelia was eighteen, and it was agreed that Cordelia should accompany him and his three daughters on a trip to Switzerland the following summer.

Which she did. With the result that Mr. Copplestone somehow or other lost his rose-tinted spectacles, on a mountaintop perhaps, where the perspective is so different and the view so much clearer, or maybe they were stolen by his daughters. At any rate, he suddenly recovered from his infatuation, and with the speedy efficiency of long legal experience in other men's idiocies, returned the goods undamaged and only metaphorically sampled, paid over a certain sum in compensation for nothing much, and went home with a gasp of astonished relief.

By then his string-pulling had tugged its repercussive course among the powers that were still being, and after a few months of further observation and final vetting, Alfred Northbrook Hayley was released from prison, on the 8th January 1900, in time to be home for his twenty-fourth birthday on the 9th. This was a special stroke of fatherly brilliance on the part of Colonel Plummer, who had tried hard to get the release through for the New Year, but failed, so kept it back two days when it did come.

Alfred Northbrook Hayley, however, did not go home for his birthday. He did go to Birmingham, but he stayed with Mrs. Ricardo instead.

He was in a state of suffused excitement when he first saw the familiar red ties of the South Western Railway guards and climbed into the opulent South Western first-class carriage at Portsmouth. The lace antimacassars, the red plush, the feel of his own leather grip, the feel of the two gold sovereigns his mother had sent him—well, one of them was already a small gold piece and some silver now, for his fare so far had cost five and fourpence—all this seemed unbelievable and intensified by his two years in prison. Every detail was new and enormous, as if his eyes had changed into magnifying glasses. *"Nixey's Black Lead,"* he murmured with great emotion as the train moved slowly then more quickly along the platform, the noise drowning his voice. *"Hinde's Curlers . . . Brooke's Soap Monkey Brand . . . SAPOLIO . . . Reckitt's Blue . . . Are Ye Washed in the Blood of the Lamb? Epp's Cocoa, Frame Food, Whelpton's Purifying Pills."* He had never thought those crude lettered placards would one day be transformed into such a truly thrilling guard of honour.

He kept his coat on at first, for it was bitterly cold, but soon the fug in the carriage increased with the carbon dioxide of four large gentlemen, two of whom were smoking. So he took it off and hung it up, although he felt very awkward in his one and only suit, which seemed to have shrunk in the Governor's keeping—far surely he hadn't put on weight in prison? Perhaps he was still growing, or perhaps he had just lost the feel of well-cut clothes. But he didn't even care, he had no desire whatsoever to talk to anybody. Not yet, anyway. Objects first, then people. Everything was so big, so bright, so familiar yet so different, as if the world and all the bits and pieces of human progress had been re-created and remade just yesterday, but slightly outsize.

He took a hansom from Waterloo, to Haxell's Little Hotel in Exeter Street, and the hansom got stuck in the Strand, behind a growler whose wheels had interlocked with those of a milk-float. Both drivers were yelling obscenities at each other and soon others joined in, a businessman going home early in his brougham, a salt-man with a donkey barrow and a Union Jack waistcoat, and the driver of a Vanguard omnibus whose horse decided to relax in a big way so that a street-orderly had to dart through the traffic with his pan and brush and nearly got run over by one of those new salmon-coloured taxis driving freely the other way. Through the artillery of traffic noise a German band could be heard from the pavement, playing *Break the News to Mother*, pierced through by the strident whistles of gentlemen calling cabs and those of errand-boys vying with each other on two fingers. The noise was of a whole army, the smell was of a stable with alien whiffs of petrol, the mud was of a farmyard. Never had anything so appalling seemed so splendid to Alfred Northbrook Hayley. He was the only person in the whole melee who wasn't shouting, on the contrary, he sat back in his hansom and laughed uncontrollably with a loud happiness that caused his driver to open the hatch and peer down to see if he was all right.

The cab cost him a shilling and a threepenny tip. Bed and breakfast at Haxell's would take anything between a crown and half a guinea at most, then there was his fare to Birmingham tomorrow and incidental expenses. That left him very nearly one whole sovereign to spend tonight. He would do himself proud—why a four course dinner at the Dieppe in Soho only cost a shilling, and he was going to do better than that, with a glass of shrub or lovage cordial at the Long Bar, then Simpson's Chophouse with a three-and-sixpenny bottle of the best champagne to celebrate. Then perhaps Terry's Theatre, or the Alhambra, why not, by cab, and a cab back, and a final whisky and lemon. There was no end to a golden sovereign, if one had it all to oneself. "All to myself," he repeated in his hotel room, as he adjusted his choker, "I owe nothing to anyone, I don't have to be nice to anybody, I shall never need or want or trust anyone again."

So much so that when he stepped out of the train at Birmingham, he stood paralysed on the platform as the travellers pushed past him, with their porters carrying great bunches of luggage strapped over their shoulders. He could not face going home. "59 Gravelley Hill," he kept muttering to himself, and it didn't sound in the least like home.

But he did need someone after all. A day, an evening, a night and another day make a large chunk of time even for the new solitude of independence that seems like a mystical experience after the peculiarly dependent and crowded solitude of prison. He wanted to see—who? The station smelt of smoke and urine—why did all stations smell just so? He wanted musk roses and cinnamon, spikenard and calamus. The hands of his mind moulded a shape that emerged as a teagown of reseda velvet with a yoke of silk guipure lace and long angel sleeves of chiffon coming out of big shoulder puffs, with loose undersleeves of pale yellow silk. Not that his mind named all these things, it only saw, but a name very quickly followed, and a face. Mrs. Ricardo, of course.

The maid was a new one, and a little insolent, Madam was not at home, she said, then, Madam was just going out. He said, Well make up your mind, and at that moment Madam did in fact emerge into the hall, wearing a floor-sweeping pelisse of black velvet with a chinchilla collar that enclosed her head like an arum lily, right up to the princely hat and its osprey curl, so that her face looked like the very heart of an exotic flower. A great deal of lace jabot cascaded over a twisting riverbed of more chincilla, down to a handspan waist, and her muff was also of chinchilla. He gasped and she said, "Well, well, if isn't Mr. Brook. And may I ask, to what do I owe this extremely unexpected call?"

"I'm so very glad you're not wearing khaki." He couldn't stop staring at her and hadn't noticed the maid's triumphant smirk. "Every woman in London is wearing khaki trimmed with red, and every shop window is filled with khaki cloth and Union Jacks. And for what? To show a group of farmers that England is mistress of the seas." The maid had gone under Mrs. Ricardo's dismissing eyebrows, so he added, "but you are mistress of my heart."

"I'm just going out to tea," she said, "but as it happens I'm a little early. You may come in for a few minutes. And explain yourself."

He followed her, full of mumbled apologies. Her drawing room flared its yellow silk at him and once again every object thrust itself on his consciousness with enormously sharp contours—the black Bechstein with its photographs of faces made, it seemed, of smoke, the overlarge flowerpiece on top of it, the tall flames under the very ornamental chimney, throwing out their glow through the brass fireguard, on the massive brass fender, the brass scuttle, the bunch of brass instruments, and the deep orange velvet curtains caught up to reveal the dark blue silk ones, themselves caught up to reveal a full length waterfall of fine lace.

He went round in a daze, touching everything.

"It's wonderful," he murmured. "Wonderful. Look. Silk. Porcelain. Leather. Velvet. Silver. And books. And ivory notes." His fingers ran up the keys. "Lace. And glass. And Petals. Silk again. Silk, satin, muslin, rags, silk; coach, carriage, wheelbarrow, donkey-cart, coach. Tinker, tailor, soldier, sailor, rich-man. Silk. Velvet. May I, oh, please, may I stroke your muff?"

She was so astonished she gave it to him, flattered perhaps at this odd show of sentimental memory.

"Thank you." He buried his face in it. "Oh, you have no idea, how soft it seems."

"Have you been abroad, then?"

"Abroad? Yes, oh yes, I've been abroad all right. Across the sea."

"South Africa?"

"South Africa, yes." He stared at her again, and though she was used to being admired she disliked intense young men, unless perhaps she was indoctrinating them.

"Look, Lovell, four years is a long time. You can't come crashing in here and assume it's all yours for the asking."

"Oh, no, I wouldn't dream—I'm sorry, I know it must seem strange. Please forgive me. I want nothing from you, except—" his mind was working again, quickly—"only a little understanding. I've just got back—my lungs, you know, I was sent home. I simply can't go straight home. My father cut me off with a shilling, you know, over some trouble I got into. Yes, love," he answered her raised eyebrows, "but it seems a foolish affair now. In London, after I left you. Rebound, they call it. He was quite right, of course, but so cruel. I volunteered as a private soldier because I couldn't afford to buy a commission. I have literally just landed at Liverpool, all I want is to be allowed to come and see you, not for anything, I assure you, just to get used to England, to escape from home, to talk to someone, someone who understands."

He had been stroking his cheek continually with her muff, sometimes talking straight into the fur. Quite suddenly she lost her hard impatient look and said gently,

"You can stay tonight if you wish. I have to go now, but I'll be back in about two hours. I will order tea for you."

Home was not quite as grim as he had pictured it, but the boarding-house at Gravelley Hill was a great shock to him, and he criticised the decision and its result most bitterly, whereupon his father could not refrain from pointing out that if anyone was to blame it was he, Northbrook. His mother, who wanted no recriminations, reproached her husband and reminded him that this had not been the main reason, Mr. Hayley's ultimate failure as a tenant-farmer lay so heavily on heart that he could not bear to be reminded of it, and blamed the government, the Great Depression and his son, so that the latter banged his fist on the table and shouted, "Oh, not *that*, again!" and flung out of the room.

Dilly, who had developed the fashionable whine and said "henk you" now, kept taunting him and saying all the time in mysterious tones that he owed his release to her. There was only one maid-of-all-work, and he kept bumping into strange boarders, women of vague outlines and uncertain ages, dropping hairpins and smelling of camphor and saying "good evening" brightly on the stairs, and small bearded men covered with snuff and tobacco, who, it seemed, wanted only to be lifted down, dusted and replaced.

The only person who was glad to see him, apart, of course from the overwhelming gladness of his mother, was Muriel.

"Was it nice, at Hotel Seaview?" she asked with the sweetest smile, one day when he was playing *Jerusalem* with angry consecutive chords on the little brown piano. "I hope the air did you lots and lots of good."

He stopped and turned on the stool, suddenly grateful. Muriel was only two years his junior, and he sometimes felt closer to her than anyone, although she had his father's eyes.

"It did do me lots and lots of good, Moo. Do you think I look gooder?"

She stretched her arm with her thumb out, and measured him like an artist, smiling with one closed eye that twisted her mouth upwards.

"No. You're gooder on one side and badder on the other."

"So it all comes right in the end?"

"In the very end, I expect so."

"Oh, Moo, you don't want me to die yet, do you?"

She looked at him, puzzled.

"You mean, like Lovell?"

"Yes. Like Lovell."

"It wouldn't be exactly like Lovell, would it? Besides, you wouldn't really miss me."

"Oh, but I would. To tell you the truth, Moo," he said in sudden gush of self-pity and family hatred, "you're the only person I really missed, down in the Isle of Wight."

"Was I? How nice. But you never do tell the truth, do you, Narboo?"

She was Muriel, so he couldn't be angry. He gave a sheepish grin instead, which didn't quite come off because he really was a little peeved.

"You've been listening to tales about me."

"Oh, yes, there's plenty of tales everywhere. Everybody's always telling tales, about everybody else, because everybody else is so much more their business, you see, than everybody unelse, that they don't mind. I mean their business is, well I mean," she suddenly got confused about just where the words had led her, and ended lamely, "they're all so interested, you see."

"I know what you mean, Moo," he said with prickly tears in his eyes. "That's just the way families are."

That was what Reggie Smith said to him too, when he complained. Reggie came back in May, on leave from South Africa where he had been wounded in the fighting at Kimberley, and Northbrook sought him out quickly, spending much time with him and questioning him in great detail, and counter-boasting about the precociousness of his sexual experiences, which included all Cordelia's governesses in turn and Miss Marjorie Lockhart, one of two sisters who ran the boarding school in Birmingham where they had all been. But even Reggie got on his nerves, especially when he talked of his brother William, who was doing brilliantly at Cambridge and had just been offered a Fellowship at King's. Then William himself came home, and after a struggle couldn't help renewing his flirtation with Dilly, who suddenly became angelic, so that everybody said what a charming couple and assumed they were unofficially engaged, though Mrs. Smith kept repeating to him with meaningful regret that William would have to give up the Fellowship if he married Cordelia. She made Cordelia, rather than just marriage, sound like the stumbling block.

So he escaped from the family and the family friends as much as possible, disappearing for days on end and refusing to discuss his future. For Mrs. Ricardo had other plans, at least for spring and Summer. And when she was just sufficiently tired of him to make the parting an exquisite pang for herself, and not either a painful wrench or a vulgar sigh of relief —her timing was always perfect—she introduced him to a man called Shand, who was in Birmingham England on business and pleasure, his pleasure being Mrs. Ricardo.

16

IT WAS Father Biretto who suggested he should discuss his future with Father Gaveston, and he offered to write a letter on his behalf. Northbrook was about to say that he knew Father Gaveston well, for was he not a grandson of Lord Chafford and the third son of The Hon. George Gaveston, M.P. for South Warwickshire, who had married Lord Weirwood's sister Lady Charlotte, and of course the Weirwoods and the Hayleys were very close friends. But quick reflection told him that in the circumstances a letter from Father Biretto might be more useful with Father Gaveston, whom he had only heard spoken of, than all the family connecting links he could bloat up.

Father Biretta had his parish at Sutton Leigh, about three miles South of Over Marstaple, towards Weirwood in fact, where they had lived before, some eight or ten miles further South. Northbrook couldn't stand the church at Over Marstaple, or indeed the Reverend Archibald Stanton, who had once threatened to sue him for libel. So he would walk to Sutton Leigh and have long talks with Father Biretto, much to the annoyance of Mr. Hayley.

Armed with the letter, Northbrook marched home with glory in his heart, raced up to his room, collected all the cash he had, packed a very few things in a small grip worthy of Dick Whittington, bade such a fast farewell to his mother she had no time for protest or distress, and adventurously set off on the road to London, the railroad of course.

He was twenty-one, and yet bewildered, for London was enormous. He had been here before, with his father, on his way to France, but that was different, being brought by cab to a fixed address then away by cab again. Now that it was his alone to conquer, he felt confused in this jungle, with its wild fauna and barrows, victorias and hansoms, four-wheelers called

Quicksilver, Defiance, Rapid, Reliable, and horse-buses of various colours called the Atlas, which was green, the Favourite, the Royal Blue, the Arrow. How could one possibly find anything or anywhere? Even one fixed address produced a list of complicated directives. But beyond all the confusion was the shock, shock at the crowds, shock at the paraded poverty of street beggars, shock at the dirt, and at what he saw from the grimy train as it emerged out of the smoke-arbour of Fenchurch Street with a loud hiss of steam. Nor did the ride on top of the Plaistow horse-bus give him the feeling that the streets of London were paved with gold. The slums of Birmingham were nothing to this, and his arrogant young heart quickly turned the horror into an ardent pride in his own nobility, not altogether unmingled, however, with compassion. But Father Gaveston had quite enough Holy Young Men to fill his Franciscan community in Plaistow. Slumming was all the rage among the Holy Young Men—who were called HYMns, though some said the plural was HYMen—especially if they could wear a robe and a pair of sandals, and be very very nice to very poor boys, bringing into their lives a little of the richness and colour they had themselves found in the true way to God. Father Gaveston, therefore, after a short talk to this particular Holy Young Man, gave him another letter, to his friend David Huxley, known among Anglo-Cats as Brother Cynewulf, O.S.L.

It was in the year 1110 that Saint Lambert of Alfringham had appeared to the Blessed Cynewulf on the very spot where he himself had died in his own hermitage, and told him to found an Abbey there which was to house a new English order, whose Rule he then dictated in all the complexity usually required for the stark and simple life. The Order of Saint Lambert developed quickly and Alfringham became famous especially for the miraculous cures effected at the Rock of Truth. Lying and thieving children were brought there by anxious parents, and even petty thieves and poachers were reputed never to steal again once they reached and touched the Rock, so that soon the law had to recognise the place as a sanctuary and abandon its pursuits at the great gate. Neither the divine nor the legal privilege, however, extended to more serious criminals, few of whom in any case had any real desire for so unprofitable a solution. Indeed even the Abbey found the business unrewarding, since the rich did not admit to lying or stealing. So the monks began to pray to Saint Lambert to include in his wondrous understanding of the human heart at least those physical diseases, from dumbness to toothache and from paralysis of the arm to chilblains, which could be traced, however remotely, to a one-time theft, however childish, or a one-time lie, however white. The donations rolled in, and after two centuries Alfringham had rather lost sight of the stark and simple life. Then the royal thief took over, and the monks escaped simply and starkly to France and the Spanish Netherlands, where by now they had two abbeys. So ended the glorious history of Alfringham, but the Lambertines survived, expanded and flourished, with enormous respectability throughout Europe, perhaps out of sheer uniqueness, being the only one of the great orders with an English origin.

It was on 29th April 1893 that David Huxley, a young student of architecture, having just read all about the Blessed Cynewulf of Alfringham in an old book on the monasteries of England, began to dream of reviving the Order of Saint Lambert in the Church of England, which was, of course, the Catholic Church before Rome had so unreasonably dissented. He read all the right books and served in all the right churches, where it was fun to dress up in a red cassock and zuchetto and bear a bedizened banner or swing a thurible; he stayed in all the right communities, from the Cistercians on Mount St. Bernard in Lincolnshire, to the new Anglican Benedictine nunnery in Ealing, and slowly he joined all the right secret societies, from the Societas Sanctae Crucis, known as S.S.C., to the Confraternity of the Blessed Sacrament, the Guild of All Souls and the Society of the Holy Rosary; he saw, above all, the right people, and by 1894 he had gathered around him a small group of young men who shared his ardent vision and his delight in the picturesque white habit he had designed, with a black scapular, departing a little from the strict black of the Lambertines. By 1895 he had persuaded the Rev. Charles Taplow to persuade the Archbishop, whose knowledge of the Canon Law as regards postulants and novices was naturally a little hazy after so many centuries of not having any, to permit his tonsure and solemn profession as a Lambertine monk. So he wrote out the whole Rule of St. Lambert in a beautiful script on vellum, enlarging it considerably with bits from the Cistercians and bits from the Carmelites and bits from the Benedictines. But the oblates had nowhere to go, and met in the parlour of his mother's small and brand new house in Deodar Road, Putney, which overlooked the river and was thus also very picturesque, though the dog always became neuralgic at the sight of them and barked from the garden all the way through their Gregorian chant. By 1895, most of the oblates had deserted him, just about at the time when he met Father Gaveston and saw that his true vocation was to work among slum boys, so that Father Gaveston introduced him to the Vicar of St. Luke's in the dockland parish of Strathmond, who offered this strange new recruit to the Anglican Underworld a cold old-house for his community in Lower Wharf Road, Strathmond. He moved in with two of his monks, on 29th April 1896.

By a pure coincidence which Brother Cynewulf, as he now called himself, could only regard as a sign from the Blessed Founder Himself, Northbrook Hayley turned up at The Priory, Lower Wharf Road, on the 29th April 1897, with a letter of introduction from Father Gaveston, a leather grip, and a silver snuff-box from which he took discreet and delicate pinches as he talked. Both men were slight, one in a silken grey suit and wing poke collar, the other in a flowing black and white habit; and Northbrook's countenance was as fresh and clean as Brother Cynewulf's was smooth and swarthy, his hair stuck up like a brush and was as sandy as Brother Cynewulf's was tonsured and dark, his eyes were as hypnotically blue as Brother Cynewulf's were hypnotically black.

"You won't be allowed to keep that, I'm afraid," said Brother Cynewulf, pointing to the silver snuffbox. "No private ownership, it's the Rule."

"Ah, yes of course, Father, I'll send it home."

"Good. And by the way, although I am in a sense the Prior here, I am not a priest. You must call me Brother Cynewulf." He gestured with his hand as he spoke, holding two fingers papally together. "It is, of course, my dearest wish to be ordained one day, as it is also to take my little community back to its rightful inheritance at Alfringham—those 'bare ruined choirs', you know, 'where late the sweet birds sang.' But in the meantime, we must follow the call of more immediate needs, here among the poor boys, some of whom may one day sing in just those very choirs."

Northbrook decided quite spontaneously to take the name of Brother Sebastian, much to Cynewulf's mingled disappointment and admiration. The disappointment he expressed: all the Brothers had chosen native saints, he said, it was a tradition in the order, but the new arrival was strangely elated about Sebastian. The admiration, however, was less concise, something remotely apprehended about naked Italian youths and arrows of desire. He even began to hum "Jerusalem" as he walked out of his tiny office in front of the newly accepted postulant, to introduce him to the community.

The three other monks, apart from the Prior, were Brother Cuthbert, Brother Alban and Brother Theobald, Brother Theobald being really the Vicar of St. Luke's, and therefore allowed to keep his real name as a non-resident and only part-time monk. Brother Sebastian said he was delighted to be the fifth, which was his lucky number. Very soon after his arrival, two more came, a fact which Brother Cynewulf regarded as following directly from the arrival of Brother Sebastian, who was quite clearly a miraculous omen of good luck sent by St. Lambert, and who for his part was immensely pleased to be promoted so quickly from new boy to older inmate. The newcomers were called Brother Asaph and Brother Boniface. The latter, however, was a Cockney boy of seventeen, whose face was so pale that nobody could manage the Prior's name for him without giggling, so that he soon insisted on sticking to his own, which was Felix, a perfectly good saint, he said and Brother Felix he remained, though Brother Sebastian soon began to call him Brer Fox. Brother Felix disliked Brother Sebastian on sight, and called him Brer Wolf, but only behind his back.

But Brother Sebastian's spiritual longings soon began to wane. The so-called Priory was a two-storied house of smoked yellow brick, facing North and standing back from the road behind a high brick wall with a wooden door. It had probably once been a more well-to-do house in the road, which consisted of low slums, dark and back to back, liaising the families of seamen or dock workers. The screech of cranes, the hoot of sirens and the clang of swing bridges going up to let a ship pass in or out of the dock, could all be heard, as well as the milk-woman with her cans on a yoke, shouting *Mee-yal-koo*, which they never bought. And the house was very old. It was also bare of any but the most rudimentary furniture. The Prior's tiny office which had been a vestibule—contained a desk he had brought from his own home, but otherwise only two stools. The kitchen and refectory had a trestle table each, benches and a stone floor. The two common rooms were quite empty and were used mostly as rough-play rooms for local boys. Upstairs was a clubroom for them, with a few stools and benches, a small wooden table and a shelf of tattered books. The two rooms opposite had been transformed into a chapel, and on the second floor, were the "cells", artificially divided from each other by wooden walls, with planks for beds and strawsacks for mattresses. The food was entirely vegetarian, chiefly lentils, dried, peas or beans with macaroni, and a bowl of black coffee for breakfast, one spoonful of sugar and a hunk of dry bread.

Brother Sebastian didn't like this part of it one bit. His original vision of the monastic life, even in the slums, had been late rather than early mediaeval—as indeed had Brother Cynewulf's, who was beginning to feel that he had been led astray into all this Boys Brigade stuff, away from the true Lambertine vocation. And Brother Cynewulf confided some of these doubts to Brother Sebastian, who had become, within a matter of almost days, his most trusted adviser, much to the annoyance of some members of the community, who called him the amateur nobleman. But Brother Cynewulf was most excellently pleased with Brother Sebastian. They were well matched, these two, with their big ideas and their splendid ancestry, their pretences which yet were not pretences, their absolute faith in themselves which they sincerely believed was an absolute faith in God. Very soon Brother Sebastian had represented himself as a man of many contacts, who had given up "the world" for his vocation but who would not be averse to re-contacting those contacts in that world for the sake of the higher ideal. The Prior, of course, had his community to look after, and it would look a little odd if he went around too much, especially begging, but he, Brother Sebastian, could be as it were his ambassador-at-large.

At large it was.

For of course, Brother Sebastian had very few contacts, apart from Father Gaveston, whom he visited frequently in his parish, and who was willing enough to help him and Cynewulf by introducing him to his own friends in society. Brother Sebastian in fact, represented himself in "the world"—the one he had given up—as a person of some consequence at the Strathmond Lambertine Community—and an engaging young scholar in a monk's habit was after all quite an amusing guest to have at one's less frivolous dinners or weekends, at least in High Church circles. Even in society proper, or rather in certain literary and aesthetic sections of society, there was a vogue for having dog-collared guests whom one called "Father" in a loud voice, but a real monk, that was truly unusual, and some of the more decolletées ladies liked to come up to him and touch his sleeve or kiss his scapular. The young men were more remotely fascinated, but he enjoyed that too.

He was seldom at the Priory, and when he was, he stayed mostly in his room, except for the offices, in which he enjoyed singing, for he had a good voice and liked to startle the others with his solo responses. He occasionally took the boys on Saturday trips into Kent, and became very friendly with two of them especially, who worshipped him and behaved badly when he was absent, but otherwise he took no part in the Priory's activities, was extremely rude and uppish to guests and never cleaned his room.

"Where does he get the money for all them trips, that's what I'd like to know," said Brother Felix. "It can't be from the Prior, I'm sure of that."

"Indeed, not," said Brother Cuthbert primly, who was one of the original faithfuls and loathed Brother Sebastian. "Brother Cynewulf has precisely £40 a year from his mother, which isn't much on which to support a community of seven, now is it?"

"Brother Sebastian told me his mother ran a posh sort of boarding-house in Rottingdean, oh very superior, he made that ever so clear. And his sister, what came here with her governess to see him, she was an uppish young lady all right, *owe Northbrook*, she says, it smells *sowe hhorrid*, just like *gowets*, *hhow doo you beaar* it? Kid of twelve or thirteen, I ask you. If he don't like it here what's he staying for? He ain't got no more vocation in him than a blind sparrow, that's what."

"Fear not therefore: better are ye than many sparrows," Brother Cuthbert quoted pointlessly and Brother Felix said, "Oh, Brother, what a lark."

The boardinghouse in Rottingdean was actually a young man called Hugh Walford, who lived the life of an aesthetic solitary in a lonely house near Roedean Shack. He had met Brother Sebastian at Canon Grant's and been more than rather fascinated, so that he said in effect, come and see my rubbings, for they shared a passionate interest in monumental brasses. And the odd thing was, they really did talk of monumental brasses, the weekend being wondrous and worshipful and monumentally innocent, at least on Brother Sebastian's side, who merely wanted the love of everyone he met, no less, and without knowing it sparked his mind from the hidden desires of men like Hugh Walford, and as for Hugh, well, even he felt peculiarly overawed by the postulant's flowing black robe and the holy gestures.

Brother Sebastian, in fact, was sincere. Or rather, he had already developed to a fine art, and without any conscious intention of doing so, that useful gift we all have of using sincerity as a mask, by detaching one aspect of the truth as we see it from another, both being equally true at different moments. He genuinely believed in his vocation, in his devotion to God and to the Lambertine ideal of meditation and prayer, towards which he was working by winning the sympathy of so many useful people. But he also believed in himself, a penniless young student who needed free lodgings, however uncomfortable, a place where he could improve himself by reading, and of course by prayer, and where he had already written a succinct and learned article on the Church Brasses of Warwickshire, which had been accepted by *The West of England Antiquary* for the princely sum of one guinea, as yet unpaid. He was getting on very splendidly, and many people in High Anglican Places thought well of him. But he needed money. He had come to the end of his savings and Brother Cynewulf allowed him only the occasional crown or half-crown. Even a monk could not beg for everything. There were fares, for though calced he did not relish walking to Brighton, for example, or Sittingbourne, nor could he travel third-class. Even in the London Underground and the Metropolitan Railway he owed himself at least a second-class compartment. Then there were the tips to the endless servants who did not unpack his non-existent luggage. It was incredible how trivial worldly things and trivial worldly people could impinge upon his plans, even now, in this elected silence, this chosen devotion to himself and God alone.

It was during Compline one September evening that Brother Cynewulf first noticed the small hole in the wooden cross where the diamond had been. He went on singing as he glanced quickly at each monk in turn, and the eyes of each monk were carefully following the notation of Solesme, and the lips of each monk were reverently singing.

In spite of his anxiety, Brother Cynewulf couldn't help the glow of pride that swept over him every time he looked at his achievement, four of them in black and white, the novices in white, the postulants in black and the three new oblates in brown. The oblate Sylvan, especially, looked charmingly Franciscan. And Brother Sebastian in black, with his fresh complexion. Yes, he was very pleased with Brother Sebastian, who was being very kind to Sylvan. But the diamond. He had bought that cross himself when St. Austin's Priory in the New Kent Road went up for auction. But no. His monks were all Caesar's wives, above suspicion.

When the office was over he asked everyone except the oblates to stay behind, and showed them the hole in the cross.

"Oh dear," said Brother Cuthbert, "what shall we do? The Y cross is worthless now."

"I noticed it in the middle of the *In manus tuas*," said Brother Felix, "never had such a fright in all me life."

"Well, you're responsible for the chapel, Brer Fox, you should have noticed it before."

"Don't you Brer Fox me, Brother Sebastian. I looks after the chapel better'n you looks after your own cell. I'd like to know something of what goes on up there I would."

"Come, come, brothers in Christ, no bickering, now," said the Prior. "We must find this diamond. It may be exceedingly awkward if one of the local lads has stolen it."

"Very likely, I should think," said Brother Sebastian.

"It's the poor what gets the blame," said Brother Felix.

"Well we can't have any litigation. We must move with great circumspection."

"I suggest we first move with circumspection over the chapel floor," Brother Sebastian said with sudden firmness. "I expect it just fell out. It's probably under the altar carpet."

"I beat the carpet out myself only this morning," said Brother Felix indignantly.

But the monks got down on their hands and knees on the floorboards, and after a while a small ping was heard and Brother Felix leapt up and shouted.

"Northbrook, you humbug!"

"What do you mean? Here it is! I've found it! It fell out of the fold as I moved the carpet."

"I saw you, you had it in your hand all the time. I always said there was something crooked about you. What are you in, Brother Sebastian, diamond smuggling?"

"I *will* not be spoken to like that. You shall apologise, Brother Felix. Here's your diamond, and look after it properly from now on."

He swept from the holy place like an angry prophet, and the monks filed out after him looking sheepish, Brother Felix muttering angrily, "I saw him, I tell you, I saw him. Bloomin' shame, I calls it. It's the poor what gets the blame, that's what."

But Brother Sebastian went to see Brother Cynewulf, who believed him, and no more was said. And when Brother Sebastian was clothed as a novice, he decided suddenly to change his name to Austin. His mother, he said, had a great devotion to St. Austin, and wished him to be known by that name. "Pity," Brother Cynewulf murmured, "we had all got used to Sebastian, so suitable, somehow, Sebastian."

By November, however, Brother Cynewulf was beginning to wonder about Brother Austin alias Sebastian. He was going about rather a lot. There was that visit to a friend in Worcester College—well, he *was* the son of a Bishop. And in early October he went to stay with Canon Grant in Brighton. That was business in a way, and he was given some community money. But then at the end of the month he shot off without permission to Birmingham for a week, taking seven and tenpence and asking Brother Cuthbert to inform the Prior that he had gone because his father was ill. The Prior had to be quite stern with him afterwards. "No community money for travelling except on business, I made it a Rule myself always to obtain expenses from those people whom we visit, but of course there are exceptions. This is not one." Then Brother Austin explained that the seven and tenpence was not for his visit to Over Marstaple but for reimbursement of money he advanced to Brother Felix for housekeeping on October 11th. Finally, one afternoon a young nurse called Nancy Weymouth turned up at the Priory and asked to see Father Austin.

"You mean Brother Austin, my child."

"Oh, no, Father, I mean Father Alfred Austin. The son of the poet, you know."

"There must be some mistake. We are none of us priests, here."

"Oh I know, Father, not Roman priests. I know all about that. Alfred explained to me, about Anglicans, you see, we're going to be married, I mean, he said, he promised . . ."

"But my child, we only have a Brother Austin here. He's a monk; not a pr—not a clergyman. You understand the difference, don't you? We practise celibacy."

"Celibacy?"

The girl looked both puzzled and frightened. She had seen the word only that afternoon, oddly enough, in *The Strathmond Protestant Banner* someone was reading on the tram, a big headline that read "Bishop practises open celibacy."

"We take vows not to marry," the Prior explained gently.

"But, but, but he's got to marry me," the young nurse exclaimed. "He said, he promised. Oh, no!"

"Sit down, my child. Now, don't cry. Tell me all about it. You see, I have to know. What does this Father Austin look like?"

She sniffed and wailed and sobbed and dabbed her eyes as she told the dismal tale he fully expected to hear. It was in the Jubilee crowds. She had got lost and he had been so kind and seen her home by tram. She lived in Camberwell. He said he was a clergyman, working in the slums. He hoped to get his own parish soon. She was a nurse, and a respectable girl, and worked hard to help her mother, who had six younger children. It had seemed so wonderful, meeting him, and a clergyman too. And such a real gentleman. He never so much as touched her except her arm perhaps, to help her across the street. And then he knew so much, too, about churches and things. And then in the summer, no September it was, they went on a trip once, into Kent, she had the afternoon off. He wanted to show her some brasses or coppers or something in a church there. And then somehow—she buried her eyes in her handkerchief here—it started on the top of the horse bus, they were tucked together under the waterproof rug, and he got her feeling all funny, and it was such a lovely day, and then they walked arm in arm through the fields, and then they sat under a tree, and she felt more and more, well, funny, and he begged, and he promised, and then— The obvious rest was lost in sobs and tears.

When Brother Austin was sent for, and came in, he looked furious at first, and then got very excited. He ignored the girl and made a long speech to the Prior, reproaching him for taking this unknown woman's word against his, couldn't he see she was a Nice Protestant girl being used by the Protestant Association, who loathed the High Anglican Party and all this monkery as they called it? Couldn't he see through all this Mrs. Henry Wood stuff, why it was a wonder she hadn't come in rags, clutching a baby at her breast on a stormy night. What did he take him for, a blade? As a matter of fact he did know her, he had noticed her as a shorthand writer at a gathering in Mr. George Fenton's house, yes, Mr. Fenton, the secretary of the Protestant Association, with whom he had made friends for the very purpose of doing a little scouting—and did Brother Cynewulf know, for example, that the Protestant Association now had a complete list of all the members of the S.S.C. as well as the Acta of the S.S.C. Synod, which they were about to publish? He was just going to report this startling discovery to his superior, but found his superior listening to the prattle of a shorthand clerk and typewriter.

The girl looked completely bewildered during this tirade, and even Brother Cynewulf was nonplussed.

"It's all very well, Brother Sebastian, I mean, Brother Austin," he said angelically, "but don't you see that if you're telling the truth then it hardly matters whether or not the girl is lying?"

"Oh, I'm not lying, Father, I assure you."

"My child, you must not interrupt me. Don't you see, Brother Austin, that they will use such a scandal against us, anyway? Providing of course that there really is an infant on the way. And the girl's story is convincing enough. Though I must admit, this Father Austin business sounds too childish for words, and very like them, very like them indeed. No understanding at all. I can visualise it all so easily—not the Lambertines, the Libertines, and so forth. Dear me." He shuddered. "What a nuisance."

"Well, if that's all you're worrying over, I can handle it. Leave the politics to me, Brother Cynewulf, I am your ambassador-at-large, remember? All I care about is your good opinion of me, and that my word should be trusted. How else can I be a religious under you?" He had taken a sheet of paper from the prior's desk and was writing on it as he spoke. Then he turned to Nancy Weymouth and said very gently, with the softest look in his eyes.

"My dear child, you have been most ill-used, and perhaps a little foolish, but far be it from me to condemn or criticise. I do assure you that the Prior here, and I, understand just what you are going through and why you came here, and you have all our sympathy. But you must believe me when I tell you that there are things going on in high circles which you cannot possibly understand, though I can explain them to you later, if you wish. You have been an instrument in these machinations, and it may well be that these machinations could finish not only my career but the careers of all those dedicated men around me, whom I love most dearly. You wouldn't really want that would you?" She shook her head, the tears still burning her eyes. "Then you will be a good girl and sign this paper, won't you? Please trust me. Everything will come right in the end, I promise."

The girl signed, like an automaton.

But she heard his small sigh of relief, and understood the essential fact every woman always understands in a flash, even those who refuse to face it. She faced it at once and with a sudden dignity that transcended her red nose and weepy eyes and half askew hat, she rose and went to the door, addressing only the Prior:

"I know I signed, Father, but it was him all the same."

Brother Cynewulf was very perturbed by the incident, and prayed through Christmas for guidance. He talked to Brother Theobald, the Vicar of St. Luke's, Strathmond, and Brother Theobald also prayed for guidance, and talked to Brother Cuthbert. So that when the January number of *The Church Vigilant* did in fact publish the list of all the members of the Societas Sanctae Crucis, together with the Acta for July, August and October, and the full report of the September Synod, Brother Cynewulf sighed with relief and thought, dear Brother Sebastian, he was telling the truth, but how very wicked of them. Brother Cuthbert, however, at once consulted Brother Theobald, who said, There is a traitor in the camp, and without pausing to genuflect by the chapel, padded up to Brother Austin's cell, followed by Brother Cuthbert. The door was locked, so Brother Cuthbert trotted down to the kitchen and asked Brother Felix for a screwdriver, and Brother Felix left the lentils to stew and followed him up on being told excitedly what it was for.

The room was indeed a mess. Books and papers were scattered all over the plank bed, as if it had been used as a desk, and a *prie-dieu* Brother Austin had bought for a shilling from the rag-and-bone man was turned unprayingly towards the bed. The washstand was strewn with toilet bottles and the slops were unemptied. In the corner a Gladstone bag was opened out on the floor, and on it about a dozen books were carefully ranged.

"That's the bag what came for him, by the railway company," said Brother Felix. "Last October it was. He unpacked it downstairs and he told me Canon Grant had given him all them books, for the Priory. All about Church Brasses, he said they was."

"Very pretty, too," said Brother Cuthbert. "Oh, look, what a shame, one has a lot of pages torn out."

"Brother Cuthbert, come and have a look at this," Brother Theobald called from the bed, holding a letter he had found, and his voice was so ominous as he read it that Brother Felix stayed quite still, crouched on his haunches, holding a book on Fourteenth Century Figurines.

"The Protestant Association, 14, Dean Farrar Court, Strand, London, W.C.," Brother Theobald read out, "16 November 1897. Dear Sir, Thank you for your letter which I have not been able to answer until now. Your first offer of S.S.C. Acta I did not care for. It is not easy to judge the value of the Report of the Synod without seeing it, as the contents of these documents vary. I should be willing to offer you a guinea or 25s. for it, and if you post it to me I will send you a remittance by return. Yours truly, George Fenton, Secretary."

"Oh, Brother Theobald, the man's a scamp!" Brother Cuthbert was very shocked.

"Blimey!" said Brother Felix, "the dirty rotter."

But Brother Theobald took control at once, and said, rather unfraternally, "Collect all the papers, you two, and take them to the Vicarage. Leave the books. I am going to see the Prior."

The Prior, however, was sitting with Canon Grant, who was in a state of great distress. Twenty-two books, some of them rare, had vanished from his valuable ecclesiastical library after the visit of a young monk from the Lambertine community, called Brother Sebastian. Such a nice young man too, serious and well-spoken, and quite an authority on mediaeval brasses. The servants had seen him leave with a Gladstone bag he had borrowed from one of them. And some of the books had been traced by the police to Messrs. Bull & Auvache, a firm of booksellers in Bloomsbury, who had bought them for six guineas from a young monk who would not accept a cheque, but who signed a receipt as Austin O.S.L. They had his address in their books, and frequently did business with him, he was interested in mediaeval brasses, they said.

Brother Cynewulf was appalled, and begged the Canon not to prosecute. The Canon only wanted his books back, he was very, very sorry, very disturbed, distressed, oh dear. But when Brother Theobald came in with the letter, the distress of the Canon spread quickly. What other secret papers had he stolen? They went up to the cell, where the Canon identified his library marks on the books, and then to the Vicarage, where Brother Theobald looked up his own S.S.C. membership papers and other documents of other ritualistic secret societies. The S.S.C. Acta for July, August and October were missing, as well as the full report of the September Synod for that year.

All this clerical distress, however, was as nothing compared to the distress of Brother Austin when he returned. For Brother Austin became quite hysterical. He could not clear his name, he said, without inculpating someone else, and when pressed, this someone else became more and more remote, until quite suddenly this someone else took shape in his mind, and began to emerge—slowly, in spite of great reluctance, as someone else whose memory he valued too greatly, no he couldn't say it, someone who had given him the books, which he said he had received as a gift from the Canon. He himself hadn't yet had a moment to look at the books, had no idea that other documents were inside them, and surely the Canon would remember, and regret the whole incident, but if not, well, it wasn't for him to say how this other person had got hold of them, even at the cost of his own reputation, and so forth. The Canon said,

"You mean, my very dear friend, the Reverend Williams?"

Brother Austin hid his face in his hands.

"I have named no one."

"The Reverend Douglas Williams died in November," the Canon said to the Prior. "He could have had any of the books for the asking. He knew that." He turned to Brother Austin. "Do you realise that you are accusing a dead man?"

"I have named no one."

It was extremely foolish of Brother Theobald, the Vicar of St. Luke's, to try and force the Canon to prosecute by refusing to return the books, but Brother Theobald and Brother Cuthbert were determined to have the traitor both punished and silenced. It was even more foolish of Mr. Ernest Copplestone, solicitor for the Protestant Association, to advise the young monk who had sold them the S.S.C. Acta to issue a writ against Brother Theobald and Brother Cuthbert, for the return of his papers which they had taken from his cell after breaking into it. But the Protestant Association were determined to drag into the public eye the existence of all those romanising secret societies within the Church of England, of which the public eye was in their opinion still too unaware.

On the 19th January therefore, the warrant issued by the distressed and reluctant Canon was executed, and Brother Austin was arrested and taken down to Brighton. He was by then extremely confident, so confident that poor Brother Cynewulf began to be tormented once again with doubts. Brother Austin simply *knew* his own innocence, and was quite sure the judge would believe him. But alas, he was innocent, if not of larceny, certainly of court procedure. Scarcely a fortnight had passed since the Lord Chancellor, Lord Halsbury, had moved the second reading of a Bill to amend the law of Criminal Evidence, whereby prisoners would in future be allowed to go into the witness-box. But there wasn't a chance of it becoming law for months, indeed, it was already two years ago that

Lord Halsbury had introduced an exactly similar Bill, announcing that he had said all he had to say of it at least five times in previous Sessions, and that though the Lords had made no difficulties it had failed to pass through the Commons on account of pressure of other business. It had eventually had its first reading in the Commons but had never made the second, and had been withdrawn at the end of the Session. Perhaps only the echoes of it had reached Brother Austin in his remote contemplative life, at any rate he had felt entirely certain of his dramatic appearance in the witness-box, and of his ability to convince the judge, all on his magical own. But the splendid speeches and gestures he had rehearsed availed him nothing as a prisoner in the dock.

The litigation in the Brighton Police Court was not in fact a mere case of petty theft, it was a struggle as enraged as most religious wars, between the High Church Union, who engaged Mr. Richard Barlowe, and the Protestant Association, who engaged Mr. Arnold Pettigrew. The Stipendiary Magistrate was very bewildered.

"What has all this to do with the question?" he asked when Mr. Pettigrew had cross-examined the poor Canon about all the ritualistic societies in turn.

"I am going to show you that behind all this is one of the most bitter pieces of religious persecution that we have had for many years."

"What difference would it make if it were so?"

"I will show that this gentleman is an involuntary instrument in the hands of these men, forced to prosecute against his own will, and wishing it to be withdrawn. I have it in his own handwriting, in a letter to the prisoner's mother."

"Will that make any difference?"

"Of course you will not allow this Court to be used for altogether ulterior objects?"

"But if a case is made out, I shall have to commit for trial, even if the prosecution be undertaken from the most petty motives of vindictive spite."

"Are you prepared to rule that, even if I establish that this prosecution was not instituted by Canon Grant at all, but was started by one of the Members of this so-called Holy Cross Society for the purpose of shutting this prisoner's mouth, or preventing the publication of documents which they feared, and as a revenge for the prisoner having published certain documents already—if I satisfy you as to that, would you still commit for trial?"

"Even then it would be a question for a jury. Of course, if there were anything in that to inspire me with doubt as to whether the evidence as regards larceny is true that would be another thing."

The poor Canon was put through it by Pettigrew, especially on the fallibility of his memory and the likelihood of his having given the books to the Reverend Douglas Williams. A letter was produced from the prisoner to his mother, dated October 12th, in which the prisoner said that the Reverend Douglas Williams had given him a lot of books on mediaeval brasses. The prisoner was admitted to have been very much under the influence of the man they called Brother Cynewulf. And all the monks were put through it, from the Prior to the Rev. Theobald Simpkins, who was made to look very foolish over the vice of private ownership and whether he owned his pocket handkerchief.

The Stipendiary Magistrate became irascible. "Are you trying to show that if the men in this fraternity are not allowed private ownership the prisoner could not therefore be in possession of the stolen books?"

"No, sir," said Pettigrew, as if shocked by the judge's sophistry. "I am trying to find out by what religious rule the Reverend Simpkins appropriated the prisoner's property. I have the Rules here, on 'the baneful vice of private ownership', which is to be 'cut off from the Monastery by the roots'." He read out. " 'But if anyone shall be found to indulge in this most baneful vice . . .' then there follows a lot of Latin."

"What is the correction for this baneful vice?" the Stipendiary Magistrate asked with sudden interest.

"I don't know," said Mr. Pettigrew, like a schoolboy caught out on his construing. "Are you a member of the Church of England?" he asked the witness brusquely.

"I said that I was a clergyman."

"I asked you if you were a member of the Church of England."

"Surely we are not going to have a theological discussion," the magistrate said petulantly. "I am not going to allow it."

"Here is a man on whom I say the whole of the prosecution rests. I want to test the credit of the witness. Surely this is no theological question?"

"I am a member of the Church of England," said the Reverend Simpkins like a repentant Peter.

"Are you a member of the Society of the Holy Cross?"

"You can say so." The Reverend Simpkins was clearly imitating one greater than himself.

"Are you a member of the Confraternity of the Blessed Sacrament?"

"I am."

"Are you also a member of the English Church Union?"

"Yes."

"Also the Society of the Holy Rosary?"

"Yes."

"Did you break into the prisoner's room?"

"I opened his room door."

"Did you make a list of all you found there?"

"I did, and you have it."

"Did you find a letter from the Reverend Douglas Williams?"

"No."

"That you swear?"

"I can't say it was not there. I did not find it."

"But you found a letter from Mr. George Fenton, relating to the S.S.C. Acta?"

"Yes."

"What were the S.S.C. Acta?"

"You have a copy before you."

"They are the transactions of the Society of the Holy Cross. That is the Society that published the book called *The Priest in Absolution* in 1871?"

"No."

"What! Mr. Grant said so."

"Mr. Grant did not."

"Canon Grant said that the Society published it."

"What on earth has that to do with the case?" the Magistrate asked again.

"Everything. This man is the instigator of the prosecution, because the transactions of this Society were published in *The Church Vigilant.* Were you annoyed by it?"

"I was not."

"Was the Society annoyed by it?"

"No, they were rather pleased than otherwise. It was a good advertisement for them."

"Do you suggest they were pleased? Do you know that the letter that you yourself had stolen was published in extenso, omitting only the name, in *The Church Times?*"

"I never stole any letter."

"This letter that you took possession of then."

"No, I did not take possession of it. It was simply in my custody."

"You are indeed a casuist."

"Don't raise theological questions," said the Magistrate. By the time the prisoner was committed for trial at Lewes Assizes, the newspaper had got hold of the weird and picturesque story. "Monk in Court," a few bored and bewildered paragraphs announced hopefully, though in fact only Brother Felix had worn his habit, because he had no suit. Mercifully *The Times* gave it only one paragraph well tucked away, for the Dreyfus case and the trial of Mr. Zola in France were attracting much more attention, and as for home litigation, Lord William Nevill, accused of fraud, naturally occupied most of the space. Other papers even had drawings of him, which was very unfair. The Church papers, however, went to town on the Monk case. *The Rock* got hold of back verbatim reports and splashed it all over their most important pages. *The Church Times* said that the Protestant Association were Jesuits in disguise and *The Church Vigilant* said that the Church Union were Romanist spies sent by the Pope. The prisoner, in all this, was almost forgotten.

He was not, however, forgotten at Lewes Assizes, when the whole farce was gone through again, before Mr. Justice Hoyden, who was a High Church Anglican notorious for allowing his personal prejudices to play havoc with the rules of evidence. He said that the prisoner was a wolf in sheep's clothing. Mr. Richard Barlow, summing up for the prosecution, said his learned friend had endeavoured to confuse the simple issues of the case by introducing bitter theological controversies. Mr. Arnold Petti-grew, for the defence, said it was clear that if the prisoner had not issued a writ against the Reverend Simpkins to recover the incriminating letters he would not have been prosecuted. It was not for the theft of books he was being prosecuted but because he took it upon himself to start legal proceedings against these members of the Church of England who masqueraded as monks. It was indeed a sad thing that in these days when the Church had enough enemies outside it should divide itself into hostile forces, because, he added aptly, forgetting the original subject of the quotation, a house divided against itself could not stand. In this case the prosecution would not have been started had it not been discovered that there was "a traitor in the camp", an expression which was the last word in vituperation against anybody. Mr. Pettigrew went on to point out that the prisoner had taken the books openly to a bookseller where he was well-known, and gave his proper name and address. Mr. Barlow, he said, had grown pathetic on the subject of accusing a dead man, but this was the prisoner's defence, not that advised by his counsel. The prisoner gasped at this piece of treachery.

His lordship had a great deal to say on the improper use of documents, for some private letters from the Prior to the prisoner's mother and to the Reverend Simpkins had apparently been handed over to a representative of the Star, by Mr. Copplestone himself, the solicitor for the Protestant Association, and been used as a basis for a virulent attack on the various societies of which the Reverend Simpkins was a member, in an article headed *A Lambertine 'Sell'*. The article was written in the interests of the Protestant Association, and it did seem as if there was some ulterior motive in handing the letters over, especially one which had not been submitted in Court and said, "Brother Austin's game is up now. You need not be alarmed by his threat of legal proceedings. I have the whole affair in my hands and I shall get rid of him as quietly and as quickly as possible." If the Protestant Association had been trafficking with a spy, and inducing a member of their Society to betray its secrets, they must not be surprised if the view taken of their conduct was unfavourable. The whole affair had raised an unnecessary cloud and the simple question for the jury to decide was whether the books were stolen by the prisoner.

The jury found the prisoner guilty.

After which Mr. Barlow revealed—and was unpardonably allowed by the judge to reveal—that the prisoner had visited the rooms of Bishop Johnson's son at Oxford, and, he alleged, stolen from there a valuable book on brasses, which had been sold to Messrs. Bull & Auvache.

Mr. Pettigrew said it was a strange thing, but he had a most extraordinary good character of the prisoner from Mr. Johnson.

Mr. Barlow said he also had information that an action had been brought against the prisoner at Manchester for the return of a book of stamps valued at £59. The verdict went against him, and he had never paid a farthing. Then in July he had packed up a box of books and sent them to the Midlands Educational Agency, who were then pressing him for money. He also sent them a £5 note, and though it could not absolutely be traced, Mr. Huxley had lost a £5 note about that time. The prisoner had long had a career of religious duplicity. It did not matter how kind people had been to him, he had taken advantage of them in every possible way. There could be little doubt that from the first he had palmed himself off on generous people.

Mr. Pettigrew said that with regard to the action at Manchester he had a letter from well-known solicitors saying that the prisoner had only lost his case because he could not prove postage, and that no one suggested that the stamps had been sold or otherwise disposed of. He then repeated that the prisoner had insisted on a defence which in counsel's view was untenable. Mr. Copplestone had also done his best to induce the prisoner to throw himself on the mercy of Canon Grant. The prisoner seemed extraordinarily excitable, and was a very difficult person to deal with, and he seemed to have acted in a singular way during the last two years.

His lordship, in passing sentence, said that the prisoner had been found guilty of one of the worst crimes he could conceive—stealing books from one friend and endeavouring to throw the blame on another friend who was dead. It was very rarely he had had any case before him which had given him so much pain, and the prisoner thought, what a lucky lordship. His lordship therefore, in the prisoner's own interest, and so on.

As soon as they saw which way the sentence was going, the gaolers quietly laid hands on the prisoner, who didn't move but stared fixedly at Brother Cynewulf, without flinching even when he heard the very prejudicial sentence of three years' penal servitude. Then he turned soldierly on his heels and marched out, head high.

After the prisoner had been removed his lordship said with petulance that he had looked at the rules of the Society mentioned by Mr. Pettigrew, and had found to his, surprise that they were a translation of the rules of Saint Lambert, who had lived about 630. He had thought they were rules promulgated recently, under the authority of the Archbishop of Canterbury. What therefore, his lordship seemed to say, was all the fuss about?

The prison ink was a corrective red, with which the prisoner underlined Isaiah Eli, 7.8: *He was oppressed, and he was afflicted, yet he opened not his mouth: he is brought as a lamb to the slaughter, and as a sheep before her shearers is dumb, so he openeth not his mouth. He was taken from prison and from judgment: and who shall declare his generation?*

Then he wrote a long red letter to the Prior, as it were in his own blood, on the Byronic spectacle of his bleeding heart, ending with the virulent hope that every time Brother Cynewulf sang Terce and came to the line "false witnesses did rise up, they laid to my charge things I knew not", he would suffer great anguish in his soul and remember the man whom he so unjustly caused to be wrongly accused.

As Brother Cynewulf said afterwards to Vernon Manning—a young protégé of Canon Grant's who joined the Order a few months later, by which time the publicity of the case had prompted a rich businessman to help them buy back the ruins of Alfringham Abbey—as Brother Cynewulf said: he wasn't sure, even now, Brother Austin was so very convincing.

But the clerical press fed on it for two more months, the high and low parties insulting each other, in acidly ecclesiastical terms. *The Church Vigilant* for March published the whole correspondence between the Secretary and the Judge, who had apologised for accusing them of trafficking with a spy, as well as the original letter from "a totally unknown young man" called Northbrook Hayley, headed Over Marstaple, November 1897, offering the S.S.C. Acta, which "a friend of his" was anxious to sell. There was also a brief little article on "The Perils of Confirmation", in which "the case of a Young Monk, now undergoing penal servitude", was dragged in as illustration. "His parents, of the yeoman class, are good Protestants, but at Confirmation time their son, whom they describe as having been till then truthful and upright, fell under the spiritual sway of a Ritualistic priest." From which all else, naturally, followed.

17

"HE MAY mean to be upright and truthful, but he's nothing more than a downright liar. Which I could even forgive him if at least he could work, do something, just one thing that would impress me. But he's useless and incompetent as well."

Mr. Hayley sat back angrily in the winged chair that was his in the corner of the dining room by the fire. He was resting after tea, for he was not, at fifty-four, as strong a man as he should have been for a farmer with an outdoor life—but that is often the fate of men with tireless wives. He looked ruddy enough but knew the virtue of taking rest. She knew the virtue of being always on her feet, a virtue often tiring to other people.

She was on her feet now, in a slightly trailing umbrella skirt, very black beside the pile of table-linen she was examining piece by piece for mending. She wore a gold watch pinned above her plump bosom. The maid had cleared the tea things, though the plumcake had been forgotten and Mrs. Hayley had placed it temporarily on the sideboard, with the silver sugar basin and tongs, which were also waiting to be put away.

"You're a little severe on him, dear, he really is ill, you know."

"Of course he's ill. He's always ill when there's anything unpleasant to face. Remember when we asked him to get up at the same time as we do and work the separator before breakfast, when we first bought it? He was on holiday from school, had nothing to do and what happened? Haemorrhage of the lungs. And during that trouble at school? Haemorrhage of the lungs. And now—"

"Oh, Alfred, you're not suggesting, surely, that he's shamming?"

"No, no, my dear, of course not. Just trying to explain my feelings of exasperation. I don't mean to be severe and I know he's not strong. Never intended him for fanning, of course, indeed, he can't even stand the pig-killing. But then, farming's gone to the dogs these days. Ever since that Corn Law nonsense. No, no. But it is strange all the same. Haemorrhage of the lungs. If only I could get inside that boy's mind. I simply cannot understand him, Mary Ann."

"I think you do, dear. You're no early Victorian father, you're very kind and loving, and strict where strictness is called for. It's only a difficult stage between boyhood and manhood, when perhaps a mother is a little closer and more needed."

Mr. Hayley frowned.

"Maybe. But I didn't behave like that. I didn't put on a grand manner or quarrel with people, least of all with my own father, I would never have dared to dispute my father's authority on points of religion. I didn't write interfering and unpleasant letters to people I met on trains."

"Perhaps you didn't meet people on trains?"

"Oh, come, Mary Ann, this is no joking matter. Lovell isn't like that, Dilly isn't like that. Northbrook is our eldest son, he should be our pride and joy. He's intelligent. He can be sensible and polite and very agreeable when he wishes, then suddenly—off he goes at a tangent. Why? What have I done to deserve this?"

Mrs. Hayley was silent, for the imputation was obvious, if perhaps unintentional, that the peculiarity came from her side of the family. Her own sister Emily had been simple, like Muriel, and because of the responsibility Mary Ann had not been free to marry, after her mother's death, until her thirtieth year, when Emily herself died. She knew only too well the split behaviour which he so resentfully described, and to her inmost self she even admitted that all her children were like that, to a different degree. Dilly certainly, who was already at ten far more spiteful than any of the others, and yet could be as sweet as golden syrup. Lovell was the only one who took completely after his father, and yet oddly enough his father said at times he was devoid of character, quiet, gentle Lovell, though the very shyness could also rouse his deepest tenderness. But even Lovell in his secretive way might also be said to go off at a tangent.

When people are plump, their silences often seem bigger, and Mr. Hayley was a little disconcerted.

"Well," he said a little brusquely, "I really don't know what we're going to do about Mr. Stanton. He really is threatening to sue. And so would I, in his place. I saw the letter. With some of the others I gave Northbrook the benefit of the doubt, but not this time. What gets into him, Mary Ann, why can't he let good people be? Or bad people for that matter? He is not their keeper."

"I think Mr. Stanton will see his way to forgiving and forgetting, dear," said Mrs. Hayley placidly. "I had a little talk with him this afternoon."

Mr. Hayley was both taken aback and annoyed.

"You're incorrigible, my dear," he said at last, very gently. But he sighed with relief all the same.

She put the last table-napkin on the all-right pile which she carried to the sideboard, where she first put the sugar bowl away, in a small cupboard above and then the linen in another below.

"At least he feels these religious questions deeply, you must admit."

"There shouldn't be any religious questions. All that was settled centuries ago. But there always are people who want to attract attention. In my day it was the Oxford Movement, and they were bad enough. Turned over to Rome, most of them, which just goes to show. It doesn't do to take too much notice of these things. The Religion of the Church of England has been handed down from father to son for generations, and that's what makes it what it is."

"It jolly well isn't so there," Northbrook muttered to himself outside the door. He was in his dressing gown and had been eavesdropping on the last bit of their conversation as he returned from the lavatory. He started swiftly up the stairs when he heard his mother's steps moving towards the door after a murmured agreement. But he was still rather weak.

"Northbrook, what *are* you doing on the stairs?"

"Visiting Lord Tennyson."

Mrs. Hayley was shocked, for although his euphemism had been used by the children for years she had never really approved of it, and now Lord Tennyson had died only such a short while ago, and all the newspapers had been edged with black, as for a king.

"You've no business to go outside in your condition. You're perfectly well provided in your own room. Go back to bed at once."

"I'm sorry, Mother. But I do feel a little better." Then he said in a loud stage whisper, "I *hate* Jeremiahs."

"Go back to bed, there's a good boy."

"Come and talk to me, Mother."

"I will very soon. I must see to the supper first. I'll bring you up some nice hot broth. Now run along."

"And a tiny bit of boiled mutton with caper sauce, Mother?"

"We'll see. Get back to bed at once."

But Northbrook found he had nothing to say to his mother when she did come up. His little expedition had exhausted him and he could hardly even drink the broth. He lay in bed, holding her hand, with his eyes shut, and she lowered the lamp, which spluttered and smelt, so she turned it right down and sat quietly in the autumn dusk and the glow from the specially lit sickroom fire. When he was asleep she crept out, taking the supper things.

But he was not asleep, quite, or else half woke when the door clicked to. His brass bedstead glittered in the firelight and the roses on the wall were winking. He felt oddly aware of the entire house below, on top and on either side of him. There he was inside his bed, like a bee in a hole of a honeycomb in a hive.

Below him, the dining room, and his parents' voices. Behind that the kitchen, and the maids. Opposite that the dairy, the smell of which he hated, and in front of that the parlour, where they sang hymns round the piano on Sunday nights, and where visitors were received. Next door to him now, the master bedroom, with its half-tester and its mystery and the glimpses of his mother at her dressing table. Opposite that, the schoolroom, all inkwells and blotting pads and penwipers and bits of india-rubber, and opposite him, the spareroom, into which Lovell had been moved because of their room being a sickroom now. Above him, Miss Bell, whom sometimes he heard walking about as she undressed, if he was awake late enough. Behind her the maids and opposite both the girls' rooms, one room for Dilly and Muriel, one for the boarders, Joan and Fanny Wharton and Lilly Abraham. A whole floor of femininity up there. A whole houseful of family. And he thought, John was the only person in the world who understood me. We shared everything, John and I. There wasn't one secret of my inmost soul I didn't tell John. Even my unfaithfulness with Miss Lockhart I confessed to John. He was hurt, but he understood. And I think he admired me for it. Oh how I loved him, my brother Jonathan. And he fell asleep loving and loathing his brother Jonathan, loving and loathing Sheba's breasts, which Miss Marjorie Lockhart, a spinster of thirty, had, after much pleading, allowed him to see and touch.

Miss Lockhart was one of the sisters who ran a small private school near Birmingham where he and his friend John had boarded before they were each sent to St. Austin's College at Hullesmere. But Northbrook always came back with a haemorrhage and soon it was decided he should rather do his school work at home, with short periods for general guidance as an older boarder at the Lockharts, which was nearer; and the Reverend Archibald Stanton agreed to take him for Latin and Greek. At first he managed to meet John in the holidays, but after a year John became more distant, and talked of things and people he had barely or never heard of, *Sesame and Lilies* and a novelist Pelladau and some painter called Preraphael and another called Beardsley. And though they read Christina Rosetti together it wasn't the same. Then Lovell, who had started that year at St. Austin's, told Northbrook that John was a blood and a topper, and inseparable from a boy called Sylvester Gant, who had worn one of the new double collars at half-term. So he fell in love with Miss Lockhart, who had advanced ideas and read French novels and thought she was the mature, experienced woman instructing the virgin boy, but who in fact was almost as innocent and secretly excited at having, after all, a man in her life, however young. She let him kiss her, and lifted her skirts to show her black, colour-embroidered stockings, her petticoats and drawers, then lowered them and slowly unbuttoned her bodice. After which she sent him away in sudden remorse and terror, convinced that she would now be an expectant mother, indeed a fallen woman. As for him he had been horrified by the feel of those flabby white jellyfish under that camisole, and had cluttered down the stairs as fast as he could to weep for his brother Jonathan. If it hadn't been for Father Biretto, Northbrook would have spent the most miserable summer in his life. And now he was to go to Birmingham, as an articled clerk in the Regal Life Insurance Company, starting from October 1st. At sixteen and nine months, he was truly the unhappiest person in the whole world, and his dreams were edged in black, like those of a widowed king.

The next day Lovell was going back to school, and came in to say good-bye in his blue serge suit and Shakespeare collar. He had his father's brown eyes, into which a lank fringe of brown hair fell perpetually, though he kept pushing it back. He was just fourteen and so shy that even his brother found it hard to talk to him, except in a bullying mood, which he felt too weak for now.

"Shall I give John any message for you, Northbrook?"

"Oh, I don't know. Yes, you might. Well, no, perhaps not. Are you allowed to talk to him? He'll be in the Fifth now, won't he?"

"Upper Fifth," said Lovell with great reverence, and Northbrook was pleased, because he would have been there too, but then he felt annoyed.

"Hmm-hmm!" he said ambiguously.

"I could talk to him. I mean, if I had a special message. If you liked, that is."

"Well, you could tell him I'm going to the city, and I shall become very rich."

"That's a little difficult, Northbrook, I mean, it's the sort of thing one says casually, not a special message, is it? I mean, I'd have to go to his study, and knock, and all that."

"Yes, of course." In a state of health he would have said, don't be such a funk and what rot, have you got no guts, but he felt too tired, and suddenly didn't care. "What would you say was an extra good special message, Lovell?"

"You want me to give you one, to give to him from you, you mean?"

"Yes, give me a special message, Lovell."

"Perhaps—" he thought hard, and ended lamely, "your love."

"My love. I wonder if that's special enough, any more."

"Perhaps you found a very good brass somewhere, you could tell him about? I could take him a rubbing if you like."

"His belly and his thighs were of brass, his legs of iron, his feet of clay," Northbrook murmured wearily.

"I have a friend, too," Lovell said shyly after a silence. Then with great courage he added, "his name is Bernard. We tell each other everything."

"Do you?" said Northbrook without interest and stared glumly at the pine tree branches that brushed the sky just outside the window. "Is the squirrel still in the tree?"

"Yes, and Dilly was lying in the hammock all yesterday afternoon, watching the hole."

"Wasn't it too cold?"

"No, the sun was out yesterday, and besides Mother came and made us wear our jackets. I was there too. But not in the hammock."

"Yes, I heard your voices. Did she talk about me?"

"No," Lovell lied, for Dilly had said to him, "I don't think Northbrook is one of us, is he Lovell?" and he had shushed her, pointing to the window. "We talked about the squirrel."

"I'm tired. Go away."

"Well, goodbye, Northbrook, I hope you'll be better soon."

"Goodbye. Oh, and Lovell." The boy turned at the door. "I have no special message for anyone."

Later, Miss Bell came in to see him. He was always surprised, after an absence, at the darkness of her nut-coloured hair, which she wore in basket plaits, for her eyes were light blue like his, and her skin as fair, and her nose as large, so that he remembered her more as an older sister than his real sisters. She was a feminine edition of himself, though his hair was sandy. And she pulled very funny faces.

"Hello, Northbrook, I'm back. The holidays are over."

"Not for me, I'm the studious type." He smiled and showed her Buckle's

History, which he was half reading half dozing over. On his bedside table also lay a privately bound red leather volume entitled in gold, *Guesses at Truth, by Two Brothers.* Also Harmsworth's Fortnightly, A Literary Self-Educator complete in thirty fortnightly parts, 7d. Net. "You just missed Lovell," he added indifferently.

"No. I saw him at the station. His train left twenty minutes after mine so your father took him in the phaeton and met me all in one trip. It was so nice to see Whiskers the pony again. And Mr. Hayley of course."

"How are you, Miss Bell? Had a nice holiday?"

"Fairly nice, thank you. My mother wasn't too well, but apart from that —" She never talked much about her home. Three generations from clogs to clogs, her mother always said: the grandfather makes the money, the father enjoys it, the son loses it. Harriet's schoolmistress had suggested that one of the girls should "go out", and she was seventeen when she answered an advertisement in *The Birmingham Post*, which had been put in by Mrs. Hayley. Mrs. Hayley was impressed by the schoolmistress's recommendation, for it praised Harriet as "the daughter of such a mother" even more than in her own right. The odd thing was that the Hayleys were not very much better off than the Bells, but this she never said. Mrs. Hayley took in other children for Miss Bell to teach with Cordelia and Muriel, in order to pay for Miss Bell. There were two living-in maids but Mrs. Hayley did much of the cooking and all the household work and sewing. A Mrs. Clark came in from another farm to do the washing. Miss Bell, however, was treated very much as an equal. The only domestic duty required of her was going round with Mrs. Hayley to make the beds, during which journey many family matters were discussed but not, of course, all.

Northbrook was so often at home in term time she had got to know him well, for he was less surly and argumentative with her than with his parents, and less arrogant than with his brother and sisters. But the distance between sixteen and nineteen is a much more respectful one, especially in friendships, than that between, say, sixteen and fifty-four; three years of knowledge seems amazing, making the last of the big childhood gaps.

He was not, as a matter of fact, at all interested in her home life. When away, she didn't exist, when here, she belonged to them.

"I'm going out to work, too," he grumbled. "As a clerk, it can you imagine me as a clerk?"

"You'll do very well in insurance. It's a wonderful opening."

"What rot, Miss Bell. Have you been making the beds with Mother already?"

"Of course not, I've only just arrived." She made a prunes-and-prism face. "What do you mean?"

He smiled wryly. "Oh, nothing. Mother's always talking of wonderful openings, as if the world was a chain of magical caves, or a row of Sesames. Have you read Ruskin, Miss Bell?"

"A little, yes. Rather a tiresome old man."

"Oh, he's old, is he? Oh, well, I won't bother. Have you read a fellow called Beau de l'Air?"

She was embarrassed, for she had heard of him as very wicked, and connected him vaguely with Bowdlerised Shakespeare. So Northbrook promptly resolved to get hold of him. She prevaricated.

"He's dead, I think." She said it with her Dickens-reading-little-Nell face, and he laughed, then sighed.

"All the most interesting people seem to be dead. Except Newman, and he's so old he's as good as dead. Look, Miss Bell. I had the *Apologia* bound up together with Francis Newman's *Phases of Faith*. Don't you think my title is apt? After the brothers Hare, you know. But it was all so long ago, Miss Bell, and still I don't know the truth. I wish I lived in the Middle Ages. Why is our time so dreary? Why doesn't anybody *do* anything?"

"Perhaps you will, Northbrook. You have a great deal of talent. You should write."

"I do in secret," he said shyly. "Shall I show you one of my poems?"

The Regal Life Insurance Company was much more fun than he had expected. He was put in the Renewal Department. The office was dark but he had a small roll-top desk all to himself, with a private drawer and locker, in a row of roll-top desks that stood back to back, each of whose clerks became more and more important, so that those at the other end hardly spoke to him, and two even more important persons had large desks to themselves, and one of the partners had a separate office behind a glass door. But he was above the office boys and his mentor was not a gentleman, which helped to ease the panic of the first few weeks, when he couldn't understand a word of what he was supposed to be working at. It was soothing to be reassured of one's innate superiority over a man like Albert Hodge, who wore a patent waterproof collar and even sometimes a dicky, and paper over his cuffs while he worked, and a suit of shiny black cloth; who knew every thing about premiums, but nothing of *En Priamus. Sunt hic etiam sua praemia laudi*; who understood every clause and sub-clause of every insurance scheme, but was incapable of cutting down on the subordinate clauses in his own native speech, carefully modelled as it was on the complex language of the documents he read all day; who gave a wink whenever the maturing of a policy was mentioned, but had never heard of the policies of Archbishop Laud. Yet he was by no means illiterate. He knew all about books, as the Midlanders so enchantingly stretch the word to include everything from encyclopaedias to penny populars. For he too, thought himself not as other men, not, that is, like the other clerks who talked only of music halls and girls, kept singing *Ta-ra-ra-boomdeay,* and exchanged the latest jokes all day, so that the office was perpetually crackling with native wit—a gentleman said to another gentleman, mistaking him for a porter, Call me a cab . . . I said, call me a cab. All right, sir, you are a cab—and so forth, down to mothers-in-law and Gay Old Boys with their lady friends. Albert Hodge, on the other hand, read all the great novelists, like Christie Murray and John Strange Winter and James Payn and Mrs. Oliphant and Edna Lyall. He read, moreover, *The Saturday Review, The Spectator,* and *The World* and even sometimes *The Athenaeum,* and knew that those top anonymous critics in London praised these authors highly and thought them Very Important. But he couldn't organise his knowledge, except on Insurance, and his mind jostled with bits of Samuel Smiles, Dickens, Childe Harold, Ruskin, Tyndall and *The Adventures of Mr. Verdant Green*; all about a young man at Oxford, a sixpenny paper volume which Northbrook promptly noted and went out to buy.

Yes, it was pleasant to know for once and for certain that his own education, however imperfect, was yet incomparably superior, that though his parents said dinner and parlour where the Weirwoods and such said luncheon and drawing room, nevertheless he spoke the Queen's English in his cradle and was treated quite differently by the head of the firm, he and the only other son of a gentleman there, a young man called Tallant, who sat opposite him. They were altogether several cuts above the others, and Intended for Higher Things. He really didn't get on with the other clerks at all and they didn't seem to take to him, which showed that they felt he had nothing in common with them. They Knew Their Place.

It was exciting, also, to have money of his own, twelve whole shillings and sixpence a week, after the first three months at half a sovereign. When he got his rise he started to live in Birmingham during the week and went home at weekends. His very modest lodgings cost him four and sixpence with breakfasts, and there were plenty of little places where he could get a three-course lunch of simple, homely food for ninepence, and an evening bowl of soup with a large chunk of bread for threepence. Nine and sixpence or at most ten shillings a week all told and half a crown for extras. Algerian cigarettes were five a penny, though they were pretty foul and unofferable, and once a week he bought Duke's Cameos at fivepence for ten. Of course his parents clothed him, and well. And gave him three and sixpence for his return fare home every weekend. And above all they were there, in the background. But he was as self-supporting as any young man of seventeen could be, and it made him feel a hell of a fellow, almost a swell, a Johnnie, a master, a blade. Would there ever be anything quite so sweet as that first taste of economic independence, however stark the life, however hard and dull the work, oneself the treasurer and administrator of all one's pleasures? And the town so crowded, with its gentlemen in frock-coats and silk hats, its fine ladies in broughams, its young mashers in such tight trousers, imitating London, its office girls in black or navy blue, neat and severe, its factory girls in black straw hats, with earrings and Mizpah brooches, and hair in rolls over their ears.

There was no end to what half-a-crown could buy in one's imagination. And soon he began to earn more by working in a bookshop in the evenings, and the born bargainer in him perfected the technique of selling for three and sixpence what he had bought for two and tenpence, which he had learnt from his earlier love *The Exchange and Mart*, through which boys could indulge their craze for swapping all manner of goods from school prize copies of *In Memoriam* to stamps, coins, birds' eggs and cricket bats. He made new friends, and his family hardly saw him, even at home. On Saturday afternoons he went round the country for brasses, talking to the clergymen about church history, and being asked to stay for tea. And on Sundays he stalked off to Father Biretto, Signor Pirouetto as Mr. Hayley called him, for Northbrook's insistence on Sutton Leigh Church infuriated him.

"Isn't it a little High?" he had said at first, and Northbrook had answered rudely, "You talk of religion as if it were venison." But Mr. Hayley had his own brand of repartee and said, "It's you who's making game of it, my boy."

It was true that Father Biretto was extremely proud of the fact that his name had appeared in a book called *Ritualistic Priests in the Church of England—9000 Roman Traitors,* followed by all, not just some, of the mystical signs—*e* for eastward position, *i* for use of incense, *r* for reservation, *c* for candles, etc., and of course all the secret societies. Never had he been given so many letters after his name.

And indeed, Father Biretto was the next best thing to a University one could wish for. He was full of delightful Latin jokes, and talked of the Scare'm Missal and of having just got through a Marathon Rosary, and when Northbrook objected to the Rosary's ten Hail Mary's for one Our Father, saying "Our Father doesn't come very well out of it, does He?" Father Biretto said, "Oh well, it's a woman's world-to-come, you know. Man sinned through woman. God redeems through a woman." He called the delicately carved communion bell God's signature, because it always stood at the bottom right-hand corner of the altar steps, so that strangers would know where they were. And he said the Sacrament in its frame of golden sunrays was like a blank-faced clock, out of time, you see. But above all, he told Northbrook what to read, Mallock's *New Republic* as the best shortcut to everybody's views, well, everybody that mattered. "But Church History is the thing, don't forget Church History. *Tracts for the Times*, especially No. 90." And, even more important for a bewildered young man, he told him what not to read. "Oh, no!" he would say as if absolving him from further responsibility. "Not Robert Ellesmere! Clergymen's doubts are right out, my dear boy, since Butler's article. We simply don't, any more, have doubts. It's a little Low, you know, or at any rate, Broad."

"Mr. Stanton says, 'The word of God plus my own experience of Christ must harmonise, if they do, then I am right.' " Northbrook was a good mimic and liked to please Father Biretto by making fun of the Reverend Archibald Stanton. "So I said, 'what about other experiences of Christ and other readings of the word of God? What about, for that matter, the Buddhists, or the Mohammedans, they believe they're right?' And he said, 'Oh no, the buddhists are wrong'—he pronounced them as if they believed in buds—'I'm very sorry for them of course,' he said, 'I wouldn't persecute them, but they are wrong.' "

"Well, of course, these people know so little of Church History, do they not? To them the Reformation is the only thing that has ever happened since Jesus Christ."

And Father Biretto gave him a little lecture on Church History, rather as if the early Fathers and the later Saints and some of the pleasanter Popes were exclusive Anglican property. For Anglo-Catholics rather liked, sometimes, to talk of following Saint Bernard, or Saint Bonaventure, or Saint Anselm, or even Saint Thomas Aquinas, without necessarily having read them.

And so did Northbrook, having read much much less, use this great Communion of the Saints as a glorified cricket eleven to bat against his own father, scoring more and more centuries, the second, the fourth, and the thirteenth especially. But never sure enough of his ground to counter Mr. Hayley's plain common sense, so that in the end he too would resort to more contemporary facts.

He had thoroughly irritated his father at the beginning of Sunday supper by making an ostentatious shoulder-to-shoulder sign of the cross as grace was said. Mr. Hayley knew perfectly well that he was only trying to impress or shock the Wilsons, who had come over for the afternoon, but in fact Molly Wilson had been to Somerville College and was used to ostentation in all forms, and her brother Jack was too busy pretending to flirt with Cordelia, who at eleven years old looked frail, fair and minute next to him. It was only Mr. Hayley who was shocked, and a long argument ensued.

"All right," Northbrook said at last, passing up the cold beef, "but last Sunday, just to please you, I went to church at Over Marstaple; granted I was a little late, but do you know what happened? The new curate, who didn't know me, was standing outside and said, 'You can't go in, there's a communion service going on.' I ask you!"

"Very right and proper, too. You've no business being late for church."

"Christ would never have said that."

"Don't you take it upon yourself to know what Our Lord would have said. I suppose you were wearing one of your aesthetic ties, or your corduroys, no wonder Mr. Hilton was wary."

"Ahlaw, Ahlaw," Northbrook imitated his father. "You sound so Chapel."

"Northbrook, you will apologise to your father at once." Mrs. Hayley was scandalised. Why did he always choose Sunday night, when supper was earlier and the girls had it downstairs with the family? And today there were guests, as well! "You're becoming extremely vulgar."

"All right, I'm sorry."

"And stop these ridiculous arguments. You're wearing your father out, he has quite enough cares and troubles without these eternal discussions. I suppose you haven't even heard that Dundreary died?"

"The Lord have mercy on its dreary soul."

His father was livid. There were only four farm horses and Dundreary was the first he had bought when he took on Monwode Farm. He had got it young and cheap only four years before, in Weirwood, when the livestock and implements of Manor Farm went up for auction after Mr. Braddon's death. He even remembered Northbrook seated on the roller that was hanging on the chain under the waggon, watching how the sale was going, making a note of all the prices, and getting very excited when he was bidding for Dundreary. And now Dundreary was dead and Northbrook didn't even care. They had all spent the whole of Saturday trying to get it to its feet, for he believed that if a horse lay down when ill it died. But it had died all the same, and the loss was severe.

He said in a voice full of controlled rage:

"I will not stand any more of this. Leave the room at once."

Northbrook shrugged his shoulders and got up with much scraping of his chair on the wooden floor. It was Mrs. Hayley's only complaint that she had such bare and such few carpets for this ten-roomed house. He ostentatiously cut himself a piece of cake from the sideboard and went out.

"What have I done to deserve such a son?" Mr. Hayley muttered half to himself.

"You had a Great Depression when he was born, didn't you, Father?" Muriel spoke shyly, thinking that he wanted an answer to his question, and that this was it, and that everyone knew it but had forgotten, except her.

He made an impatient movement.

"You have me," said Cordelia happily. "I'm your Dilly darling."

"Cordelia, don't try and benefit by your brother's disgrace," said Mrs. Hayley. "We love you all equally, even when one of you does wrong."

Cordelia pouted. Lilly Abraham and the two Wharton girls said nothing.

Molly Wilson, who was working on a dialect dictionary, tried to engage Mr. Hayley on Warwickshire antiquities, which led to heraldry and genealogy, but young bluestockings are seldom the soul of tact, and Molly Wilson insisted that in the old days many tenants on the big estates had taken the name of the lord who owned the estate, just as they did in Scotland with clans. She was always being asked by Americans to find their missing links with the Warwick family but the missing links were always missing. Mr. Hayley, who was still only a tenant farmer but had had his genealogy traced back to the Hayleys of Kilbrae, was hardly mollified.

Miss Bell was trying to sign to Molly, and found herself uncomfortably aware of Molly's brother Jack as a very handsome man who seemed amused by everything. And in order not to think of Jack Wilson, who wasn't looking at her anyway, Miss Bell thought rather of the empty chair between herself and Mr. Hayley, and pondered on the pitfalls of parent-hood. They're such a sweet and kind and devoted couple, and they haven't a notion how to bring up their sons and daughters. They treat them either as naughty children or, when all goes well, as equals, no, as honoured guests, gentleman to gentleman with the boys, and "Cordelia darling, won't you have just a little of this nice chicken breast?" when Cordelia would happily eat the lot. Then they're angry and disappointed when something goes wrong. A good smacking, and proper punishment from the beginning, that's what was needed. But she was interrupted from her maidenly theories by Mrs. Hayley.

"The girls are to help clear away and wash-up. You too, Muriel."

This was unusual. It was Sunday and the maids were out, but the chil-dren were rarely asked to help, even so, and besides, there were two guests, but they were clearly excluded. Muriel anyway was no good at washing up or drying, she got it all wrong. Both Dilly and Muriel felt they were being penalised for Northbrook's misdemeanor, and the work was done in a long silent grudge.

The Wilsons left soon after supper and the family trooped into the par-lour where Mrs. Hayley played the piano and they all sang, *And Now O Father Mindful of Thy Love*, which was Mrs. Hayley's favourite, and *Through the Night of Doubt and Sorrow*, which was Lovell's, Lovell being away at school. And many others. Northbrook wasn't there. He had left earlier to catch the 7.42 to Birmingham. He plays more sweetly, Miss Bell thought, and more lively, too. She suddenly remembered the Sunday when North-brook had played the organ in church at Over Marstaple and accompanied *And Now O Father of Thy Love* with *Daddy wouldn't buy me a Bow-wow* in the left hand. She started to giggle and Mrs. Hayley looked up at her, rather hurt. But Miss Bell knew that after she had gone up to the schoolroom with the girls and then put them to bed, she would come down and find Mrs. Hayley, who wasn't very good at chess, playing cribbage with Mr. Hayley, and waiting to play chess with her, who would by then be tired, so that she could beat her. Miss Bell knew all this, and many small things besides, and loved every single member of the Hayley family, nevertheless. She also knew that Jack Wilson had not taken the same fancy to her as she had to him, no fancy at all, come to that.

Northbrook received the telegram on the morning of May 13th and felt nothing whatsoever. He went to the office and saw Mr. Colville, who had one of the big roll-top desks too. Mr. Colville meladded him and condoled, and Northbrook thanked him, but still felt nothing.

He was not met at the station and had to walk. His mother had left for St. Austin's College to bring back the body, Miss Bell told him. But still he felt nothing. His father had gone with the horse and trap to Birmingham to sell the butter as usual, for it was Thursday. "He took it very badly," Miss Bell said, "be gentle with him, Northbrook dear." And Northbrook felt something at last, but only a sudden tenderness shot with anger. Surely his father should have been sitting in his wing chair, staring at the empty grate, prostrate with grief. Or gone with his mother? Supposing it had been him, and not Lovell?

"What exactly happened?" he asked Miss Bell in a flat voice as they walked together in the little orchard just behind the farm-sheds and stables. There were no lessons that morning but Muriel was up in the schoolroom and the boarder girls had been sent home. Dilly was sitting quietly by herself under a plum-tree, swaying to and fro as she sang to an old-discarded doll she had fetched out of the toy-cupboard. The doll wore a long dress of white lace, and the weaker branches of the plum-tree were propped up on both sides with forked poles. For a second Northbrook saw Calvary, and the Virgin Mary cradling the dead Christ. But at once it was the plum-tree again, and Cordelia and a doll.

"Apparently he was digging a cave," Miss Bell was saying, "in an earth mound at the end of the playing fields with another boy called Bernard Hopkins. The whole thing collapsed on them. Some other boys were there and rushed for help. The Hopkins boy was got out alive, but not Lovell."

"A cave!" Northbrook closed his eyes and muttered, "My God!"

"I can't see how they dug it to begin with, it seems impossible."

"I know how."

"They sent two telegrams, the first saying <u>lie</u> was seriously hurt. To prepare them, I suppose. He must have been dead already. It came just after tea. Then the second one came about ten. The girls were in bed, but Dilly heard the knock and woke up. I went in to her and she said 'Lovell's dead, isn't he?' I was so upset myself I could hardly comfort her." Miss Bell wiped a tear with the corner of her handkerchief.

There was no laying-out of the body, for St. Austin's College provided the coffin and even paid for the transport home. The body waited in the parish church of Over Marstaple, and Northbrook prayed a long time, after lunch on the day before the funeral, the only hour when he could be sure no one of the family could be there. The funeral was quiet and very simple, and on foot they walked home with Muriel and Cordelia, who both looked startling in the plain black dresses Mrs. Clark had quickly made for them, and with deep black velvet ribbons round their hats.

"I saw Lovell," Cordelia said, "at the same moment he died."

"Don't talk nonsense, what do you mean?"

"It's true. I was out walking with Miss Bell along the road but running ahead. And suddenly I saw Lovell walking towards us, he was as near as that tree. I said 'Hello, Lovell, are you back from school?' I thought he was back, you see. But he didn't answer and I was so puzzled. Then he vanished."

"You're lying. How did he vanish? Gradually?"

She frowned, as if trying to remember.

"No. Suddenly. That is, I'm not sure, because I looked back to see if Miss Bell had caught me up, but she was still about ten yards behind and was looking at the Ibbotsons' house. When I turned my head again Lovell was gone."

"You're making all this up, Cordelia. I know when you're lying."

"I'm not, I'm not. Am I, Muriel? Didn't I tell you about it that same evening, before the telegram came? Tell him, Muriel, didn't I?"

"Before the second telegram, you said something about Lovell, but I can't remember what it was."

"There you are, you see!" Cordelia and Northbrook both exclaimed at once, and Northbrook immediately added, "Oh, go to hell."

Then suddenly his heart turned over and he felt sick with fear. Those were the last words he had spoken to Lovell. During the Easter holidays. Good Friday. His father had forbidden him to go over to Sutton Leigh for the beautiful three-hour service there, which he had been so looking forward to. *Popule meus quid feci tibi?* he kept quoting at his father. "I hate Good Friday here, it's so dreary." And Lovell had said, rather primly, "I don't suppose Jesus enjoyed it much, either." And he had said, "Oh go to hell and don't be so cocky." His father was furious at his language, and there had been another row. So that he had spent most of Easter at Sutton Leigh or roaming around, certainly he hadn't seen Lovell again, and then he had gone back to Birmingham. And Lovell had appeared to Dilly, not him.

Muriel was talking and he hadn't heard a word. But it wasn't to him, it was to Dilly, and Dilly was crying. He looked back at his parents, who were walking slowly arm in arm, very black against the dusty white road, and Miss Bell, slim and black beside them, a little apart. Just ahead of him the road forked and he could see their tall square house on the hill to the left, edged with white quoins, just behind the poplars, and with the pine-tree in the front garden and the outlying sheds behind, overlooking the two hundred or so Hayley acres of corn and pasture. There were just two strips of white cloud over the house, like frowning eyebrows in a clear blue sky. Suddenly Northbrook cut away quickly from his sisters, and almost before they had noticed he was on the right hand road, the road that went South towards Weirwood Abbey, over Sutton Leigh where he had at all costs to talk to Father Biretto.

That summer the three Smith children came to stay as usual, and for once Northbrook didn't want them there at all. They had always been a little like poor relations, for Mr. Smith had had only a very small business in Birmingham before he died and left Hannah Smith in what Mrs. Hayley called reduced circumstances, though Northbrook always said he didn't see what they could have been reduced from. But now William was going up to Cambridge, on a scholarship, and Reggie was working to win a place at a London Technical College, and Maud was top of her form at school. Whereas he had to work in an office throughout the summer and come home at weekends. He hated them now, except Maud.

But one day in the fields they all promised to marry one another. William would marry Dilly, who already at thirteen was ardently in love, and a clever flirt; Northbrook would marry Maud, who was pretty but long faced and not in the least disposed to love and obey him, which made him furious; and Reggie would marry Muriel, who said, "You don't have to really, of course, because I'm not clever, but thank you very much." And when Reggie said, "No it's true, Muriel, I love you and I want to marry you, then it's all in the family," she said, "What about Lovell?" And everyone was embarrassed because they thought she had forgotten. But she knew, it was they who had forgotten and she was very upset that she hadn't managed to do as they did. She liked to imitate Northbrook, so she walked away towards the Weirwood and Sutton Leigh road he had taken after the funeral, muttering to herself, "Four became three so fast, so fast. But then, I am rather slow-witted, you see, my dear, I am not quite like the others."

18

THE BELLS of Weirwood parish church rang loud, Grandsire Triples, treble met in three, four, dodge in six, seven, up, etc., for Lord Weirwood's forty-fifth birthday on the 17th January, 1887.

"Are those the church bells, Letitia?" Lord Weirwood asked his wife in the apple-green Hepplewhite breakfast room a mile away in Weirwood Abbey.

"I can't hear anything, dear. Oh. Why, yes, I believe they are. Indeed, dear, they must be, since it's your birthday."

"How very thoughtful of Canon Willoughby," said Lord Weirwood as if surprised, though he had been listening for the bells, and was extremely pleased. This happened every year and Canon Willoughby had "Tell Verger bells for Lord W., 9.30" jotted down in his diary.

"One would have heard them better from the morning room. What a pity." Lady Letitia's tone implied that the Canon's thoughtfulness might have included waiting until they had finished their breakfast. As a matter of fact the Canon's thoughtfulness had included this, but what with the good wishes from all the servants after morning prayers, it was already nine-thirty now. The presents from the family were still to come, indeed they were already waiting in the morning room, piled on the rosewood Pembroke table by the french windows, colourful packages in the wintry sun which was rivalling the yellow newness of the flames in the huge Adam chimney. The children had had their breakfast in the nursery before prayers, and were waiting in the schoolroom for the sign to come down again.

Lord Weirwood was as pleased as punch at the prospect.

He looked across the oval table at his wife, who at thirty-seven looked mature but delicious against the white and gold and apple-green of the room, in a pale blue breakfast gown and long close-fitting suede gloves. Such English beauty, so fair, so creamy, almost, one might say, at least to oneself, a milkmaid complexion and a milkmaid bosom, almost, one might say, at least to oneself, too luscious for a lady, and yet she *was* one, in her own right, an earl's daughter, though he himself was only a viscount, how lucky he was to have the best of both worlds. "I think they've stopped," he said regretfully. "I must thank the Canon, though, so thoughtful of him."

"Shall we adjourn?" said Lady Letitia.

"Indeed, my dear, I am quite ready." He got up and walked towards her to escort her out. "Oh, and by the way, Letitia, don't forget to have a piece of my cake sent down for the little Hayley girl."

"Ah, yes. Thank you for reminding me, dear. How thoughtful of you. I had otherwise quite forgot."

"Oh, those bells!" said Mrs. Hayley in the big kitchen of the Old Vicarage, which stood just next to the church. "One can't hear oneself speak."

"They're for me, they're for me!" Dilly hugged her new doll and danced round the table where her mother was squeezing the icing to write "Dilly" in pink over the birthday cake she had made the day before. Five coloured candles and five pins with frilly holders were waiting on the table.

"Dilly darling, you're shaking everything. And don't stay in the kitchen, dearest, you'll get your best dress soiled. Go up to the nursery, or in to the parlour if you like."

"The bells are ringing for me, for me!" She burst into the parlour, where Northbrook was sitting by the fire, in his Eton collar and Norfolk suit, working at his Latin. He looked rather big and grown-up, though his hair was sticking out, so she stopped suddenly.

"Oh, go away, Dilly, you're interrupting."

"But it's my birthday, Norny, I'm five."

"Well I wished you many happy returns, didn't I? And you got a nice doll. And don't call me Norny."

"Arboo, then, Arboo, Arboo."

"Not Arboo, either. Now, off with you. Go and play. I'm busy."

Dilly felt that birthdays were rather a swindle, nobody wanted her. Muriel and Lovell had gone to the Vicarage for their lessons as usual. Her father had gone to Manor Farm as usual. Her mother was in the kitchen as usual. Northbrook was reading books with no pictures as usual. Why didn't the summer come back, when everyone was outside and speakable-to?

"All the same, the bells are for me! Me and Lord Weirwood, he told me so."

"What do you mean, he told you so? When did *you* speak with Lord Weirwood?"

"He told me so." She repeated obstinately. "When we went to tea last summer. Because I was born on his birthday."

"All right, they're for you." He was rather annoyed because his own eleventh birthday the week before had passed without any bells. But he didn't want to be unkind, since she was, after all, five today, and her blue eyes were shining. "Now be a good girl and let me read. You can sit down there, if you like, and play with your doll. But keep quiet."

"Her name's Lady Letitia," Dilly explained, "but she's very delicate, and wants to rest now." She put the doll down among the cushions of the other chintz armchair and looked thoughtfully at her brother. "Norny." She came up to him and looked wistful. "Won't you read to me out of my new books? Please, Norny, just today, it's my birthday?"

"Oh, all right, then." He put away his Caesar, regretfully, for Latin was the only subject he really loved. "What did you get?"

"I don't know."

She brought three toy-sized books to him with great eagerness. Her mother had started reading-lessons with her that year but the presents were really for future promise rather than achievement.

"*Peep of Day, Line upon Line, Daddy Darwin's Dovecot.* Which would you rather?"

"Which do you think, Norny?"

"Well those two are holy, this one's pretty."

"Let's have this one, then."

So he read her the story of Daddy Darwin's Dovecot.

". . . one gaffer in workday clothes, not unpicturesque of form and hue. Grey home-knit stockings, and coat and knee-breeches of corduroy which takes tints from Time and Weather as harmoniously as wooden palings do . . ."

Dilly couldn't understand a word of all this.

". . . D'y see yon chap?" (one of the gaffers apparently said to the other). How horridly boring these gaffers were.

"Oh, Norny, let's stop. Teach me a tune on the piano, please, Norny."

By the end of the morning she could play Little Miss Muffet with one finger and thought herself the happiest girl in the whole of England. Birthdays were enormous fun after all.

In spite of having no bells Northbrook felt very superior because one of the books he had received for his birthday was in Latin, and he could understand everything. It was The Book of Common Prayer which had belonged to his mother's father, Dr. Davies, who had used it as a boy when at school in Paris. Northbrook was deeply excited by it and in a few weeks had learnt his first Latin Collect by heart, *Tenebras Nostras Illumine*, and the *Pater Noster*, the Nicene Creed, the Prayer of humble access and the *Veni Creator*. He used the book incessantly in church and tears came to his eyes at the first effect of the *Vere dignum* followed by the *Sanctus*. What was actually being said in English by Canon Willoughby, and the hymns sung by the congregation, were as nothing compared to the emotion in Northbrook's heart as he murmured all those lovely new words to himself, staring at the large and square pew full of Weirwoods near the altar, and all the Weirwoods' winter breaths as they sang in the flickering candlelight from the tall lantern holders at each corner of their pew. And all the high wooden pews down in the nave had tall sputtering candles too, and everybody else had winter breath as well, just like the Weirwoods. And the Weirwood household staff in front on the other side, they had winter breath too, as had Mr. James, Lord Weirwood's estate agent. And so, as far as he could see behind Mrs. Braddon's black woollen cloak, so had the Templetons from Weirwood Hall, in the front pew on this side, and the Farleys, from Taunton Manor, and so had Mr. Braddon himself. The Hayley pew was just behind the Braddon pew, his father being bailiff to Mr. Braddon, which Northbrook always thought sounded very grand, for Mr. Braddon lived at Manor Farm, up towards the Vicarage, and Manor Farm had lots and lots of beams, like Tudor palaces in history books.

"Hear ye what comfortable words our Saviour Christ saith unto all that truly turn to him."

The comfortable Words always made Northbrook feel most uncomfortable. He never travailed and was never heavy laden. He did not feel that he would perish or needed an Advocate. And some of the words in the big Bible his mother had given him for his birthday were far from comfortable. "Let the dead bury their dead," Jesus had said, and all that stuff about forsaking home and father and mother and sisters for His sake. What did it mean? "Thy navel is like a round goblet," he had opened at random and read, what did that mean? It had made him giggle, but now he felt afraid. "Gentle Jesus meek and mild, Listen to a little child . . ." He repeated the whole prayer to himself in sudden panic. "Jesu gentle shepherd hear me. . ."

He hadn't really behaved very well about Jack-the-Shepherd up by the weir. Those swans had been so fierce, he would have drowned, he might not be alive at all if it hadn't been for Jack-the-Shepherd. And he had told no one, hardly thanked him he was so shaken, and so annoyed, too, at not getting those eggs. No comfortable words could make up for the loss of those eggs.

"Do this in remembrance of me."

Northbrook bowed his head suddenly and put his face in his hands. *In Remembrance,* the Canon had stressed so much at Bible Class, it is *not* God himself, though the Papists believe it is. We cannot make God appear at will. But Northbrook always peeped between his fingers, just in case he could see God, or a Burning Bush perhaps. Only Moses had seen God but still that was before Jesus. But no, Canon Thornton was quite right—

there was nothing. "Do this in remembrance of me," said the Canon for the second time. In remembrance. *In memoriam,* his own Latin book said. Like Prince Albert. Like those stones in the churchyard, In loving memory. Naturally, since Jesus was dead, and up in heaven now. *In memoriam quod Christus mortuus est pro te.* "Jesu gentle shepherd hear me."

But then, what could he have done about Jack-the-Shepherd? The eggs were lost and his life was saved, but life was after all something he possessed already. He couldn't owe it to someone like Jack-the-Shepherd. It was true that in Eric or Little by Little gentlemen's sons sat side by side with plebeians at the local grammar school, and Eric exchanged friendly greetings with the glazier's son. But would the glazier's son have been welcome in Dean Farrar's drawing room? They never had the Fardons to tea, who lived next door, nor did Tom Baines ever step inside their parlour. He played with them in the village, at least, when there was no one else, like his cousin Percy, around.

Suddenly the service was over and he had hardly listened. Lord Weirwood and Lady Letitia were bowing graciously on both sides as they walked down the aisle, followed by their two sons, the Honourable Robert Henley, who was the heir to the title, and the Honourable William, and their two little daughters, the Honourable Imogen and the Honourable Claire. The household staff followed and started at once in the direction of the Abbey, but the Weirwood family waited with Canon Willoughby outside before climbing into their carriage, so as to greet the local gentry and the village people as they came out, in strict order of precedence, and to inquire politely after their health. First the Templetons, then the Parleys and the Braddons, then the Hayleys, whose small daughter Cordelia curtsied very prettily to Lord Weirwood and thanked him for the piece of cake he had sent down on his and her birthday, "our birthday" she called it, without shyness, and he was charmed. After the Hayleys it was chiefly brief curtseys from the women and raised hats from the men, unless a specific ailment or disaster had to be asked about. Then the victoria drove them all away. And very soon they went off to the South of France for the rest of the winter, the Lady Letitia being sensitive to cold.

Mrs. Braddon died suddenly in the middle of the Golden Jubilee, and Mr. and Mrs. Hayley talked a great deal of poor Mr. Braddon, who was getting on, and was not so strong as he used to be, and had no one now to leave Manor Farm to. Except perhaps his brother, who was a ne'er-do-well, at any rate he had emigrated somewhere and had got Mr. Baines the carpenter to make him a lot of packing cases, then gone off without paying him, "And it seems," said Mr. Baines, "as if I wasn't the only victim, he's a bad egg, is Mr. Braddon's brother."

"Even so, blood comes first," said Mrs. Hayley to her husband at dinnertime. "We mustn't expect anything."

"No, no, of course not. I suppose I could always rent a farm somewhere if the worst came to the worst. Still, I must say, a little something would be nice, considering all I did for the farm through those bad harvests from '76 on. Dear me, it's over ten years ago, how time does fly, and the Depression with us still. Farming never recovered and I doubt whether it will unless the government does something Intelligent for a change."

"Was it very bad, Father, ten years ago?"

"Very bad, my boy, the worse year was '76."

"That's the year I was born."

"So it is, so it is. Well, your arrival didn't make things easier, I can tell you."

Northbrook couldn't see what things had not been made easier by his birth. Up at Manor Farm his father had a little brick but which was his office, with shelves and a table and a fire, and it stood just beyond the muddy quadrangle of stables, pigsties, barns and sheds behind the farm, where the fields began. His father always carried a spud and when he walked over the farm he would every now and again stop and spud a thistle or a dock. That is, when he wasn't on horseback. Or carrying a gun. Tom Baines had told him how his father had come along when he and Jim Walton the carrier's son were picking acorns on Mr. Braddon's ground last autumn, and how it was too late to run, so that they waited, and how Mr. Hayley had spoken kindly and asked if there were many acorns down, and how he had fired with both barrels into the tree so that down came a shower of acorns which kept them busy for two hours, and their pigs happy for days. Or there was the time when the corn started disappearing at Manor Farm, and Mr. Hayley had kept watch and caught Jack Thomas the waggoner pinching it for the horses, to make them sleek and shiny. But how had these things, which seemed so easy, been made less easy by his birth? So he asked:

"Are they easier, now, Father?"

"Yes, yes, a little easier, son, a little easier."

He was relieved to hear that his growing up had not been in vain.

"What would you like to be if you weren't bailiff to Mr. Braddon, Father?"

Mr. Hayley looked surprised, then dreamy.

"As a matter of fact, I think I'd like to be an antiquary."

"Is that to do with horses, too?"

"No, no. It's a man who collects and sells antiques. Old and valuable things from old houses."

"Oh, I see, like me and birds' eggs?" Northbrook saw an unconvincing image of his father creeping stealthily into old houses and helping himself to old things, which was of course not stealing, because they were old, and because it was his father. Besides, Eric in the book had turned out not to be a thief at all, though everybody thought he was.

"A bit, yes," Mr. Hayley tussled the sandy brush on his son's head. "And what would you like to be when you grow up?"

Northbrook thought.

"I think I'd like to be a lord. A Latin lord," he added so as to bring in his latest love.

"Ho-ho! A bishop, no less!"

"Are bishops Latin?"

"Well, not exactly. But they have to know Latin."

"I'll be a bishop, then."

"I shouldn't be a bit surprised," said his father proudly. "You'd have to start at the beginning, though, as a curate."

"Oh, I see," said Northbrook and privately resolved to become a Latin lord without starting at the beginning.

"Your grandmother would be very pleased to hear you say so."

"Oh I see," Northbrook repeated, and changed his plans completely. He had once been taken to see old Mrs. Hayley, who lived in Warwick, and he didn't like to be reminded of her existence. She was a gaunt woman in black, who wore her caps as a branch wears a blossom about to fade, and who kept pinching his cheek, which he hated, and saying, "Thomas, you should have been called. The first son of the first son should always honour the grandfather. But Alfred always was pigheaded. Northbrook! That's no name for a boy. That's where we've lived for generations. Did you know that, boy?" Suddenly she was proud of the name, after all, at least as a place, a cradle of Hayleys. "It was there at the time of the Gunpowder Plot, some of the conspirators hid there, did you know that, boy?" And she would pinch his cheek again, forgetting to let go as she cackled on and on, tugging at the flesh for emphasis. "Your father was born there. So was your Aunt Tilly, but she went off to Liverpool. Septimus is the only one who stayed. Now there's a man, your Uncle Septimus. And he called his first boy Thomas, Thomas Hayley, there's a good solid name for you Northbrook indeed But Alfred always was pigheaded. Went haring off after a fine young lady in Hamberton, doctor's daughter she was, did you know that, boy? And then she kept him dangling for seven years, a real Rachel, your mother. And not above a flirtation or two on the side meanwhile. Fair broke your father's heart at times. These modern hussies. Now Septimus, there's a man for you."

Northbrook was almost as frightened of his Uncle Septimus as he was of his grandmother, more so even, for Uncle Septimus used to come to the Old Vicarage on long visits, and was huge, with red hair and a red beard, like the giant in Jack and the Beanstalk. His cousin Thomas was also rough and tough, and much more popular with the village boys. Northbrook much preferred his cousin Percy, Aunt Tilly's son, a pale town boy who was very sophisticated about all sorts of things Northbrook had never heard, like Beatty's Herod, with two driving wheels, single front, and outside as well as inside cylinder, or Stirling's Great Northern eight foot single-wheeler, four-two-two, and the Gladstone type, two-two-two; or how he'd given up telling lies for Lent because no one had ever given up sin for longer than that; and how a man called Hazlitt had said that *Paul and Virginia* had kept him awake, which showed he was a very dull man, since it was a very dull book; and how if you got up suddenly from the bathtub it made the same noise as the Holy Ghost at Pentecost, though of course one had to be careful not to get the nursery floor too wet. Northbrook worshipped him and when Percy came he dropped all the village boys and spent the whole time in the woods with Percy—well not the whole, because Percy had a way of disappearing and saying "See you in no time at all", which could mean never, and always drove Northbrook into a frenzy of self-accusation as to what he had done wrong. But they made a private den in the churchyard where a clump of trees formed almost a but with a large yew tree and a little help from a derelict tombstone and a few stolen branches. And there Percy told him how babies were born, and demonstrated, leaving, however, a great deal unexplained. And there they invented a game called Blood Brothers, who had millions of adventures together. And there Northbrook wept when Percy went home after a month in the country which had seemed to Northbrook like all eternity, as did his sorrow now. Two days later, however, he was playing once again with the boys in the village, for it was pleasant after all, to be a ringleader again.

"What about Lovell?" said Tom Baines, the eleven-year-old son of the village carpenter, wheelwright and undertaker. "We could use him."

"Don't be silly, he's only eight," said Northbrook. "He can't play with us."

They were crouched behind the high bank on the road to Weirwood Abbey, at the junction of the village main street, which climbed widely away from them up to the triangular hillock of grass at the top where the road forked off in three directions—on the right towards Birmingham, in the middle to Manor Farm, Tom Baines house and the Vicarage, on the left to the parish church and the Old Vicarage, with its wisteria and its tall yew hedge. The Old Vicarage was in fact the centre of the feud, for it was really one long house divided into two, with the Hayleys in one half, on the church side, and the Fardons in the other. Mr. Fardon was an ornamental iron-worker as well as the blacksmith. At this moment he was in his smithy under the big chestnut tree on that very hillock of grass, which stood like an island at the top of the village. It was the best outlook post, from which one could see in all directions, and it was held, not unnaturally, by the Fardon children and their band. From down below they could hardly be seen, for the blacksmith was rather busy today.

Northbrook was the chief, and consulted with Tom Baines, who though six months older was his second-in-command, and Jim Walton, the deputy second. The "men", or rest of the band, consisted only of Willy Perkins, the Outdoor Licenser's son, so he listened in but kept his counsel.

The great problem was how to get up the village street and back to the Hayleys' house without being spotted by the Fardon band and showered with catapults. They could, of course, go down the Weirwood Road towards the bridge and up through the wood, then across the fields to the back of the Old Vicarage, but that was no fun at all. Lovell had just come down the street and entered the Co-op, no doubt on an errand for his mother. At the same moment they spotted Telegraph Tim, who was wobbling towards them from Weirwood on his new safety—the most mechanised postman in England, he called himself, as swift as the telegraph, and the name had stuck. A unanimous nod from the counsel and Northbrook darted Indianwise behind the bank, then out on the road as soon as he was beyond the angle of vision from the smithy. He waved wildly at Telegraph Tim, who was not as mechanised as all that about brakes, and who ran his bicycle straight into the bank, which was the only way he could stop.

"Listen, Tim, you're going up to the Co-op, now, aren't you?" The Co-op was the village shop and also the post-office. "Well my kid brother's in there. Hurry, and give him this message. He's to go home, and when he walks past the smithy, he's to tell the Fardon boys, very casually, that his brother's already at home, in the garden, with his band. Got that? Now hurry or you'll miss him."

Lovell was very frightened at having to shout to the big boys over the din of the smithy, and he walked shyly past at first, hugging the syrup of squills he was carrying, but then plucked up his courage and walked back. At first the Fardon band didn't believe him, and said, why are you a traitor, anyway? But Dick Fardon looked down the village street and everything was so still on the Weirwood Road, and Lovell's brown eyes looked so innocent he thought the band must have gone home the other way. So he said, "Oh come on, this game's boring, let's go up to the hayloft on Manor Farm, and jump down on the hay." So a strategic withdrawal was carried out according to plan.

When Northbrook's band entered the back garden of the Old Vicarage in triumph, Lovell was rewarded only with brief thanks and a lofty word of praise, but not by admission to the exalted circle, even on a temporary basis. He sat on the steps, watching enviously as the boys got down into the cave which was their headquarters. They had dug it deep down, then boarded it over, and covered the boards with the earth thrown out. Here the band had all their conferences, and could shelter from the Fardon catapults that so often shot over the garden fence. There was even a little hole with a pipe for a chimney, and they had lit fires in there at first until Mr. Hayley forbade it, on account of the hayrick in the field just behind. Lovell didn't dare ask to be invited in, so he just sat there hoping. But then they came out, and went upstairs into the loft, which was shared with the Fardons, with only a beam in between. And a small pile of last year's apples was still there, so they formed a chain and passed them over one by one, and piled them again on the Hayley side, then sat down to eat them all. In the garden meanwhile, Lovell had entered their cave, and sat alone inside on a packing-case, giving orders to his men.

When the theft of the apples was discovered by Mr. Fardon two days later, the elder Hayley boy was so obviously the culprit, or at any rate, the chief of all possible culprits, that complaint was made in, as Mrs. Fardon put it, no uncertain terms. The worst punishment Mr. and Mrs. Hayley could think of, however, was to send him up to bed without any supper, for they were model and modern parents, who believed in love, not the rod. They had, in fact, very little idea of degrees in punishment. Two months earlier Northbrook had locked Dilly in the cellar for three hours when the house was empty, his parents having gone into Birmingham with Lovell and Muriel to buy them new boots. He had let her out just before they returned, but though her black overall had protected her dress, her white stockings and her face and hands were all smeared with coal and she was in a state of shock. So it had all come out and he had also been sent up to bed without any supper.

But Northbrook liked his room and liked his bed, and snuggled down to read. He hesitated. *Paradise Lost?* It was beautifully bound and also a present on his eleventh birthday, but from his father. He decided for *Frank Fairleigh*, for he had just reached the bit when Frank saves Freddy Coleman's life: Freddy Coleman laughs it off, then creeps to Frank's room at night to thank him in private. *"For when I feel deeply I hate to show it, but indeed (and the tears stood M his eyes while he spoke) indeed I am not ungrateful."* Then Frank says he has only one request to make. *"What is that?" Replied he quickly, "Do not forget to thank Him, whose instrument I was, for having so mercifully preserved your life." A silent pressure of the hand was the only answer, and we parted for the night.* How fine that was! Northbrook felt he was both Frank and Freddy. Then he remembered Jack-the-Shepherd and thought, why didn't I behave like that with him? But what could one expect from Jack-the-Shepherd, with his scruffy yellow hair and dirty hands? Jesu gentle Shepherd hear me. Suddenly Northbrook felt like reading *Paradise Lost* after all, and put *Frank Fairleigh* away. He had already got to Book Nine, having skipped through several summaries of arguments, and though it was an abridged edition, he revelled in the Fall, muttering the Noble Verse to himself with sensuous pleasure, loving the sounds of the words perhaps more than the contents but still absorbing images of fruit, serpents and nakedness.

After a while, though, he heard voices outside and got out of bed to see. A group of village boys and girls were standing at the church gate, talking and laughing and pushing each other. There was Tom Baines, and Jim

Walton, too. And Dick Pardon, by Jove. He got up on the windowsill in his nightshirt, and suddenly the chattering stopped as they all looked up at the thin little figure like a living statue in the window-frame, rosy in the setting-sun, with his nightshirt pulled right up to his chin, showing, as they said afterwards, all that he had got. Which, Tom Baines added knowledgeably, was considerable. The laughter drowned the girlish giggles and a cheer went up as Northbrook bowed, smiled and then retired, gratified by his success. Oh, happy sin, whose punishment is so sweet.

Like Northbrook with the village boys, so the Weirwoods kept somewhat aloof during the summer months when numerous relatives came to stay, Lord and Lady Chafford and their children, Sir James and Lady Darlington and theirs, Lady Evelyn and Brigadier Walsh, and distinguished guests like Lord Salisbury and Mr. Balfour for occasional weekends, and even the unfortunate Lord Randolph Churchill. And of course the Warwicks, the Kenilworths, the Leighs from Stoneleigh Abbey, and many other weekend combinations of people who mattered, resting from the glorious exertions of the London season.

When they had all departed, however, Lady Letitia would allow a suitable interval to pass for recovery, whereupon the winter, which was apt to arrive early in the Midlands would suddenly be upon them, and of course one could not have these things encroach on the preparations for Christmas, the annual journey abroad, or the London season. But in early June or thereabouts, before it all began again, she would set aside a few duty teas for the local gentry and others.

Canon Willoughby was a widower, and neither the Farleys nor the Templetons took much part in the village activities, for they lived some distance away. In practice therefore, the role of the vicar's wife fell upon Mrs. Hayley, who organised all the jumble sales, the garden-parties and the local charities, and loved it. Until the Honourable Imogen grew up and got smitten with good works, Mrs. Hayley it was who went round the very poor with bowls of soup, rice-pudding remains, cross-over-shawls and flannel petticoats, and the not so poor with homemade porkpies the very poor could well have done with.

Mr. and Mrs. Hayley were thus much respected in the village, for though Mrs. Hayley was considered strait-laced and standoffish by some, most of them thought she had a heart of gold, which was the usual way of saying she was on the whole a good sort, though a lady. She was indeed a lady, who always let it be felt, without ever saying or indeed, probably even thinking, that she had married very, very slightly beneath her, both culturally and socially, though in fact Mr. Hayley read quite as much as she did, and had if anything better manners with the village people. She was the one, at any rate, and in her own quite unpondered conviction, who felt at home with and was sought by, the nicest people, the best families, with good names, the Farleys, for instance, and the Templetons, and of course, the Weirwoods. She was therefore always very thrilled when the invitation to tea came from the Abbey, by hand, and on horseback.

The usual euphemistic excuse was made for Muriel, who tended to drop her tea-cup, or bread-and-butter face down on the carpet. But Northbrook and Lovell in their best suits, and Cordelia in her prettiest white frock with stiffened frills, all said how do you do very exquisitely to Lady Letitia, who wore gloves a size too small, a green silk skirt sweeping the floor, and a rich green satin bustle. The Honourable Imogen and the Honourable Claire had tiny bustles sewn into their dresses, and looked very pleased to be encased in little boned corsets. The Honourable Robert Henley took Northbrook's hand and bowed most politely, and so did The Honourable William Henley. It was the Children's Hour, when they all came down anyway with their best toys, in their best clothes and with hair fresh from the curling tongs, to meet their parents in the drawing room—the chintz drawing room of course, not the velvet drawing room or the silk drawing room which was all Chinese—and to play games like Happy Families or Grab. So they were delighted to find other children there, for a change. Young Henley, in fact, soon asked for permission to take his guests up to the schoolroom or the nursery, and his mother graciously assented. Mrs. Hayley was left alone with Canon Willoughby and Lady Letitia, which was quite delightful, she said afterwards. And later, Lord

Weirwood looked in, wearing a smoking jacket of purple velvet.

Northbrook was always overawed by the Abbey. There were rows of Chinese Chippendale chairs outside each big white and golden door along the carpeted corridor, and enormous pictures and gilt-edged mirrors and golden candelabras. The entrance hall was immense and so was the centre staircase, also carpeted in red. But they didn't use it. There were unpolished oak stairs at both ends of the long passage, one to the nursery quarters and one to his mother's apartments, said The Honourable Robert Henley. Oh no, the servants' stairs were the other side. Even in the nurseries the armchairs were Hepplewhite, in pale blue with frail-looking cane seats. All this splendour, which he couldn't even name, put him off his stride and into his stride at one and the same time. He felt very excited. The Honourable Robert Henley, heir to the Weirwood title, he kept thinking silently, Henley, Hayley, only two letters changed and here I would be. He started to limp, like Richard III.

"Hurt yourself?" said Robert Henley kindly.

"No, no, it's all right. Just twisted my ankle on the stairs but it's gone now."

"Look here, Hayley, let's go off, you and I. Both our kid brothers'll be happy with the girls. I want to show you something."

"Oh, right-ho, then." Northbrook was flattered by all this lordly fellowship, for although he was nearly two whole years older than Robert Henley, he felt considerably less self-possessed, and was awed by his undeniable superiority as a Weirwood, and heir to the title.

The kid brothers hardly noticed their departure: the Honourable William had pledged his troth to Cordelia and they were being married with great ceremony by Lovell, who was dressed up in a paper dog collar and a long black pinafore belonging to the Honourable Imogen. Imogen and Claire were bridesmaids, after which they all swapped round and Lovell married Claire. The Honourable Imogen was a little ungainly and, rather like Muriel on similar occasions, had already grasped the fact that nobody ever married her, and was very good-natured about it.

So Northbrook and Robert Henley slipped away and along the passage again, then up the oak-stairs at the end, which got more and more narrowly spiral.

"This is my den. The pater let me have it all to myself, on my tenth birthday."

They were in the newest part, a mid-Victorian addition to the building, all turrets and towers and Moorish galleries. He took a key out of his pocket and opened a door into a small octagonal room, well, minute by Abbey standards but in fact almost as large as Northbrook's and Lovell's bedroom. Three of the walls formed a bow-window with crisscross-leaded panes, and the rest of the room had the most extraordinary scheme of interior decoration he had ever seen. The ceiling had been painted red, and the wall to the left of the bow window was hung with a big Union Jack. The wall to the right was hung with a Turkish rug, which, he explained, was a trophy, won from the Russians at Sevastopol. The wall to the left of the door was covered with maps to eye level, then a framed portrait of the Queen as Empress of India, then a daguerreotype of last year's Golden Jubilee, and another of Lord Roberts in a martial moment. The wall to the right of the door supported a whole armoury of toy rifles, swords, daggers, even bows and arrows. A huge toy cannon stood in the window, on a rickety wooden table beside a real telescope mounted separately on a tripod. The wooden floor was bare, save for a moth-eaten lion-skin that welcomed them open-jawed. The only bits of furniture were an old toy-cupboard, bursting with discarded instruments of war, and another table covered with more maps and plans and compasses. Northbrook stood in the doorway astonished.

"Well, come on in," Robert said a trifle impatiently. "I haven't all day, you know." But he showed his guest round very proudly, explaining every detail of his campaigns, which were sometimes against Napoleon and the French, sometimes in India on the North West Frontier, and sometimes against the Russians in Crimea, especially during the winter months, when the sick man of Europe had to be defended and Northbrook visualised him with haemorrhage of the lungs, consumption, cholera and a bloody cold.

Robert went to the window and looked out.

"Oh good, he's there."

"Who?"

"My man, my batman, you know."

Northbrook looked out as well, to see this curious creature with wings. The turret gave onto the stables at the back of the Abbey, but they were so high the stables looked quite small. In the middle of the yard a groom was brushing a fine black horse.

"I tell you what, we'll send him a message, and order him up."

"How?"

"You'll see."

Robert went to his desk and wrote on a piece of paper: "Proceed to H.Q. without delay, By Order of Captain Henley." He was modest in the rank he assumed, but then he knew that the generals were never heroes, except only the very top general, who commanded the whole show. Otherwise the heroes were usually heroic despite the generals, who were nevertheless useful to recommend them for V.C.'s and such, and then he could turn himself into a general just for the occasion.

Northbrook was very intrigued to see him tie this message to an arrow and go to the open window with a large bow. For a moment he quite expected him to die, like Robin Hood, shot in the heart within a castle room from the nearby forest. He went up to the window and stood gingerly by as the boy took aim.

"Supposing you kill him?"

"I never miss," said Robert ambiguously and away went the arrow with a twang that made Northbrook jump back with fright. Then he looked out and was amazed. The arrow was quivering in the ground with its white message like a butterfly, just a yard away from the groom, and the horse was rearing dangerously. The groom caught it by the mane and soothed it as he looked up, grinned and shook his fist up at the window. When the horse was quiet again he went over to the arrow and read the message, with excruciating slowness as the boys waited impatiently. Then he looked up again, pointed to the horse, opened out his five fingers, closed them again, saluted smartly.

"He'll come in five minutes," said the boy, rather annoyed. "I'll have him court-martialled, I will."

"What's his name?" Northbrook asked, not daring to ask the meaning of court-martial.

"Jonas. He's my aide-de-camp as well as my batman, though that's a little irregular. You can be my aide-de-camp for this afternoon and he'll be our batman. And sergeant-major of course, one must have a sergeant-major."

"Him or me?"

"Jonas of course. He's very adaptable. He's the coachman's son, actually, and there's absolutely nothing he doesn't know about horses. He taught me to ride. He's fourteen, you know. Pretty ripping chap, really."

"Fourteen, good heavens!" Northbrook was always frightened of older boys and felt more ill at ease than ever.

"Oh Jonas is all right. He does everything I say. My every wish is his command, and of course up here it's all commands. We're going to have a big war now."

He looked out at the horizon dreamily.

"What a nice view," said Northbrook politely as they waited.

The Honourable Robert thought him a bit of a nincompoop and was beginning to regret his decision, and to wish Jonas would make haste. Yes, he really would court-martial him, or beat him perhaps. But he was well brought up, so he said,

"Oh yes, would you like to look through the telescope? You can see right over into Worcestershire."

He turned in a bored way and saw to his relief that Jonas was at the door, standing to attention with a smart salute.

"You scoundrel," said the boy furiously. "Don't you know every soldier has to obey orders at once, and unquestioningly, in Her Majesty's Fusiliers?"

19

WE ALL see through a glass darkly, and sometimes for one brief second, through a glass lightly. As for me, I was seeing through a glass wetly as I sat in the B.E.A. bus on my dismal way through the new slums of surburbia to London Airport. A lady behind me was saying in an old world voice, "The shops in Bond Street are so awful now, it's just like Shaftesbury Avenue. Curzon Street still has a few nice ones." She was obviously refusing to look at the ugliness we were driving through. We never quite catch up I thought, we improve, we rebuild, rehouse, bright and brittle, but always the rot sets in again, the ugliness and shabbiness of humanity. And with the suburban part of my own mind I wondered, what will the neighbours think, all those visitors from abroad whom we try so hard to impress with our Newborn Baby Britain, no longer a solemn old Mother-Country but a gay gurgling little thing waving its rattle at all its aunts and uncles? Instead of taking these visitors underground, at least, straight to the postcard London of Westminster or Tower Bridge, instead of introducing ourselves like other towns, in our best finery and with our hair properly curled, we let ourselves be caught like this in torn and dirty underwear. But then, I reflected, it probably always was so, from Waterloo 6 St. Pancras, and even in the old stagecoach. Life, I said with startling originality as I stepped out of the bus in my mackintosh, is like that.

And occasionally life is even more so, weaving its senseless patterns of incidence, coincidence and obeisance, at any rate, I felt very tense as I went up the escalator, carrying only a briefcase, then through the Customs, the Passport Control and into the departure lounge. I glanced at the other passengers in their scattered armchairs. They all seemed very calm, and yet there is always a subdued excitement in any group of people about to take off for an altitude of nineteen thousand feet and upwards. I have flown to many places on brief holidays, and a plane to me is just a container into which one is sealed for a varying number of hours with nothing but meals to relieve the monotony. Yet each time I catch myself out feeling grand and rich, smart, modern and casual; then insignificant and tripperish as more and more flights are announced, like busloads, leaving every few minutes, rows and rows of loungefuls one after another, Flight 203 for Rome—Athens—Istanbul, passengers by Air France to Nice, Scandinavian Air Lines for Copenhagen and Oslo, the muffled voice continued to relay its disembodied orders for unreal destinations, castles in the air, mere blobs at the end of very straight and thick red lines superposed on maps of Europe as it used to be, with mountains and rivers and roads.

I was glad of the trip. I had been suffering from a boxed-in feeling recently while the house in which I had my flat was being painted. It was like being on the stage. The scaffolding outside my window made me nervous, as did the reproachful presence of workers watching me have my breakfast, and the Irish tenor who thought the block must somewhere contain a film or television producer, so that he sang *Across the Irish Sea* at the nasal top of his voice from eight o'clock in the morning until I left at 9.45. Besides, I had immense difficulty in getting my scooter out now, on account of the workers' cars parked bumper to bumper. I hoped they would all be gone by the time I got back.

"B.E.A. flight 704 to Brussels, now waiting in Departure Lounge No.7. Will Mr. Austin Weymouth please report to the centre desk immediately. There is an urgent message at the centre desk for Mr. Austin Weymouth. Will Mr. Austin Weymouth please report to the centre desk immediately."

A little bald man of sixty or so got up hurriedly, in buff suede shoes and very narrow trousers. He was wearing one of the new very short overcoats of light tweed and a narrow shantung tie with irregular horizontal stripes in sky-blue and coffee-cream. He had removed his Robin Hood hat and now jammed it on, which took twenty years off his age, in spite of the thick-lensed spectacles. I guessed idly; new kind of aerial commercial traveller, no, third assistant to small film company's wardrobe mistress, no, television ads, a bright-ideas-fellow, could be. Suddenly I thought, my God, no not my God, my half brother. But when he came back I looked straight into his thick little lenses and said aloud, no, definitely no, much to the raised eyebrows of a mildly exhibitionist dark girl in sunglasses and the very latest line of fashion, who sat in the other armchair at my table, wearing pigskin gloves and smoking through a very long holder.

There always is a mildly exhibitionist girl wearing sunglasses and the latest fashion in every flight at every airport, even on a rainy day, and she always quietly attaches herself to me. I am not in the least good-looking, or rather, my features are regular but dull and I look pale, uninteresting and, even on holiday, very like a lawyer. But that type can spot an older bachelor, a divorcé or an unfaithful married man from twenty-thousand feet. What is more, I like being thus spotted by just that type, though I al- ways regret it later. The routine of the performance fascinates me, or, as I prefer to call it, the beautiful inevitability of it all. This one had evidently been driven straight to the airport, for I had not seen her on the bus, but I had recognised her type of luggage at the Customs, three matching pieces and a hatbox in white and gold luxury leather, long before she swept in all television smiles and scent.

Television, damn, I looked again at Mr. Austin Weymouth, who seemed mightily pleased with the message he had just received, no doubt about the latest slogan to be flashed at our tired subliminal selves and our tedi- ous subliminal urges, then I successfully dismissed him from my thoughts.

Wild speculations, if I had to indulge in them, were best directed upon that exquisite lost creature with the hard red mouth and the thin nervous hands, who was trying like so many of us to attract the world's attention as a substitute for the world in a grain of sand. It occurred to me in one of those blinding glimpses of the obvious that the age of chivalry had well and truly died, that it was now always the women who did the chasing, so much so that this had become routine in, for example, American films, where always the girl first gave that revelation look, invented the first ex- cuse to talk, stood unaccountably close with upshot breasts and parted lips, or, in face of real obtuseness, frankly declared her love, whereupon the genial male suddenly and overwhelmingly discovered his. And I wondered whether women were any more at peace with themselves, now that failure, in spite or perhaps because of this freedom, really meant failure and not that society hadn't given them a chance. The most serene women seemed to be on the contrary, the proverbially frustrated ones, the unlovely and unmarried who obeyed all the rules and loved their cats.

Be that as it might, I knew how it would go. Our flight would be called. The ground-hostess would wait at the lounge door then take us to the primitive little yellow bus that drives passengers out to the aircraft. But Madam would sit at the other end, in mysterious solitude, looking carefully at no persons and no aeroplanes but at her glove-button, or a letter, or one corner of her lip in a handbag mirror. But afterwards if I got into the plane first, she would come up casually and say, "Is this seat free? Oh, thank you," then strap herself in knowledgeably, and without another word start reading *The Times* or *The New Yorker*. And if she got in first I would come up casually and go through precisely the same ritual. And it was so. She had the seat by the window, and an hour to work in, by which time we would have had our cold Lyon's salad and she would draw my attention to the fact that we were now over Belgium, flying so high that the green and brown strips of field looked like mere brush-strokes, and then, as we came down over Brussels, to the atomium, with its five silver globes shining in the sun. And I would lean across her, pleasurably, to see. And it was so.

But I didn't care. I let it all go, and let her sail through the Customs and into the Autorail for the centre of the town, without more than a shade of regret. For Mr. Austin Weymouth had shaken me more than I had realised, and although he was met, at Melsbroeck, by a chauffeur-driven Mercedes, and swept out of my life for ever, the dismissal I had performed in my mind on the plane had not been as successful as I had supposed, and Mr. Austin Weymouth who had so disconcertingly shared my plane like a sperm in a male organ, became quite a stock character in my interesting dream life, interesting, that is, to my psychiatrist. He tended, moreover, to enter it in various guises, but always uttering a string of unrelated comparatives, as if these made up his Dickensian character-motif, as optimistic as Mr. Micawber's. Better, Swifter, Easier, Whiter, Warmer, Easier, Softer, Bigger, Tastier, Easier, Quicker, Easier—harmless enough in themselves, but alarming in the context of some of the dreams I have.

Besides my briefcase, I was carrying only a zip-bag, and took the next autorail to town, emerging at a huge open space that had once been funny little climbing streets round Sainte Gudule, almost at the bottom of the hollow where lies the old city of Brussels. But the creamy yellow trams were still there, more streamlined, except for a few old models, one of which I promptly chose for my slow, screeching, bumping and tinkling ascent out of the centre to the Cinquantenaire, where I changed for a No. 40. And the No. 40 was more thrilling to me than any Viscount, Comet or Pioneer Rocket to the moon, for it raced along the Avenue de Tervueren, swinging and clanging at a tremendous speed beneath the endless roof of chestnut trees, past the tall rich houses and the pond in the park of Woluwe where I had skated as a boy, through the Forêt de Soignes, so swiftly that the spattered sun on the tall, tall trunks of the beech trees flashed like messages of golden morse. And I stood on the platform, though plenty of the wooden seats inside were free, and I held on to the rail and leant out, so that the wind swept back my hair and I was ten, out for an afternoon with Marcel, his mother perhaps inside, or mine, or perhaps we were alone, on trust not to stray too far into the forest on our dangerous adventures. On, on, past Quatre-Bras, then another café-cluster the name of which I had forgotten, still in the golden-green woods and then at last, Ter-mi-nus! Tervueren.

Just as I had not, in town, called on my uncle Maurice at the smart offices of *Voyages Bertrand*, or on my successful cousin, now a nuclear physicist, and his rich Belgian wife, in the Avenue Louise, so I did not now go into the big park or visit the Colonial Museum, with its stuffed crocodiles and its dummy negroes paddling down the painted plaster Congo in their canoes. I was not trying to materialise old memories; either of school expeditions or of family; for childhood comes back only in evanescent glimpses, brought about perhaps by the touch of a worn out curtain, a light behind yellow fringes falling on a brown velvet table top, a holiday whiff of dung or the smell of quinces cooking for jam, apples with a tang of strawberry and strawberries with a tang of melon, a taste of wine in water, or Alpine bilberries with sugar and cream.

I walked instead along a cobbled road that led slightly up hill, past flat-fronted little brick houses and towards the woods again. And here a glimpse of childhood did occur, in the artificial silk and cotton-covered bottoms of two housewives or charwomen scrubbing their piece of pavement, as all housewives did, by law, every Friday, all over Belgium—les *gros derrières' fleurís*, as my grandfather called them, looking forward to them every Friday. It was strange to see them again, and out here, too, where I had not lived.

Then the pavement became hard earth and the honks more sparse, hidden away in gardens behind tall trees. At last I came to a familiar hedge and an open gate, with a small painted notice, which read, first in English, then in French, *St. Lambert's Priory, Prieuré de Saint Lathbert,* followed by the hours of the Masses and Benedictions in the chapel.

I walked up towards the house, which was tall and gloomy with gables and pointed roofs and jutting bow-windows, and a side-stair climbing up to a first floor door, which was the chapel.

Below the side-stair was another door, where I rang the bell. After a while the small window opened behind the grill and a pair of eyes in a white face peered out, their querying eyebrows almost disappearing into the white band below the wimple.

"Good afternoon, Sister. May I see the Reverend Mother?"

"Ooh! It's Philip! Ooh, how exciting!" said the portress in a thrilled Irish whisper, and the door was unlocked with the consecutive clanging of bars, chains and keys.

"How are you?" she asked breathlessly, as she showed me into the dark little parlour. I put my bag down on the stone floor and my hat on the brown plush-covered table in the middle. "Did you have a rough sea, now? Ooh, but you'll never be seasick I'm sure, a strong young man like you."

At my age, this was sheer flattery.

"As a matter of fact, I flew, Sister."

"Ooh, how exciting I I'd love to fly now. But what am I doing chattering all this time? I must run and tell the Reverend Mother you've arrived. Ooh, she will be happy."

I sat down at the table and felt both touched and uneasy. It was pleasing to have one's much expected arrival treated like an astonishing miracle of divine grace, which, for all I knew, it may well have been. But the parlour always made me nervous. There was a small statue of Saint Theresa in one corner, and a large crucifix in another, a picture of the Sacred Heart of one wall and a photograph of the Holy Father John XXIII on the other, back to back, I knew, with Pius XII who had now been moved to the corridor, but not removed altogether, on account of some of the nuns having special devotions to him. Along the third wall was a glass cabinet full of holy pictures cut out or painted or embroidered by the nuns, little saints made of wool and wood, painted 'shrines, cards with prayers beautifully written out in red and black script, rosary-purses hand-sewn in soft leather and lined with silk, as well as lay objects, dolls, pincushions, handkerchiefs, bookmarks and lavender bags. For the nuns were extremely poor and worked hard for a little extra money. But few people came this far out and no one seemed to know of the convent's existence. Donations were as scarce as new vocations.

The parlour was icy cold, too, with its stone floor, indeed it had once been the scullery of the house, and now it was two tiny rooms, this one where the priest had his breakfast after Mass, and the next where guests could sleep, or any priest in charge of the Annual Retreat. Père Van Gruendebeek, as I knew to my cost, came at five-fifty every morning, on a motorbike, and the nuns called him *le curé motorisé*, and I had to lie very quiet in bed, staring either at the lifesize plaster statue of Our Lady in the corner, who held out her hands at me, modest but alarming, or at the photograph of Cardinal Newman, over my bed, looking both stern and gentle above the motto *Cor ad cor loquitur*, while the priest had his breakfast at seven o'clock in the next room.

Then a door opened, and another, and suddenly she was here, tall in her flowing black habit, her features small beneath the white starch that supported the black veil—like having a draper's shop on your head, she had called it once during a heatwave.

Always it was awkward at first. She kissed me, we sat and talked, and she knitted, for she was not allowed to waste a single moment, even on worldly sons.

Always I was surprised how young and serene she looked, with her grey hair quite out of sight, probably almost white by now, and her eyes so calm and brown. I couldn't even remember her age, over sixty I assumed, but how little over I kept forgetting, for with the veil she had also assumed a timelessness, like a small advance on eternity. I could see it all now, and felt happy for her, but when she had first made the decision, shortly after the war, it had been for me like death without the sentimental thrill of un-seen presence watching, or the consolation of angels and cherubs wafting her soul to heaven, or even the certitude of slow forgetfulness. A mere re-moval from the world, without the paraphernalia of death. And now, already twelve years later, here she was, The Reverend Mother Prioress, or Mother St. Thomas, O.S.L., alias Mrs. Alfred Hayley, alias Laura Ber-trand.

"It's rather grand, your being Prioress," I said, for it had only happened a few months ago at the last Chapter. Even so, it had been remarkably quick: I could remember visiting her in a shabby house at Notting Hill Gate, when she was a fifty-two-year-old postulant called Sister Laura, who couldn't keep her wimple clean and tidy and kept catching her veil on a rosebush in the minute garden during the Rosary Walk; when the minor sacrifices like cigarettes, face-powder and mirrors seemed almost insu-perable, and when the hardest penance still was having to talk to the oth-er nuns in the recreation half-hour.

She smiled.

"It was pure chance, really. I was sent out here when this house opened, because I spoke French, and Mother St. Cuthbert was so often ill that in practice I've been Acting Prioress for some time."

"I hope they all respect you like mad?"

"It's only for five years, you know. Power corrupts, and all that."

"Is it a lot of work?"

"Well, yes." Her dark eyes lit up suddenly with the odd mixture of holy anger and merriment so peculiarly hers. "There are so few of us, you see, and alas, vocations don't entail competence. The librarian is almost blind so I have to do the cataloguing for her. Mother St. Austin's grammar is wonky, so I have to go through her translations. My Sub-Prioress doesn't speak French, so I have to deal with all tradesmen and other outside business. The vestry-mistress has eczema and the kitchen sister can't cook, so that I have to make all the unusual things, Feast-day meals for instance. They can't do heavy work, or say they can't, so the Sub-Prioress and I have to move furniture and such. I am sixty-six. The peace of the cloister, my goodness!" And she laughed with what seemed like secret delight.

"But Mummy, why don't you order them?" I was horrified. "It's not so easy. They're very old, most of them, except for Mother St. Alban, the Sub-Prioress. Older than I am, and far less gifted with energy, or capability." She spoke simply, and the phrase was no boast but a thanksgiving. "It hasn't really been a very successful experiment," she went on, "opening a house here. It's too far and we're not getting the vocations. We haven't enough money and even to live sparsely in Brussels costs like luxury in London. We may all pack up and go back."

"May I smoke?"

"Yes, of course. They can smell me three rooms away when I've been with you. You've no idea how it clings to these robes. Tobacco Thomasina, they call me then, or even Tobacco Tom, well, they used to before I became Prioress."

She had chosen St. Thomas the Doubter at her Solemn Profession because, as she told me then, she had procrastinated so long with her Vocation doubting it and being afraid. I hadn't taken much interest at the time —indeed it now occurred to me that my sullen absence from the ceremony may well have been her last disappointment in the worldly desires she was offering up for the sins of that same world. But now at last I wanted to break that barrier, that spiritual grille between us, and I wanted as well to ask a thousand things, which yet I knew I would not ask and she would never answer.

"Tell me, Mummy, what exactly made you become a Lambertine? I mean, why not a Carmelite, or a Benedictine, or a Poor Claire?"

"Well, darling, it's just one of those things. Each order has its own task, reflecting some aspect of Christ's life on earth—teaching, healing, praying, and so forth. One is directed, that's all. I had known Mother St, Jerome as long ago as my early married years in London. She died in January, you know, at ninety-three. As a matter of fact I believe your father first took me there."

"Did you know he was a Lambertine monk, in 1897?"

"No, really? How very strange."

But she didn't seem as interested as I had hoped.

"An Anglican Lambertine," I went on, insistently, "you know, there was an attempt to revive the Order within the Church of England, in the 'nineties, and they got hold of Alfringham Abbey, with a lot of donations from rich Anglicans. But then the whole show became untenable on Anglican terms, everything was in Latin, of course, with Exposition, Reservation, the lot—they even had the Feast of the Assumption, and some bishop was so shocked he refused to be Visitor. So the whole community went over to Rome, in 1908, I think it was. That's how Alfringham happened, didn't you know? It's part of the European Lambertine Order now. Abbot Cynewulf Huxley. He was allowed to remain an Abbot and was rushed through some telescoped novitiate or something, all very irregular because he had nominated himself Prior, then Abbot, without even having been a novice, properly speaking. He died during the war."

"Oh yes," she said vaguely. "I have heard of him."

"I went to stay at Alfringham," I said, and she looked up, surprised and hopeful. "A terrible place, you've no idea, all glamorous and mock mediaeval, with monks in white cowls and charabancs of pilgrims pouring in daily and the present Abbot behaving like a film-star with everyone telling him he's sure to be canonised and asking him for bits of his habit or snips of his hair."

"Every place has its purpose," she said, counting the stitches at the heel of a long black sock.

"But Mummy, this one is immoral. The monks have the easiest time you can imagine, they live extremely well, they come up to London and see their friends whenever they feel like it, they say they're a mendicant or-der—which isn't strictly true of Lambertines—and invite themselves everywhere, and get buckets of money but pay no taxes, my goodness, I think I'll take a vow of poverty, it's the only way to be comfortable and se-cure for the rest of one's life."

"Now, darling, that's no way to talk. We don't pay taxes either, for that matter, at least not on donations."

"Yes, but look how simply you live, and how hard you work. Why, you weren't even allowed to keep a silver thimble when you went in. You're not allowed out, and if you have to travel to London you must wear blinkers, figuratively speaking, like a horse, and not diverge two inches from your route. Do you know these monks go on holiday every year? Holidays from what, God? You haven't had a day's rest for twelve years."

The Reverend Mother Prioress smiled at my puritan indignation.

"Monks always have an easier time of it, at least, as far as those things are concerned," she said quietly. "It's traditional, and after all, it's the men who started the whole thing. You may be sure that they have it more difficult in other ways. I must fly now, it's Compline in three minutes. I'll get Sister St. Kevin to bring you some tea."

Out she went, and I knew I wouldn't see her till six, and that by special dispensation to herself.

"How did you think Mother was looking?" whispered Sister St. Kevin as she put the big tray down.

"Well, very well. Perhaps a little pale."

"Ooh, she works ever so hard, Mother does. And she's so good to us, you know. But here's your tea, and a little bit of apricot jam Mother made her-self. Ooh, she's such a good cook, Mother is. We miss her in the kitchen now she's so busy. And she thought you'd like this pain de peace. It's Belgian, you know."

I adored pain d'épice, and said so.

She thought she had to entertain me as I ate, and stood there small and pink-faced in her brown habit.

"Tell me, Sister, do you believe a dead person can guide a living person they loved into a sort of compensation, a penance, you would probably call it, for their own life?"

"*Cor ad cor loquitur*," she murmured. "One never knows, Philip boy, one never knows who is doing penance for what, or just which life needs praying for, and what dead soul, the ways of God being inscrutable. The more prayer, the better, that's what I believe, or the scales go down on the side of evil."

"Don't you think they've gone down anyway, Sister?"

"Ooh, what an idea! You'd be surprised, Philip boy, how much prayer there is in the atmosphere. All those scientists can never measure that, now."

"No, I suppose not." It was one of those remarks one couldn't argue about. But I was trying to thrash out something other than the problem of evil. "Do you think, Sister, that somebody can leave a sort of spiritual testament behind, giving as it were unseen directions, to their sons, for instance?"

"You mean, like a legacy, but of the spirit?"

"Yes, in a way. A legacy of guilt, rather, which has to be worked out, I mean, atoned?"

She flashed an Irish grin at me. "One never knows, one never knows. Ooh, I should have thought our own legacy of guilt from Adam was enough to cope with, now. And who are we to decide the guilt of others whom God has forgiven more than likely, and atoned for many a time, for all mankind indeed."

"You don't think, then, that one is responsible for one's legacy, immediate legacy, I mean, from one's father, for instance?"

She looked sharply at me, like a bird.

"Ooh, I wouldn't say that, Philip boy, I wouldn't say that. But you just pray for the sins you'll be visiting on others, and the sins visited upon you will be taken care of."

"I can't pray at all, Sister."

She looked at me in silence.

"Perhaps," she said after a moment, "that is your legacy. Of course, you know, one can always refuse a legacy, or give it away. You should make an offering of it, Philip, boy, make an offering of your lack of faith."